HEART OF A SCOUNDREL
Heart of a Duke Series

For more information about the author:
www.christicaldwellauthor.com
christicaldwellauthor@gmail.com
Twitter: @ChristiCaldwell
Or on Facebook at: Christi Caldwell Author

For first glimpse at covers, excerpts, and free bonus material, be sure to sign up for my monthly newsletter!

Printed in the USA.

Cover Design and Interior Format
© The Killion Group Inc.

The Heart of a Scoundrel

Heart of a Duke
THE SERIES

USA Today Bestseller

CHRISTI CALDWELL©

Other Titles by Christi Caldwell

THE HEART OF A SCANDAL

In Need of a Knight—Prequel Novella
Schooling the Duke
Heart of a Duke
In Need of a Duke—Prequel Novella
For Love of the Duke
More than a Duke
The Love of a Rogue
Loved by a Duke
To Love a Lord
The Heart of a Scoundrel
To Wed His Christmas Lady
To Trust a Rogue
The Lure of a Rake
To Woo a Widow

LORDS OF HONOR

Seduced by a Lady's Heart
Captivated by a Lady's Charm
Rescued by a Lady's Love
Tempted by a Lady's Smile

SCANDALOUS SEASONS

Forever Betrothed, Never the Bride
Never Courted, Suddenly Wed
Always Proper, Suddenly Scandalous
Always a Rogue, Forever Her Love
A Marquess for Christmas
Once a Wallflower, at Last His Love

SINFUL BRIDES
The Rogue's Wager
The Scoundrel's Honor

THE THEODOSIA SWORD
Only for His Lady

DANBY
A Season of Hope
Winning a Lady's Heart

BRETHREN OF THE LORDS
My Lady of Deception
Memoir: Non-Fiction
Uninterrupted Joy

DEDICATION

To Nana Lil

For years and years, my Nana Lil was my cheerleader and champion. When things seemed impossible, she assured me my world would open up. She used to say: "I wish I'm around to someday see it." I would tease her and say; "I hope I'm around to see it, too, Nana."

Two years ago, my cheerleader and champion was diagnosed with dementia. She no longer knows I'm her granddaughter. When I visit her, she smiles and loves to speak with "the young author who writes romance novels." Of all she's lost in terms of her beautiful, cherished memories of our family, she recalls my stories.

And for that, and for everything you've been to me and for me—Nana Lil—this one is for you.

ACKNOWLEDGEMENTS

A very special thank-you to the dear Carol Cork for all her patience, and all the valuable time she spent answering my questions on Wales. Carol, you are a champion of romance authors and a fountain of information! Thank you!

CHAPTER 1

London, England
Spring 1817

THE LADY WORE AN IVORY, lace-trimmed, cashmere shawl. Such details generally only applied to an interest in how that delicate slip of material could be used for dark acts behind chamber doors. In this particular instance, that tedious, ladylike fabric would serve an entirely different purpose.

Seated behind his mahogany desk in the comforts of his own office, Edmund Deering, the Marquess of Rutland, absently rubbed his thumb and forefinger over the old, silken black tress. Such an act would be considered sentimental in any other gentleman. A hard smile turned the corner of his lips. Then, he was not most gentlemen. Ladies, dowagers, widows, and the husbands of a whole host of discontented wives would, in fact, say he was no gentleman at all.

And they would all be right.

The tress had been clipped a lifetime ago. Given to him as a token of affection, it had ultimately come to signify empty promises and the indefatigable truth—women were faithless, fickle creatures who'd splay their legs for the right title and not a thing more.

As if in agreement, the muscles of his right thigh tightened. He rubbed the old wound, welcoming the sharp reminder of his own past weakness.

A knock sounded at the office door and he stopped rubbing his leg. In one fluid movement, he tossed that scrap of hair into the rubbish bin at the side of his desk. He shifted his gaze to the clock. Odd, he'd not expect a wastrel to also be perfunctory. "Enter," he drawled. His butler, Wallace, a loyal fellow who'd served Edmund's father, entered. "The Viscount Waters to see you, my lord."

Viscount Waters hovered at the threshold of the room.

Wordlessly, Edmund inclined his head and the servant backed out of the room, closing the door behind him, and leaving Edmund and Lord Waters alone.

The short, pudgy nobleman with a bulbous nose and, even more importantly, an enormous debt to Edmund shifted on his stout legs. "R-rutland," he stammered. He tugged at his stark white cravat, highlighting the crimson red of his flushed cheeks. "Y-you summoned me?"

Dispensing with formalities, Edmund sprawled back in his chair. "Come in, come in," he murmured resting his arms over the sides of his chair.

The balding viscount swallowed audibly and cast a desperate glance over his shoulder at the path the butler had retreated.

"I said come in," Edmund said on a lethal whisper.

Lord Waters jumped. "Er, yes, of course, of course." And yet, still, he lingered before stiffly moving forward. Perspiration dotted the man's brow, which Edmund suspected had little to do with the exertions of his movement and everything to do with his unease.

The man feared him. Anxiety bled from his eyes, seeped from his lips. Fear made Edmund powerful. Weakened others. Yes, fear was good. Very good.

Lord Waters paused in front of his desk. He yanked a white handkerchief, embroidered with his initials, from the front of his pocket and dabbed at his brow, smartly silent. Likely the only thing which the man had ever been smart about.

"You have a daughter," Edmund said, a steely edge to his words.

The older viscount blinked several times at the unexpected pronouncement. Always leave others unsuspecting. Unsettled individuals were careless and Edmund thrived off that the way he did fear. "A daughter?" the man squawked. Then a slow understanding glinted in his eyes. He paused mid-dab and thrust his handkerchief back into the front of his jacket. "Er, yes. Lovely, lovely gel. Quite lovely," he rambled. "She'd make you a splendid—"

Edmund leaned forward and laid his forearms upon his desk. "I've no intention of making a match with your daughter." He peeled his lip back in a sneer.

The man's skin went ashen and he tugged out the kerchief once more. "Er, uh, yes…well, you'd have me settle our debt in other ways then, will you? Very well…"

A dark, ugly laugh rumbled up from Edmund's chest cutting into the man's offer. Lord Waters would sell his daughter. The darkness in people's souls had ceased to surprise him long ago. "I've little desire in tupping your virginal daughter," he snarled. Virgins didn't interest him. Simpering young debutantes, innocent misses, held little appeal. He'd wait until they were wedded, bedded, and craving real lessons on passion.

"Oh." The viscount rocked back on his heels. "May I sit?" He gave his lapels another tug.

Edmund arched an eyebrow at the man's unexpected show of courage. He pointed to the leather winged back chair and the fat, fleshy lord ambled over then sank into the seat. The leather groaned in protest to the man's hefty weight.

With deliberate, methodical slowness Edmund pulled open his desk drawer. He withdrew the leather folio inside.

The man's skin turned white and he gulped. "Y-you have a b-book." It was a statement of fact—a confirmation of a detail he'd likely heard bandied about at his clubs and gaming hells but had, until now, taken it as a rumor.

"Surely, you do not imagine you're the only person indebted to me?" He made a clicking noise with his tongue. No, a whole host of gentlemen owed Edmund in some way or another. Exorbitant debts, promises made, favors pledged. Lord Waters was but one of those many and the man would now pay his debt. He opened the leather book, never taking his gaze from the viscount. "You owe me quite a vast sum."

Waters wet his lips but said nothing.

"Five thousand pounds, your unentailed property in Hampshire." Though Edmund had little interest or need in a country property. He didn't leave the glittering filth of London. "Your pathetic wife's jewelry." The man winced. "Your eldest daughter's dowry."

"Have you called to collect?"

He strained to hear the man's whisper. Edmund spread his arms wide. "Indeed, I have."

The man closed his eyes a moment. "And you're sure you wouldn't want my daughter. Quite beautiful she is, quite—"

"I'm quite certain," Edmund said, placing mocking emphasis at the man's redundant choice of words. "I've little interest in your simpering—"

"Oh, no," Waters gave his head a frantic shake. "Not simpering at all. If you care for feisty, spirited gels, my Phoebe will—"

"I've already stated, I have no interest in your virginal daughter," he whispered. Though an unholy humor twisted inside him at the truth that, for a bag of coin, a man would sell even his daughter.

The viscount closed his mouth quickly and gave a jerky nod.

Edmund reclined in his seat. He captured his chin between his thumb and forefinger. He did, however, have an interest in one virgin. A particular virgin with nondescript, brown hair, a slightly crooked lower row of teeth, and a pair of dull, brown eyes. In short, an uninteresting lady who'd never hold even the hint of appeal for a practiced rogue such as himself. The only thing to set the lady apart from all other ladies—her name: Miss Honoria Fairfax. The beloved niece of Margaret, the Duchess of Monteith. That love would lead to the girl's ruin. Another icy grin pulled at his lips. He stood, unfolding his length to display the towering six-foot four-inches that terrified lesser men, such as this coward before him.

Waters recoiled, burrowing deep into the folds of his chair.

"You see," Edmund began, wandering casually over to the sideboard at the corner of his office. "There is something I will require of you." He selected the nearest decanter, a half-empty bottle of brandy. He pulled out the stopper and tossed it upon the table where it landed with a thunk.

The viscount remained silent. He hungrily eyed the crystal decanter in Edmund's hands. Only the man's ragged, panicked breaths and the splash of liquor streaming into the crystal glass split the quiet. Bottle and brandy in hand, Edmund wandered back over to his desk and propped a hip on the edge. He took a sip. "Miss Fairfax," he said at last.

The man cocked his head and with confused eyes, looked about as though expecting to find the lady in question there. "Miss Fairfax?" he repeated.

Edmund swirled the contents of his glass. "I'd like something that belongs to Miss Fairfax." Her good name. Her virtue, and more—the agony of Margaret knowing her beloved niece would be forever bound to the man she'd thrown over for another. A thrill ran through him as the sweet taste of revenge danced within his grasp. Unfortunately for Miss Fairfax, she had rotten blood running through her veins and, as such, would pay the ultimate price for her aunt's crimes.

"I don't know a Miss Fairfax," the man blurted.

Edmund stilled his hand mid-movement and he peered at the viscount over the rim of his brandy. It, of course, did not surprise him the man should fail to note those minute details of his daughter's life. Likely, his lack of notice would result in that quite lovely daughter he'd described with her legs spread wide for some unscrupulous rogue.

"Beg p-pardon," the man said on a panicky rush. "I—"

"Miss Fairfax is a friend of your daughter's," he interrupted. He glanced across the room at the long-case clock, ready to be done with this exchange.

Lord Waters scratched his brow. "She is?" He frowned and Edmund could practically see the wheels of the man's empty mind turning. Then, an understanding lit his unintelligent eyes.

"Not the beautiful one," he said of the other young woman Waters' daughter considered a friend. It really was quite unfortunate the stunning Lady Gillian Farendale, whose sister had been jilted by some worthless cad, was not, in fact, the one he sought. He'd have delighted in taking his pleasure in that lady's body.

"Ah, the other one." The man guffawed. "A taste for the ugly ones, do you?" he said with a crude laugh. "Then, they're all the same when you have them under you." He dissolved into a paroxysm of laughter. "That one has lovely bosom." That fact likely accounted for the modest scrap of hideous fabric the lady donned with a nauseating regularity. A shame the young lady went through the trouble to hide her one mentionable attribute. Though convenient, considering the important plans he had for Miss Fairfax and her shawl. He eyed the man through hooded lashes until the demmed fool registered Edmund's dark displeasure.

His laughter faded and he swallowed audibly once more. "I

know the one," he said. He gave his cravat a tug. "Th-though my daughter has large bosom as well and is far prettier than the Fairfax chit. Are you sure—?"

Edmund fixed an icy glower on the man that forced him into silence. Then, he took a long, slow swallow of his drink and set the empty glass down. Folding his arms across his chest, Edmund stood over the man in a method he'd long used to rouse terror in much stronger men than this coward before him. "She wears a shawl." He dropped his voice to a hushed whisper. "I would like that shawl." Once he had that piece of fabric in his possession, it would set his calculated plan into motion. And from there, he would have more. A devilish excitement stirred in his chest.

"Eh? A shawl?" The older man fixed his gaze on the empty glass of brandy and then cast a longing glance over at the sideboard. The man was a drunkard. He wore his need for liquor upon his person the way a fat dowager doused herself in too fragrant perfume on a hot summer day. Relishing the other man's inherent weakness, Edmund picked up the decanter and splashed several fingerfuls into the glass. That failing had cost the viscount a small fortune, property, and, inevitably, his daughter's good standing in Society. He held the glass up in salute and took another swallow.

Lord Waters closed his eyes momentarily. Sweat rolled down his brow. This time, he did away with all hint of politeness and dragged the back of his sleeve across his head. "Why should I help you, Rutland? What are the benefits in me collecting anything for you? You already have enough."

Edmund passed over his half-empty glass. "Ahh, because I'm prepared to forgive a portion of your debt each time you gather information about Miss Fairfax." Waters hungrily eyed the glass and then greedily grasped at the offering.

Waters accepted the glass with trembling fingers. Liquid droplets splashed over the rim as he raised the tumbler to his lips and took a slow, savoring sip. "Why should I trust you?" he finally asked, eying Edmund with not nearly enough suspicion in his bleary eyes.

"The way I see it, Waters, you've little choice."

Lord Waters downed the remaining contents of his glass and then eyed the amber droplets clinging to the rim. Then like the base animal he was, he licked the remaining liquid from the edge and set the snifter down. "You'll forgive my debts, then."

"Each time you help." Though he suspected those debts would be promptly owed him once more when they sat down behind a faro table at Forbidden Pleasures.

The man scratched at his paunch. "Very well. The chit's shawl." He dusted his arm over his perspiring brow once again. "How do you expect me to collect this scrap?"

Edmund cracked his knuckles. "That is for you to worry about." He strode around his desk and reclaimed his seat. "We're done here," he said, coolly dismissing the viscount. With an unholy delight in the other man's discomposure, he pulled out the folio that contained Waters and a whole host of other gentleman in his debt, and proceeded to review the names, dismissing the fat viscount.

"But..."

Edmund slowly raised his gaze, daring the man to speak.

The man sketched a jerky bow and then all but sprinted from the room, knocking over the furniture in his haste to be free.

He sat back, looking down at a whole host of names of men who'd already realized that one could never truly be free of Edmund, the Marquess of Rutland—unless he wished it. And unfortunately for Miss Honoria Fairfax, she was what he wished for.

With a dark laugh that would have roused unholy terror in the unwitting young lady, he returned his attention to the men in his debt.

CHAPTER 2

SEATED UPON A GILT ROPE chair at the far back wall of Lady Delenworth's ballroom, alongside her two dearest, oft-bickering friends, Miss Phoebe Barrett surveyed the dancers assembling for the latest set. Dubbed, the Scandalous Row, she, Miss Honoria Fairfax, and Lady Gillian Farendale, had found friendship early in the Season. Born to notorious families, who Society still spoke of with scandalized whispers, there had been something less lonely, something special in finding other scandalous sisters in this cold, heartless world. For the short time they'd known one another, they'd forged a bond stronger than most familial connections.

Phoebe proceeded to study the crowd with no little boredom and a great deal of tedium.

Then the orchestra struck up the chords of the next set.

As the daughter to one of the society's most reprehensible letches, Phoebe really *should* crave that tedium. And yet...eying the twirling waltzers, she perched on the edge of the seat hungering for more.

Ignoring her friends' prattling, Phoebe's gaze snagged upon one couple. A tall gentleman angled the lady in his arms closer and whispered something into her ear that brought a blush to the young woman's cheeks. Phoebe's heart doubled its beat. A wistful sigh escaped her. To be the recipient of that—

Honoria stuck her hand out and waved it before Phoebe's eyes, startling her into a soft gasp. "Hullo? Are you listening?" she asked with the same exasperation as a governess dealing with a recalcitrant charge.

Phoebe stole a final peak at the lord and lady and returned her attention to her far more predictable, far less exciting life. "Er, no I'm afraid I was woolgathering."

"Phoebe," Gillian wagged a finger. "You shan't capture a single gentleman's interest if you're forever woolgathering."

She frowned. "I'm not forever woolgathering," she said a touch defensively. Simultaneously, her friends arched a single eyebrow. She sighed. "Well, perhaps a bit," she conceded. "About the waltz." And being the recipient of such a gentleman's devotion.

Gillian gave her a smile of agreement. "I find it romantic, as well." A twinkle lit her eyes. "Particularly if one has the right gentleman to—oomph," she grunted as Honoria buried her elbow into her side. "There is nothing romantic about a waltz," Honoria scolded. "It is only an opportunity for notorious scoundrels to place their hands—" Honoria continued over Gillian's shocked gasp, "on a lady's person. Cads all of them." She jerked her chin. "Especially that one."

They followed her stare to Lord Allswood who brazenly eyed Phoebe, even over the head of his golden dance partner.

Phoebe swallowed a groan. "Oh, blast." Gillian patted her hand. "It is because you are so lovely."

"It is because he is so loathsome," she muttered. She shifted in her seat, presenting the scoundrel with her shoulder. "My father likely owes him a debt." After all, her father owed most gentlemen, and some not so gentlemanly men, one form of debt or another. The vile wastrel.

"I daresay you require something such as Honoria's hideous shawl to detract from your beauty."

Honoria touched the edges of the fabric. "I like this particular piece," she said, defending the garment. She bristled with indignation. "Furthermore, we all conceal our…" she colored. "Er, attributes."

Phoebe reached over and gave the piece a bold tug. "Well, I, for one, think it is a silly habit for a young lady to fall into. Such protective garments should only be donned by aging ladies or ladies desperate to avoid attention." She stuck her finger up. "Nor should a lady hide who she truly is."

Honoria pursed her lips. "I, for one, do not care for a gentleman who'd be so captivated by…by…" Her cheeks reddened.

"Your charms," Gillian supplied, her gaze still surveying the crowd.

Though, it would be scandalous for any of them to say as much, they all knew what Gillian implied—Phoebe, too, needed to conceal her large bosom. Frustration ran through her at a world where women were seen for the connections they could make and their physical attributes and not the power of their minds or the beauty of their soul.

A beleaguered sigh escaped Gillian. "Even honorable gentlemen are interested in…in…" She motioned to Phoebe. "That," she substituted for which Phoebe was immensely grateful. It would hardly benefit any of their reputations to be discussing their… charms in the midst of Lady Delenworth's crowded ballroom.

"Regardless," Honoria pursed her lips. "Well, we shall not allow him to approach you."

Phoebe stole a sideways peek at the still leering lord. He was nothing if not persistent in his intentions, intentions that were anything but proper.

"No, you deserve an honorable and good gentleman," Gillian said with a loyalty that pulled at Phoebe's heart.

An inelegant snort burst from Honoria. "There is no such thing."

She gave silent thanks when the strands of the waltz drew to a finish and the couples upon the dance floor glided back to their respective places in a flurry of satin skirts and brightly colored breeches. Phoebe worried the flesh of her lower lip. The tediousness of this whole husband-hunting thing was well and truly grating. She didn't doubt she must make a match. It was inevitable. After all, there were few options for an unwed lady and one of scandalous origins, no less. Still, she held to firm ideals in the gentleman who would ultimately become her husband. Honorable. Respectable. Good-hearted. In short, a man nothing like her father.

She studied the fashionable noblemen escorting their ladies out to the dance floor for the next set. The orchestra struck up a lively country reel and the couples whirred past in an explosion of vibrant satin skirts. Surely, there was a decent, honorable fellow among the lot. She cast a sideways glance down the row at her friends. Or rather, three. They required three gentlemen, more specifically. "Not all gentlemen are rogues," Phoebe felt inclined to point out.

Honoria let out a beleaguered sigh. "You are a hopeless romantic, Phoebe."

She frowned, not caring to be painted with their black and white brush. "Perhaps I am romantic," she said, tilting her chin back. "But I'll not judge everyone and anyone because of several dissolute men." At her careless words, she bit the inside of her cheek.

A pall of silence descended over their trio. Gillian, with her pale blonde hair and piercing green eyes was by far the most striking of the friends, and yet a scandal involving her sister jilted at the altar by a "rogue" had marked her as less than marriageable material. They took care not to speak of the scandal in her past—unless Gillian herself cared to discuss it. Which invariably, she did not.

The country reel came to a rousing finish met by an explosion of applause.

"Which dance is next?" Gillian arched her neck, in an attempt to see the orchestra as though in doing so she might find the answer to her question.

"Consult your card," Honoria said on a sigh. "Never mind," she added and scanned her empty card. "A quadrille."

A gentleman, one of the roguish sorts with unfashionably long locks and a lascivious glint in his eyes, started toward Gillian.

The three women fixed matching glares on him and sent him scurrying away.

"He'd approach you without even a formal introduction." Honoria jerked her chin toward the fast-fleeing rogue. "I told you. Nigh impossible to find the honorable gentleman you speak of."

Phoebe certainly hoped her friend was wrong in this regard, and she'd wager, if she were the wagering sort, which she assuredly was not, that both Honoria and Gillian hoped she was wrong, too. Gillian did not rise to Honoria's baiting. "I know such a man exists." Her eyes grew distant, hinting at secrets there. Widening her eyes, Phoebe stared at her friend. By the saints in heaven, some gentleman had captured Gillian's attention? A blush stained the other lady's cheeks and she rushed to speak. "Have *you* found such a gentleman?" Hope filled her almost lyrical words. From her pale whitish-blonde hair to the soft clarity of her voice, there was an almost otherworldly quality to the woman.

Phoebe warmed under their scrutiny. "No, I hope to." A gentleman who'd encourage her love of travel and welcome a lady who'd see the world beyond the dark, gray confines of their superficial London world.

A wave of restlessness stirred in her and she fiddled with her ruffled ivory satin skirts. She surveyed the room once more and a shiver of distaste ran along the column of her spine. Lord Allswood, with his latest dance partner, continued to eye her with that lascivious gleam in his bloodshot eyes. Likely from too much drink. Gillian groaned and, for a moment, Phoebe believed her friend had noted horrid Lord Allswood's unwanted attention. Then she looked out at the crowd.

Gillian's plump mother, the Marchioness of Ellsworth, marched through the ballroom with fleshy cheeks and a determined purpose in her stride. She had her fingers wrapped about the forearm of a reed thin, too-tall dandy in pink satin knee breeches.

"Knee breeches, for the love of God and all the saints in heaven," Gillian complained, mouthing a prayer to the heavens. "What gentleman wears knee breeches?"

"Pink knee breeches, no less," Honoria pointed out unhelpfully.

Phoebe jabbed her in the side with her elbow. "Ouch." The other lady winced. "I was merely pointing out…" Her words trailed off as the Marchioness of Ellsworth stopped before them. She peered down her broad nose at the ladies her daughter had marked as friends, in clear disapproval. Then with a dismissive once over, turned to her daughter. "Gillian, please allow me to introduce you to Lord Appleby Hargrove."

At the prolonged awkward pall of silence, Phoebe discreetly nudged the suddenly laconic lady with her knee.

Gillian sprung to her feet with a pink blush. "My lord," she murmured, dropping a curtsy.

He tugged at the lapels of his mauve coat. "Lady Gillian," he said in a nasal tone that caused all three young ladies to wince. The gentleman's valet who'd let him go out with pink breeches and a mauve coat should be sacked first thing, Phoebe thought dryly. "A pleasure," he said, his gaze lingering overly on Gillian's generous hips as though she were a broodmare he was sizing up. Phoebe's fingers twitched involuntary with a need to plant a facer in the letch's face. Surely, the marchioness recognized even with the scandal in their family's past, Gillian deserved a good deal better than a suitor more interested in her friend's generous endowments?

The marchioness reluctantly looked to her daughter's companions. Phoebe wasn't certain if the lady's disapproval stemmed from their scandalous pasts or their status as mere misses. "Lord Hargrove, may I also present to you Miss Phoebe Barrett and Miss Henrietta—?"

"Honoria," her daughter corrected.

"—Fairfax," she went on as though Gillian hadn't spoken.

The young gentleman flicked his gaze disinterestedly over Honoria's trim frame and ivory skirts. "Charmed."

"Undoubtedly," she muttered under her breath.

Pride swelled in Phoebe's breast at her friend's unerring pride in the face of the rude young nobleman.

Next, Lord Hargrove passed his blue-eyed stare over Phoebe. His gaze fell to her décolletage, his eyes lingering overly long on her too-generous bosom. When he looked at her, a glint of lust reflected in the depths of his eyes. She shivered, willing to trade her left hand in this moment for her friend's cashmere shawl.

"I was mentioning how very graceful you are, Gillian," the marchioness said sharply. By the hard glint in her eyes as she alternated her gaze between Phoebe and Lord Hargrove, she'd detected the dishonorable gentleman's interest in a woman other than her daughter. "His Lordship has asked that I coordinate an introduction so he might ask you to dance."

With seeming reluctance, he returned his attention to the by far loveliest of the scandalous trio. "My lady, will you do me the honor of partnering me in the next set."

A desperate glint lit the young lady's eyes, but then her mother fixed a black glare on her and Gillian spoke on a rush. "It would be a pleasure, my lord." He held his arm out. Gillian hesitated a moment and then with the same enthusiasm as Marie Antoinette being marched to the guillotine, she placed her fingertips upon his satin coat sleeve and allowed him to escort her off.

The marchioness stared after the departing couple and then without a backward glance for her daughter's wayward friends, turned on a huff, and beat a hasty retreat.

"A lovely lady," Honoria said. "Why, I give thanks every day that it is just my aunt, so I do not have to contend with an overbearing mama and her scheming ways." She gave a mock shudder. "A mother who would turn her daughter over to such a dandified fop, a shame, indeed."

Phoebe opened her mouth to agree just as her gaze collided with Lord Allswood. She bit back a curse.

"What is it?"

She ignored her friend's quietly spoken question. The determined gentleman moved through the crowd with a singular purpose in his step. Phoebe hopped to her feet. Honoria looked up at her and then followed her attention across the ballroom. She immediately rose in a flurry of white skirts. Having made too many hasty escapes from the determined Lord Allswood, they immediately sought refuge behind the towering Doric column, and proceeded to skirt the edge of the crowded ballroom. Their ivory and white skirts pressed together, they made their way to the back of the ballroom and slipped past the crimson red drapes, into an alcove.

The ladies shared a conspiratorial smile. "I wish we could stay in here forever," Phoebe whispered. Or at the very least until Lord Allswood took himself off to the card tables set up in Lady Delenworth's back room. "Why does he persist?"

"Because you're perfectly lovely and clever."

She snorted. A cad such as Lord Allswood would hardly care whether she was as empty between the ears as a plaster wall. He was, if nothing else, tenacious.

"We cannot remain here all night."

No, no they couldn't.

A spark glinted in Honoria's eyes and then she fiddled with her haircombs while chewing her lower lip in deep concentration.

Phoebe furrowed her brow. "What are you—?"

"Aha," she said, with a pleased smile as she managed to untangle the haircombs from her dark tresses. She stuck them between her teeth and spun Phoebe around.

"What—?" She winced as with her hasty efforts, Honoria tugged too hard at her hair. She gave one more tug and tears sprung to Phoebe's eyes.

Engrossed, Honoria tossed the butterfly combs onto the small, velvet chair where they landed with a soft thump. She took the rose, diamond-encrusted combs worth more than any and every bauble shared by Phoebe and her younger sister, Justina, combined and tucked one into Phoebe's brown hair. "Gentlemen do not look carefully enough," she carefully arranged the other diamond-encrusted comb. "They see white skirts and certain garments." She removed her ivory cashmere shawl and draped it over Phoebe's shoulders, and then guided her around. "Such as my shawl, and then don't see beyond that."

Phoebe widened her eyes as her friend's efforts made sense. Honoria thought to deter Lord Allswood's efforts. She made a sound of protest. "I cannot take this from you," she said, shrugging the delicate slip of fabric from her shoulders. As long as she'd known the other woman, this scrap of cashmere had been the dearest item in her friend's possession. She was never without the garment.

"You're wearing it incorrectly," Honoria scolded, ignoring Phoebe's concerns. She carefully arranged it just below Phoebe's shoulders. "And yes, you can. Come. I imagine he's since gone and now you may move freely." They slipped outside the curtained alcove and startled gasps escaped them.

"Father," Phoebe murmured, dropping a hasty curtsy. Her friend followed suit.

He ignored their polite greeting, his frown deepened as he looked between them. "There you are, gel," he said at last. "Been looking for you," he snapped.

Having learned long ago to not rile him, as he was always unpredictable in his temperaments, she calmly said, "I'd torn my hem and it required repairing." The lie came effortlessly.

He ignored her words, turning to Honoria. "Miss Fairfax," he said.

"My lord," she returned.

Wordlessly his beady blue eyes went to her décolletage and Phoebe fisted her hands at her side, knowing there was supposed to be a sin in putting one's hands upon one's father, but, by God, she wanted to bloody his bulbous nose for the way he leered at Honoria. Guilt at having commandeered the other woman's shawl filled her.

Sorry, she mouthed as regret and mortified embarrassment lapped at her conscience.

Except, when the viscount picked up his gaze there was a

detached coolness there. "Come along," he commanded and wrapped his fingers about Phoebe's wrist, all but dragging her away. "There is someone I wish for you to meet."

She cast a longing glance back at her friend who stood staring commiseratively after her, and then returned her attention forward to where Lord Allswood waited, a triumphant grin on his hard lips.

"...Lord Allswood..."

Phoebe groaned. "No." She dug her heels in, either forcing him to stop or drag her to the floor.

He stopped and scowled at her.

"I require a moment of air," she said quickly, her mind turning entirely too slowly.

Her traitorous father scratched his bald, sweating pate. "Air?" he said it as though she sought the king's crown.

Nonetheless, she nodded once. "Air. The heat of the ballroom is too much," she finished lamely.

Before he could issue protest, she spun swiftly on her heel in a flurry of whispery skirts and all but sprinted away from her father, away from Lord Allswood and away from the ballroom—in desperate search of peace.

CHAPTER 3

EDMUND PASSED A CYNICAL GAZE over the tedious activity of the crowded ballroom. Foppish swains converged upon the Diamonds of the First Water. Couples twirled in a kaleidoscope of colorful satins. The tinkling of giggling ladies grated. He'd quite studiously avoided such infernal crushes. Not for the reason of avoiding the marriage trap. Even the simpering ladies knew better than to seek his favor. He belonged less in this polite world than the devil did in that fabled heaven.

The rare appearances he made were never without purpose and certainly not without reason. This night was no exception. He skimmed a hard stare over the lords and ladies present. White gown upon white gown created an almost cloud-like effect of debutantes. The unfortunate lady he'd selected as the lead player in his scheme was no exception. He eyed the dark-haired young woman with her nondescript features, brown eyes, white gown, and that silly shawl. Though in fairness to that otherwise useless scrap of fabric, tonight it had served its purpose. So, this was Miss Honoria Fairfax, Margaret's niece, and also the young woman he'd wed.

From her narrow-waisted frame, to her pale complexion, there was nothing that roused even the hint of lust in the young woman. A hard smile played on his lips, which sent a dandy in yellow satin breeches who'd been passing too close, scurrying in the opposite direction. The taste of revenge, however, would serve as a potent aphrodisiac when the time came to ruin her. One of Lady Delenworth's liveried servants stepped into his line of vision, holding out his silver tray of champagne flutes. Edmund flicked an icy stare over the young fool who'd dared interrupt him. The man stumbled back, nearly upending his burden, and then scrambled off.

Edmund returned his attention to the drab wallflower he'd eventually take to wife, but the pale blonde beauty on her right leaned forward, restricting his view. He'd taken care to learn everything and anything about Margaret's niece; he knew she donned that silly shawl, as though to protect herself from leering eyes. He scoffed. As though one would leer at one such as her. The lady enjoyed reading. And she'd made the fatal mistake of taking two women as her close friends and confidantes. The sad creature had yet to realize that those ties to other people, be it friends, family, or lovers, invariably weakened one. She would learn, and then she'd never again make the same careless mistake.

The blonde beauty more suited to his tastes, leaned back and revealed the other dark-haired young lady—Viscount Waters' daughter, Miss Phoebe Barrett. He passed a quick, methodical gaze on the woman whose familial connection would lead him to Miss Honoria Fairfax. A delicate jaw, high cheeks, and a pert nose, she may as well have been any other young English woman. He made to return his attention to the woman he'd trap, when Miss Barrett's full lips turned down at the corner. Even with the space between them, he detected the hard, disapproving glint in her eyes. For one moment he believed she'd noted his scrutiny, which was, of course, preposterous. One such as she could never glean a hint of his treachery. He followed her stare.

Unaware of his scrutiny, she boldly glared at Lord Allswood. A mirthless chuckle rumbled up from Edmund's chest as the two studied one another. Ah, so the lady had a lover, and by the furious set to her mouth—she was an angry lover. Then, he looked to the fop, Lord Allswood, and followed the other man's gaze to the woman's generous décolletage. A wave of unexpected lust slammed into Edmund. The otherwise ordinary lady possessed the lush, tempting form he'd long admired. An angry, lush, lover. Never before would he believe himself capable of envying that fool Allswood. He did in that moment.

As though she felt his gaze upon her, Miss Barrett snapped her head up and looked about. Edmund shifted behind the column, escaping her notice…and waited. He'd grown adept at waiting. For triumph and victory was made all the sweeter with the wait. In addition to the lesson on weakness he'd learned as a youth, he'd also come to know the importance of masterful timing, and so he remained fixed to the marble floor, behind the column, occasionally shifting so he might steal furtive glances at the lady he sought.

Edmund swallowed back a curse at the now empty row of chairs. He quickly scanned the ballroom for a glimpse of the lady and found her in moments. Others might have failed to note the rapidly fleeing Miss Honoria Fairfax as she made her way down the perimeter of the ballroom, but as one who'd perfected subterfuge, he recognized it in another. He immediately started moving after those nauseating white skirts. He gave thanks for that ivory cashmere shawl; the one identifier of the dark-haired woman who represented all on his quest for revenge.

With a purposeful step, he strode through the thick crush of bodies. Gentlemen paled as he cut a swath through the crowd. The married ones frowned, pulling their wives closer. The mamas glowered, pulling their innocent daughters even closer. A hard smile formed on his lips. Then, one of the benefits of being the most feared, unrelenting lord was that it spared him from inane company and made his orchestrated meeting with Miss Fairfax all the easier.

Edmund exited the ballroom and strode down the narrow, dimly lit corridor just as the lady turned down the end of the hall. He quickened his step and then a splash of ivory caught his notice. He drew to a slow stop, a humorless grin turning his lips upward at the corner.

Fate proved once again the undeniable truth—the devil loved a sinner. He swiped the modest fabric off the thin carpet and without breaking stride, stuffed it into the front pocket of his jacket and continued walking forward, after the unsuspecting young lady. Edmund turned at the end of the hall and silently cursed. He ducked back as the dark-haired debutante froze. "Hullo," she called out.

Either the lady met her lover or courted her own ruin. He paused, counting his good fortune. He'd interrupt any possible assignation between the lady and the young swain she'd meet.

There was also the surprising good piece in not requiring the viscount's assistance in this, maintaining the debt he held over the man. Edmund waited several moments and then peered around the corner. But for the handful of shadows playing off the floors from the lit sconces at each end of the hall, the corridor remained empty. If he were meeting a lover, where would he arrange that assignation? Just another benefit of having taken countless lovers in countless ballrooms in countless trysting spots. Edmund started down the hall, bypassing doors already passed by the lady herself. He made his way to the row of floor-length windows, hardly conducive to concealment, but certainly beneficial when one welcomed the pleasure of a voyeur.

With excitement thrumming through his veins, he silently pressed the handle. He shoved the door open and wordlessly stepped out onto the stone terrace.

"Blast."

He stilled.

A flurry of cursing rent the quiet of the night. *Riiiiip.* "Bloody hell."

And for the first time since he'd set his scheme into motion involving the dull, hideously plain Miss Honoria Fairfax he felt the faint stirring of interest. And if he were a less cynical, less practiced rogue, he'd have been intrigued by the cursing, too loud for a tryst, young lady at the far end of the terrace.

"Is that you?"

He wandered down the stone patio, the tread of his boots noiseless, silent as the dead.

"Oh, do hurry, Honoria." Edmund drew to a sudden, jarring stop, a black frown on his lips. *Honoria*? Then who was the white-skirted creature he'd been erroneously chasing after? He growled. Bloody hell, he'd followed the blasted wrong chit. Cursing his ill luck he spun on his heel and started back toward the double doors, when the lady called out.

"I'm afraid I've snagged my gown on Lord Delenworth's spear."

That gave Edmund pause and, despite himself, for the first time in more than a score of years, an honest grin pulled at his lips. He quickly flattened them into a familiar, hard line.

"I'm here," Miss Phoebe Barrett quietly called, "and this is certainly not as pleasurable as I'd imagined."

Edmund tamped down any amusement at the lady's unwitting innuendo. He strode closer. The thick clouds, obscuring the moon, shifted and cast a pale glow of white light upon the terrace to the lone figure of Miss Phoebe Barrett bent over the balustrade with her derriere presented for his viewing pleasure, buttocks far more generous than he'd previously credited.

He stopped beside the lady angling her neck about to catch a glimpse of her friend. Their gazes collided. "Hullo," he drawled on a silken whisper.

Her eyebrows shot to her hairline as her eyes formed round moons. "Uh-er, hello," she finished weakly.

He closed the distance between them and layered his hands upon the stone ledge. "Do you require assistance?" Though, in actuality, the lady was a good deal more appealing with her backside presented to him like a generous offering.

"Assistance?" She squiggled and squirmed and an unexpected wave of lust hit him. Then she stilled and he cursed the fates for stealing his fleeting enjoyment of the evening. She sighed. "Yes. I believe I've dropped something over the edge." She bit her lip and scanned the darkened grounds. "My shawl. I suspect the wind may have carried it off when I was looking at the grounds below." She suspected *wrong*. "Because there really is no other accounting, for it's gone missing." Ah, unfortunate for the lady there was one accounting for it. "I would have noticed it gone before this moment," she carried on.

He winced at her inane ramblings. God, he detested the infernal prattling of the innocent misses. Only... He eyed her with a renewed interest; this woman who could, nay would, lead him to her friend and, ultimately, that friend's ruination. He'd be served by ingratiating himself to the lady. In so doing, it would lessen his dependence on the lady's drunken, whore-mongering father.

"Hullo?" she called out, a question in her tone.

Drawing on the hint of remembrance of the charming, youthful man who'd once inspired smiles in a lady, he said in a teasing voice, "I gather you're unable to free yourself."

She nodded, the movement awkward at the upended angle of her body. "Indeed," she said, with an almost eagerness that he'd followed the direction of her thoughts. "Only, I leaned too far, and how was I to know Lord Delenworth should have a cherub with a spear jutting out from the edge of the balustrade?" He rubbed his temples to dull a sudden megrim brought on by the lady's prattling. "Alas, I've caught a lace ruffle of my gown upon the—"

"Will you not shut up?" he bit out. Her innocent ramblings came to an immediate cessation. He closed his eyes and prayed to a God he didn't believe in for patience.

"Did you tell me to shut up?" Her indignant question slashed into his thoughts.

Despite the outrage in her tone, her question provided the opportunity to rectify his rash misstep. Edmund leaned over the edge and the lady flinched at his nearness. "Indeed not, my lady." She hesitated, unblinking like an owl. "I'd asked if you needed help getting up."

"Oh." Then she smiled widely and in that moment, he was struck by the staggering truth that the lady was a good deal more interesting than the plain, unmemorable creature he'd eyed in the ballroom. She was rather…pleasant. Granted, rather pleasant had never roused any great desire inside him, but it made his intentions to spend time with Miss Honoria Fairfax's friend, at least…palatable. "Oh, well, of course, that makes a good deal more sense than you being so rude as to tell me to shut up." If she thought a mere shut up was rude, the lady's head would spin if she knew even a hint of his debauched behaviors through the years. "Forgive me." He'd forgive her anything if she ceased her infernal carrying on.

With a tug, he freed the lady's gown from Delenworth's spear. Or rather the man's cherub's spear.

"Splendid," the lady exclaimed.

He didn't care to think about old, portly Delenworth plowing this one over the side of this same balustrade. An unlikely pairing those two would be. He scowled. Why in blazes should he care whether Miss Phoebe Barrett was plowed by anyone? The lady fiddled with her hideously ruffled ivory skirts, drawing his gaze downward and providing him a welcome diversion from his confounded thoughts. He lingered a moment upon that generous bosom. Creamy white. Lush. Begging for a man's attention.

"I…forgive me, I…thank you," she said quietly.

He sketched a bow. "Might I have the honor of knowing the lady I've rescued from a vicious spearing, my lady?" Edmund's shaft stirred with delightful images of giving the young lady a vicious spearing. What manner of bloody madness was this, lusting after this one?

"I'm not a lady."

All the better. He arched a single eyebrow in invitation.

Her cheeks burned red. "I mean, I'm not a 'my lady'. I'm a miss." She dropped a curtsy. "Miss Phoebe Barrett."

A detail he'd already gathered. "Ah," he said noncommittally.

She cast a glance over her shoulder, out into the darkened London night. When she returned her gaze to his, an unexpected wariness gleamed in her blue eyes. "If you'll excuse me," she said, stiffly polite. Did he imagine the previous chit chattering more than a magpie? "It wouldn't do for us to be discovered together."

"No, it wouldn't." He schooled his expression into that of concerned gentleman. "Forgive me." He made to leave.

"Wait," she called out.

They always did. Some inherent darkness she and every other young lady didn't even know they carried invariably drove back logic and caution and replaced them with recklessness. He turned and looked questioningly back at her. "I don't know your name," she blurted.

He sketched a bow. "Edmund Deering, the 5th Marquess of Rutland." Scandalized shock did not replace the too-trusting openness of her expression. Instead, she continued to evaluate him in that curious manner; an unlikely pairing of innocence and boldness.

Then her expression grew shuttered. Ah, so she'd heard of him. Of course she had. Even though he studiously avoided polite *ton* events if they didn't serve some grander scheme, ladies old and young alike had heard of him—and knew to avoid him. For the unsophistication of one such as Miss Phoebe Barrett in her ivory skirts, there was also that unexpected guardedness that likely came in her connection to that fat, reprobate Waters. "I should leave."

Wiser words were never spoken. "Yes," he concurred.

The lady stepped right. He matched her movements. She stepped left. He followed suit, blocking her exit.

Alarm lined Miss Barrett's face. A hand fluttered to her breast and he buried a black humor at that ineffectual, defensive gesture. "My lord?" She looked quizzically up at him.

Her instincts were sharp. "Surely, you do not intend to leave without rescuing your shawl?" As though that hand could protect her from his legendary prowess. His was an arrogance based on years of bringing lonely, eager ladies to great heights of pleasure.

His words proved the correct ones. She caught her plump, lower lip between even pearl white teeth and angled back around. Miss Barrett had made her first of many missteps around him—she'd demonstrated a weakness. The shawl, an item belonging to Miss Honoria Fairfax, meant nothing to this woman, and yet she'd risk her reputation, safety, and well-being in his, a stranger's, presence... but for her friend's shawl. This hopeless devotion demonstrated her weakness—she cared that much about Miss Fairfax and that would prove useful. He pressed, unrelenting. "I gather it is an important article to you," he said in soft tones. It was also a fact he intended to put to valuable use. He held out his arm. "Allow me to lend my assistance."

Except, she narrowed her eyes suspiciously. "I...it wouldn't be proper," she said at last.

He'd not given the lady enough credit. With her caution and hesitancy, she'd already demonstrated more reserve than he expected of an innocent. Edmund bowed his head. "Of course," he agreed. "Forgive me." He backed away once again. He turned to leave while counting silently to five. He made it no higher than three. "Wait!" she called out, bringing him to a halt. "Perhaps if you remain here while I search below then I might freely conduct my search. That way, if any interlopers," trysting couples, "should happen by, then you might send them on their way."

A slow grin formed on his lips that would have likely chilled Miss Barrett's heart should she have seen it. He schooled his features and turned back around. "It would be my pleasure."

She gave him a wide, unfettered smile. This was not the guarded, icy, seductive smile worn by the lovers he took to his bed, but rather an expression that spoke to her artlessness. Odd, she should retain even a shred of innocence with her bastard of a father. The viscount's daughter sprinted for the end of the terrace with a speed anything but ladylike. She raced down the steps and disappeared into the gardens below.

Edmund strolled closer, damning the thick cloud coverage overhead that blotted the moon and obscured the lady from his vision. She moved noisily through the plants. Then the moon's glow penetrated the passing clouds, illuminating her. "Do you see it, Miss

Barrett?" he called down.

She paused and frowned up at him. "Hush," she scolded as though she dealt with a naughty child and not the most black-hearted scoundrel in London. She held a finger to her lips. Her tone was far gentler, almost apologetic when she again spoke. "Mustn't be discovered, you know."

"No," he called quietly down. Discovery with this one would prove disastrous. It would prevent him from the revenge he intended to exact upon Margaret, the Duchess of Monteith. "If you require my assistance, you need but ask."

THE STRANGER'S SOFTLY SPOKEN PROMISE carried down into Lord Delenworth's gardens. Phoebe lingered, staring up at the dashing stranger far longer than was appropriate and then gave her head a clearing shake. She resumed her search for a splash of ivory fabric amidst the darkened landscape. Though in truth, her efforts, her attention, which should be reserved for the very important task at hand were instead reserved for the gentleman, a man whose name was even more talked about than her own.

Phoebe picked her way down a row of expertly pruned circular boxwoods. Then, a gentleman of his stunning beauty well knew the risk faced of being discovered, unchaperoned with a lady. He had the face and form that hinted at a masculine perfection that made a lady do foolish things...such as forgetting she was alone. With a gentleman. In a garden. Under the pale moonlight.

She cast one glance back up at the marquess with his broad, powerful back presented to her while he stood sentry, then...she wasn't most ladies. She was one of the Scandalous Row of ladies from illicit families. A flash of white snagged her notice and hope stirred in her chest, drawing her steps in that direction. She paused beside a full rosebush of white blooms, tightly closed from the evening's chill. Only, he'd displayed no outward reaction to her given name. No shock had flared to life in his eyes at her connection to the lecherous Lord Waters and his excessive drinking and wagering.

She sighed, shaking aside the poignant musings and scanned the grounds for the fabric given her by her devoted, loyal friend.

Phoebe knew but pieces of the story behind the shawl but it was a cherished gift and all that remained of her friend's departed father. And now it was gone because of Phoebe's carelessness. She stopped and surveyed the grounds for a hint of white in the inky darkness. Gone, all because she'd rushed off in an attempt to avoid loathsome Lord Allswood and—

A shadow fell over her shoulder. It blotted out the moon's light and she shrieked, but the soft cry died on her lips at the length of ivory cashmere dangling before her eyes. Phoebe whirled around and impulsively plucked the muddied shawl from the gentleman's fingers. She crushed it to her chest. "How... Where...?" Her throat worked convulsively. "Thank you," she said, her voice roughened with emotion.

The marquess' hard lips turned up in a grin, the only softening of the harsh, angular planes of his chiseled cheeks. "Alas, I fear it is more rough for the wear," he said sympathetically. He shot a hand out and captured the edge of the cashmere, rubbing the soft material between his thumb and forefinger.

"Thank you," she said once more, studying his powerful hands encased in gloves. Something appealed in those slight distracted movements of his long fingers.

He released it suddenly. "The garment is so very important that you'd risk your reputation with me, a stranger." His was not a question but rather an observation of a man with an intelligent gleam in his brown eyes.

She nodded anyway. "It belongs to H..." *Honoria.* "My friend," she settled for, rightfully cautious.

Silence descended. The intermittent cry of a night bird split the quiet. She should have left long ago. Her father shut away in those card rooms would never note her absence. Her loving mama, on the other hand, would very well note she'd gone missing, as would her friends, and still she remained.

"Well," they spoke in unison.

"Thank you," she said softly. "I am in your debt."

He swept a respectful bow. "It was, indeed, nothing, Miss Barrett."

"Phoebe." At her own boldness, embarrassed heat slapped her cheeks. There was nothing polite or proper in giving him leave to use her given name, and yet by the nature of their meeting and her debt to him, there seemed a bond of sorts between them. "Considering the kindness you've shown, I thought it appropriate you call me by my Christian name." He said nothing, just continued to study her in that inscrutable manner until a pained awkwardness replaced the ease that had existed between her and this tall stranger only moments ago. Phoebe toyed with the fabric of Honoria's shawl and cleared her throat.

"Edmund."

She cocked her head. "Edmund," she murmured. There was nothing proper or appropriate in knowing him by his Christian name. She'd but heard the faintest whispers of this man; whispers she'd taken care to avoid. As victim to that same gossip, she detested any talk about other people. Though, there was nothing proper or appropriate in any of this exchange.

He gave her a gentle smile. "You should go," he said quietly.

Phoebe gave a reluctant nod. "I should." And yet, perhaps she was more of her shameful father's daughter than she'd ever feared because her feet remained fixed to the ground.

Edmund closed the space between them with languidly elegant movements. She swallowed hard as the gentle gleam in his eyes darkened, replaced with a harsh, angry glint. Then he blinked, so she thought she merely imagined the frigidity there. He angled his head down and touched his lips to hers.

A startled squeak escaped her and she danced out of reach. Her heart threatened to pound out of her chest. "What are you doing?" Her voice emerged as a breathless, barely-there whisper.

He opened his mouth.

Phoebe continued her retreat, never taking her gaze from his piercing brown eyes. She knocked against a stone statue and grunted.

Edmund took a step forward.

She jabbed a finger in his direction. "Stop." He froze. He'd intended to kiss her. She'd seen as much in his eyes. Gentlemen didn't kiss her, even those who'd determined her worth of little value for her connection to the lecherous, reprobate Viscount Waters. But this gentleman had. She kept her finger outstretched, warding him off.

"Forgive me." There was a harsh, almost gravelly quality to that whispered response. "I was taken by your beauty."

Phoebe knocked into a fountain and an inelegant snort escaped her. And gentlemen certainly were not taken by her *beauty*. She didn't possess the otherworldly exquisiteness of Gillian, or even the blonde prettiness associated with a proper English miss. Nor did she believe a stunning model of masculine perfection such as Edmund, 5th Marquess of Rutland, would be overcome with passion for one such as her.

A frown formed on his hard lips. "I don't know what you believe of me." The marquess folded his arms. "But I am not…" Heat blazed a path up her neck and burned her cheeks. He quirked an eyebrow.

"Immoral," she said on an angry whisper and then glanced about to be certain they weren't discovered and she was indeed forever labeled exactly that.

Edmund spread his arms wide. "It was never my intention to disrespect you. Perhaps I was caught in the moonlit moment or perhaps it was the splendor of these grounds, for I assure you, madam, I am not a gentleman to be so unwise as to give my attentions to a respectable lady, particularly an uninterested lady." He sketched a stiff bow. "Forgive me."

Guilt roiled in her belly and mixed with shame over the staggering truth—she'd not been uninterested. Which only made her body's awareness of a mysterious stranger all the more alarming.

He made to leave.

"Wait!"

He immediately halted at her exclamation.

"I didn't mean to question your motives." Up to that faintest meeting of lips, his intentions had been honorable and good. "Thank you for your assistance."

Edmund turned back and searched her face with his gaze once more, as though seeking the veracity of that apology. He gave a curt nod and then stalked over with a languid, almost panther-like sleekness that again sent warning bells clamoring. Or was that the rapid beat of her pulse? Her heart fluttered as he came to a stop beside her and she detested this inexplicable awareness of him that defied logic—something she'd always prided herself upon. He ran his knuckles over her cheek and her heart skipped several beats. "You wear your doubts upon your face, Miss Barrett. You're guarded."

She wet her lips, uncomfortable with that unerring accuracy. A mere stranger, he'd seen so very much to know... What he couldn't know is that having been born to a disloyal, black-hearted bastard such as her father, she'd learned long ago to be wary of a man's motives, while hopefully daring to believe there were men of honor.

"You say nothing, which is your confirmation," he admonished.

Unnerved by his ability to seemingly know her thoughts, she retreated, placing much needed space between them. Desperate to give her fingers some task, she ran them over the pink peonies, curled tightly in rest for the spring night. "I've learned to be cautious where a gentleman is concerned." She leaned forward and drew in the sweet, fragrant scent of the bud.

He narrowed his eyes to impenetrable slits, following her every movement. "And has there been a man who has hurt your heart, Phoebe?"

Phoebe, he called her Phoebe again, and that menacing, possessive whisper that was her name hinted of a man who'd likely stalk off and cut the cad if she gave a name. "Just—" *my father.* She pressed her lips into a tight line. "No one," she said at last, unwilling to trust this man she'd only just met with those protective pieces she carried close to her heart. "No one has hurt me."

"You wear a frown," he said quietly, boldly touching a finger to the corner of her lips. "A young woman such as you should not know this sadness."

A protestation sprung to her lips. She wasn't sad. She had a loving mother who was more friend than anything else. She had a brother and sister she would have walked across the coals of hell for, and she knew would do the same for her. And yet...there was sadness. The gold flecks in his eyes glinted with knowing, but he said nothing, for which she was grateful. Instead, he bent down, and she studied him curiously as he fiddled with something upon the ground, and then he stood. She widened her eyes at the rose he'd managed to free from the bush. "What is that?" she blurted.

The subtle twitching of his lips was incongruously hard with that gentle movement. "It is a rose. To remember our meeting." He held it out. He set his mouth in a serious line, driving back all earlier teasing. "I'd not have there be sadness between us, Phoebe."

She eyed it cautiously. "And should I remember this meeting?"

Her cheeks warmed at the boldness of her own question.

"Undoubtedly," he said in that smooth baritone that washed over her.

She claimed the flower and drew it close to her heart. The sweet, fragrant hint of the bloom wafted about the air, wrapping her in this magic pull, a product of the spring night and the forbiddenness of their exchange.

"She is not here," a young lady's impatient voice cut through the quiet.

"But I saw her go down the hall. Where else would she be?"

God love her friends for being so devoted as to set out in search of her. And yet, why was there this tug of regret?

Gillian spoke on a hushed whisper. "You do not believe something sinister has befallen—"

Honoria snorted. "You're so fanciful, Gillian. Nothing sinister happened to her and she is not here. We've walked the entire length and she's not…"

Had anyone else discovered her with Edmund, the Marquess of Rutland, there would be nothing but a hasty union based on her own ruin.

Silence.

Then the shuffling of slippered feet as the two ladies scrambled down the stone steps and stole into Lady Delenworth's gardens. She looked about, momentarily contemplating escape, but too late. Her friends found her. They staggered to a stop with their mouths agape, their eyes widened in a blend of horror and shock.

Heat splashed Phoebe's cheeks and she unwittingly took a step closer to the marquess.

"Phoebe?" Gillian asked. There was skepticism in that one-word utterance.

"The same," Phoebe said, in an attempt at nonchalance.

Honoria's wide, brown eyes alternated rapidly between Edmund and Phoebe. "What is the meaning of this?" she hissed. "Come away from him this instance, Phoebe Eloise Barrett," she snapped in the same angry tones of a mama who'd discovered her daughter… well…just as Phoebe had been discovered—in a compromising position.

Edmund remained stoically silent. His dark gaze lingered upon Honoria and then he returned his attention to Phoebe. "I should leave," he admitted, taking a step away.

"Yes, you should," Honoria tossed back with an unexpected cruelty in her tone that Phoebe didn't remember of her friend.

"Honoria," she chided. "I lost your shawl and he merely found it and returned it to me."

Fire flared in her friend's eyes.

She opened her mouth to say something, but Edmund touched his hand to hers, silencing the defense of him on her lips. Gillian stifled a gasp with her fingers.

"If you'll excuse me," he requested and sketched a deep, deferential bow to her and her friends, and then walked briskly off.

Honoria launched into a stinging rebuke. "What are you doing with one such as him? Do you have any idea who he is?"

Actually, she'd never before seen a glimpse of the dark, dashing stranger. There had been something menacing there in his eyes, and yet for the momentary flash, there had been warmth, something more that told a tale, and God help her for always longing for the story. "No," she said. Though that was not altogether true. "Well, now—"

"The Marquess of Rutland," Honoria hissed once more.

"Yes, he said as much." And he'd said a good deal more. *Edmund.*

Gillian widened her eyes to the size of moons. "You exchanged greetings." She shook her head disapprovingly, sending a golden-white curl falling over her eye. "That is not at all appropriate."

Phoebe bristled. At what point had her scheming, oft trouble-seeking friends become this stodgy, judgmental pair? "It was a chance meeting—"

Honoria jabbed a finger out. "Nothing about the Marquess of Rutland is a matter of chance. He is a heartless scoundrel."

She hesitated. Her friend's words borne of abhorrence spoke of a familiarity. "Do you know him?"

The too cynical for her years, young woman pursed her lips. "Not per se," she said with a touch of reluctance.

Phoebe released a breath.

At the knowing look given her by Phoebe, she added. "But I know enough of him."

"I've not seen him at any *ton* functions this entire Season."

"Nor will you," Gillian said, interrupting before Honoria could reply. "The marquess quite studiously avoids polite events. He is on Mama's list of gentlemen to avoid."

Ah, the infamous, ever growing list of suitors her daughter was not to look at, talk to, dance with, or breathe around. After her eldest daughter's elopement, she'd attended with far greater care the reputation of her other children.

"As he should be," Honoria snapped. She began to pace a small path along the row of peach rose bushes. "There is nothing honorable about him. He is dark, vile, evil, and…" She paused mid-stride and leaned close. "And he is rumored to tie his ladies up."

Phoebe furrowed her brow. "Whyever would he tie a lady up?" There really was no end to the limitless, shameful gossip put forth by Polite Society.

A blush stained Honoria's cheeks. "Well, for…for reasons that aren't appropriate." Her words so whisper soft that Phoebe strained to hear.

Gillian scratched her forehead. "I daresay I agree with Phoebe. The man might be whispered about, but I don't think any polite lady would take to being tied up."

Honoria's lips turned downward in a frown. "Regardless of his odd proclivities, he only enters Society when there is some poor person he'd destroy. The scandal sheets say he takes pleasure in destroying anyone and everything." At that impassioned speech by her friend, Phoebe scoffed. Honoria made Edmund out to be an utterly horrid beast, and yet the man who'd waited patiently above while she searched for the lost shawl, and then tried to beat a hasty retreat, surely was incapable of deception. "We do not read the scandal sheets," she politely reminded her only pairing of friends. Nor had Honoria been one to possess a fanciful imagination.

Honoria tossed her hands up. "Your fancifulness will mean your ruin."

There was an almost prophetic quality to that pledge that caused a chill to race down Phoebe's spine. She tipped her chin up. "I understand we have reason to be cautious where gentlemen are concerned." She looked at Gillian first, until the young woman shifted on her feet, and then turned her attention to the other young lady. Honoria, however, in her unflinching opinion, remained proudly fixed to her spot. "However, I still say I far prefer a world where you are cautious and yet still trust in the goodness of man." Because to believe the alternative…that there was no trustworthy, honorable figure, would make for a very dark world, with little reason for hope in the sentiments of love she and her friends and so many other young ladies secretly aspired to.

Honoria gave her head a pitying shake. "Then you're a fool," she said, wringing a shocked gasp from Gillian.

Phoebe ignored the other young woman's scandalized expression and gave Honoria a sad smile. "Perhaps, but I'd rather be a fool than a cynic who doesn't see the goodness in people."

"He is not a man, he is a monster," Honoria insisted, unrelenting.

Phoebe squared her jaw. "Lord Rutland has given me no reason to believe he is a monster."

"He makes a scandal of himself with widows and wicked ladies," her friend said on a loud whisper, and then she looked about as though fearing they'd been discovered.

Phoebe's lips tingled in remembrance of that hot, fleeting kiss. Honoria flicked her on the arm. "Ouch." She winced.

"Get that look out of your eyes, Phoebe Barrett, this instant."

"Can we not return?" Gillian pleaded.

For once, the voice of reason to their troublesome trio, Honoria and Phoebe ended the debate on the Marquess of Rutland's humanity. Folding her fingers over the small peach rose in her hand, she trailed along at a slower pace behind her more cynical, world-wary friends, wondering about the Marquess of Rutland...

CHAPTER 4

COLD. CALCULATED. RATIONAL. METHODICAL. THOSE were but a handful of words loudly whispered of Edmund, the Marquess of Rutland. He frequently heard them uttered by scandalized mamas and sighing, lonely wives. He'd always relished the image he'd crafted as a coldhearted bastard. His was no mere image, however. Edmund truly was a coldhearted bastard and that was the more generous of insults hurled at him.

The following evening, seated at his private table at Forbidden Pleasures, he sipped his brandy and reflected on his chance meeting with Miss Phoebe Barrett. His first opinion of the lady had proven erroneous. With her generous décolletage and auburn tresses and lips made for the devil's delight, she belonged in a man's bed—his bed. He swirled the contents of his glass. There had been a shimmer in her blue eyes that had spoken to the lady's interest.

He frowned into the contents of his glass as he shifted his thoughts to the woman who'd been the central figure of his scheme in his quest for revenge against Margaret. In Miss Honoria Fairfax's eyes, there had been little hint of the warmth and intrigue from her too-trusting friend. Instead, there had been guardedness and a cynicism he'd not expected in one who'd only just made her Come Out one, nay two, years ago.

He'd been impatient and rash. Two words that were not often ascribed to him. In his youth, perhaps. Back when he'd foolishly imagined he had a heart and believed that heart belonged to just one woman. Edmund thrust aside remembrances of Margaret and instead focused his energy upon his plans for Miss Fairfax—plans that, considering the go-to-hell look in her eyes, would not make his efforts of ruining and ultimately forcing her into marriage as easy as he'd expected.

Edmund took another swallow of his brandy. The lady's friend, on the other hand, Miss Barrett, with her breathless sighs and moon-eyed looks had demonstrated a physical awareness of him that was more conducive with his plans of revenge. He smelled lust and the lady had desired him. He'd have staked all his possessions and all the debt owed him on that fact, and it was a pleasure he'd gladly act upon. There was something intriguing about the prospect of laying down the trusting innocent, parting her legs, and teaching her the pleasure one could find in darkness.

"My lord is there anything you desire?"

Edmund glanced up at the owner of that sultry whisper. He flicked a bored gaze over the blowzy blonde woman with rouged lips and a promise in her eyes. Life had taught him the perils of distraction. Margaret had been a distraction. She'd been the last. Wordlessly, he waved the barely-clad woman away. She departed on a flounce of crimson skirts.

Any other day, any other moment, he'd have gladly welcomed a diversion with one or two of the warm, willing women of Forbidden Pleasures. Not since his meeting with *Phoebe*, as the young lady had insisted he call her—a rather silly, ladylike name. More specifically, not since his encounter with Miss Honoria Fairfax. Following that meeting, he'd come to the rather surprising revelation it would be a good deal harder to slip into that lady's good graces and lure her away from respectability. Such a woman would take care to avoid being alone in Edmund's company, which, in turn, would make ruining the pinch-mouthed miss difficult. His mouth tightened. No, he'd not earn himself Miss Fairfax's favors, but he *could* earn the favors of the more trusting, naïve Phoebe Barrett.

Edmund tapped his fingers along the edge of his tumbler. The lady's friend was an altogether different matter. No, the prickly, pinch-mouthed Miss Fairfax would be the one he was saddled with. He gave a shudder at the prospect of shackling himself to that one; though revenge would certainly sweeten the otherwise unpalatable prospect of having her for his wife.

After he'd taken his leave of the ball last evening, he'd immediately realized he must alter his plans. Miss Honoria Fairfax could not be easily seduced away from respectability. No, the lady's defenses could only be broken down if he ingratiated himself to Phoebe Barrett. Through her friend's affiliation with Edmund, Miss Fairfax would slowly come to realize his trustworthiness. He'd crumple the walls of her reservations, and when she at last trusted—as they all inevitably did—he would trap her and, at that, have his revenge. His plans now all hinged upon another woman—Miss Phoebe Barrett.

He scanned the crowded, noisy club. His gaze alighted upon a familiar, bumbling form as he ambled past the other patrons. Lord Waters lurched his large frame through Forbidden Pleasures, carelessly shouldering younger dandies in his haste to get to his tables. The man's lecherous gaze lingered upon the women scattered about the club, plying their trades. He paused and a brown-haired beauty sidled up to the fat viscount. Edmund studied the woman almost dispassionately. Never one to desire a brown-haired beauty, he'd long favored blonde creatures and the ladies with midnight black locks, as Margaret's.

There had been something faintly *interesting* about Miss Phoebe Barrett's tresses. What would those strands look like spread upon his satin sheets? He gave his head a brusque shake. Where in the hell had that bloody idea come from? He didn't dally with innocents, but preferred his women as skilled and jaded as himself. A scantily clad woman leaned up and flicked her tongue over Waters' ear. Edmund eyed Phoebe's father disinterestedly. Give a lady some coin and it mattered not who she took to her bed. The Prince Regent, a pauper who'd found a purse or, in this case, the paunchy Viscount Waters.

Growing impatient while the man took his pleasures there, Edmund downed his brandy.

The viscount stiffened. His back straightened and like a buck caught in a hunter's snare, he scanned the room. His beady eyes collided with Edmund's and then he stumbled away from the brown-haired beauty. He walked with a far brisker pace than Edmund would've believed the man possible of, drawing to a stop at Edmund's table. "R-rutland." The lecherous beast directed that greeting to Edmund's partially empty bottle.

With a deliberate glee for the man's weakness, he picked up the bottle and poured another glass to the rim. "Sit," he commanded.

Lord Waters hefted his corpulent frame into a seat.

"There is something more I require of you."

The other man planted his elbows on the table and the furniture shifted with the abrupt movement, rattling the bottle. He shot a hand out, righting it before it tipped. "I couldn't get the shawl," he said on a wheedling tone.

He flicked a piece of imaginary lint from his sleeve. "As such, you've only increased your debt to be paid back with interest."

The viscount swiped a hand through his sparse hair. "And you'll forgive my debts if I help you with the ugly miss?"

Edmund yawned. "A fat, foul bastard such as yourself has little right to cast aspersions upon the lady's attributes." His was spoken as a matter of fact. Crassness had ceased to bother him since he'd become the jaded boy of seven who'd been forced to witness his mother and her lover—a man who also happened to be her brother-in-law. Red suffused the viscount's fleshy cheeks. It mattered not that the lady in question would one day be his wife. "I need to know the lady's whereabouts."

Lord Waters shifted his enormous belly. "I imagine the Fairfax girl is at some ball or another."

He leaned across the table. "Not this moment, you fat fool."

The man whitened, but then a knowing glint reflected in his eyes. "Eh, you want to court the gel?" He reached for the bottle. "My daughter would make you a lovely wife." An image as Phoebe had been last evening, the moon's light bathing her face in a soft glow, came to mind. Her full lips parted with an unwitting invite in her eyes.

The viscount noted that imperceptible pause. "Pretty girl, my Phoebe is." He scratched his paunch. "My younger daughter is even prettier. You're welcome to either of them. Prettier than the Fairfax chit. That one's mother was a whore. My wife knew her proper place, gave me a son and allows me to carry on as I will. My girls will do the same."

Edmund drew his bottle back, unfazed by the man's blunt cruelness in talking of his family. Then, when one's father forced you to watch your mother being tupped by her brother-in-law, everything else ceased to shock. "It matters not if she's a whore," he drawled. He expected when they were wed, the lady would have any string of lovers in her bed. That was the way of their world of false propriety.

Waters frowned at Edmund's lack of interest in Miss Fairfax's gentility. "You're certain you don't want my Phoebe?" His breath came in little wheezes from the exertion of speaking. "You wed the Fairfax girl and she'll only give you a bastard. Everyone knows…" Edmund fixed a glare on the man that left those words unfinished. Yes, all of Society knew the scandal that had whirred about of the lady's family. Honoria Fairfax's mother had been rumored to spread her thighs for footmen and dukes and everyone in between. Perhaps with their like pasts, they'd suit after all. He didn't have an interest in innocence. It was the one thing he did not know how to handle, but for the corrupting of it. "I've no interest in your daughter," he said flatly, which wasn't altogether true. He had very specific interests in the lady, that all connected to the pound of flesh he'd exact.

A beleaguered sigh escaped the viscount. "Can't you just court the Fairfax chit as any other of the gents?"

No, his connection to Miss Fairfax's aunt made that an impossibility. He leveled the man with an icy stare that silenced any further recommendations or presumptions.

"Er…right." He eyed Edmund's brandy once more and smacked his lips.

"How often does your daughter see Miss Fairfax?" he asked in hushed undertones lest any passerby foolish enough to come close might hear.

"Not altogether certain," he mumbled.

"How long has she known her?"

The man scratched his creased brow. "I don't quite know—"

"How do the young ladies spend their time together?" This would prove useful and spare him the tedium of having to find anything out about the rambling miss with her delectable derriere.

Lord Waters sat back in his chair and folded his hands over his paunch. "Do you know, I've no idea how those three occupy themselves?"

"Then start. I want to know where your daughter goes, and with whom, and what her interests are."

"Her interests?" Edmund fixed a dark glower that had the man nodding. "Er, right…I'll find out her interests."

The nearly destitute man failed to realize his inattentiveness would mean the ultimate ruin of his already doomed daughter. Those unattended young ladies invariably found themselves with their ivory skirts tossed up and a rutting lord between their legs. The image merely drew up the memory of Miss Barrett bent over the rail, a piece of her gown caught in Lord Delenworth's spear. An unwitting smile played about his lips.

"Er, have I said something amusing?" Lord Waters asked, puffing out his chest with pride.

His smile died. "No," he seethed. The man deflated. It would take a good deal more than this bumbling fool to elicit any amusement on his part. Delighting in tormenting the viscount, Edmund picked up his brandy and downed another glass. He welcomed the fiery trail it blazed down his throat. Edmund shoved back his chair and stood.

"You're leaving? May I finish your b—?"

He ignored the other man and started through the club, winding his way past drunken fops, who nearly fell over themselves in their haste to be free of the Marquess of Rutland. Except one.

A tall figure stepped into his path. Edmund flicked a cold gaze over the blond-haired gentleman with bloodshot eyes. The man had been drinking. "What do you want?" he asked on a silken whisper that would have sent most any other man fleeing. This one remained.

"You do not even know who I am?"

Oh, he knew the man. The Viscount Brewer. Up to his neck in debt, with creditors knocking, and a miserably unhappy wife. The occasionally visible bruise worn by the viscountess in Polite Society indicated just why the lady was so unhappy. That discontent had driven her to seek a place in Edmund's bed several weeks past. "Do you expect I should know you?" And he'd been happy to oblige the woman.

The viscount snapped his eyebrows together in a furious line. His cheeks turned a mottled red.

Edmund peeled his lip back in a sneer. "Say what it is you'd say or step out of my way."

Lord Brewer's momentary courage seemed to flag, for he fell

silent, and with a sound of impatience, Edmund stepped around him. "My wife." The other man called after him.

Edmund turned around with a deliberate nonchalance. He dusted a fleck of imaginary lint from his sleeve. "What of your wife?" He'd had the young viscountess in his bed for that one exchange, but took an abiding pleasure in taunting her sniveling coward of a husband. "I've had so many men's wives in my bed, surely you don't expect me to remember yours?"

The man opened and closed his mouth several times, and when he still said nothing, Edmund continued on, and dismissed the drunken bastard from his thoughts. Instead, as he reached the entrance and accepted his cloak from a servant, he returned his attentions to the delectable Miss Barrett. Prior to their exchange on the terrace, she'd merely represented the key to his plan in lowering Miss Honoria Fairfax's defenses. He shrugged into his cloak and then the majordomo pulled the door open. He stepped outside and a cool blast of wind slapped his face. *I suspected the wind might have carried it off when I was looking at the grounds below…*

The whispery soft quality of Miss Phoebe Barrett's voice slipped into his mind. Now she occupied his thoughts for entirely different reasons. Her sultry tones were best reserved for wicked games upon satin bedsheets and a familiar stirring of lust struck him. Edmund strode down the handful of steps to his waiting carriage.

The liveried driver yanked the door open.

"Home," he commanded in clipped tones. He climbed inside and sat upon the crimson squabs. The door closed with a firm click behind him and then the carriage dipped with the young driver scrambling atop his box. A moment later, the black lacquer conveyance rocked into motion. He peeled back the edge of the curtain and peered out at the passing unfashionable, seedy streets. He'd long preferred the sordid London hells to the respectable, polite White's and Brooke's. The world of dark and deception was, at least, sincere in what it represented unlike the façade of polite, wedded lords and ladies who'd simultaneously gasp with outrage at the fabric of a person's garments while taking their pleasure with another.

He considered his meeting with Lord Waters. The greed and desperation gleaming in the man's eyes indicated he'd do anything and everything Edmund required of him. Though this particular meeting had proven useless, avarice was a powerful motivator. What the old, fat letch didn't know of Miss Fairfax, he soon would.

From the crystal windowpane, his evilly grinning visage stared back at him. An unsought-after creature such as Phoebe Barrett would welcome any hint of attention bestowed upon her. No, it would take no effort at all for a scoundrel like Edmund to slip through her defenses so he might, in turn, ruin her friend.

The carriage continued to rattle down the cobbled roads. His smile dissolved into a scowl. However, the lady he intended to bind himself to had proven herself suitably guarded and cynical. Such a woman was the perfect match for an emotionless bastard like him. How ironical to find he preferred the idea of bedding that prattling lady with her well-rounded buttocks presented on Lord Delenworth's balustrade, all the more.

His carriage rocked to a slow stop before his fashionable Mayfair townhouse. He didn't await his coachman's assistance, instead he shoved the door open and jumped out. With purposeful steps, he strode down the pavement and up the stairs of the white townhouse. His butler, an older man with white hair, pulled the door open.

"Lord Rutland," he greeted. Despite his stooped and aged form, he sketched a flawless bow.

He frowned. "Wallace," he said tersely. "I told you, you needn't bow," he snapped as the old servant closed the door behind him.

A twinkle lit the man's rheumy blue eyes. "It is good for my constitution."

Edmund snorted and shrugged out of his cloak. Wallace held his hand out. He eyed the gnarled fingers and thick, dark green veins jutting at the top of the man's hand. The loyal servant should have retired twenty years ago. Sheer pride and no small amount of obstinance kept him at his post. Edmund had offered him a sizeable pension at some point ten years ago, and continued to present the offer, but the man refused. Edmund suspected the old, withered figure would die at the damned doorway.

Wallace followed his gaze and cleared his throat. "It's merely the cool weather," he confided.

Edmund released his cloak into those ancient hands. Tightening his jaw, he said nothing. It was age and rheumatism. He'd not debate the merits on the man keeping his position at this late hour.

He started up the winding, white marble staircase.

"I understand you've begun attending respectable events, my lord?"

Alas, old, bold, and mouthy Wallace had little point in allowing Edmund his much-welcomed, solitary presence. "You learned long ago I don't answer questions," he said with far more patience than the man deserved. Edmund didn't answer to anyone. Cheeky servants. Cloying mistresses. Eager young ladies with a taste for darkness. Powerful peers. He owed nothing to anyone.

Edmund reached the top landing and turned down the corridor, making his way to his office, the vexing Wallace forgotten. He stopped beside his sanctuary and pressed the door handle, stepping inside the ominous room. He closed the door behind him and locked it, welcoming the hum of quiet and the eerie shadows that danced off the plaster walls. This room, once belonging to his father, held many dark memories. He'd learned long ago to embrace those memories. They'd shaped him into the man he'd become, driven all weakness from him, and transformed him into the cold, powerful nobleman who roused terror in the hearts of most. How many years had he spent despising his parents for the pain of his past? Yet, his selfish parents had shaped him. Strengthened him in a way that he could not be hurt. That was the greatest gift they could have ever given, not that useless sentiment people called love.

He strode over to his desk and settled into the familiar folds of his winged back chair—his only addition to the office. This was his. The single piece of dark leather furniture represented his conquering of the old, long-dead marquess' hold—upon this room, and more, his hold upon Edmund. With deliberate movements, he pulled open the top drawer and removed his leather folio. He flipped open the book and shuffled through pages.

Lord Exeter. Weakness Faro and French mistresses. Debt one thousand pounds.

He flipped to the next.

Lord Donaldson. Weakness diddling his servants. Whist. Debt country cottage in Devonshire.

He skimmed the following names and then stuck his finger in the book to halt the pages turning.

Miss Honoria Fairfax?

He picked up a pen and dipped it into the crystal inkwell and added one more name.

Miss Phoebe Barrett.

Edmund proceeded to mark notes upon the pages of his leather folio and then sat back in his seat. The lady's weakness was her friends, and that weakness would guide him to Miss Fairfax, the woman he'd ruin and wed. Last night, he'd seen Miss Phoebe Barrett as a vexing interference in his plans for another woman. After he'd taken his leave of her, however, he'd realized the serendipitous meeting with the too-trusting miss. With her regard for Honoria Fairfax, Phoebe would ultimately aid him in his quest for revenge.

His attention should be devoted to the woman he'd make his marchioness, and yet... He drummed his fingertips on the arms of his chair, studying the most recent addition to his folio. Phoebe remained firmly entrenched in his thoughts, for reasons that did not have anything to do with revenge. No, it had to do with her lithe frame and well-rounded buttocks.

With a growl, he forcibly thrust back thoughts of the woman and focused on Honoria Fairfax, whom he'd gathered little about. By her lineage alone, he knew she was surely a title-grasping, scheming miss who'd part her legs and sell her soul for the title of duchess. After all, hadn't he himself been cut of the same cheap fabric as his sire? He'd little doubt Miss Fairfax was any different than her mother. The muscles of his stomach clenched. Or her aunt.

Edmund drew in a slow, steadying breath, detesting the slight showing of weakness that proved Margaret's defection still rankled. Ah, Margaret. The lady who'd won his heart and made his twenty-one year old self believe he could know love when his parents had not. The hopefully optimistic, lovesick swain had merely been a two-month interlude from reality. For in the end, she'd chosen another—a duke. A now dead duke. And Edmund had become that which he'd always be—an emotionally deadened, heartless scoundrel who took his pleasures where he would. He trained his eyes on the name of Margaret's niece. Then eight years later, she returned from her period of mourning and the foolish hope he'd not known he carried that she'd come to him had died. She'd returned to London and chosen another. Again.

He had little doubt she'd come to regret that decision. An ugly laugh rumbled up from his chest. He closed his folio.

CHAPTER 5

SEATED ON THE COMFORTABLE IVORY cushion of the parlor windowseat, Phoebe studied the street below. Her books on Captain Cook's explorations lay scattered at her feet, untouched since her world had been thrown into upheaval. Lords and ladies walked arm-in-arm while carriages rattled by. She absently played with the cashmere textured dupioni curtains thinking of another slip of cashmere—an object retrieved by a mysterious gentleman. The same gentleman who'd kissed her. Her first kiss. Quick, because she'd ended it. Hot, because, even now, warmth swirled in her belly in remembrance of it. And she'd insulted him. Because for as much as he'd insisted on being captivated by her beauty, she knew what she was and what she looked like and was quite comfortable in that. A gentleman who possessed such luxuriant, chestnut hair with tones of black, and brown eyes the color of warmed chocolate did not…well…he did not go about kissing ladies such as she.

And ladies such as she, who'd taken care to protect her name, virtue, and respectability since she'd learned the extent of her father's vile ways and the words whispered about him, and their entire family. She had pledged to never be so enticed by a gentleman who might go about kissing her. She dropped her head back against the wall.

"What has you so quiet, my dear?"

A startled shriek escaped her at the sudden, unexpected appearance of her oft-smiling mother. "Mother," she greeted the gentle-spirited woman who'd been all things good and loving to her children, when their father had been absent and, oftentimes, vicious with his words. She swung her legs over the edge of her seat and made to rise, but her mother waved her off.

"Do not bother yourself. Not on my account," she said softly and slid into the seat beside her." She glanced down at the books Phoebe had abandoned reading a long while ago. "You're not reading," she said it with a faint accusatory edge underscoring her words. She bent and retrieved one of the books and held it up, as though there might be a question as to what books she referred to.

"No. I'm…just… thinking." *About a gentleman, a stranger, who stole into the gardens and has since captured my thoughts.*

Her mother lowered the book of travels onto her lap. "You?" she scoffed. "Unable to think of traveling?" Yes, for as horrid and uncaring and all things unfeeling as Papa was, her mother had long been devoted to each of her children's interests. When other mothers would have burned the pages of works that documented the journeys of powerful, brave, and bold explorers, her mother had given Phoebe her own pin money so she could read more and learn more. "What, nothing to say?" her mother prodded, bringing her back to the moment. A twinkle lit her kindly blue eyes. "Only one thing can account for this sudden, inexplicable inability to read, as you are wont to do."

Please do not say it.

"You've met a gentleman."

She'd said it.

Phoebe glanced away from the smiling question in her mother's eye. "No." Even as the word left her mouth, she realized how half-hearted the belated response was. "Yes," she amended. Her mother's eyebrows shot to her hairline. "Not in a way that was inappropriate." Except, as soon as those words left her mouth, she recognized how damning they truly sounded. "Er…I dropped something and he retrieved it and…" She fell silent. Her mother continued to sit there, eying her in that knowing way. "But there's not more there." Other than her first kiss, which would be memorable to any lady regardless of whom the kissing gentleman was, or ever would be. "It was just a fortuitous meeting in which he rescued Honoria's shawl," she said, more to herself.

Her mother's lips pulled up in the corner. Phoebe froze a

moment wondering how a woman who lived an existence with a cad like the Viscount Waters as her husband should ever manage such a beautiful and alive smile. "It is never a chance meeting. There is no such thing," she said with a widening smile.

How was the other woman able to smile? How could she do it so freely and sincerely and beautifully when she remained trapped in marriage to a vile reprobate? And more, how could she believe in the dream of love and romance for others, when life had so cruelly stolen the hope of those emotions from her?

Suddenly uncomfortable with thoughts about her mother's marriage and Phoebe's heart, she swallowed back the question that would only cause the other woman pain. A knock sounded at the door and she glanced up. From the entrance of the room, the butler cleared his throat. "Lady Gillian and Miss Honoria." He sketched a respectful bow and backed out of the room.

Phoebe scrambled to her feet, never more glad for the sudden appearance of two people. These two people, particularly. The young ladies filed into the parlor like a pair of geese and dipped matching curtsies. "My lady," they said in unison.

"Good morning, Gillian. Honoria." Her mother greeted them with a smile and then a twinkle lit her eyes. No doubt she knew her daughter well enough to detect the relief at the young ladies' interruption. With a quick kiss on Phoebe's cheek, the older woman sailed from the room in a flurry of skirts.

Ever garrulous Gillian broke the silence. "Shall we be going? Honoria is not permitted to remain out long. She has—oomph." Gillian glared at Honoria. "Did you kick me?"

"I daresay that should be fairly obvious," Honoria muttered.

Phoebe looked questioningly between her friends.

When it became clear Honoria intended to say nothing else, Gillian explained. "It is Lord Thistlewait." The gentleman in question had made no secret of his interest in Honoria. And Honoria had made no secret of her *disinterest* in that gentleman. Gillian skipped over and claimed a spot on the gold upholstered sofa. "I've heard horrid things of Lord Thistlewait," she said on a conspiratorial whisper. "They say he is a stodgy bore." Which in no way explained a priggish gentleman's attention on one of the most notorious, unwed young ladies.

Honoria patted her brown curls. "I've not heard any *truly* ill thoughts on the gentleman." She stifled a yawn with her fingers. "He is a bore." She wrinkled her nose, ruining her whole affected attempt at maturity. "Which I would suppose constitutes an ill thought," she muttered under her breath.

What would Phoebe's two friends say about her unwitting fascination with the Marquess of Rutland? Heat spiraled through her as she recalled his kiss. There was nothing staid or stodgy about the marquess. And with the desire he stirred, staid and stodgy were a good deal safer.

"Why are you looking like that?" Gillian cocked her head and then looked to Honoria. "Why is she looking like that?"

Phoebe's cheeks warmed. "Shall we go before Honoria is forced to return and be courted by Lord Thistlewait?"

The lady in mention narrowed her eyes and then opened her mouth as though she wished to say something on Phoebe's deliberate evasiveness. But Phoebe implored her with her eyes and Honoria gave an imperceptible nod.

A short carriage ride later, with no further talk of Lord Thistlewait or questions about Phoebe's peculiar reaction, the ladies and a rightfully wary maid made their way not shopping but through the broad columns of Egyptian Hall.

Phoebe glanced up at the sweeping ceiling of the darkened Egyptian-style space. Hieroglyphics marked the walls of the famed place constructed by Mr. Bullock. She paused beside the menagerie of stuffed creatures at the central portion of the hall and, reaching up on tiptoe, craned her head about in search of the items belonging to the famed Captain James Cook. From the corner of her eye, she noted Honoria grip Gillian by the forearm, staying their forward movement. Her friends paused and looked back at her.

"I do not see them," Phoebe murmured, turning a small circle in search of the display of those revered items returned by Captain Cook's crew.

"I imagine that is the fun in coming here, taking the time to look." Honoria paused. "At everything."

Gillian nodded her agreement. "Oh, yes. I daresay the ferocious snakes eating their prey is a good deal more interesting than some horridly boring explorer who—"

Phoebe frowned, personally offended for the gentleman. "He

is not boring," she said defensively of the legendary explorer and cartographer. She rather resented Gillian filing the Captain Cooks of the world into the company with the Lord Thistlewaits of the world.

"Come along," Honoria urged, motioning Phoebe forward. "We shall search. Gillian shall enjoy her horrific snakes, I shall have the opportunity to appreciate the gold recovered from…from… wherever it was recovered from and you may have your Captain Cook."

Phoebe returned to her friend's side and, maid in tow, fell into step beside the young women, all the while scanning the enormous space for those famed artifacts. The story of Captain Cook had intrigued her from the time she'd been a small girl. Her mother had regaled her with those fascinating stories of the man and his great, fascinating explorations. And though she'd known even then the foolishness in imagining a life of exploration and adventure, excitement had stirred in her heart at the dream of it. Now she realized her mother had likely dreamed of escape for herself. Selfishly she'd not given thought to the woman her mother had been prior to the marriage arranged by Phoebe's grandfather. Had she dreamed of escape even then? Or had she willingly ceded over all control unquestioningly as the dutiful daughter and that longing for escape came later? Regret stuck in her chest. She would never cede control over to a gentleman strictly because her father commanded it. No, she would steal her happiness when and where she could…and be the sole controller of her fate.

She turned to her maid. "Marissa, you may take yourself about the museum. No harm shall come to us," she said when the young woman hesitated. But then she dropped a curtsy and hurried off.

"That was well done of you," Honoria complimented. "I only wish my aunt's maids were as obliging."

Phoebe's father's servants were loyal to the Viscountess Waters and her children. That devotion was likely a product of pity for the horrid father and spouse the Barrett family suffered through. It was well known that the servants in Honoria's aunt's employ were loyal to her harridan of an aunt and not much more.

From the corner of her eye, a ray of sunshine slashed through the windows at the top of the room and splashed light off a glass display case. She squinted down the length of the room at the wide map contained within that particular exhibit.

Gillian followed her gaze and groaned. "There is hardly anything interesting in a map. Bah, what does it show?" She jabbed her finger toward the stuffed snake. "As opposed to that magnificent—"

"Go." Phoebe laughed. "I'll not be long." Still they hesitated. "I assure you the nefarious sort is hardly lurking about the Egyptian Hall." Not allowing the young ladies an opportunity to issue protest, she started down the hall for Captain Cook's collection.

AT LAST THE YOUNG LADIES were alone. Invariably, those scheming ladies with scandalous families ultimately found a way to disentangle themselves from their chaperones.

From where he stood behind the massive Doric column, Edmund tucked away the note from the lady's father, a bald, greedy Judas, and lazily studied Miss Barrett's hurried steps. She cast a longing gaze forward, walking with purposeful strides. He narrowed his eyes. She met a lover. There was no other accounting for her solitary presence in Lord Delenworth's gardens a few days ago and now the eager glint in her brown eyes.

Never taking his gaze from the young lady, Edmund moved with slow, stealthy steps along the perimeter of the famed Egyptian Hall. He strode past the handful of visitors present, those other patrons foolishly engrossed in the useless artifacts collected about the room.

It mattered not that there was some other gentleman who'd ensnared her notice. He'd seen the stirring of interest in her eyes, the breathless whisper of a sigh as his lips touched hers. Then, she stopped abruptly before a broad, crystal case. She cast several furtive glances about, her gaze lingering upon her two friends thoroughly engrossed with the massive, coiled serpent and the prey the frozen snake intended to devour. Phoebe turned her attention back to the case and he strode forward. With the same ruthless speed of a lethal serpent, he stopped just behind her.

Her shoulders stiffened and her singular focus shifted from one of Cook's worthless artifacts to his hovering presence. She spun around, hand to her breast, and then a smile wreathed her cheeks. "You." Her eyes made her more transparent than the crystal panes of the case. Shocked pleasure lit her blue irises and then the familiar wariness replaced her earlier excitement. "My lord," she said again, this time more composed.

He sketched a bow. "Hello, Miss Barrett. What an unexpected pleasure." He lied. There was nothing unexpected in this meeting. This had been carefully planned since Lord Waters had sent round a missive detailing the ladies' plans for that week. He angled his head toward the case. "Never tell me you are also an admirer of the legendary Captain Cook."

Flecks of gold danced in her eyes. "Oh, quite!" Ah, so she didn't meet a lover. Her love was for a dead explorer. How singularly… odd. He'd never before known a woman who'd worn that silly, starry look about anything other than a bauble or the promise of passion between the sheets. He shifted, disconcerted in a world where he was always only sure. She gestured to the map. "This is…" Her words trailed off. "You're an admirer of Captain Cook?" she whispered.

He was, now. With her breathless question, he was restored to the ruthless Edmund. He made a show of studying the display case. "I must confess it is not Captain Cook who has singularly captured my attention."

She widened her eyes and a hand fluttered up to her breast. "It isn't?"

With a deliberate slowness, he returned his attention to her. "No," he murmured. He dropped his gaze to her lips, studying them, remembering the taste and contour of the plump flesh. And just then he was ensnared by his own game, wanting to take her mouth under his and explore the hot depths of her and more. He blinked back the momentary lapse in sanity. "Travel," he managed at last.

Phoebe tipped her head, the passion dipped and faded from her eyes, replaced by the thick haze of befuddlement.

"I find myself fascinated by exploration and those who've traveled and been places and seen the wonders and magnificence beyond the confines of the stifling London Society."

Her breath caught.

Everyone had their weaknesses. The trick to life was identifying those weaknesses and exploiting them; taking them and twisting them to suit one's uses for that person. He grinned. This was the moment where he'd effectively trapped Phoebe Barrett. "What of you, Phoebe? Do you, too, dream of far-off places and escaping," he gestured about the walls of the museum. "This?"

She followed his gesture and then ultimately fixed her gaze upon that map trapped behind its crystal confines. "I do," she said softly.

He put his lips close to her ear. "It begs the question, what would you escape from?" The safe answer she wasn't aware of was, in fact, him.

Her brow creased. "That is a rather intimate question." There was a faint hesitancy to those words that hinted at a logical, practical woman of some caution. She angled her head back, craning to look at him. "What if I were to say I'm not escaping but searching?" she asked, instead, proving she was not cautious enough, not when those unguarded words let him, a stranger, far more into her world than she should ever dare allow.

"And what are you searching for?" For the span of a heartbeat that question was borne of a desire to know what would make a polished, English lady seek a life beyond the glittering world of their London Society. Why, when ladies were mercenary creatures, driven by greed and a lust for the material and their own pleasures?

Her expression grew shuttered. "I..." She flicked her gaze about and then settled her stare on his cravat.

He'd unnerved her. A triumphant sense of power filled him. It was entirely too easy.

"Do you know what I am searching for, Phoebe?" *Revenge. Domination. Control.*

She gave her head a little shake and again looked up at him.

"The thrill of knowing more," he said on a soft, gentle whisper he'd not believed himself capable of any longer.

She folded her hands together and then stared down at the interlocked digits. "I understand that." Those quietly spoken words barely reached his ears. "I believe we are kindred souls in that way, my lord."

"Edmund," he automatically corrected. The lady was wrong in that regard as well—everyone knew the devil didn't have a soul.

"Edmund," she whispered. Phoebe stole a glance about. Ah, so she had at least some sense to know they shouldn't be viewed conversing, unchaperoned, in this public manner. She slipped by him and walked the length of the giant elephant, running her gloved fingertips over the ropes about the massive creature.

He trailed after her, allowing her the freedom of the slight distance, and the sense of control she strove for—strove and failed.

When she reached the back middle portion of the gray beast, she froze beside a tall column.

Edmund stopped and stared at her expectantly.

"Would you find me silly if I say I detest London?"

He frowned as she confirmed his earlier suppositions. "I would say you are truthful and wise," he said, giving her the first truthful words he'd spoken in either of their exchanges up to this point. He closed the remaining distance between them and then stopped when but the span of a hand separated them. "I also detest London." And that was the second truthful piece he'd imparted. A sudden unease filtered through him at this sense of being exposed before her—when he never laid any part of himself bare before anyone.

She clung to his words. "The insincerity, the glittering opulence, the cruel gossips, and unkind words and whispers. What person would prefer such a place?"

In short, she spoke of a world Edmund had always been suited for. An increasingly familiar disquiet continued to roll through him; powerful and volatile and all the more terrifying for it. "If you could go anywhere, Phoebe," he said, shifting the conversation to this woman who represented a means to an end of the one chapter in his life that had seen him defeated.

A wistful smile played upon her lips and he stilled at the sincerity of that unabashed expression. Had he ever been so unrestrained? One time, yes. Before he'd confronted the vile depravity of his own parents, and then everyone else around him.

"Wales."

Wales. When presented the possibility, even imagined, to go anywhere—the decadent halls of Paris, the crystalline waters of the Caribbean, the wonders of the Orient—she would choose Wales. It spoke to the lady's imagination…or rather lack, thereof.

Merriment danced in her eyes. "By your expression you find exception with my choice." Hers was a statement.

Edmund leaned against the pillar. "I gather there is nothing you do without purpose, and certainly a woman of reason…has her… reasons."

She dropped her voice to a soft, husky whisper. "Anglesey." That whisper washed over him, drowned out her word, his question, their discourse. All he heard, felt, or saw was her and the eager gleam in her eyes. Some unidentifiable force of emotion slammed into him, something more potent than lust for the unfamiliarity of it—a desire to crave something with such ferocity for nothing more than the mere unjaded want of it; sentiments not driven by revenge or power.

Desperate to fill the void left by her whispery soft utterance, he repeated, "Anglesey."

With a widening smile on her lips, she nodded once. "The great Vikings and their raid upon Anglesey, and Rhodri Mawr's ultimate defeat of the leader Gorm."

He flicked a gaze over her, discovering the new, next, unexpected bit about Phoebe Barrett. She was a bloodthirsty thing. "And you are intrigued by the ruthlessness of the Vikings?"

"Not their ruthlessness." She gesticulated wildly with her hands until he had to look away or become dizzy from her frantic movements. "They were seafarers."

"They were raiders," he said bluntly.

"And traders," she continued as though he'd not spoken.

Ah, it made sense. The lady would make something romantic of a bloodthirsty, savage lot bent upon conquering and destruction. A thrill of inevitable victory coursed through him. Where Miss Honoria Fairfax would wisely and safely keep him at arm's length, Phoebe, in her unjaded innocence and naiveté would wander into the darkened corners of the Egyptian Hall and weave romantic tales of savages who'd slaughter, rape and pillage.

By the slight downturn of her lips at the corner, she'd followed the direction of his thoughts on her Viking raiders. "They traveled the Mediterranean and North Africa, the Middle East and Central Asia."

She spoke with the same excitement and enthusiasm as a tutor imparting a favorite lesson to his charges. The muscles of his lips tugged and pulled and then, for the first time in more years than he remembered, an honest smile formed, tight and stiff from the lack of use.

"What is it?" she blurted.

Edmund schooled his features. He ran the pad of his thumb over her plump, lower lip. "Oh, Phoebe, you'd go to Wales to be closer to your Vikings, instead of spreading your wings and daring to dream of those sapphire waters of the Mediterranean or the opulent beauty of the Far East." He relished the rapid rise and fall of her chest that hinted at her body's awareness of him. "You deserve more in your dreams and for them," he said quietly and claimed her lips in a faint kiss.

This meeting of mouths was only part of his ultimate plan to ensnare her in his trap. Yet, if that were so, then why did desire course through him, filling him with this pained hunger to make her his, to mark her when he'd learned to never want anything of a woman beyond the immediacy of his and his lover's immediate desires? Phoebe leaned into him, reaching up on tiptoe and returning his kiss with boldness no innocent had a right to. He wrapped his hand about her and dragged her closer to his chest, so that the generous mounds of her breasts crushed against him. A desperate little moan escaped her and Edmund angled his head, deepening the kiss and swallowing that breathy sound of her desire. He wanted her. Now. He wanted to layer her to the pillar that served as her only protection from ruin and take her here, hard and fast, so that her moans became screams as she found fulfillment.

The tinkling giggles of ladies from somewhere within the museum penetrated the momentary spell Phoebe had cast upon him. Reality reared its unpleasant head. He set her away with alacrity. Panic pounded in his chest as he, who prided himself on his mastery over self-control, had succumbed to his hungering for the breathless, wide-eyed innocent before him. "Go," he commanded gruffly.

"I—"

"Go," he ordered again, his tone harsher than he intended.

She squared her jaw and, for a moment, it appeared as though she intended to defy his orders. And for an even briefer moment, he wanted her to do exactly that. But then she spun on her heel and ran from him as though the devil trailed on her heels…and as Edmund stared after her, he supposed the devil, in fact, did.

CHAPTER 6

PHOEBE STRODE QUICKLY DOWN THE perimeter of Egyptian Hall, returning to Captain Cook's map and the other handful of artifacts that no longer sung to her soul, called back this time by the words Edmund had revealed—words that had served as a window into his troubled soul—that had proven they were kindred spirits, of sorts. She paused beside a column, borrowing strength from the massive, white pillar, all the while praying her friends were so engrossed in their own explorations they'd not noted her disappearance. Her skin pricked with awareness and she brought her shoulders back—he studied her. He'd commanded her to leave, but he hovered in the shadows, his gaze burning a mark onto her skin. She closed her eyes a moment. Her friends were correct. This senseless attraction to Edmund was imprudent and dangerous and all things rash. Yet, when he spoke to her, his own thoughts echoing her heart's wishes and sentiments, she forgot the need to use caution where the famed rogue was concerned.

Her friends stepped into her path.

"Where were you?" Honoria snapped.

Phoebe pressed a hand to her racing heart. "You frightened me," she said, praying her world-wary friend did not take in the color on her cheeks and piece together some man, nay, a specific man she'd expressly warned her against, had set her pulse to racing once again.

Honoria planted her arms akimbo and took another step closer.

"Why are you blushing?" Of course, ever the guarded one of their trio, she missed few details.

Their friend, Gillian, ever the maker of peace within their group, shifted nervously back and forth upon her feet, glancing at the ceiling, the column behind Phoebe, Captain Cook's map—anywhere but at her friends who never quarreled—until now. Now it seemed they did it with a staggering frequency.

Honoria clearly tired of Phoebe's silence. "I saw him," she hissed. "I saw him in the museum moments ago."

"I don't know what you're talking about," she returned, as with that one lie, Phoebe descended into some dark, unfamiliar plane of her and Honoria's friendship. Her friend narrowed her eyes.

"You would lie to me?" Shock, hurt, and pain all underscored that question.

Even Gillian, who strove to avoid any and all conflicts, pursed her lips. "Not well-done of you, Phoebe." She shook her head. "Not well-done of you at all."

Guilt rolled through her. "What would you have me say?" She held her palms up. "You've already judged him just as the rest of Society has and found him lacking."

"Not lacking." Honoria held a finger up. "Evil. Vile. Reprehensible—"

"Stop," Phoebe cut in, her tone sharper than she intended. As the victim of Society's cruel gossip through the years, she'd long ago vowed not to listen to the gossips' opinion on another person's worthiness or, in this case, *unworthiness*. "Who are we to pass judgment?" She stole a glance about to be sure there were no interlopers in this charged exchange. "My father is one of the most reprehensible letches in London. He is a faithless coward, a profligate gambler, and by Society's accounts, I am no better than he because of my connection to him." She paused, as the familiar hurt of living in the whispers of her father's scandals struck at her with a pain she suspected would always be there. "We've all been judged," she said softly to her friends. Not once had anyone looked at her, truly looked at her, as anything more than an extension of the dishonorable man who'd sired her. Phoebe folded her arms and hugged herself. There had been nothing in Edmund's eyes or his kiss, which had given any hint that he'd judged her worthiness by her father's shameful ways. "He is no different than any of us," she said, looking between her friends. By the tightness of their lips and the concern in their eyes, they appeared unfazed by her passionate defense of the gentleman.

"He is nothing like us," Honoria spat. "It is not his family members' worthiness that is called into question, but the gentleman himself. The papers purport he's done scandalous things with scandalous women and—" She drew in a slow, steadying breath and stole a glance about at their very public surroundings. Young ladies did not speak of scandalous things and scandalous women as Honoria now did. "Stay away from him, Phoebe. No good can ever come to be with a dark devil such as Rutland."

Phoebe set her jaw at a mutinous angle. Gillian placed a staying hand upon her, stopping the rebuttal on her lips. "We do not want to see you hurt."

Oh, dear. She was being schooled on matters of practicality by Gillian. "I'll not be unwise," she reassured them.

"You already have been. Twice," Honoria stated her words as matter-of-fact with no real malice. "For the Marquess of Rutland."

Gillian gently squeezed her hand, calling Phoebe's attention away from the disgust in Honoria's eyes. "He is not rumored to be a nice gentleman, Phoebe."

She pulled her hand back and Gillian flinched as though she'd been struck physically. "Rumors," Phoebe said again, annoyed with her friends' inability to see that in their unfavorable opinion of the marquess, they were no different than every other arbiter who'd come before them, holding others in judgment, and ultimately finding them wanting for crimes not truly known—crimes that might not truly be crimes, but manipulated truths. "I do not doubt there are dark pieces to the marquess," she conceded. The hard glint in those brown eyes, the gold flecks hinted at something desolate, and even as that raised the guards she'd built about her these years to protect herself, the walls were flimsy, because the gentle touch of his lips and his whispered words revealed more and, God help her, she wanted to know all.

"And?" Honoria prodded.

Phoebe gave her head a clearing shake. "And I will be cautious." She glanced over Gillian's shoulder at the Captain Cook exhibit. "Nor has the marquess expressed any interest in me." Though, that wasn't altogether true. There had been his kiss. Nay, his two kisses.

"Good," Gillian said.

"Not good," Honoria corrected, frowning at Gillian. "Don't you see, Phoebe, if he was an honorable gentleman, if he was good and trustworthy and desiring something meaningful with you, he'd not meet you in these clandestine spots and steal away with you. He'd court you openly, publicly. He'd pay you visits and bring you flowers and make those honorable intentions clear."

Phoebe troubled the flesh of her lower lip. There was truth to her friend's words and yet, "Our meetings have been mere chance. He does not steal away with me." A dangerous excitement swirled inside.

Honoria took a step closer. "Nothing *he* does is by chance and without purpose." The unease roused by her friend's pronouncement stirred to life Phoebe's misgivings once more.

"What purpose could he have of me or with me?" She knew him not at all. Until their meeting in Lady Delenworth's gardens, she'd never paid attention to the man whispered about. She didn't have time for whispers.

Honoria lifted her shoulders in a shrug. "One can never be certain where the marquess is concerned." She leaned close, lowering her voice. "But he toys with people's lives as though they are pawns upon a chessboard."

Phoebe resisted the urge to roll her eyes at her friend's over-dramatic statements on the powerful Marquess of Rutland. "I will be careful," she promised, desperate to put to rest the matter of Edmund's suitability or integrity. "I will not be hurt." Nor was it likely their paths would cross again.

"Come along," Gillian murmured, ending any further discourse. "There is still much to see."

Phoebe trailed along at a slower, contemplative pace behind her friends. It was unlikely she and the marquess would again meet. For a rogue did not have any use or need of an innocent young lady in the market for a husband. And she'd wager her very own happiness that he had little interest in marriage. She stole a last glance back at that enormous pillar they'd hidden behind a short while ago. They might have shared interests and passions, but it was as Honoria said, a confirmed bachelor who studiously avoided *ton* events had little use for one such as Phoebe.

EVEN WITH PHOEBE AND HER friends' furtive whispers, from his place in the shadows of the museum, Edmund was aware of every word exchanged.

Her erroneous defense of him and his intentions, and her friend, the woman he'd ultimately trap—the cynical, mistrustful Miss Honoria Fairfax. With the exception of their dark coloring, the ladies were foils in every way. Margaret's niece with her cynicism was a vastly better match for a monster who'd ruin anyone and everyone on his quest for revenge.

He used the ladies' distraction to take in Phoebe. She folded her arms close to her person, as though shielding herself from her friend's disapproving words. Any other moment before this one, with any other woman, his gaze would be drawn to the generous expanse of her breasts, mentally stripping her of those modest white skirts. Instead, he fixed on that protective way in which she held herself. Mayhap she sought to shield herself from the truth she knew…a trusting hope in him, that he had no right to, while ultimately knowing as someone inherently good that there was no good in his soul, even as she willed there to be more of him.

Phoebe moved her gaze about the museum, searching, lingering on the place they'd stolen to a short while ago. She thought of him. Unwisely, he thrilled at her preoccupation with him, and for reasons that somehow moved deeper, beyond the revenge he'd exact upon Margaret and the niece she so loved—the woman who, when this plan was complete, would find herself his wife.

He eyed Honoria with an objective eye. Brown hair, lean frame, yet a large bosom, nondescript features. His gaze wandered back to Phoebe, whose luxuriant, silken tresses put to mind images of those chocolate waves cascading over his sheets, wrapped about them in a silken curtain. He wanted her and, by the flare of desire in her eyes and the bold way in which she'd returned his kiss, the lady wanted him as well. Suddenly, the annoyance she'd represented, the necessary pawn upon his chessboard, as Honoria had accurately stated mere moments ago, proved a welcome diversion.

Edmund stayed along the perimeter of Egyptian Hall as he made his way out of the museum. When he stepped outside the building, it took a moment for his eyes to adjust to the brightness of the afternoon sun. He scanned the clogged roadways in search of his carriage and then bounded down the steps toward the waiting conveyance. His driver pulled the door open.

"My clubs," Edmund said in clipped tones as he climbed inside the carriage.

The old servant nodded once and then closed the door with a quiet click. A moment later, the black lacquer carriage lurched forward, moving slowly through the busy London streets. Edmund yanked open the curtain and eyed the passing roads until the fashionable streets gave way to the vicious, seamy side of the city. Some of the tension pressing on his chest since he'd momentarily envisioned more with Miss Phoebe Barrett eased with the familiarity of the dark underbelly of the world where no sensible person dared venture. Pickpockets lurked in the streets. Whores lingered on the corners, lifting their tattered skirts to those who'd risk their life and foolishly stroll these streets unarmed. This was his world. This was the world he'd truly been born to and comfortably belonged.

Because…lords, ladies, or common thieves and whores in the den of sin—ultimately they were all the same. All that mattered was survival—social survival, one's actual physical survival, and in some cases, emotional survival.

A small boy with a black cap darted out into the streets, his cheeks gaunt and smudged with dirt and soot. Not much older than Edmund had been when the carefully constructed lies of his life had been kicked out from under him, and he'd been forced to confront reality—his parents' faithlessness to one another, the scandalous parties thrown for all the most lecherous reprobates of London Society, and their usage of their own son as an instrument of revenge. He gave his head a shake, dispelling reminders of the naïve boy he'd once been. Edmund eyed another child in the streets who effortlessly raced past a foppish dandy in gold satin breeches, easily divesting the man of his purse. A hard, cynical grin formed on his lips. The man likely wouldn't know of his carefully removed possessions until he was comfortably ensconced in his clubs. How much stronger that child was and ever had been than Edmund's younger, foolish self who'd been born innocent and then been corrupted. He almost envied the lad who'd never had grand illusions of what life is or should be.

The carriage jerked to a halt before the stucco façade of Forbidden Pleasures. Without waiting for his aging driver, he tossed open the carriage door and jumped from the carriage, his boots noiseless on the grimy pavement. He didn't require his loyal, aging servants to cater to him any more than they'd made it a habit of doing so through the years. Nothing he'd done had merited such devotion, but, at the very least, if they were too foolish to accept their pensions, he'd see to his own blasted responsibilities of opening doors without assistance. He strode to the front of the establishment and the black double-doors were thrown open.

Edmund left the light of day and sailed through the threshold into the dark of the devil's den. It took his eyes a moment to adjust to the thick cheroot smoke that hung in a heavy cloud over the establishment. The raucous laughter of drunken gentlemen blended with the tinkling of coins being tossed upon the gaming tables. He scanned the hall of dissolute lords, waving off the lush, golden beauty who sidled up to him. She turned away on a flounce and went in search of some interested, bored nobleman who'd tup her for a handful of coins. He'd little doubt the loathsome lord he sought was here. He was always here. It was how Edmund had managed to fleece him of a small fortune, including the man's eldest daughter's dowry.

He curled his fingers into a reflexive ball, his fingers digging crescent marks into the flesh of his hands. One of those daughters meant nothing to Edmund in the scheme of his revenge. The other was no longer a shiftless, shapeless lady in white skirts. The now dowerless young woman was Phoebe Barrett with cautious eyes belied by a trusting smile and her damned dreams of exploration. Edmund abhorred himself for the guilt that snaked through him for being the man who'd stripped her of her dowry. A growl worked its way up his throat. Just then, he located Phoebe's father, seated at a faro table; a buxom, brown-haired, young woman who might as well have been his own daughter's age upon his lap.

Why should he note such a detail? And why should that detail matter so very much? What in hell madness was this? He thrust back the peculiar thoughts. The wistful woman's loathsome father was to blame. If it hadn't been Edmund, it would have been some other who'd bested the viscount in faro, and he was all the richer for that defeat. Except, there was no sense of triumph in that rationale. Bloody hell, he didn't want to feel guilt or regret or any emotion—feelings weakened a man.

Fueling the icy fury coursing through him and the tumult of emotions he couldn't put to sorts, Edmund stalked through the club. Young gentlemen gulped and ducked out of his way, cutting a wide path for him. He drew to a stop beside the viscount's chair. The old man fondled the dark beauty's breast, cupping the pale mound of flesh that spilled over her lacy top. "Waters," he said on a slow, lethal whisper.

Viscount Waters scrambled to his feet so quickly he upended the woman on his lap. "R-Rutland." The woman caught herself against the table and then with her lips pursed in displeasure at her partner's careless handling, turned and sought companionship with another. "D-Did you want to s-see me?" Those bulging, bug-like eyes darted about, unable to meet Edmund's gaze. How very different this shiftless, spineless coward was from his daughter who met Edmund's gaze unapologetically. Then, would she if she knew who he was—*truly* knew who he was?

"Walk with me." Not waiting to see if Waters followed, Edmund turned on his heel and stalked through the crowd, toward his empty tables at the far back corner of the club.

The viscount lengthened his shorter stride in a bid to keep pace. "H-Have I done something w-wrong? Was my daughter not where she said she'd be?" He wheezed from the exertion of his efforts.

Oh, the lady had been where the viscount had promised. Staring wide-eyed at that damned map and dreaming of travels to Wales, when other ladies would have been lusting after the latest French fabrics and baubles. He wanted nothing to do with those damned too-trusting eyes. Edmund jerked out a chair and claimed a seat with his back pressed against the wall. The position allowed him the advantage of surveying the crowd, without being vulnerable with his back exposed.

Having been unable to match Edmund's long, quick stride, Waters hurried over belatedly and made to pull out the seat opposite him. He hesitated and eyed Edmund with a nervous glimmer in his blue eyes.

Edmund started.

"May I?"

But for the bug-like bulge—the color was Phoebe's and it roused reminders of the woman he'd taken his leave of a short while ago. Instead of the greed and fear in her sire's eyes, however, Phoebe's had sparked with intelligence, hinting at a keen wit that threw into question how she could possibly share the blood of one such as Waters. "Sit," he snapped.

The viscount immediately hefted his bulky frame into the chair opposite Edmund. The wood groaned in protest.

He'd learned long ago the other man's weakness; his almost rabid fear of Edmund and so he toyed with Waters the way a cat did its prey. He deliberately motioned forward a scantily clad, ethereal beauty with a silver tray. She moved with slow, languid steps; a deliberate sway of her generous hips meant to entice. He eyed her dispassionately, from the interest in her green eyes to the manner in which she darted the pink tip of her tongue out, trailing it along the seam of her lips.

The man smacked his lips. Waters' second vice. Women.

The woman stopped beside the table. "My lord," she purred and set down her tray with a bottle of fine, French brandy and two glasses. She fingered the crevice between the enormous mounds of her abundant breasts, an invitation in her eyes.

"That will be all," he said coolly.

He waved her off. With a pout, she sauntered away.

The viscount groaned, alternating his gaze between the departing beauty and the full bottle of spirits. "What have I done now?" he asked, sounding more like a petulant child than an aging viscount.

Edmund yanked off his gloves then tossed them aside while studying Waters through narrowed eyes; this man whose daughter dreamed of escaping. Was it a wonder when she'd been forced into a miserable existence with this fiend as her father? To keep from dragging the other man across the table and choking the air from his lungs, Edmund gripped the edges of the table so hard his fingernails marred the smooth, mahogany wood. Relishing the viscount's discomfiture, he forced himself to lighten his grip. He reached with deliberate slowness for the bottle. He splashed several fingerfuls of brandy into his glass and then, knowing it would drive the other man to near madness, filled it to the remainder of the brim.

Tired of the man's presence, Edmund brought them 'round to

the reason for this meeting. "I'm here to discuss your daughter."

"Eh?" Waters scratched his furrowed brow. "I thought you wanted the ugly one, the Fairfax girl." At the further narrowing of Edmund's eyes, he continued on a rush. "Of course you're welcome to my daughter, either of my daughters," he amended. He wrinkled his nose, giving him the look of a small rodent. "Though, if you take my youngest daughter, Justina, then I can let Allswood have Phoebe and my debts to that man…"

Edmund set his glass down and reached across the table. Lip pulled back in a snarl, he clasped Phoebe's father about the neck, effectively cutting off air flow and silencing the man. The viscount's words roused images of Allswood laying claim to Phoebe. "Shut your goddamn mouth, Waters," he hissed. All the while an icy rage seared through him. No one dared tread upon that which he had already claimed. Even in the spirit of pretend courtships.

He released the man with such alacrity, Waters collapsed back in his seat, taking great, heaving gasps of air. It was a testament to the evil that went on in this place that only mildly curious glances were tossed their way. "I'd charged you the task of finding out her interests."

What if I were to say I'm not escaping but searching…

Waters rubbed his neck where Edmund had so roughly handled him. "The gel likes her travel books, I told you," he whined.

In short, the man didn't know a jot about his daughter beyond that. Edmund layered his elbows upon the table and leaned across the smooth, mahogany surface, shrinking the gap between them. "I intend to find out for myself, Waters."

The viscount's cheeks turned ruddy and then in a shocking display of courage and boldness, he said, "You aren't going to ruin the chit, now are you?" Ah, so there was a bit of fatherly loyalty to the woman. Waters' beady eyes darted about the club and then returned to Edmund once more. "Can't have you ruining her. Not when I can use her to make a match." Of course, that would account for any father's sense of concern for his daughter's virtue.

Edmund downed the contents of his brandy in a long, slow swallow and set the glass down hard. With a last, disdainful glance at the corpulent lord, he shoved back his chair and stood.

"Rutland?" the viscount's pleading voice called after him.

He ignored the other man and continued his path through the

clubs with renewed purpose for Phoebe Barrett. The viscount asked him not to ruin his daughter, failing to know she'd been ruined the moment she'd made friends with Miss Honoria Fairfax.

Silently he catalogued the viscount's newest revealed weakness—using his own daughter as a pawn.

CHAPTER 7

THE FOLLOWING MORNING, PHOEBE, INSIDE the Viscount Waters' carriage, rolled slowly through crowded London streets. She fiddled with her reticule. At any other moment, and any other time before, an eager excitement would have consumed her every thought so all she might think about was this trip she now made.

You'd go to Wales to be closer to your Vikings, instead of spreading your wings and daring to dream...you deserve more in your dreams and for them...

Edmund, a mere stranger to her just three days ago, had somehow reached inside her and seen both the hopes she carried and, more, the secrets she kept, even from herself. "Oh, it is ever so exciting." Her sister's lyrical sing-song voice called her to the moment. Justina fairly bounced on the edge of her seat. At seventeen, there was still an honest innocence to her younger sister's happiness. "New shops, new books." A wistful expression stole over her face. "Oh, I cannot wait until I make my Come Out."

There was a romantic, faraway glimmer in her sister's lovely blue eyes that gave her pause. This whimsical dreamer remained somehow untouched by their father's darkness. Unease stirred in Phoebe. With her golden blonde curls and trusting spirit, Justina would be easy prey to any manner of roguish gentlemen with dishonorable intentions who'd take advantage of that trusting spirit.

Feeling her stare, Justina's smile dipped. "What is it?"

Phoebe shoved aside concerns for the future. There would be

time enough for worrying when Justina made her Come Out. "I'm merely thinking of the books I'll find," she lied.

Justina dropped her chin into her hand and sighed. "You are so clever and bookish."

Her lips twitched at the compliment given that would have not been construed as such by most any other lady. "You too are clever," she said.

Her sister wrinkled her mouth. "Not like you. I've tried to read your books of exploration and I find my mind drifts to romance and dashing knights and scandalous loves and…" She prattled on and on, raising the warning bells once again of the perils of sending Justina out into London Society. She would need to be carefully guarded.

Phoebe stared out at the passing London streets, the crowds thinning as they disappeared deeper down to the less traveled parts of North Bond Street, while thinking of another—a gentleman whom her friends vigorously attacked with their words and urged caution of.

Edmund, the Marquess of Rutland—a gentleman whom Society saw in one light, while in truth he, too, possessed a traveler's soul, longing to break free from the strict confines of their gilded world and know life beyond the cage they'd been trapped within. Only, as a gentleman, he could travel and explore and go…and yet he did not. Just like her. What was it that held him here?

"Oh, dear, you have the look again."

She released the curtain and it fluttered back into place. "What is that, dear?" she asked, returning her attention to Justina.

A twinkle lit her sister's pretty eyes. "The look," she whispered as though fearing the driver and the footman perched atop the box might hear her over the loud churning of the carriage wheels. "It is a gentleman, as Mother said." Phoebe widened her eyes and made a choking sound. Her sister's smile widened. "The look of longing…" She choked again. *The look of longing?* "And you wearing the expression a person has the moment they try their first ice at Gunter's."

"I do not," she said, drawing her shoulders back in indignation. She was practical and logical and didn't have dreamy eyes and faraway expressions.

Justina nodded as though the matter were settled on fact. "Oh, yes." Then as the ultimate insult, she leaned over and patted Phoebe's knee. "Nor did you deny there is a gentleman."

"There is no gentleman," she replied automatically…and belatedly. Warmth burned her cheeks.

Her sister gave her an entirely too mature of a sudden, sympathetic smile. "I am sure he is splendid."

He was splendid; a magnificence that defied the hard, chiseled planes of his cheeks and a noble, square jaw with a slight cleft, the only hint of softness in a face that may as well have been chiseled of stone. Even with but their two meetings, Edmund asked questions of her interests as though seeing someone more than any other lady who'd made her Come Out and sought a respectable match.

"You've the look of longing again."

Blessedly, the carriage rocked to a halt alongside their destination. "I do not have a look of longing," she muttered, grateful when the footman tugged open the carriage doors and effectively interrupted her sister's response.

Phoebe allowed him to hand her down with a murmur of thanks and paused to look at the corner establishment. She shielded her eyes against the sun's glaring brightness. Her sister came to a stop beside her and followed her gaze. From the corner of her eye, she detected the skepticism stamped on her face. "This is the shop?"

"This is the shop." She remained rooted to the spot while eying the sign that hung haphazardly, swaying in the spring breeze.

"It hardly seems er…" Justina scratched her brow. "The fashionable shop to contain those travel items you so love." The shop in question was, in fact, one she'd never before visited. After Edmund's inadvertent challenge of her dreams and love of exploration, she'd resolved to look beyond the safe, expected books offered at the more fashionable shops.

She eyed the building with the same skepticism in her sister's suddenly wary eyes. "I have it on good authority it is a reputable establishment with original artifacts and books."

"On *whose* good authority?"

Phoebe pretended not to hear Justina's question. She could hardly say her loyal maid had put inquiries to some other nobleman's hopefully loyal servants and had been given this particular shop. "Come along, then," she said with forced cheer and started toward the Unique Treasures and Artifacts Shop.

"Not at all a clever name for a shop," her sister mumbled as she followed Phoebe into the dark and cluttered shop.

Phoebe skimmed the expansive space, with floor-length shelving of books and tables scattered about the room and brimming with unfamiliar objects; some of them shining and lethal in appearance. Her heart kicked up a beat with excitement.

"Perhaps it isn't a gentleman, after all," her sister said at her side. She glanced at Phoebe questioningly. "You have the same look of longing." She groaned. "Never tell me you've gone and fallen in love with your tiresome artifacts."

Phoebe laughed and took her by the shoulders, then steered her off. "Go. Shop."

"You're trying to be rid of me." Her sister slapped a hand to her chest in feigned hurt.

Phoebe winked. "Indeed, I am."

"Very well," Justina said on a prolonged sigh and then skipped off with the exuberance better reserved for a younger child.

Free of her oddly knowing younger sister, Phoebe returned her attention to the shop, and scanned her gaze over the collection of exotic creatures petrified. A black panther with a lethal gleam in his frozen, yellow eyes pulled at her. "Hullo?" she called out softly. She looked about for a shopkeeper and, at finding none, ventured deeper into the shop, drawn to the massive panther in the corner. Phoebe touched a tentative hand out and stroked his satiny smooth head. Regret tugged at her. This is not the adventure and exploration she craved. She didn't long for a world where creatures were captured, killed, and forever memorialized as a token of one person's dominance in a world different than the natural world they belonged to.

"Oh, hullo, there."

Phoebe started and dropped her hand. She spun around. "Hello." A bespectacled, tall, lean man with a shock of red hair stared back at her as though she were as rare as one of those exotic creatures on display in his establishment.

"Do you require assistance?" Though the faintly pleading way in which he studied her suggested a greater desire for a lady like her to remove herself from his shop. She took in the armful of books in his arms.

"Er..."

"Because I can help you," he said with a touch of annoyance in his tone.

"Th—"

"But I am helping another patron at the moment." With that, he spun on his heel and marched off.

Well. She supposed she should be offended by his surly unpleasantness. Her lips twitched instead with suppressed amusement. Phoebe returned her attention to the black panther. "You poor thing, you," she said softly. Not only being plunged into a world in which he didn't belong, but being consigned to a life with the foul, miserable shopkeeper.

The panther's lips peeled back in that perpetual growl, indicated the same displeasure as the shopkeeper with her presence.

"It is hardly your fault you're so miserable," she said, stroking him on the head one more time. The world saw a beast to be feared and not revered. What a lonely way for any being to go through life, merely existing and not living.

The shopkeeper's flat, nasally tone carried over to her from within the shop, cutting into Phoebe's musings. "...Captain Cook, indeed, I do, my lord."

Her ears pricked. Drawn by those first two words, she abandoned the angry panther and moved down the aisle, picking her way around the tables filled with oddities from all over the world.

"Yes, the very same." That deep, gravelly, very familiar baritone brought her to an abrupt stop.

Her heart kicked up a funny rhythm that had nothing to do with any of the artifacts, items, or books in the curiosity shop. *Edmund.* "I am looking for a book on the history of his ship, the *Resolution*," he spoke in quiet tones that continued to do funny things to the organ beating too hard inside her chest.

She touched her hand to the shelving and peeked around the floor-length unit just as he accepted a book from the crotchety shopkeeper. That subtle movement caused the midnight fabric of his expertly tailored coat to pull across his impressive frame, highlighting the muscles of his back. Her mouth went dry. Gentlemen were not supposed to have broad-muscled physiques. They were supposed to be padded and proper, and not at all...well, so very masculine.

The shopkeeper glanced up and caught her gaping at them. "Can I help you?" he snapped.

Phoebe gulped and dipped back behind the shelf. She pressed herself against the mahogany structure, her heart hammering. Mortified heat burned a trail across her body. Still, for the miserable man's notice, Edmund hadn't noted her impolite scrutiny. No. He—

"Miss Barrett."

A strangled squeak escaped her at the unexpectedness of that silken whisper. If that black panther had been given a voice, this is how it would have sounded. Dangerous and oddly warm at the same time. "Ed—m-my lord," she swiftly corrected at the ghost of a smile upon his hard lips. "I—" Have nothing to say. There were no words. Phoebe remained with her back pressed against the shelf, borrowing support. "Hullo," she settled for. After all, what else could a young lady who'd been caught gawking and eavesdropping say?

The shopkeeper took a step toward them, but Edmund leveled the reed-thin man with a frigid look that sent him shuffling off in the opposite direction. When the marquess returned his attention to her, his firm lips were turned up in a seductive grin that drove back all reason and logic that reminded her the folly in being here, alone, with him.

Though she wasn't really alone. Not truly. Her sister even now perused the aisles. So, Phoebe remained rooted to her spot.

She and Edmund spoke in unison.

"What brings you here?"

They shared a smile and he held up a small, leather volume with one word emblazoned in gold across the front. *Resolution.*

She reached out reverent fingers and then caught herself, lowering her hands back to her side.

"Here," he urged, holding out the copy.

With a tentative hand, Phoebe reached for his offering. He placed the copy in her trembling grip. Their fingers brushed and even through the kidskin of her gloves, her skin burned from the heated intensity of his touch. Desperate to give her fingers something to do, she fanned the jagged, ivory pages and then stopped at a random page. *Do just once what others say you can't do and you will never pay attention to their limitations again…*

Edmund tugged off his gloves and beat them together. "You've come to discover those pieces beyond your Wales." His was more a statement than a question, spoken with an unerring accuracy. How could he know her thoughts so clearly when they'd but met?

"I have."

Her breath hitched as he reached an arm out, but he merely deposited his leather gloves onto the dusty shelf above her head. "And to look at Mr. McDaniel's curiosities to bring you closer to those exotic places you now long to explore?"

Flecks of silvery dust danced about them. "There is nothing that says I need forget Wales for some other far-flung place." Disquieted by his knowing, she turned a question to him instead. "Why are you here, Edmund?"

He ran his piercing brown gaze, flecked with gold, over her face. "Do you know, Phoebe, when I arrived here a short while ago, I would have said my desire to find more of Cook's great artifacts is what drew me here."

Phoebe dragged the small volume close to her chest. "A-and now?" she whispered.

Her pulse drummed loudly in her ears as Edmund dusted his knuckles over her cheek. "And now?" He lowered his lips closer to hers. "Now, I would say, I'm sure it was you. The hand of fate throwing us together again and again."

"Do you believe in fate?" Her words emerged breathless. "You do not strike me as one to believe in matters of fate." Her lashes fluttered wildly and she hated that despite her friends' warnings about Edmund, the Marquess of Rutland's suitability, she wanted him. Wanted him when she knew nothing of him beyond their shared love of discovery, and his kiss, a kiss she'd now known twice.

He ran the pad of his thumb over the flesh of her lower lip. "At one time I would have sneered at talk of fate."

God how she wanted to know his kiss a third time. "And now?" she repeated once again.

He dipped his head lower, so close their lips nearly brushed. The faint hint of brandy clung to his breath, his sandalwood scent wrapped about her, intoxicating in its masculine power. "Now, I'd be mad to not believe." Phoebe forced her eyes open, holding his intense stare with her own.

"Do you know, I've been warned against you?" She set aside his book upon the nearest shelf.

He stiffened, drawing back so she mourned even that slight parting. "You would be wise to heed such warnings." He spoke in an emotionally deadened tone that chilled her, chasing away all earlier warmth. At the desolateness in his eyes, sadness pricked at her heart. What must it be like to go through life, whispered about *and* alone? As painful as it was to be the talked of viscount's daughter, Phoebe had a loving mama and brother and sister, and loyal friends.

Phoebe ran her palm over his cheek and he jerked erect as though she'd run him through. "I learned long ago to not place much heed in the words of gossip."

For a moment his thick dark lashes swept down and concealed the brown depths of his eyes. When he opened them, a whirl of tumult swirled in their depths. "You should," he said on a gruff whisper. "You should steer far and clear of me, Phoebe Barrett, and seek out respectability instead of the ugliness that surrounds me." She expected him to push her away. Instead, he leaned his cheek into her hand, as though craving her touch. "We are very different people. I am the thunder to your sunshine."

He was wrong; just as she herself had been wrong mere moments ago. They shared far more than she or he had acknowledged until this moment. They both knew the pain of Society's condemnation. It united them in a bond that could only be experienced and shared by two who'd been scorned and whispered about by the cruel, merciless members of polite Society. "I don't believe you want me to leave," she said softly. She stroked her thumb over his lip, mimicking his earlier movements. Even in her innocence, she recognized the flare of desire in his eyes. "After all, even a gentle flower requires both the storms and the sunshine to survive, doesn't it, Edmund?"

GOD HELP HIM. SHE WAS a pawn; nothing more than a tool to guide him into the graces of the woman he would bind himself to. Phoebe had never been more than another person to be used to exact his revenge upon the one woman, nay the only person, who'd never paid the price for betraying him and shaming him before all. The numb muscles of his upper thigh from that long ago duel fought for the right to the lady's heart, throbbed in a mocking remembrance. And yet, where was the vitriol? Where was the hungering for revenge? Instead, desire burned inside him for this innocent slip of a woman with hope in her eyes and a dream on her lips. Panic squeezed the air from his lungs.

Then she stepped away, putting the distance he himself should have between them and he breathed again. She wandered past the shelving, touching the cluttered tables with artifacts he cared not a jot about, and then she crooked a finger. Drawn to her like a moth to flame, Edmund followed after her, forgetting every lesson he'd learned about the perils of fire.

She stopped in the corner of the shop and then tossed a glance over her shoulder back at him. Did she think he'd not wander down whatever path she led him on? How could the lady not know her own appeal? She had a more potent hold upon him than the sirens drawing those poor fools out to sea. An encouraging smile on her lips, she crooked her finger again, urging him the remainder of the way. No, the lady did not know her allure. He stopped beside her with a deliberate closeness so his thigh crushed the fabric of her skirts.

Her smile dipped, the muscles of her throat working. "It is magnificent."

He ran his gaze along the crown of her silky, auburn tresses and the delicate planes of her heart-shaped face. "Yes, magnificent."

"Though my heart breaks for him," she said, not taking her eyes from the smooth, black panther stuffed for his efforts—frozen in his last furious state of battle.

Edmund's gaze caught the golden-yellow of the beast's stare. The snarling creature jeered at him for having dared to forget for even one moment that he was no different than the cold, emotionless creature on display before them. "Your heart would break for a beast with no heart," he said, his tone coolly dispassionate.

With a frown, she raised her eyes to his. "He once lived, and knew freedom and joy—"

"He is an animal," he bit out, tired of her naiveté, for with every honest smile and wide-eyed glance, pricks of something a more human, worthy man might have construed as guilt dug at his skin.

Her smile deepened and she studied the stuffed creature with greater attention. "Perhaps," she murmured to herself. "But I prefer to think of him as he once was."

"There you are."

Phoebe started and spun around, a guilty flush on her cheeks. Edmund followed her stare and took in with a lazy interest the blonde-haired, plump young lady with blue eyes. The young lady couldn't be more than sixteen or seventeen. She smiled—Phoebe's smile.

The sister.

"Justina," Phoebe said and stepped away from him.

The wide-eyed girl looked back and forth between them and then her smile grew, dimpling her cheeks. "Oh, hello." She loosened the strings of a ridiculously large, garish, purple bonnet then lowered it.

Splotches of red slapped Phoebe's cheeks.

When it became apparent Phoebe intended to say nothing further, Edmund filled the silence. He threw his arms wide and sketched a respectful bow. "The Marquess of Rutland. It is a pleasure."

A merry light twinkled in the girl's eyes. This one would be ruined with far more swiftness than her sister had managed. The young lady dropped a curtsy. "My lord." She looked to Phoebe and cleared her throat.

"Oh, er…yes…my lord, this is my sister, Miss Justina Barrett."

"Miss Barrett, how do you do?"

A tittering giggle bubbled past her lips. "Very well."

Phoebe's blue eyes darkened and she frowned at the both of them. Ah, the lady was jealous. Her sister. In his mind, he mentally ticked off another of the lady's weaknesses.

The young Miss Barrett sidled closer to her sister and slipped her arm through Phoebe's, interlocking them at the elbows. "Is he the one?" she whispered loudly.

"Justina," Phoebe bit out. The color of her cheeks deepened to the shade of a crimson berry and he suddenly had a taste for the sweet, summer fruit.

He gave a crooked grin and reclined against the bookshelf, taking in the exchange with renewed interest. The one? The lady had been speaking to her sister of him, only confirming the supposition he'd come to yesterday morn—he'd fully ensnared Phoebe in his trap. This oddly light sensation in his chest felt a good deal different than the rush of victory he was accustomed to. Perhaps when she served her ultimate purpose and he ingratiated himself into Miss Honoria Fairfax's graces and thoroughly ruined Margaret's beloved niece—then there would be the sense of triumph. As it was, there was an otherwise inexplicable thrill in knowing she spoke of him to her sister. "Have you spoken of me, Miss Barrett?" he asked of Phoebe. And then, rusty from ill-use, the muscles of his mouth quirked up in a grin.

The ladies responded as one. "No."

Justina Barrett leaned closer. "She just has the look."

"The look?" he spoke over Phoebe's protestations, interested to know more about this look the younger sister spoke of, particularly as it pertained to Phoebe.

"The longin—ouch." She swung a wounded, accusatory gaze at Phoebe. "Did you pinch me?"

Phoebe darted out the pink tip of her tongue and trailed it over her lips. Another surge of lust slammed into him; once again filling him with a desire to lay claim to that mouth and more. She cleared her throat. "Er…yes…but only because I'd meant to ask whether you'd seen the display of Captain Cook's hats at the back of the shop?"

Joy lit the young woman's eyes and she jammed her bonnet onto her head. "Indeed? I do not know how I missed such a thing." Likely because there was no such display. He said nothing on that score as he was eager to be rid of the other Barrett sister. "I've been wandering around this infernal shop, but haven't seen anything of remote interest, to me that is."

He winced as the young woman prattled on and on. This was his punishment for involving the Barrett sisters in his plans for revenge. This young woman and her infernal jabbering.

"Oh, yes," Phoebe said, her features schooled in a mask. "It was several rows back, down the bookshelf." He eyed her. All creatures practiced deception. Even she. Only some, however, were skilled in matters of treachery and untruthfulness.

"I shall go have another search." Justina Barrett dropped another curtsy. "It was a pleasure, my lord."

"The pleasure was all mine," he said with the same trace of the charming gentleman he'd demonstrated years ago.

The young lady skipped off, leaving him and Phoebe alone—yet again. When he returned his gaze to her, he found her staring after her sister. She troubled the flesh of her lower lip, lost in thought. "I fear the day she makes her entrance into Society," she said quietly, more to herself. "With her beauty and…" She gave her head a brusque shake, remembering herself, and likely remembering too late that, but for a handful of carefully orchestrated meetings, he was little more than a stranger to her. "Forgive me," she apologized, clasping her hands together.

Odd, she should worry after her own sister's naiveté and fail to realize she was nothing more than a pawn in his scheme for revenge. *Is she…?* He forcibly thrust back the fool question. Of course, she was. If there had been no betrayal by Miss Margaret Dunn, there would have been no duel, and humiliation and moment of weakness in caring for anyone other than himself. Then there would have been no Miss Fairfax. He dipped his gaze down Phoebe's lean frame, lingering on the generous swell of her breasts, and then raising it to meet her eyes. And there would have been no Phoebe. *What a travesty that would have been.*

He wandered closer. "There is nothing to forgive." Not where she was concerned. Edmund lowered his lips to her ear. He inhaled, drawing in the fragrant scent of lilies that clung to her skin, the innocent scent crisp and clean, putting him in mind of things long forgotten—lush countrysides and pure, blue skies, the shade of her eyes. What madness was this? With their bodies' nearness, he detected the faint tremble of her frame. "I wish to see you again, Phoebe. Not in stolen corners of establishments and museums in meetings of happenstance. Will you permit me to call upon you?"

For the fraction of a moment, he wanted her to say no. Wanted her to study him with the jaded cynicism he was deserving of. But for an equally terrifying moment, he wanted her to say yes. A panicky viselike pressure squeezed the breath from his lungs at his own apparent weakness for the innocent Miss Phoebe Barrett.

"Yes," she whispered.

Edmund claimed her lips in a quick, hard kiss. He wrapped his arm about her waist and tugged her against him, aching to worship every curve of her glorious form with his mouth. She whimpered and he swallowed that breathless entreaty with his lips.

"Phoebe?" Her sister called from somewhere within the shop.

He swallowed back a curse and set her aside, placing three deliberate steps between them. Edmund yanked out a nearby book and thrust it into her shaking fingers. She eyed it in confusion just as her sister turned the corner.

"There you are," she said with that same silly smile. "I cannot find the hats. Would you please help me?" The youngest Miss Barrett dropped her voice to a low whisper. "The shopkeeper is quite the curmudgeon."

"Of course, sweet," she said and then handed the book over to him, her hands far steadier than he would have imagined. "Thank you, my lord. It was a pleasure." She spoke with a sincerity that ran ragged through him. No one welcomed his presence, nor desired his company. Within the depths of her unjaded eyes, however, there was warmth and a genuine desire for more than his body or the material things he might give—which was all he *had* to give. It drew him, more powerful than a serpent's venom.

"The same, Miss Barrett." He accepted the book with a murmur of thanks, deliberately brushing his fingers against hers.

Phoebe hesitated a moment, and then without a backward glance, hurried after her sister.

CHAPTER 8

THE WHOLE OF THE CARRIAGE ride home, Justina's excited chattering filled the quiet and saved Phoebe from contributing to the discussion, that wasn't really much of a discussion, about the shops they'd visited that morn. All the while, her mind raced to meet the speed of her thundering heart. He wanted to court her. The Marquess of Rutland, unkindly whispered about by all, desired more than just their fateful meetings. With that honorable request, so went all the reservations she'd carried after Honoria's warning.

Yet, for all the harsh words spoken by her friends and gossips, she knew Edmund to be more—a man who, for all of the *tons'* ill-opinion, believed in fate and dreamed of a life beyond their glittering, cruel Society. Their shared love of Captain Cook and the wonders of the world united them, just as their position as gossiped-about figures of the peerage bound them.

A smile pulled at her lips. The carriage drew to a stop and she looked with some surprise to the window, realizing they'd arrived home.

"We're home." Justina clapped her hands together. "I cannot wait to tell Mama of all the bonnets and hats we saw at the milliner."

Roger, the liveried footman who accompanied them on their travels, pulled the door open and helped Justina down first, and then reached a hand up. "Thank you," Phoebe said. She trailed along at a slower pace behind her excited sister.

The butler pulled the door open and greeted them both with a grin on his wizened cheeks. "Hullo, Manfred." Justina tugged at her bonnet strings and handed the revered item over to the ancient servant, a testament to her faith in his care. She didn't trust her hats with just anyone.

"Miss Barrett, Miss Justina." A twinkle gleamed in his eyes. "Master Andrew is—"

Justina's eager shriek cut into his announcement and she went tearing down the hall that would have sent more staid mamas into histrionics. Mindful of appearances where her younger sister still was not, Phoebe followed along at a more sedate, though still quickened, pace.

Andrew was home. Two years younger than Phoebe, with his keen wit and brotherly devotion these years, he was everything their father had never been. The loud squeals of her sister's laughter stirred emotion in Phoebe's chest and, damning propriety, she raced the remainder of the way. She stepped inside the parlor.

He spun Justina around in a flurry of white skirts and then over her shoulder caught Phoebe in the doorway. "Ah, my sensible, protective, elder sister," he said by way of greeting and set down Justina.

The youngest Barrett sibling slapped him on the arm. "Oh, do hush."

"Andrew, it is ever so good to see you." Skirts snapping noisily, she rushed over and flung her arms about him. But for her mother and sister, there was no one she loved more than her brother. For as horrid an existence they'd known as the children to the shameful Viscount Waters, they'd had one another, and the love shared had made everything else bearable.

Andrew enfolded her in his embrace. "Still unwed?"

She pinched him on the arm and stepped back. "You're insufferable."

Justina giggled. "I do not expect she'll be unwed for long."

Phoebe glared her into silence. Her efforts proved futile.

As one who'd delighted in vexing his two sisters, Andrew winged a blond eyebrow upward. "Oh?"

"There is a gentleman who has captured her notice."

Heat scorched Phoebe's neck and burned a trail up her cheeks. "There is no—" She promptly pressed her lips together. By

Edmund's own request just earlier that morning, he had every intention of launching a courtship and, as such, his presence would no longer be a secret to her brother or any of polite Society.

Andrew's teasing grin slipped and he studied her with more maturity than she'd come to expect of him through the years. "You're flying your colors, Phoebe."

"My colors?" She furrowed her brow and looked questioningly to her sister, but Justina only lifted her shoulders in a little shrug. An equally befuddled expression marred her face.

The only Barrett son demonstrated the same relentless determination that he had with spillikins. "Come now, are you intending to become a tenant for life?"

An inelegant snort escaped her. He'd gone off to university and returned speaking a foreign language. "A *what*?" She buried a laugh in her fingers. But then, wasn't that the way of young men?

Folding his arms across his wiry chest, he stared expectantly back at her. "Married," he said, in the tones their nursemaid had practiced upon them as young children in the nursery. "*Wedded*." Andrew took a step closer and tapped her on the nose. "And you've still not answered just who it is—"

At his subtle movement, a scent, a mixture of lavender and spiced wood wafted about, tickling her nose. "He's…" She sniffed the air. "Egads, whatever are you wearing?" Phoebe scrubbed her nose in a bid to drive back a sneeze. "Achoo."

Their sister's unrestrained laugh filled the room and Andrew bristled with indignation. "This is all the scent."

"All the what scent? The one to drive young ladies into a fit of sneezing?" Phoebe joined in her sister's merriment.

Despite his eighteen, very nearly nineteen, years, he jutted his lower lip out the way he'd done as a young boy, unwanting to share his toy soldiers with two blood-thirsty sisters. Through her mirth, she took him in. Nearly a foot taller than her, at some point he'd grown from chubby young boy into this lean, tall figure she hardly recognized. "Oh, come, I'm only teasing." She leaned up on tiptoe and ruffled his blond locks, arranged in the "frightened owl" fashion. Amusement tugged at her lips. "Er…"

"It is hair wax." By the defensive note, she suspected she should let the matter rest.

"I feel that." Then, having delighted in teasing one another through the years, she couldn't very well cease now. "I feel a very good deal of that wax." Phoebe dusted her hands together to rid her palms of the residue. He danced out of her reach, which only drew attention to the garish, canary yellow satin breeches. A groan escaped her as she took him in.

"What?" he sniffed the air, as if in search of that scent that had called attention to the transformation that had overtaken him this past semester at university.

"You're a dandy," she wailed, covering her eyes with her palm and shaking her head back and forth.

"Who is a dandy?" their mother called from the doorway, bringing the trio of siblings' attention to the entrance of the room.

"Mama," he took a quick step forward as though eager for a motherly hug as he'd been as a child, but remembered himself.

"Andrew," she cried out and rushed forward.

He cleared his throat. "Mama." Giving his garish lapels a tug, he rocked back on his heels. Phoebe stole a peek down, assessing those heels. Heels. Not boots. She sighed. Yes, a dandy, indeed.

Then, mothers were permitted liberties young men would never afford another. Mama clasped his face between her palms and leaned up on tiptoe and planted a kiss upon his cheek. "You've come home."

His nose twitched. The movement so subtle anyone else might have failed to see, but she'd known Andrew better than anyone. "*Why* are you home?"

Crimson splotches of color stained his cheeks. "Can a son not return to see his mother?" He looked to his sisters. "Or a brother return to see his sisters?"

Justina skipped over and claimed his hand. "Do come sit," she urged, tugging him over to the sofa. "I want to hear all your stories of university and the dashing, wonderful, young men you've met."

Puffing his chest out with pride, Andrew claimed a seat and proceeded to speak on all the noblemen he'd come to call friend. Mama sat in the mahogany shell chair and seemed the only one to note that Phoebe remained standing. "Will you not sit?"

"I wished to read, Mama," she replied.

Andrew ceased mid-sentence, a grin on his lips. "Your Captain Cook?"

Yes, her Captain Cook, but now another gentleman, one very

much alive, occupied the better part of her thoughts these past three days. She inclined her head. "The very same. Will you excuse me?"

Just then, Justina asked her brother a question, calling his attention back and Phoebe slipped from the room. The tread of her slippers marked a silent path upon the carpeted corridors as she made her way to the pink parlor. She slipped inside. The stack of books neatly arranged into a pile on the mahogany, rose-inlaid table beckoned her. Not breaking stride, she swept the leather volume atop the small heap and carried it across the room.

Fanning the pages with her fingers, Phoebe slid onto the windowseat.

May I have permission to court you…?

The notorious nobleman, Edmund, Lord Rutland, wanted to court her. She'd resolved early on to never wed a reprobate such as her father and yet this man, with his tortured eyes and ability to speak of hope and share in her love of travel, had proven himself to be so very different than her father. For her friends' warnings and Society's whispers, she wanted to know more of him, ached to know all there was to know, and then learn those whispery secrets he kept even from himself, buried in the corners of his soul he didn't realize existed within him.

Phoebe drew her legs to her chest and knocked her head against the leather volume. What madness had he wrought upon her that he'd so fully captivated her and ensnared her senses? A knock sounded at the door. "You've a visitor," Manfred said from the entrance of the room, bringing her head up.

Likely Honoria arrived to debate once more the merits of Edmund's worth. Drawing in a slow breath, she braced for the impending argument. "Honor—" The greeting died upon her lips at the sudden, unexpected appearance of the tall, commanding marquess. "Edmund," she whispered.

A scowl formed on the normally stoic servant's face. Edmund had clearly grown accustomed to those glowers of disapproval through the years, for he stepped past the other man and entered the room, a small package tucked under his arm. He passed a quick gaze about and then finding the parlor empty but for her, he fixed his intense stare upon her.

Phoebe hopped belatedly to her feet and dropped a curtsy.

A wry grin pulled at his hard lips. "Come, Phoebe, there is no need for such formality between us." He winged an eyebrow upward. "Were you expecting another?" Even with the space between them, she detected the dark flare of emotion light his eyes.

Was he jealous? "Just my friend, Honoria," she assured him. Her mind spun at his sudden appearance.

The flecks of gold glinted with a hardness that gave her pause, sending off a distant warning bell. She smoothed her palms over the front of her skirts, unable to account for his cool response to her admission, as in this moment he was transformed into the dark, dangerous figure her friends had warned her against. "M-my lord?"

His smile was back in place and he strolled over with long, slow steps. He tossed the small package upon a nearby table while not breaking his forward stride. Phoebe dropped her gaze, noting the slight hitch of his right leg. For the effortless grace with which he moved, there was a hint of a limp. How had she not noticed such a small but important detail about him before now? He came to a stop before her.

When she raised her stare to meet his, he peered at her through thick, dark, hooded lashes; the icy glint in his eyes at odds with the words upon his lips. Again, this stranger did not match with the grinning man she'd come to know. *But do I really know him? We've met but a handful of times.* And still for those three meetings, now four, there was a sense of knowing.

He captured her chin between his thumb and forefinger. "A lady bold enough to wander on Lady Delenworth's terrace in the midst of a ball and who seeks out curiosity shops surely will ask the question."

At that, she wet her lips, suddenly uneasy around him in a way she'd not been since their first unexpected meeting. "Th-the question?" Yet, for the unease, a pain tugged at her heart, as she confronted the truth: the indomitable, proud Marquess of Rutland feared by all, talked about in shocked and scandalized whispers, was insecure of his injured leg. No different than a wounded creature, snarling its fury while secretly nursing its hurts. Coward that she was, she asked, "What are you doing here?"

Edmund brushed his thumb over her lip with an impropriety

surely deserving of a slap across his cheek. "Tsk, tsk, I'd taken you for a woman of courage." He released her and stepped past her, disappointment stamped in the chiseled planes of his face. He stood at her shoulder, peering out the windows, down into the streets below. "What happened to your leg?" At her quietly spoken question, he stiffened. It was not merely morbid curiosity but rather an almost physical need to glean every last detail that had shaped him into this man he'd become.

When he looked back to her once again, there was a grudging respect in his eyes. "I dueled for a lady's heart."

At the unexpectedness of those words, Phoebe's breath hitched painfully and she preferred the not knowing, blissful ignorance of Society's tales of the dark Marquess of Rutland. An empty, mirthless grin turned his lips ever so slightly at the corner; all the more telling for the bitterness there. For if his heart was no longer engaged, there would be no stinging resentment. She stretched a hand out to him. "I am so very sorry, Edmund."

THE LADY'S FRAGILE HEART SHOWED itself once more.

Yet, this telling of Margaret's betrayal had not been a crafty attempt to slip even further into Phoebe's affections. The stories of his past, of the one woman he'd trusted was not a part he opened to anyone. Ultimately, Margaret had revealed a weakness in him that he'd since striven to strike from the remembrance of Society members who happened to recall a distant time when he'd foolishly allowed himself that momentary lapse and hoped for the elusive dream of happiness.

Staring out the window, his back presented to Phoebe, he fought for the stable footing he'd become accustomed to through the years; one in which he didn't feel the sting of hurt, embarrassment, shame—any of it. To be emotionally deadened was far safer, far more preferable than…this being flayed open and exposed before a young lady who really was nothing more than a stranger.

Gentle fingers slid into his and he started, staring numbly down at their interlocked digits. The olive hue of Phoebe's skin spoke to her Roman ancestry. Her hand, delicate and soft, and yet possessed of an inexplicable strength, drew him. Something shifted in his chest. *Pull away, you blasted, pathetic lackwit.* The muscles of his stomach clenched and he could no sooner relinquish the connection than he could sever off his duel-scarred leg.

Perhaps in this scheme of revenge he'd drawn her into, he was the only weak one, for she came closer, when his mind rebelled and urged retreat, and then Phoebe stopped so her chest brushed against his.

"Do you still love her?"

By the tentativeness in those words his answer mattered very much to her and he thrilled at that for reasons that moved beyond his plans for Miss Fairfax. "I do not love her." The harsh, guttural response intended to send her fleeing only brought her head back and a contemplative glimmer lit her eyes.

A sad, little smile pulled at her lips. "Oh, Edmund, surely you realize if that were true you'd not be so very angry still."

By the wistfulness in the lines of her heart-shaped face, she certainly believed the veracity of her own statement. Yet… He frowned. Who he was and who he'd become had nothing to do with Margaret, but rather a collection of experiences that went back to a dark, gloomy, and very real childhood. "I assure you, I do not love her." Or anyone. Love was dangerous. Love destroyed.

"I believe you try to convince yourself as much."

Her adamancy set his teeth on edge and he stepped away from her. "You speak as though you know me and yet what do you really know?" Nothing. She knew nothing. Not even the miserable creatures who'd given him life had known him…or cared to. A muscle ticked at the corner of his eye.

She arched a thin, brown eyebrow. "I know enough."

Hardly anything at all. For if she truly gleaned the black mark upon his soul, she'd not have that warmth in her eyes whenever she looked at him, just as she did now. Edmund growled. "How trusting you are," he spat the words dripping with scorn for Phoebe because of her misguided faith and trust, because of him for his deceitfulness, but more for caring about this treachery when he'd never cared before. "You would see good where there is none." As soon as the words left his mouth, he recognized that irrational attempt to have her shut him out of her life and then he'd be done with his plan.

"Perhaps." Phoebe took a step closer; the prey now turned predator. "And yet, I also realize a person can claim to be angry ten times to Sunday but if the smile on their lips meets one's eyes, there is happiness somewhere deep inside." Coming to a stop before him, she claimed his hands in a boldness that would have shocked any dowager, matron, and mama. She turned them over studying his gloveless palms.

A garbled sound lodged in his throat. "Is that what you believe, that I'm smiling?" All laughter had died from his life twenty-five years ago.

"Here." Phoebe ran her finger over the right corner of his lip, shocking him with the innocent seductiveness of that faint touch. Her caress somehow more erotic than any of the scandalous, forbidden games he'd played behind chamber doors. "You smile, and then it is as though you remind yourself you do not want to smile and this muscle twitches," she said, having no idea the havoc she now wrought upon his senses.

Edmund shot a hand out and encircled it about her wrist, capturing the delicate flesh in his unrelenting grip. "What have you to smile for?" His words were not to taunt, but rather a desperate desire to know how she'd risen from the ugliness of life, the daughter of Waters to become...*this* woman who spoke of laughter and hope and happiness. It was too much. He dragged her wrist to his mouth and touched his lips to the wildly fluttering pulse there. Phoebe's thick, nearly black lashes swept down as he continued to worship the soft skin, nipping at the juncture where her hand met wrist.

Then, as though it were a physical exertion, she forced her eyes open and peered at him with an intensity of emotion that robbed him of logical thought. "I can go through life bemoaning the circumstances of my life." Her lecherous sire. "Or I can choose to smile and celebrate where I can." She met his gaze squarely. "I choose to celebrate, Edmund."

When she spoke with that resolve, she made him believe he, too, could try again at life and, as she said, smile where he could and bury the memories of the shameful deeds no child should ever bear witness to.

Edmund lowered his head, to claim her lips under his once more and stamp the sincerity of her promise upon his soul. He took her mouth in a gentle meeting. There was none of the violent, desperate passion he reserved for every lover to come before her. With a whispery sigh, she leaned up and wrapped her arms about his neck, availing herself to him and all he could offer. Emboldened by her eagerness, he deepened the kiss, devouring her mouth with his, over and over. Gentleness gone, he parted her lips and mated with her tongue in a bold thrust and parry. He swallowed her moan of desire, catching her to him as her body collapsed against his. "I want you, Phoebe Barrett," he said harshly against her lips and, guiding her to the edge of the wall, he anchored her with his chest. He trailed his lips down her neck then kissed the silken shell of her earlobe.

Phoebe captured her lower lip between her teeth, her head falling back. "M-my maid—"

"Can go hang," he whispered, worshiping the long, graceful stretch of her neck. He'd never worried about discovery before and he didn't now. He drew her flesh between his teeth, gently nipping until she was moaning with unrestrained desire.

In this moment, nothing but they two mattered. Not his plans for Miss Fairfax or his use of Phoebe's father to advance that plan. What if there could be more between them? What if he abandoned this driving need for retribution? The curtain fell agape. It was as though the fates jeered his momentary weakening.

Through the crack in the velvet curtains, his gaze snagged upon Miss Honoria Fairfax, the woman he'd take to wife, the sole reason he was even now with Phoebe, as she stepped down from her carriage, a mutinous set to her mouth. The pale-haired Lady Gillian followed along behind her. With a curse, Edmund wrenched away.

Phoebe's chest heaved with the force of her desire and it was all he could do to keep from conquering her mouth once again. He quickly set her hair to rights, adjusting the floral, jewel-encrusted combs woven into her hair. The light reflected off the too-dull gem and his gut tightened with the truth that she wore nothing more than paste baubles. And he who'd never felt an ounce of remorse, shame, or regret in his life, was consumed by a numbing guilt. He'd divested the lady of her dowry.

"Wh-what i-is it?" Hesitancy underscored that question.

He steeled his jaw. Nay, the lady's father was responsible for those crimes. There were many other sins that could be laid at Edmund's feet. "You've visitors," he murmured, deliberately misinterpreting the question she put to him.

They looked to the door just as her maid rushed into the room, head downcast. The young woman lifted her eyes a moment and a flush stained her cheeks as she continued to the corner of the parlor, swiftly claiming a seat. Ah, the loyal maid had allowed her mistress that scandalous privacy. She'd see Phoebe ruined.

No, I'll see her ruined…

Footsteps fell in the corridor, punctuated by the excited chatter of one of those visiting ladies. Conditioned to living in the shadows, Edmund backed away. The surly and rightfully wary butler reappeared and announced Phoebe's two friends.

Lady Gillian stepped into the room with a wide, innocent smile. "Hullo, Phoe—" The warm greeting withered on her lips as she caught sight of Edmund. Silence marched out long and stilted between them.

He broke the quiet. "Lady Gillian, Miss Fairfax." Despite his polite greeting, Miss Fairfax lingered in the doorway with a staying hand rested upon her other friend's forearm, as though she'd been unable to adequately protect Phoebe but would not so fail the innocent, golden-haired lady.

Phoebe looked between them and then rushed over to greet the woman he'd take as his wife. Why was the taste for retribution less potent than this hungering to claim another? He slid his gaze over Phoebe's lean frame, taking in the gracefulness of her back.

"Gillian, Honoria." Only one as deaf as a dowager would fail to hear the forced cheer in her tone. She motioned them to sit. "Will you see to refreshments?" she called to the maid in the corner. The too-obedient young woman hovering in the corner of the room raced to do her mistress' bidding. "Lord Rutland was just visiting."

"Why?" the tart-mouth shrew who'd find herself his bride, snapped.

Lady Gillian gasped, stifling the sound with her fingers. "Honoria," she chided.

Alas, it would seem there was but one sensible woman of their lot—a cynical, wary creature with loathing in her eyes. Yes, in temperament and cynicism she would make him the perfect wife. Why did that thought leave him strangely hollow? "If you'll excuse me," he murmured. "I'll leave you to your visit." He sketched another bow.

"No," Phoebe cried out. Her friends rounded their eyes in response. Color bloomed on her cheeks and she ran her palms over the front of the gown. When she spoke, her words emerged far steadier. "That is…" She wet her lips and then looked about as though in search of some desperate device to keep him here amongst two young women who appeared as if they'd rather have his head on a platter than his company for tea. Her gaze alighted on the small, rose-inlaid side table and she rushed over in a flurry of white skirts. "Your package, Ed—" Lady Gillian's shocked gasp cut into that impropriety. "That is, you've forgotten your package, my lord." With fingers atremble, Phoebe rescued the wrapped package and held it out. She lifted her gaze to his. Entreaty, apology, and a whole host of sentiments he was undeserving of, lit her expressive eyes.

Edmund held his hands up. "You're mistaken." He lowered his voice, speaking in hushed tones. "It is yours." Running his gaze over her face once more, he sketched another bow and adjusted his awkward gait then took his leave. He made his way out of Viscount Waters' townhouse and away from Phoebe. This scheme he'd forced her into plunged Edmund into a realm in which he could never be redeemed.

His lips turned up in a smile that likely would have chilled her back into a logical miss. Then, there was no redemption for a blackguard such as he.

CHAPTER 9

PHOEBE STARED DOWN AT THE small, wrapped package in her hands. It was the height of impropriety to accept a gift from a gentleman. It was the level of scandalousness that saw a lady ruined, and when said gift was given by Lord Rutland, she might as well don crimson skirts and declare herself the next Harriette Wilson.

"What have you done, Phoebe?" The desperation infused in Honoria's tone brought her attention up.

Had she been the furious, guarded, snapping young woman she'd been since she'd stepped onto Lady Delenworth's terrace and discovered Phoebe and Edmund together, that would be easier to bear than this pitying, alarmed figure. "He wants to court me."

Her friends spoke in unison. "He wants to court you?" The young ladies, her confidantes these two years, shared a look.

"Is that so difficult to believe?" She could not keep the affront from her voice.

"Yes." This from Gillian, the most hopeful romantic one of their lot.

Honoria pounced, throwing support behind Gillian. "Don't you see?" She swept over and stopped before Phoebe. "The Marquess of Rutland is a monster."

Gillian gave a hesitant nod. "It is true. He is."

The more cynical of her friends pursed her lips. "He doesn't court young ladies."

Again, the world saw in Edmund what they chose to see. They

looked at the veneer of him constructed of whispers and rumors alone, and failed to see a man who believed in hope, and dreamed of escape from the rigid confines of their cruel world. "You're wrong." Phoebe promptly pressed her lips into a firm line. Honoria bristled and settled her hands on her hips. "My aunt knew him well and…" she wrinkled her nose. "Though she's not provided me details about *how* she knew him, it is enough to know the gossips are indeed correct about the man."

Her *aunt*? She gritted her teeth. "You'd expect me to condemn the gentleman based on tales you do not know, and on nothing more than your aunt's words alone?" Disappointment filled her. Given each of their circumstances, she expected more honor from her friend. "Come, what manner of person would I be to judge another so." She gave Honoria a deliberate look.

Honoria had the good grace to flush.

Surprisingly, it was Gillian who shattered the quiet. "Look at you, both, arguing." She sailed over in a flurry of noisy taffeta skirts and positioned herself directly between Honoria and Phoebe. "Perhaps there is good in him, Honoria."

The cynical one of their trio slashed the air with her hand. "Bah. There is not. He will hurt you," she said to Phoebe and then turned to Gillian. "He will hurt her. Scoundrels, rakes, and rogues are not to be trusted."

Annoyed with the ease in which Honoria fell into the ranks of every member of the *ton* who'd serve as arbiter and executioner of a person's reputation, she said, "I'll not let myself be hurt." As soon as that assurance left her mouth, she recognized the futility of that promise. Gillian and Honoria's silence said they, too, recognized it. For Phoebe couldn't *truly* protect herself—not fully. Edmund was not the monster Society painted him to be, but he was still a scarred and broken creature, and those were the most difficult to heal.

Phoebe passed the gift he'd given back and forth between her hands. His unyielding visage flashed behind her eyes. "I know he is not…the most gentle of men." She continued over Honoria's disbelieving snort. "When I am with him," she said, picking her gaze up, "I'm not the shameful Lord Waters' daughter. I'm simply Phoebe." And that is all she'd longed for people to see—not her familial connection to a letch who lived at his clubs and shamed her mother. Some of the tension left Honoria's stiffly held frame, hinting at a wavering on her part. Phoebe pressed her vantage. "Surely you see no one could ever make him do something he does not wish." *I want you, Phoebe Barrett.* "You warned me that his intentions can never be honorable and yet he wishes to court me." Phoebe drew the gift given her close, hugging the package to her chest. "Why should he do that unless he wished it?"

"I don't know." That terse admission came as though dragged from Honoria.

Phoebe continued her defense. "I will do nothing foolish where the marquess is concerned." Her friends exchanged a doubtful look and she steeled her jaw. Both women were entitled to their cynicism but she'd not have it jade her own interactions with Edmund. "Nor will I not allow myself to explore the possibilities that exist with Lord Rutland and what is within my heart."

Her maid entered bearing the tray of refreshments, effectively quashing any further discussion on Lord Rutland's intentions, for which Phoebe sent a silent prayer of thanks skyward. Marissa set her burden down and then took her leave once more.

Gillian motioned to the package in Phoebe's arms. "Well then, what has he given you?"

"I..." Did not want to open such an intimate item before anyone, even her friends. Particularly following Honoria's damning opinion about the gentleman. Clearing her throat, she wandered over to the sofa and claimed a seat. "I'm not certain," she settled for.

"Of course you aren't, silly." Gillian pointed her green eyes up. "That is, after all, the purpose of a gift." She rushed to sit beside Phoebe and the gift in question.

With a grudging reluctance Honoria joined them, taking a spot on the mahogany shell chair. "Go on, then."

The expectant stares trained on her indicated that, short of a blunt refusal, she had little choice but to comply. To issue any other protest would merely rouse their over-cautiousness where Edmund was concerned. She bent her head and slid the tip of her finger under the fold in the covering. Her skin pricked from the intensity of her friends' scrutiny. Phoebe drew the item out of its packaging, setting the brown fabric aside. Her heart started. *Resolution.* He'd given her the book he'd sought and found. Swept deeper into his hold, the same panicky fear that gripped her friends reared powerfully strong, when presented with this…considerateness. He knew her interests. Shared them.

"A book," Gillian's fallen tone conveyed her tangible disappointment. Phoebe held it up so they might read the title etched in gold lettering. The young woman retrieved a small plate and helped herself to a raisin scone. "There are no worries as to *that* selection," she said for Honoria's benefit. "After all, there is nothing at all amorous or inappropriate in," she wrinkled her nose, "Captain Cook's *Resolution*."

"There is everything inappropriate in it, for—"

"There is everything inappropriate in what?"

The ladies shrieked at the sudden, unexpected and, in this moment, very unwelcome appearance of Phoebe's brother, Andrew. Gillian's plate tumbled to the floor and landed on the Aubusson carpet, remarkably unbroken. Phoebe sighed as her friends came to their feet and greeted Andrew. She'd quite missed him when he'd been at university, but she did not miss his bothersome tendency of making havoc for her.

He strode over, arms folded. "Well, then?" he quizzed, as the ladies reclaimed their seats.

"It is…" Honoria and Phoebe glared their oft loose-lipped friend into silence. "Er…nothing. It is nothing."

Andrew narrowed his eyes and plopped into the empty King Louis XIV chair opposite Phoebe. And her book. And her disapproving friends. She tamped down a groan. This had all the makings of a headache. He drummed his fingertips along the arms of his chair and then suddenly stopped and leaned forward. Settling his palms upon his hideously garish, canary yellow satin breeches, he whispered, "Is this about the gentleman Justina claims you've been making eyes at?"

At Gillian's giggling, Phoebe frowned. "I am not making eyes at him." *Drat.*

Andrew leaned back in his seat triumphant with a gloating expression stamped on his face. Then showing the hint of boy he still was, or at least was to her, he reached over and swiped a plate and a cherry tart. He popped the sugared treat in his mouth in one bite. "Who is he?" he said after he'd swallowed.

"You've sugar on your face," she admonished.

He yanked out a kerchief and dabbed at his lips, ignoring her friends' obvious enjoyment, clearly expecting her brother would be indignant and then what? Challenge Edmund to a duel when he discovered that the notorious Marquess of Rutland intended to court his sister. "Well?"

She sighed. "Lord Rutland."

The yellow embroidered fabric slipped from his fingers and sailed forgotten to the floor. Her brother narrowed his eyes. "The Marquess of Rutland?"

"The same," Honoria said with a pleased nod.

Andrew furrowed his brow. "Not really the marrying type."

"Precisely, my—*our* concern," Honoria amended at Gillian's pointed frown.

Gillian spoke on a loud whisper. "They say he doesn't leave his clubs."

Phoebe curled her fingers about the gift, knowing implicitly the gentleman in question did, in fact, leave his clubs. Edmund visited museums and curiosity shops. And now her, he'd visited her. Gentleman did not visit ladies unless they desired more. A thrill ran through her. Detesting Andrew and her friends' seemingly know-all about Edmund, when they, in fact, knew nothing, she said, "I assure you he leaves his clubs."

Her brother shook his head. "No, Gillian's correct on this score. The man doesn't," he insisted. He puffed out his narrow chest, looking like a boy playing at powerful peer. "Even been to some of those clubs, myself."

A startled gasp escaped her lips and she buried it in her fingers. "Andrew!" she chided, glaring her giggling friends into silence.

"What?" He shifted in his seat. "I have, you know." Her brother tugged at the lapels of his jacket. "Been to those clubs." His sullen tone was more suited to a boy caught raiding Cook's kitchens than a young man having his roguish actions called into question.

Concern blotted out her earlier annoyance. With their father's reputation and the shame visited upon them as such, she expected he'd hold to a higher moral standard.

"And," Andrew continued on a hushed whisper, "I see him there quite frequently. Terrifying chap." A mottled flush stained his cheeks. "Not that I'm afraid of the man, I'm not," he said, his tone wholly lacking of conviction.

"You should be," Honoria warned. "You both should be."

Phoebe scoffed at more of her friend's cryptic, unsubstantiated warnings.

"I'm not afraid of any gentleman." Andrew's too-excited voice bounced off the walls. "Including Rutland." The color staining his cheeks deepened and he came awkwardly to his feet. "If you'll excuse me, ladies, I've business to see to."

Phoebe's lips twitched with mirth as she strained to hide her amusement. "Of course," she said. Her placating tone only elicited a scowl. At eighteen, nearly nineteen, there was not much business he had to see to, and she suspected as he sketched a bow and all but bolted from the room, his departure had more to do with embarrassment than anything else. With his absence, however she now found herself alone with her disapproving friends. She braced for their barrage of words about Edmund and his unsuitability.

Surprisingly, it was Gillian who returned them to the matter of concern. "He wants to court you?"

"He does." She reached for the small, leather volume and she flipped open the cover.

"Why?" Honoria asked and the rudeness of such a question brought Phoebe's head up. "Not because you're not lovely, because you are, and clever and kind, but Rutland does not have use for any of that." She wrinkled her nose. "Well, but for the exception of the lovely part."

Phoebe bristled. How dare Honoria presume to know anything about Edmund? "I've come to find that we have shared interests." And as two people condemned by Society, shared experiences. "He enjoys more than the world sees." Just as she, whom polite Society expected should have no interests beyond the fabric of her gown or the pursuits deemed ladylike that had never held any appeal for her. "And there is no harm in allowing him to court me and seeing if there could be more." Phoebe dropped her gaze to the book and her heart started at the two words inked upon that ivory velum page.

Dream, Phoebe…

She snapped the book closed, lest her friends see this piece she'd not share. "I do not care to debate Ed—Lord Rutland's merits with you." Not anymore. "I appreciate your concerns and will be cautious with my heart, but neither will I judge a man on rumor alone." Considering the matter settled, she sat back in her seat while her friends dutifully turned the conversation to matters that were not Edmund and, therefore, far safer.

THE GARISH DANDY IN HIS silly satin breeches had his gaze fixed on Edmund. Seated as he was, as he always was, with his back pressed against the wall, allowing him a vantage of the entire scandalous hell, he narrowed his eyes on the young man who'd been staring for the better part of an hour. The lad blanched and yanked his gaze away.

Promptly dismissing the pup, Edmund took a swallow of his brandy and instead focused his attentions on the lean, lithe young lady with thick auburn tresses who'd occupied the better part of his thoughts since he'd taken his leave of her that morning—Phoebe.

He stared into the contents of his glass seeing her. The deep shade put him in mind of her silken curls, those curls he still longed to see fanned out upon his bed. With a silent curse at those fanciful musings, musings that he, the Marquess of Rutland, certainly did not have, Edmund took another drink. His lips pulled in an involuntary grimace that had nothing to do with the burn of liquor and everything to do with those damned romantic, nonsensical thoughts about a lady and her satiny soft skin and the glimmer in her clear blue eyes… He tossed back the remaining contents of his drink.

Edmund passed the empty glass back and forth between his hands, fixing on the lingering droplets that clung to the edge of his tumbler. In this moment he could not sort out who he hated more—himself or Phoebe—for slipping past his defenses and burrowing a place inside him that he'd not known existed; a place of hope, where revenge didn't dwell.

You smile and then it is as though you remind yourself that you do not want to smile and this muscle twitches…

A chill ran through him at how eerily accurate those words had been and, more terrifying, for the truth of them. After having been forced to witness his mother tupping her husband's brother, he'd seen the inherent ugliness in life. The lesson, however, had proven a useful one. If his parents, the people who'd given him life, were capable of such vile depravity then certainly such ugliness dwelled within him, too. Time had proven that as fact. Edmund swiped the bottle of brandy from the table and splashed several fingerfuls into the glass. He wanted to hate Phoebe. Nay, he didn't want to feel anything where she was concerned. Revenge could not be fully exacted when a man felt any hint of emotion. But with four damned meetings, she'd become, God help him—a young woman. A young woman beyond her silly, white skirts and attendance at polite social functions. Now, she was a woman who dreamed of travel and her damned Vikings and the Captain Cooks of the world. What was more, when she looked at him, she didn't see the monster Society took him for, the beast he truly was. He'd infiltrated her world, much the way her marauding Vikings had, and fed her words of falsities, all to exact revenge upon her friend. And through this pretend courtship and the orchestrated meetings, some great shift had occurred, and it threatened to plunge him into the precipice of madness.

For, God help him, that foolish, careless youth who'd opened his heart to a woman and had it flayed open for all to see, still lived. Despite Edmund's confidence that he'd long ago buried the inherent weakness to feel…*anything*, Phoebe's smile and boldness and talks of love and hope proved that he still felt. His mind skirted away from just precisely what he felt.

He swirled the contents of his glass. The irony was not lost on him. He, who used every man, woman, or servant who could advance his plans for wealth or retribution through the years, would not use Phoebe. In the end, she'd defeated him. How could he truly move forward with his plans for the prickly Miss Honoria Fairfax when another brown-haired, whimsical miss would forever occupy his thoughts? In marrying Margaret's niece, nay, in trapping her, by nature of her relationship with Phoebe, he'd consign himself to a world where he would never be free of Miss Phoebe Barrett. Just like the scar he carried on his leg, she would remain a mark reminding him of his weakness.

Filled with a seething fury with himself, he picked his head up. His gaze collided with the blond dandy across the club. Even with the distance between them, he detected the up and down movement of the young man's throat. He glared at the youth. However, instead of looking away as he'd done the better part of the afternoon, the lad angled his chin up and with a shocking boldness, held Edmund's stare. Fear, trepidation, and determination warred within the young man's eyes as he shoved himself up from his seat and made his way through Forbidden Pleasures.

Edmund narrowed his gaze even further as it became apparent with the lad's long-legged gait that he sought him out. The young man stopped before his table. "H-hullo."

In a sign of deliberate disrespect, Edmund reclined in his chair and remained seated.

"M-may I?"

"May you what?" he asked on a steely whisper. But for the ladies trapped in their empty, miserable marriages who desired the wickedness found in his arms, people did not seek him out—that was unless they required something of him.

"S-sit?"

Ah, yes. It began to make sense. The lad required a favor. Favors oft proved lucrative ventures that increased his coffers and power.

Then in another surprising move, without permission granted, the young man tugged out the seat and settled himself into the chair, effectively obstructing Edmund's unrestricted view of the club.

He stared at the youth dispassionately.

"Y-you probably know who I am."

Actually, he hadn't a bloody inkling as to who this fragrance-doused dandy was. He remained silent, while the lad fidgeted back in forth, scrutinizing him through narrowed eyes. The bold yet fearful stranger couldn't be more than eighteen or nineteen years of age. With thick wax coating his blond hair, he was not someone Edmund recognized, nor cared to know. And yet… He continued to study him. There was something vaguely familiar in those cautious, yet determined, blue eyes.

At the stretch of awkward silence, the dandy cleared his throat. "Er…I expect you should know me and if you don't then it was time to introduce myself for proprietary's sake."

Proprietary's sake? Edmund gave even less of a jot about propriety as he did for the gossip hurled about him through Society's parlors and receiving rooms.

"You don't say much, do you?" he blurted. "Yet, the ladies do seem to favor you." That piece was spoken more to himself, as though he puzzled through an incongruity of life.

Edmund's lips tugged at the consternation in the boy's tone. *You smile, and then it is as though you remind yourself that you do not want to smile and this muscle twitches…* He promptly pressed his lips into a hard, comfortable, and safe line. His patience thoroughly exhausted, he snapped, "What do you want?"

The lad jumped. "M-my sister," he squeaked, his voice cracking. A flush stained his cheeks and he glanced quickly about as though determining whether anyone had heard his outburst. Which was an impossibility. Men didn't even keep tables near Edmund's. They knew to cut even a wide berth in the hells he frequented. Then the boy squared his shoulders. "I am here to speak to you about my sister."

"Your sister?" He rolled his shoulders. Ah, so he must have dallied with this protective younger brother's sister at some point. Edmund picked up his brandy and took a sip.

The young man nodded, eying the bottle of brandy a moment, and then returning his attention to Edmund. "They say you don't have honorable intentions toward ladies."

"I don't," he said flatly, eliciting a frown from the young pup. Edmund made it a point to avoid those simpering, virginal debutantes.

He scratched his brow. "That is what they warned." *They*? The gossips? The *ton*? Anyone and everyone? And more, did the blasted fop think Edmund gave a bloody damn about the unknown lady's identity? "But my sister believes you've honorable intentions toward her despite it. She says—"

"I don't," he cut in. Silence met that emotionless pronouncement. He expected the young man to leave, but he remained, frowning, drumming his fingertips on the tabletop. Edmund took another sip.

"Phoebe is usually more sensible than this."

He choked on his swallow as the boy's words registered.

"Are you all right?" Concern lined the young man's face.

He ignored the question. By God, this bold, protective lad was, in fact, Phoebe's brother. "You're Miss Barrett's brother?" Lord Waters' son?

A smile lit the other man's face—carefree and innocent. Edmund hadn't worn that expression himself in more than twenty-five years. Yet, the offspring of that reprobate Waters should. Interesting. "So, you do know her."

"I know her," he said, his tone gruff. And he wanted to know a whole lot more of her in a way that would have no brother smiling.

Then the lad's grin dipped, replaced with a perplexity. "But you're not courting her?" He scratched his brow. "Because she said..." His words trailed off and Edmund took another long sip to keep from asking what the hell Phoebe had said. The young man made to rise. "Well, if you'll excuse me. It wasn't my intention to—"

"Sit," he bit out as he, who'd been previously annoyed by the pup's presence, now gritted his teeth to keep from asking questions about Phoebe.

The young man promptly reclaimed his seat.

"I am..." he forced the remainder of that lie out through tight lips, "courting your sister." Though that false courtship was only launched to slip past her defenses and, thus, her friend's, and then orchestrate a meeting with the young woman he'd sought to trap.

"Oh." Then Phoebe's brother smiled again. "Brilliant."

Did he truly believe a man of Edmund's reputation courting his innocent, trusting and hopeful sister was brilliant? It spoke ill of the man's intelligence.

"I suppose you should call me Barrett, because of our connection and all." *Their connection?* The young man looked at him expectantly.

"Rutland," he said grudgingly.

Barrett beamed. "I suppose you're wishing to know more about my sister, if you're to properly court her and all, that is."

Young Barrett supposed a lot. And yet, what was this insatiable need to know every last detail about the innocent miss?

Without awaiting a confirmation, Phoebe's brother launched into a list about the lady's interest. "She enjoys Captain Cook," he supplied unhelpfully. Edmund had already gleaned the lady's love of travel and those great explorers. "She wishes to travel." Yes, she'd said as much. "Her favorite color is blue." A useless detail and yet...somehow oddly intriguing. It raised more questions than it answered. What did the lady like about the color? Did it put her in mind of the summer sky or the seas she only dreamed of traveling in her mind? Barret drummed his glove-encased fingertips upon the table. "What else? She detests needlepoint and is dreadful upon the pianoforte but quite appreciates taking in a performance."

As the youth prattled on and on, a slow-burning fury built steadily in Edmund's chest. Phoebe's brother would be so forthcoming with details about the lady? Would he do the same for any gentleman who came after Edmund? Perhaps the next man would be the one who lay between her legs and knew the satiny softness of her skin… A growl climbed up his throat until he wanted to choke the life out of that nameless man, as well as Barrett, for ushering in the thought of Phoebe with another. "Enough," he snapped.

Barrett went silent, his eyes unblinking in his face.

Edmund finished his brandy. The sight of Phoebe's brother and the manner in which he'd embroiled himself with this family was too much…when nothing was, or ever had been, too much. "I've business to see to." He stood, gritting his teeth at the knotted tension of the broken muscles in his leg. "If you'll excuse me."

"Of course, of course."

Mindful of the fearful stares turned on him, Edmund took his leave of Forbidden Pleasures.

Phoebe detested needlepoint, loved music, loathed playing, and she liked the color blue. And why did he hate that he would never know more of the lady than that?

CHAPTER 10

FROM HER POSITION IN THE back corner of Lord and Lady Essex's ballroom, Phoebe surveyed the crowd.

"I detest these events."

For a moment, seated between Gillian and Honoria, Phoebe believed she'd inadvertently spoken aloud.

"Oh, do hush Honoria. They are sometimes enjoyable," Gillian said with her ever cheerful optimism. Then, that like opinion on mindless events was one of the reasons she and Honoria had become fast friends early on. They both detested the inanity of being on display. Only Phoebe was openly vocal in her belief and desire for more. As her friends' squabbling filled her ears, Phoebe skimmed her gaze over to where her mother stood speaking to their hostess.

With her mother's auburn tresses and blue eyes, the viscountess and her patent smile may as well have been a reflection of an older Phoebe twenty years from this moment. A chill stole through her as she confronted the tedium of her safe, predictable existence. A passionless world known by her mother. How many balls and soirees had she attended before this very one, where she'd stared off distracted thinking of her books and far-off places she'd never herself been?

You deserve more in your dreams and for them, Phoebe…

He was her dream. That truth momentarily stunned Phoebe. Edmund, Lord Rutland, in his kisses and discourse had come to matter so very much. He'd shown her desires she carried in her own heart.

As Gillian and Honoria continued their debate on just how enjoyable these events were, Phoebe ignored them. Fiddling with the fabric of her dress, she searched the ballroom for the hint of his familiar frame. Her black panther. The frozen, forever snarling Marquess of Rutland. She smoothed her palm over her satin skirts. How was it that only she saw more of him and in him?

A man so feared and reviled by society, who did not judge her peculiar interests in Captain Cook and those oddities most lords would have scratched their heads at. Where her mother had evinced the proper, dutiful wife even as her husband scandalized the *ton* with his gaming and whoring, Phoebe wished for more than that cold, loveless match. She ached for a control of her world, when the woman who'd given her life had none of her own. And in their discourse, Edmund had demonstrated that he was, in fact, a man who would never discourage her free thoughts or bid for control of her fate. It was why she loved him. She stilled her distracted movements. Her heart thumped to a slow halt and then picked up a panicked rhythm. Phoebe closed her eyes a moment. *Oh, God. I love him.*

As though the fates were in approval, a loud buzz went up amidst the crowd.

"What is he doing here?"

There was only one person who could elicit such contempt from Honoria. Phoebe followed her friend's angry stare to the front of the room. A fluttering stirred in her belly.

Edmund. What was he doing here, this man who hid in shadows and sneered at lords and ladies? *He is here for you.* Phoebe clung to that hopeful whispering in her mind.

She stared at him with an unrepentant boldness. Attired in his familiar midnight black evening coat and breeches, he could rival the evening sky with his imposing strength. He strode down the marble stairs and did not bother with niceties for their host and hostess.

Gillian nudged Phoebe in the side. "You are staring," she whispered.

Everyone was staring. He was that sleek, black panther but very much alive and very much dangerous for the hold he possessed upon her senses and heart.

"At the very least close your mouth," Honoria said with a frown in her voice.

Phoebe immediately pressed her lips together, but it was impossible not to stare. With his towering height and broad, powerful frame, he cut an impressive figure amidst lesser lords; mere mortals in his presence. Lords and ladies stepped out of his way as he cut a purposeful swath through the crowd. All the while he flicked a hard, furious stare about the ballroom. The apathy etched in the chiseled planes of his face indicated his displeasure at being at Lady Essex's annual event. Yet, he came anyway. Why would he, if not for…?

Edmund's gaze locked on hers.

For her…

He slowed his stride. The space between them could not diminish the passion that darkened his eyes. The desire in their dark brown, nearly black, depths evoked the remembrance of the physical feeling of being in his arms while hunger had fueled their kisses and touch at the curiosity shop. She swallowed hard.

"Do not stare at him in that manner," Honoria pleaded.

"I do not generally agree with Honoria but, in this, I fear she's correct. It isn't polite to stare."

"I…" was incapable of one single, coherent thought.

"Oh, bloody hell he is coming this way." A beleaguered moan escaped Honoria.

"Of course he is," Gillian replied, thankfully filling the void left by Phoebe's silence.

"He is dangerous." There was an entreaty in Honoria's words that snapped Phoebe to the moment.

She shifted her attention from Edmund and his forward pursuit. "I…he is not." Oh, Society certainly knew him as ruthless for reasons she'd never paid attention to. "He is a better man than you or Society credits him as being."

Her friend snorted. "We do not credit him as being any kind of good. Not better. Not good. All things lethal and dangerous and…"

"Miss Barrett." That husky whisper laced with steel she'd recognize in the throes of her deepest sleep.

Phoebe gasped and swung her attention upwards the length of

Edmund's impressive height. She hopped to her feet, dimly registering her friends clamoring to a standing position beside her. They flanked her like stern mamas guarding their daughter's good name. "L-Lord Rutland." Phoebe cursed the slight stammer that set her apart from the confident, bold women he'd likely known before her. The ghost of a smile hovered on his lips as though he'd heard that tremble and reveled in his power over her. With an obvious reluctance, Edmund shifted his attention to her friends.

"Miss Fairfax." Honoria's eyes narrowed into thin slits. "Lady Farendale," he greeted a more forgiving Gillian who smiled in return.

"My lord." Gillian, the peacekeeper of the two ladies responded for both of them. "It is a pleasure to see you."

Honoria allowed her mutinous silence to stand as her denial of Gillian's polite greeting.

Just then, the lively quadrille drew to a close, amidst a smattering of applause and excited laughter. The orchestra struck up the strains of a waltz and with a boldness that would scandalize any self-respecting young lady, Edmund turned a hungry gaze on Phoebe. Her mouth went dry as warmth spiraled through her.

He held his hand out. There was no question, no request. He was in command, control, as he'd been from their first meeting. She eyed his outstretched fingers, and as he studied her through thick, dark lashes there was a flash of impatience, melded with concern in his brown irises. Did he think she would turn down his request? Phoebe drew in a slow, steadying breath, heady with the hint of his weakness—for her. For his show now, and before Society, he was not as self-possessed as all believed. She placed her fingertips in his. Edmund closed his hand over hers and momentarily held her fingers in a powerful grip. Ignoring the pointed, matching frowns worn by her friends, Phoebe allowed Edmund to guide her onto the dance floor.

He positioned them at the center of the ballroom, as though barefacedly marking her as his before the other peers present. She placed her trembling fingertips along his sleeve as he settled his hands at her waist.

The orchestra plucked the waltz and he guided her into movement. Edmund lowered his brow close. "You are trembling."

Inside and out. "I am," she said softly.

"Do you finally fear me?" The hint of a frown hovered on his lips, an indication that her answer mattered to him.

"Despite your best efforts, no, I do not." She wanted those words to come out breezy and blithe. Instead, they emerged more whisper than anything.

His eyes smiled when his lips seemed incapable of the feat. He glanced over her shoulder and as he twirled her in effortless circles, she found the subject of his attention. Or in this case, the subjects.

Honoria and Gillian stood shoulder to shoulder with their arms folded watching their every movement.

"They do not approve."

She hesitated, but would not have lies between them. "No, they do not."

"Smart young ladies."

"Do hush." Phoebe squeezed his arm and the muscles of his forearm tightened under her touch. "Would you spend your time here seeking to convince me of the danger in caring for you and trusting you?"

His body went taut, and yet effortless and graceful Edmund did not so much as miss a step in the still-scandalous dance. "Do you know what I would spend my time doing?"

Her body went hot at the husky promise of his question. She managed to shake her head. He placed his lips close her ear. "I would spend my time making love to you."

Oh, God. She momentarily slid her eyes closed. Edmund expertly righted her as she missed a step, catching her to him in a way that brought their bodies momentarily flush. Wicked warmth spiraled through her; a heady aphrodisiac lent power by the forbidden words he'd whispered here amidst the proper lords and ladies twirling about them. She wanted him. In all ways: in her arms, her heart, her life.

Phoebe could go through her life controlled by the strictures of Society and the expectations placed upon her. She located her mother at the edge of the ballroom talking to her host. Empty. Sad. Alone. Or she could become molded as her mother had been.

Edmund rubbed the pad of his thumb over her waist, burning her with his touch, even through the fabric separating them. "Nothing to say?" Edmund whispered.

As she stared up at his cynical, life-hardened eyes, she saw in their depths that he expected her to be shocked and outraged, as any young lady would.

"I would say I want you to spend your time making love to me," she whispered in return.

Hunger flared in his eyes.

The music came to an abrupt halt and they stopped amidst the other clapping dancers; strangers unknowing that Phoebe's world was coming undone before them at the hands of this man's passionate promise. They stood frozen, their breaths coming hard and fast. The forbiddenness of their exchange only fueled this maddening heat spiraling through her.

"Meet me in Lord Essex's conservatory."

His command was spoken so quietly she could have very well imagined it.

Then he dipped a short bow and stalked off. Rooted to the floor, Phoebe stared after him for seconds? Minutes? Hours? Time blurred together at the shocking words that were more order than request, he'd put to her. This scandalous promise of more in his arms was a wicked game she'd never before played and, as such, she did not know the rules or requirements. She only knew she wanted him.

Phoebe gave her head a clearing shake and walked off the dance floor. She located her friends, now locked in conversation with Gillian's father and another prospective suitor. Shifting her attention away from the two young ladies, she looked about for her mother—and found her. Phoebe's heart started. An uncharacteristically sad smile wreathed her mother's lips and reflected back such pain, it stole the air from her lungs. In looking at her, this woman with Phoebe's hair and eyes, and alike in so many ways, Phoebe saw her future…and wanted more. She wanted control of her own happiness. And sometime between Lord Delenworth's terrace and this moment, Edmund had become inextricably intertwined with her happiness.

With that, she turned on her heel and attempted to blend with the satin wallpaper along the walls. She took her leave of the ballroom and went in search of Lord Essex's conservatory. Phoebe lingered at the edge of the hall that would lead her away from respectability and into sin. She curled her toes into the soles of her slippers. To go off with him would mean ruin should she be discovered and yet…she loved him and wanted him. She wanted to know this fleeting happiness, while hoping it signified forever with him. All the while accepting that it might not. Phoebe wanted him, anyway. Through the crowd, her eyes found Honoria. Her friend no longer attended the conversation with Gillian's father. Instead, she searched the crowd and Phoebe had little doubt she sought out her improper friend on a path of ruin.

Phoebe slipped down the corridor. Her heart thundered and fear stabbed at her. She was one set of prying eyes away from discovery. As one who'd never tasted a hint of impropriety and passion before Edmund, this was a world of sentiments she was unfamiliar with. Unlike Edmund who whispered scandalous words of making love to her amidst the ballroom and then urged a meeting. Such a man was accustomed to these clandestine meetings, but in her heart she knew this was altogether different than the ones to come before. A man of Edmund's power and passion was not one who dallied with innocents…and she wanted to be the woman who broke through his cold façade and filled him with the warmth he'd lost in life. She stopped at the end of the hall and looked right and then left. Phoebe froze. The crystal doors marked Lord Essex's infamous conservatory.

She tiptoed down the hall and as her foot depressed a loose floorboard, she jumped and raced the remainder of the way. With shaky fingers, she jerked the door open and all but stumbled inside. Silence served as her only company. She turned and closed the door quietly behind her and remained frozen with her eyes trained on her fingers upon that handle. "You should not be here," she said softly. Wanting him as she did, and this moment signaling control over her happiness and fate, she could not, however, leave.

"No, you should not." Phoebe stilled as Edmund's husky baritone cascaded over her. This must have been the manner of temptation that had driven Adam and Eve to sin. Strong hands settled upon her shoulders and kicked her heart into that increasingly familiar hard rhythm. Edmund lowered his lips close to her ear and his warm breath fanned her nape. "But I am so glad you are," he whispered. His lips caressed the sensitive skin behind her ear.

Her eyes slid closed as he continued to worship the column of her neck with his skillful kiss. The shock of being pressed against the glass door, on view for any stranger or servant who might steal down this hall and see them so, should have killed this masterful hold he had upon her senses. And yet, there was a shocking thrill at the prospect of discovery. A breathless moan slid past her lips as he turned her around and guided her against the glass paneled door, rattling it in its frame. Edmund took her lips under his in a hard, demanding kiss that she returned with equal degrees of hunger and shamelessness. She opened her mouth, allowing him entry and he groaned his approval. As his tongue found hers, they mated with their mouths in a hot haze of feeling.

Edmund captured her wrists in one of his large hands and brought them above her head, pinning them to the glass door. His kiss and actions were not the ones of a gentleman gently loving a delicate lady, but rather a primitive male who sought to brand a woman forever his. She reveled in his equal need for her.

"You should not be here," he whispered as he dragged his mouth down her throat to the modest décolletage of her gown.

"No, I should not be," she managed to rasp as he lowered the fabric of her gown, exposing her skin to the cool night air. "We've already a-ascertained as much. But I want to be." And that is what truly mattered. In a world where she dreamed of passion and life through some other long dead hero's travels, she would take this journey for her and she wanted Edmund as her guide. Her eyelashes fluttered wildly open and shut. This she would take for her. Her love for him fueled her need to know him in this intimate way.

Edmund released her arms and they fell limply to her sides, but he caught her hips in his hands and dragged her to the vee of his thighs. His manhood thrust at her belly; his hardness a tumescent sign of his own need. She moaned and with a wantonness she'd not believed herself capable of, reached between them and ran her fingers over the length pressing at the front of his breeches.

An animalistic groan worked up his throat and she reveled in the helplessness of that sound. Emboldened she continued to tentatively stroke him when he suddenly caught her hand once more.

She shot a questioning look at him. For the first time, the insecurity of being with a man who knew all in the art of lovemaking, a man accustomed to equally knowledgeable partners slammed into her. "Did I do something—?"

Edmund kissed the question from her lips and in one effortless movement, swept her into his arms. He stalked through the length of the floral haven. The sweet scent of peonies and roses filled her senses. So this fragrant, floral heaven was Eden. He paused momentarily at the back of the conservatory and then pulled a door open. The crisp night air enveloped them in its fold as he stepped outside to the walled-in garden. Edmund adjusted her bodice and then set Phoebe on her feet.

She blinked, as though dazed at the abrupt cessation of his caress. "Why did you stop?"

WHY *HAD* HE STOPPED?

Somewhere between the short walk into the gardens and this moment, the small, honorable sliver of a man who still existed hoped Phoebe Barrett would come to her senses. Hope that she'd realize he was a cad undeserving of the gift she offered with her eyes, kisses, and breathless moans.

But that sliver of a man was just a fragment of who he was. The dark, selfish, hungry bastard that he was only knew he wanted her. Wanted her and planned to take what she offered.

He shrugged out of his jacket, snapped the fabric once, and then deliberately set it down beside him. A wide-eyed Phoebe followed the garment as it sailed to the ground at the side of a rose brush, taking down with it several silken petals in its fall. "You will not leave?"

She hesitated and then slowly shook her head. "I would have you take me on this journey."

Oh, God. He focused on his ragged breathing to keep from the innocent allure of that misplaced trust. Edmund stared at Phoebe through his lashes. "I am not so honorable that I will urge you to run. I have warned you, but your decision is yours."

Phoebe wet her lips. "I know that, Edmund."

That intimate use of his name on her lips drove him mad with desire and he closed the distance between them with a speed that brought a shocked gasp to those same lips. He settled his hands on her rounded hips and pulled her close. What hold did she have over him? As he took her lips in a demanding kiss, she met his desire with her own heated ardor. Edmund guided her gently to the ground and brought her down upon the fabric of his jacket. He came over her, taking in the rapid rise and fall of her chest. "Then come with me," he whispered. "I will give you your journey."

In one fluid movement, he shifted her gown and chemise down to expose her breasts once more to the moon's glow. The pink tips of her nipples puckered in the cool of the night. On a groan, he closed his mouth around the pebbled flesh and worshiped the bud. A shuddery gasp exploded from her lips and then she fisted her hands in his hair and held him close.

Encouraged and afire with a hungering need for her, Edmund continued to lave the swollen tip. He blew faint puffs of air onto her nipple and then claimed it under his lips. Over and over he repeated the patterned movement until Phoebe splayed her legs open. "Please," she begged.

Every other woman to come before Phoebe had merely been an object with which to slake his lust. There had been no bond. No connection. But rather a cold, emotionless meeting of two like beasts. He'd given pleasure and gained pleasure, but there had been none of this fiery ache inside and out to possess a woman in any way and every way she could be possessed.

Now, as he rucked up her wrinkled skirts and slid his hand between her legs to find her hot, wet center, he confronted the truth that she was different. Like a siren, she'd shaken down his defenses and tossed him onto the rocks, dazed, enraptured by her. With his hand between them, he teased the damp, auburn curls that shielded her womanhood.

Her hips shot off the ground. "Wh-what are you doing?" she gasped, but her legs fell open in an unwitting invitation.

With a slow grin, Edmund slid one fingertip into her honeyed warmth, relishing her broken cry. "I am exploring you, Phoebe. Learning what makes you cry with desire, tasting you so I never forget the taste and texture of you." He toyed with the slick, wet nub of her center and she shot a hand out, covering his with her own, holding him in place.

"D-don't stop," she pleaded, her words a breathless entreaty.

"I do not intend to, love." Fueled by the gripping need and an equal panic, he slid a finger into her dripping folds.

"Oh, my," she cried out. "Edmund."

He continued to work her, readying her for his entry and with each deliberate touch her cries took on a keening desperation that drove him to a frenzy.

The unrestrained sounds of her desire, headier than any other moment that had come before this, made every woman of his past melt away. Phoebe's innocence was an aphrodisiac; a drug he'd consumed and now it possessed him. Once he had her, he could, at last, be free of her maddening, witches hold.

He parted her thighs with his knee and palmed her center with the heel of his hand, knowing just the pressure to drive her to madness. Phoebe screamed to the skies and he swallowed that unrestrained sound with his mouth. Sweat beaded the top of his head as he warred with the unholy need to thrust himself deep and pump into her over and over until he found release. His eyes slid involuntarily closed as she raised trembling fingertips and brushed back the sweat from his brow.

Edmund reached between them and released his erect shaft from the confines of his breeches. He forced his eyes open and held her passion-glazed stare. "This is going to hurt," he said gruffly as he laid himself between the sweet envelope of her silken thighs.

"I trust you," she whispered and splayed her legs open wider. A wall of emotion slammed into him, humbling him with her unwarranted faith and trust, in light of his betrayal. Her arms came up and she wrapped them about him, holding tight.

Then with a groan he slid his length slowly inside her welcoming, hot heat. The tight walls of her virginal sheath closed about him, drawing him to the edge of ecstasy; an edge if he tumbled over, he'd never recover from.

Phoebe moaned and shifted her hips.

I am going to lose myself. I am going to spill myself like an untried youth all because of her innocence. Fighting the black thread of orgasmic ecstasy pulling at him, he moved himself deeper inside her core. With each drag of his shaft, her keening moans grew louder in volume. Edmund paused when he reached the threshold of her innocence. *Take her. Take her now.*

Warring with himself, he slid a hand to her center and stroked her until those eager moans became hungry cries. "Forgive me," he rasped and then plunged deep into the heaven of her body.

Her cry ended on a shattered scream that he silenced with his kiss. Phoebe went taut in his arms and squeezed her eyes so tight a single drop slid down her cheek, ravaging him so that the desire to drive back her tears was even greater than the need to continue pumping himself within her until he spilled his seed.

"I am so sorry," he rasped. "If I could have spared you this hurt, I would have."

She gave a jerky nod and then forced her eyes open. Pain bled through her eyes but she mustered a small smile and something shifted inside him. And because the panic pounding away inside his chest threatened to overtake him, he began to move slowly, withdrawing, and moving forward. Until the pain receded from the blues of her eyes, replaced with the haze of desire. Then she flexed her hips, almost tentatively, and he increased his pace. Phoebe folded her arms about him and matched his rhythm. Their bodies rose and fell with the sheen of sweat slicking her skin, giving her an other-worldly beauty that shattered his logic so all he wanted was to lose himself within her.

"I-I never kn-knew I could feel like this," she rasped, echoing the very thought thundering through his mind. She raked her nails lightly down his back and he squeezed his eyes shut at the pleasure-pain of both that seductive gesture and her words.

Neither did I. Agony kept those words silent. One wrong word and he would be lost—in every way.

Their thrusting took on a desperate, primitive beat and he slid his shaft in and out of her tight cavern. White light flecked behind his eyes. "Come," he urged on a hoarse command.

She arched her hips up, meeting his pounding rhythm. "Yes, take me with you," she pleaded and then her slender body went stiff in his arms. Urging her on, he reached between them again and played with her nub. With a loud, desperate cry, the folds of her sheath tightened about him and she screamed her release to the heavens. Propelled onward by her surrender, Edmund pumped harder and faster, and then with a triumphant groan, poured himself deep inside her until every last logical thought, word, or feeling was drained from him. He collapsed atop her, sated. Edmund rolled to his side and pulled her against him.

They lay there with time melting away, and instead of the sated sense of at last knowing her so he could move on from her, there was…*guilt*. He'd taken her as he would any other woman, when she'd been deserving of a bed and vows and all things good. Never before had any person's interests mattered to him more than his own—until now.

"What is it?" she whispered, as she plucked at the fabric of his shirtsleeves. She angled back and looked up at him with concern in her eyes. "Did I do something wrong?"

She'd ask that when he was the sole, vile blackguard between them? He shoved aside the stirrings of guilt at having taken her in Lord Essex's gardens and dropped a kiss atop her brow. "You did everything right." His praise elicited a pale pink blush on her cheeks. Masculine pride at being the first to know Phoebe's body filled him. Never before had he cared whether a woman had lain with another or how many lovers she'd known. This woman was different…for the idea of her sharing this with another filled him with bloodlust as a rapidly growing, insidious sentiment that felt a good deal like jealousy spiraled out of control. On the heel of that, a slow building panic spread through him. He abruptly sat up.

"Edmund?" She looked at him through confused eyes.

"Come," he commanded gruffly. "You must return or your," our, "absence will be noted."

Edmund retrieved his jacket and fished out a handkerchief. The intimacy of brushing the evidence of their loving and the traces of her innocence from her soft, inner thighs momentarily froze him. Through the years, he'd taken care to never spend himself inside a woman. In addition to not wanting to propagate the world with his bastards, he'd loathed the idea of that intimacy for the loss of control it signaled. Yet, in the moment when climax had been near, he'd wanted to brand her, Phoebe Barrett, as his. Terror ran roughshod over his muddied thoughts.

"What is it?" she pressed, concern lacing her question.

Edmund gave his head a curt shake, incapable of words. He'd thought once he'd taken Phoebe Barrett, he could purge her from his life. Loathing gripped him. In the end, she'd given a worthless bounder such as him the gift of her virtue and only fueled a growing hunger for her. He put her hair and wrinkled gown to rights, aware the whole time of her probing stare.

Not another word was uttered however as they made their way from the gardens and into the conservatory. As he pulled open the door of Essex's prized room, Phoebe hurried out of the room and back to the festivities. He stared after her.

Would he ever have his fill of Phoebe Barrett?

CHAPTER 11

He didn't come around. In fact, he hadn't come 'round in more than four days. Phoebe stared into the contents of her cup of chocolate, while her mother and sister prattled on about fabrics and shopping excursions and all manner of things that didn't matter.

Despite his request to court her, his absence these days indicated that whatever sentiments she'd imagined between them were, in fact, imagined. It was as her friends had said of Edmund—men with his notorious reputation didn't dabble in the respectable and they assuredly did not court ladies. Likely, he'd taken his leave of her and her stern-staring friends and remembered why he craved a rake's life.

Panic slapped at the edge of her mind. In a decision that had belonged entirely to her, she'd given her virginity to him. Even now, she could be carrying his child.

Nausea churned in her belly and she tightened her shaking fingers upon the cup, just as her brother sailed through the open breakfast room doors.

How could he be so carefree when her world had been so shaken by her actions at Lady Essex's?

"Mother, Phoebe, Justina," he greeted, moving with the swagger of a youth just out of university. He stopped at the sideboard and heaped a plate full of eggs, bacon, cold ham, and warm, just made bread.

Phoebe managed a lukewarm greeting and then returned her attention to her drink.

"What is the matter with her?" Andrew called across the table as he slid into a seat.

"She's sulking." Justina spoke with a maturity that brought Phoebe's head up.

"I am not sulking." Her family studied her with matching stares and she shifted in her seat. "I'm not," she said defensively. She wasn't sulking. She'd merely been reflecting on her own regrets over Edmund and what might have been and why it might not have been and… She groaned and set her cup down. When she picked her gaze up once more, she found her mother and siblings still studying her. This time, regret and pity lined their faces.

"It is about the marquess," Justina said noisily, the overly loud whisper a secret to no one.

"It is not—" They stared pointedly at her and she sighed again. It was the marquess.

"What about the marquess?" Andrew asked. With no forthcoming response from Phoebe, he turned to first his mother and then his sister. Mother nibbled at her toast while Justina made a show of buttering her bread. They were loyal, the Barrett ladies. When he looked to her again, Phoebe picked up her fork and knife and made a show of slicing her already very sliced ham. With a frown, he waved over a liveried footman. "I, for one, like the gentleman."

Phoebe's silverware clattered to the porcelain plate. "You know the marquess?" Her heart hammered wildly with this foolish desire for some additional glimpse of Edmund; the suitor who'd come and gone. But it was madness to believe he knew—

"Oh, yes, know him quite well." Suddenly, he glanced about, registering the intent stares trained on him and stretched the interminable moment out by taking a long sip of his coffee…and promptly choked.

Despite the nightmare facing her as a fallen woman, a wistful smile pulled at Phoebe's lips. For all his show, Andrew was really nothing more than a boy. That smile dipped. A boy who professed to know Edmund.

"You know the marquess?" Phoebe was grateful when her mother spoke the question, sparing her from asking that very question a second time.

"I know him, a bit," he amended.

"You merely read about him in the papers," Justina said with a bluntness that raised the color in his cheeks.

"I know him," he persisted, sounding more like an insolent child in debate about his lessons with a nursemaid. "I told him all about Phoebe."

She choked on her swallow. "You what?" Her voice emerged garbled and her mind frantically raced to put to right Andrew's words. "What did you say?" What had he said?

Suddenly registering the severity of his interference, he shifted back and forth in his seat. "I merely told him you detested needlepoint." Which didn't seem a detail Edmund would much care about.

"What else did you say?" she bit out.

He furrowed his brow. "Well…"

"Andrew," his mother snapped, with more seriousness than she'd exhibited in the course of Phoebe's twenty-one years.

"I merely sought to gauge the seriousness of his…" She groaned over her brother's words. "…intentions."

Phoebe dropped her head into her hands and shook it back and forth. *No. No. No.* But blast and double blast. Yes. Yes. Yes. Andrew had no doubt gone and discussed that very intimate part of her and Edmund's relationship, which likely accounted for why a notorious rake would suddenly cease to visit. Oh, God. Did he even now believe she'd sought to trap him into marriage? "What have you done?"

"He seemed very interested," Andrew said.

She whipped her head up. "He did?" And then her heart promptly sank. If he'd been interested, as her brother said, he would have come by, but instead he'd disappeared. The one gentleman she'd ever truly felt a connection to—a man who knew the struggle of being labeled one thing by gossips, when he was, in actuality, a very different person. A person who dreamed and hoped. And a man who, in a stolen moment of magic, she'd given her virginity to. Fear curled her toes. For she'd now given the gift expected of any gentleman's respective bride.

"Oh, yes," Andrew said after he'd taken several sips of his coffee. His lips pulled in a grimace, likely at the bitter, black brew. "He claimed he was uninterested in polite ladies."

Their mother gasped into her fingers.

"He said that?" Phoebe dropped back in her seat, her heart dipping all the further. Her friends had been correct in their suppositions of the marquess, then. She struggled to breathe through the fear and panic weighting her chest.

A twinkle glinted in Andrew's eyes. "He did, however, profess to be interested in you."

She scrambled forward, a question on her lips, as with her brother's flippant comment, hope was restored.

The words however remained unspoken, as their father chose that inopportune moment to enter the breakfast room. They stared at him in mute silence as he scratched his enormous belly. He stared at them all with a frown on his florid cheeks. "Who is interested in whom?"

Phoebe bit the inside of her cheek. She loathed the idea of her drunken, reprobate father knowing anything that mattered to her. If experience had taught her one thing about her useless sire, beyond how a marital connection could fill his rapidly depleting coffers, he had no interest in his children.

"Well," he grumbled, wandering over to the sideboard and piling a plate full of breakfast ham, sausage, kippers, and egg. He added one additional scoop of eggs and then carried his plate to the head of the table. When no response was forthcoming, he glared at his wife.

"We were speaking of Phoebe making a match," Justina said softly, even in her innocence wise enough to leave off on details.

With gusto, their father speared the meat on his plate and proceeded to shovel heaps of food into his mouth. "Oh," he spoke around his food. "A match with whom?"

Phoebe dropped her gaze to her untouched dish, repelled by the abhorrent man whose blood she shared.

He belched and helped himself to another bite. "I said—"

"The Marquess of Rutland," Andrew blurted. "Ouch." He flinched and frowned petulantly at Justina which could only mean she'd given him a deserved kick.

Father picked his bulging, wide-eyed gaze up from his plate and glanced about the table. "Rutland, you say?" A flicker of something flared in his bloodshot gaze that gave Phoebe pause; a sense of knowing, which was, of course, madness. Her father didn't know anything of her interests, hopes, or desires. He never had. And he'd assuredly not be aware of the secret of her regard for Edmund.

Their mother wrung her hands. "He is a marquess and therefore quite respectable."

Her husband snorted and opened his mouth as though to say more on it, but then promptly flattened his lips and took another bite of cold ham.

Phoebe's shoulders drooped with relief as her father once more demonstrated the same regard he had through the years, asking nothing further about Edmund or his courtship. Another tug pulled at her heart. Or his previous courtship. She shoved back her chair so quickly that it scraped along the wood floor. Her family eyed her with mixed degrees of concern and, in her father's case, apathy. "If you'll excuse me." She dropped a curtsy and walked briskly to the door, her neck burning with the stares trained on her person.

"Where are you off to, gel?"

Her father's words jerked her to a halt in the doorway. Phoebe turned slowly back around, dismayed by this unexpected inquiry. "Where am I off to?"

"Is something wrong with your hearing, girl?"

"The museum." She ran her palms over her skirts, uncomfortable with his sudden, inexplicable interest. As a girl, she'd become accustomed to his detachedness and didn't know what to do with a father who asked probing questions.

"Which museum?"

Such as that one.

"The Leverian."

He fell silent, scrunching his mouth up in deep concentration as though he sought to file away that rather uninteresting piece. Phoebe tipped her chin up. "Does that meet with your approval?"

Either too self-absorbed or too stupid to detect the mocking challenge in that question, her father waved a hand about. "I don't care how you entertain yourself, chit." With that he returned his focus to consuming his plate of breakfast meats, dismissing her.

She used the distraction to make her escape, suddenly very eager for her visit to the Leverian so she could be away from her father, her inquisitive siblings and mother, and then perhaps even away from the hurt of Edmund's defection.

CURTAINS PULLED TIGHTLY CLOSED, IT was unnaturally dark in Edmund's office. Seated on the aged, brown leather sofa with his head in his hands, he pressed the heel of his palms against his eyes in a desperate, now futile, attempt to drive Miss Phoebe Barrett from his thoughts. He'd believed that simply staying away from the dark-haired beauty would restore order to the cold, debauched life he'd lived all these years. Alas, the lady had a power more potent than the witch Medusa, for Phoebe had managed a feat no other had—she'd frozen him and muddied every belief and pledge he'd carried through the better part of his life. A vow to never know pain or care, but damn it, she had slipped past his guard and like her beloved Vikings, vanquished his sanity.

He'd resolved to not use her as part of his master scheme of revenge against Margaret Dunn. A bitter, ugly laugh rumbled up from his chest. When he'd first met Margaret, he'd fancied himself in love. After he'd been humiliated at the Earl of Stanhope's hands, fighting for the right to the lady's heart, he'd had a bloodlust for revenge. It had driven him. Consumed him. Only strengthened by the daily reminder of his own failings as a man. How very strange to realize he wanted something more than revenge—he wanted Phoebe.

It defied logic; this hungering for a lady so wholly innocent that she'd be fool enough to see good in even him. *She is not so wholly innocent anymore thanks to your selfish desires…* The muscles of his stomach clenched reflexively as something…something that felt very much like guilt swamped his senses. When he'd led Phoebe to Lord Essex's gardens, the sole intention had been to assuage his lust for the lady. He'd not given thought to anything but having his fill and purging her from his thoughts. Edmund dragged a hand down his face. Only now, in the light of a new day, having emptied his seed into her tight, virginal channel did he confront the mind-numbing truth—once would never be enough. His breath came hard and fast as terror momentarily blinded him. A knock sounded at the door bringing his head up. "Enter," he rasped out.

The door opened and his old, faithful butler shuffled slowly in bearing a missive in his hands. "M-my lord."

With a silent curse, Edmund leapt to his feet and met the man in four long strides, saving him from a lengthy walk across the expansive office. "I told you to have one of the footmen see to this task," he snapped. "If you insist on holding your damned post, you should be circumspect with your footsteps."

A smile played about the heavily wrinkled face. "The movement is—"

"If you say good for your constitution, Wallace, by God I'll sack you."

Wallace's grin deepened. "We shall say beneficial, then, my lord."

He snorted and accepted the letter held between the servant's gnarled fingers. His heart thudded to a stop in his chest at the familiar crest stamped upon the note. Edmund slid his finger under the seal and quickly scanned the hastily penned note.

She is at the Leverian.

A Judas is what the lady's father was.

And what does that make me? The temple guard at Gethsemane?

Edmund crushed the note in his hands, wrinkling it into a noisy ball. What was this? These weak feelings of regret and pain and remorse, he barely recognized within himself, sentiments he'd thought himself emotionally dead to.

"May I be so bold, my lord?"

He stiffened at the unexpected interruption, slowly returning his gaze to Wallace, who, with his dedication through the years, was the closest Edmund had ever come to friendship. "Would it matter if I said no?"

"It would not, my lord," Wallace said, inclining his head.

His lips pulled at the corner. *You smile and then it is as though you remind yourself that you do not want to smile and this muscle twitches…* He gritted his teeth so hard a pain shot up his jaw.

"But you've smiled, my lord." He waggled bushy, white brows.

"I don't…"

The old servant looked at him.

Edmund swiped a hand over his face.

"I took the liberty of having your carriage readied."

Because Wallace often knew everything and anything Edmund intended before he himself did. He glanced down at the wrinkled note and gave a curt nod of thanks. The old servant turned on his heel and shuffled through the entranceway, leaving Edmund alone. With a curse, he stalked over and tossed the note from Lord Waters upon his desk, staring down at the page.

Four days had passed since he'd last seen Phoebe and in that time this pressing desire to see her had not lifted. Instead it had, if possible, grown into a gripping desperation. As a man who'd taken what he wanted and expected everything as his due, he now knew he wanted her.

With that resolve and a short carriage ride down Blackfriar Bridge later, his driver stopped before the entrance of the Leverian. Edmund didn't wait for the servant. He tossed the carriage door open and stepped down, looking up the impressive façade of Museum Leverianum, as it was called. The most complete collection of curiosities, it boasted the efforts of Sir Ashton Lever. What manner of lady was so intrigued by such oddities? Despite a physical effort to tamp down this weakening, a dammed lightness filled his chest and he started forward, his skin prickling with the sensation of being studied by passing lords and ladies.

The gossips had already noted his interest in Miss Phoebe Barrett and likely even now tried to sort through what business the most black-hearted scoundrel had at a museum. Edmund entered through the front doors, his eyes struggling to adjust to the dark. He scanned the long rows of display cases filled with exotic creatures, and shells, and other artifacts. The irony was not lost on him—he'd now pursue a young lady and be afforded a dark museum with hidden nooks and crannies made for sinning.

Edmund strolled forward, making his way methodically down aisle after long aisle. He spared barely a glance for the shells encased in crystal for the viewing pleasure of polite Society and pressed on. Frustration grew and spread, fanning out. What if he'd missed the lady? What if her harebrained father had the wrong of it? Edmund came to the end of the row and continued on….and then froze. All the breath left his body.

Of its own volition, his hand came up to rest against the cool, solid display case, borrowing stability from the inanimate object when all his strength carefully constructed these years crashed down about him. Phoebe stood, head cocked at the side, as she studied a small, blue bird, forever trapped behind its crystal cage. An emotion pulled at him, undefinable and gripping, all at once. In their gilded world, she was not very different than the creature she now admired.

As though feeling his stare, she stiffened, and then glanced about. Their gazes collided.

Even with the length of the aisle between them, he detected the flash of shock and joy melded together in the crystalline depths of her eyes. Emotion stuck in his throat. But for fear, loathing, and disgust, no one had ever felt anything for him. Not even his own parents. Heat burned his neck and he was ashamed and humiliated by such weakness. Just then, she spoke, "Hullo." Only confirming she was far braver and more courageous than he'd ever been or ever would be.

Silently, he slipped down the row, never removing his gaze from her person; trailing it over her from the top of her thick, auburn tresses, most of those locks sadly concealed by her bonnet, down to the tips of her ridiculous, innocent, white satin slippers. He stopped beside her.

Phoebe tipped her head back to stare at him, knocking the silly, white ruffled bonnet, better suited to a shepherdess, askew. He'd long preferred the women he'd take to his bed in satin-dampened garments with plunging, wicked décolletages. How very wrong he'd been. The innocent allure of Phoebe's modest skirts was more potent than the strongest aphrodisiac. She coughed into her hand. "It was a pleasure seeing you," she said quietly. "I'll leave you to your outing." With hurried movements, she made to step around him.

His outing? He didn't go on outings. Edmund placed himself before her, deliberately blocking her path. "This meeting is no chance one. No hands of fate have been involved." Instead, the lady's own father had turned her whereabouts over, again.

"I-it isn't?"

"No."

"Then h—?"

"I've my ways," he cut in, wanting to kill the words which roused the truth that had brought them together this day. He loosened the strings of her bonnet and shoved it back, appreciating the luxuriant, silken locks, then ran his knuckles down her cheek. "I've missed you." They were the three truest words he'd ever spoken to her.

"Did you?" A bitter regret tinged her question. Yet, they should also be the only words of his she'd called into question.

He lowered his head, so that the gentle puffs of her rapid breaths fanned his lips. "I have." The memory of her had been more potent than any spirit he'd consumed and for all his resolve to set her free, he'd proven himself to be the selfish bastard he'd always been—wanting and taking. "I've tried to stay away from you." But he wanted her in a way that defied the sexual emptiness he'd known with past lovers. Edmund wanted to take her again, he wanted to lose himself in her, and meld his soul to hers until she cleansed the black vileness from him, replacing it with the shine of her goodness.

"Why?"

Their breath blended together. "You've weakened me." His chest tightened at that admission which made him vulnerable to this slip of a lady who'd occupied the better part of his thoughts, both sleeping and waking.

She caressed his cheek and he leaned into her touch, craving her naked fingers upon his skin, damning her kidskin gloves for robbing him of that simple pleasure. "Oh, Edmund. You've gone through life fearing all and trusting none, I suspect." Her words jerked him ramrod straight.

"Is that what you believe? That I live my life afraid?" he snarled, drawing back, even as that parting cost him far more. He looped an arm about her waist, applying such pressure, a startled squeak escaped her. "I assure you, Madam, I do not fear anyone. Men and women quake in my presence. I'm a vicious, dangerous, black-hearted monster and that is what has kept me away from you."

She winced; at his words? His touch? And he lightened his hold upon her. But with her reply, she proved herself the same bold, fearless creature he'd first stumbled upon at Lady Delenworth's balustrade. "There is a difference between fearing anything and fearing oneself." Phoebe ran the pad of her thumb over the bridge of his nose, broken too many times in too many fights when he'd been an equally angry boy away at Eton, fighting everyone, over everything. "And a man who warns a lady to avoid him and professes himself to be a danger isn't really that dangerous, though. Not when it hints so very loudly at caring and concern for the person you'd warn me away from."

"Why are you so determined to see more in me than I truly am?" That ragged whisper wrenched from some part deep inside.

Phoebe leaned up on tiptoe and brushed her lips against his in a fleeting, barely-there meeting of their mouths so that he wondered if he'd merely imagined the faint caress. "I think perhaps I'm the one to see the truths you hide from even yourself. Come." She took him by the hand and guided him down the aisle.

"What—?"

"Here," she said, drawing them to a stop beside the end of the crystal case. With a flick of her wrist, she motioned to a fierce vulture, trapped and frozen in time for polite Society's viewing pleasure.

Edmund furrowed his brow and looked from her to the creature and then back again.

"What do you see?"

"A revolting bird," he said flatly.

A laugh, clear as tinkling bells, bubbled past her lips. She pointed her eyes to the ceiling. "Look closer."

In a bid to see just what it was she saw in the brown creature with its red head and orangish beak, he peered and then gave a shake of his head. "If anyone sees me studying birds, I'll be ruined," he muttered.

"Do focus." She swatted his arm. "What do you see?"

Edmund took in the sharp beak and jagged claws. No one could ever possibly look at the foul creature and see anything redeeming in it. "I see a fierce, ugly, vicious beast." And he didn't see much more than that.

"Ah, yes. Of course, you do." Phoebe captured his hands, interlocking their fingers. "Do you know the vulture will never attack the living? On the outside, you are correct, they appear quite fearsome." She raised their entwined hands up. "But they're not really. When you know them, when you learn all those pieces about them that you'd not ordinarily know."

His throat worked with the force of his swallow and he trained his attention on their fingers. Ah God, she would make him into what he was not. He was not harmless and he'd spent the better part of his adult life striving to teach members of the *ton* just how fierce and ugly he was. He hastened his gaze back to hers. "If you knew the things I've done, you'd leave and never look back once." And it would destroy him. A panicky pressure closed on his chest, making it difficult to breath, to think, to move.

Instead of being warned into leaving, she squeezed his hands. "I'm stronger than you'd believe, Edmund."

Yes, she was stronger than anyone he'd ever known before. This delicate, bold, and whimsical miss had shattered his defenses and laid siege to him. In a desperate bid to reclaim order, he cleared his throat. "We might also add informed lady of bird facts to your rather impressive talents."

"Yes." A twinkle lit the blue depths of her eyes and she dropped her voice to a conspiratorial whisper. "And proficient reader." She nodded to the information card posted upon the bottom edge of the vulture's case. "I read it a short while ago."

A sudden bark of sharp, unexpected laughter burst from his chest, unfamiliar and rusty from ill-use, and it blended with her carefree, unjaded laugh. Standing there, in the crystal rows of the Leverian, Edmund thought perhaps she might be right—perhaps he was more—or, at the very least, could be more—for her. And she *deserved* more.

She deserved a proper courtship.

CHAPTER 12

IT MAY HAVE BEEN MERE moments, or perhaps even hours, that Edmund remained fixed to the marble floor, staring at the foyer door. He dusted his palms together and made another attempt to move both his legs and then promptly stopped. Though it was not his crippled limb that halted forward movement this time. With a curse, he rocked back on his heels. And continued to stare. At the door. A door that represented far more—or rather him stepping past that dark wood panel that signified far more.

Bloody hell he was not that *gentleman*. Nor was he any manner of gentleman, for that matter. He wasn't a man who collected a lady during fashionable hours and escorted her for a ride in his open carriage, declaring boldly for the world that she was his—staking his claim of possession. He closed his eyes a moment. To do this thing, ordinary to any other nobleman, would reveal to polite Society the lady had a hold upon him. And there was no greater danger than that.

Yet, he took another step toward the door and then stopped—again.

The shuffle of footsteps echoed throughout the towering foyer. "Lord—"

"Not yet," he bit out and then swiped a hand over his brow. "Not yet," he repeated in a gruff tone.

"Very well, my lord."

He drummed his fingertips alongside his leg. This madness, this spell Phoebe had cast about him, was far greater than any hold Margaret had once held over him and all the more terrifying for it. The moment he stepped through that door, he'd cease to exist as the fearless, undaunted, merciless Marquess of Rutland and instead become a man with fears, and those fears would have him at the mercy of others who'd prey upon this inherent weakness for Phoebe Barrett. "What is even the point of it?" he muttered.

"What is the point of what, my lord?"

He ignored Wallace's kindly inquiry, instead focusing on that question that begged exploring. Edmund would present himself before fashionable Society, court the lady, with no plans of revenge binding him and Phoebe as one, but for what purpose? He couldn't offer her his name. *Why can't I?* The question whispered about his consciousness, tempting and seductive and, at the same time, terrifying. As soon as the thought developed legs of possibility, he severed it at the knees. He'd spent his life insulating himself from hurts. The one time he'd faltered had proven almost fatal. Literally and, very nearly, figuratively. As though to remind him of that important detail, his leg throbbed. Edmund massaged the tense muscles of his right thigh through his breeches.

His now dead parents' union had served as lifelong testimony to the mockery of that revered state of marriage. Nor had he placed much consideration into the Rutland line after his father perished, as he frankly didn't give a jot for the reprehensible Rutlands to come before him, nor did he care for the ones who came after.

An image flitted to his mind. A small girl with thick auburn curls and Phoebe's smile, holding up a book—"Good God." Edmund dissolved into a paroxysm of coughing. There was nothing else for it.

Wallace cleared his throat.

"I'm fine," he bit out when he managed his breath. And as his whole world had been sent into a reel because of Miss Phoebe Barrett and there wasn't a soul in the world he trusted or called friend, he looked tiredly over at the faithful servant, hoping he had an answer.

A protest sprung to Edmund's lips as Wallace pulled the door open. Sunlight splashed through the entranceway and he held a hand to his eyes, shielding them from the glaring rays. "Sometimes it is easier when there is no barrier between you," Wallace said quietly.

Presented with standing there a coward, humbled before Wallace and the liveried footman waiting beside his phaeton, Edmund gritted his teeth and walked with stiff, jerky movements outside, down the steps. Not taking his gaze from the perch of his conveyance, he climbed atop and then set the carriage into motion.

Through the years, he'd studiously avoided being seen at fashionable hours, doing anything that was…fashionable. He'd devoted himself to a life of debauchery; carefully fulfilling the legacy laid out by his faithless parents and maintaining the expectations the *ton* had for one of his ilk. Now, his skin pricked with the rabid curiosity trained on him by passing lords and ladies. The rumors would circulate and just as the gossips had been right in every vile piece printed about him, now they would be correct in the seeming innocuousness of a carriage ride with Miss Phoebe Barrett. It signified his courtship. Marked her as his in a respectable way and not the way he truly longed to mark her as his.

He concentrated on maneuvering his team through the streets, onward to the Viscount Waters', for to focus on the panic swelling in his chest, threatening to choke him, would result in him guiding the blasted phaeton in the opposite direction, on to the less fashionable end of London to his familiar clubs—dens of sin where he was at ease, because that was where he truly belonged.

Only…

Edmund brought his conveyance to a stop at the pink stucco façade of the Viscount Waters' townhouse—the townhouse, that could be his if he called in his markers. At one point, revenge and greed had driven all. Yet, where was the victory in laying claim to the fat, foul nobleman's property? Because ultimately that would result in Waters wedding Phoebe off to whichever nobleman presented him with the fattest purse. He made to step down from the carriage, but the thought stirred inside, real and venomous. She'd wed. Another. A man who would lay her down in her silly skirts, yank them up her frame and take what had once been Edmund's. With a growl, he thrust back the insidious thoughts, leapt down from the carriage and handed the reins off to one of the viscount's servants who came forward. Edmund stomped up the steps and rapped once.

And waited.

And continued to wait.

Here for all fashionable passersby. He spun on his heel and passed his gaze out at the boldly gawking lords and ladies who had the good sense to yank their bloody stares elsewhere. Edmund turned swiftly back and rapped again. Bloody hell, he'd rather face his foe Stanhope in another blasted duel with his now crippled leg than be on this threshold for the *ton's* viewing pleasure.

Where the—?

The door opened.

"At last," he gritted out, before the old, wizened butler allowed him entry.

"My lord," the servant greeted, executing a respectful but painfully stiff bow. Edmund eyed the man a moment, for all his previous visits never having truly paid the servant any attention until now. Why, with his heavily wrinkled cheeks and bald pate, this one was of an age to keep retirement with Wallace. He frowned. He'd not expect the Viscount Waters, the manner of master, to inspire loyalty and devotion in his servants, particularly after the tales he'd heard of the letch diddling the younger women on his staff. Then, what had he ever done to earn Wallace's allegiance? He cast a glance about in search of Phoebe—

And found the sister. Rooted to the place the foyer met the corridor, she hovered uncertainly, a wide, overly trusting smile on her face. "Hullo," she greeted. "You are here for my sister."

As there was no question, he opted to bow and, instead, issue a cool greeting. "My lady, it is a pleasure seeing you again." He glanced up the stairs in search of the woman it would be a true pleasure to see.

"She will be down momentarily." Miss Justina Barrett dropped her voice to a whisper that carried so loudly off the foyer ceiling, her sister would have likely cringed. "She's been awaiting you all morning."

Despite his vow to never smile, a rusty grin formed on his lips, and an odd lightness filled his chest. "Has she?" Why should that matter so much to him? Perhaps because he'd gone the past thirty-two years with no one truly desiring his company.

"She has," she repeated with a nod.

The butler eyed their exchange with a wariness better suited a properly attending mama than an aged servant before stepping into the shadows, carefully watching and silent.

Wise man.

The young lady skipped forward and skidded to a stop before Edmund. "You are the gentleman I was hoping you would be."

Unwise lady. In her innocence she failed to realize her sister deserved far more than him, the monster Marquess of Rutland. "Were you?" he asked, glancing up for Phoebe, wanting this exchange over.

"Oh, yes."

Alas, the lady appeared to be demonstrating the same degree of reluctance Edmund had prior to taking his leave. Good, perhaps by now the lady had developed a suitable unease and sensed his evil. Why did that possibility leave this aching hole inside?

"Better than Lord Atwood or Allswoodson—"

"Allswood," he supplied, snapping his focus back to the young girl, now attending her quite clearly.

"Oh, yes. He—"

Would never hear the remainder of just what Allswood was or had done.

"Rutland, my friend."

Edmund stiffened and turned to greet the grinning, scent-wearing, silken garment-clad dandy. He swallowed back a sigh. So, it was to be a reunion of sorts with every one of Waters' family. Why, they only required the Barrett children's lax mama and the drunken sire to complete the happy meeting. "Barrett," he greeted, sketching a bow. He tugged out his watch fob and consulted the timepiece attached. Surely, the lady would arrive any moment?

"Here to escort my sister for a ride?" Barrett asked, rocking back on his heels. His sister shot an elbow out and nudged him in the side. "Oomph."

"Be polite," she said from the side of her mouth, while still managing a smile. All the while she maintained Edmund's stare. Did the lady suspect he could not hear her? Another grin pulled at his lips before he remembered himself.

"I am being polite. Rutland and I are good friends. Isn't that true?"

That yanked him back to the moment. Good friends? Edmund didn't have any good friends. Hell, he didn't have any friends. He had enemies aplenty. Friends? No. "Indeed," he forced out tightly.

He'd spent the better part of his life shielded and guarded. This family, who'd expose themselves and their thoughts so unabashedly, filled him with unease and a desire to flee their happy fold. What right did they have to be happy? He didn't begrudge them for having found happiness, but rather genuinely wondered how they'd managed that feat with their own foul sire.

"Perhaps we might share a drink at our club later this evening?"

Their club? The only clubs Edmund visited were not the manner of polite ones that should even be hinted at before innocent young ladies and one's young sister, no less. "Indeed," he bit out once more. Anything to be done with this blasted exchange. He glanced up…

And his breath hitched in his chest. Phoebe stood at the top. A twinkle lit the blues of her eyes. "Sorry," she mouthed.

The vise squeezed all the harder. He'd forgive her anything. Edmund followed her slow descent. Then one such as she would never be needing forgiveness. No, she was the light to his dark. The innocence to his evil. And he was nothing more than that serpent tempting naïve Eve with that apple, and she was as drawn to that succulent red object as those two weak-willed sinners in the garden had been.

"Hello, my lord," she said as she came to a stop before him. She didn't wait for his greeting, instead turned a motherly frown upon her younger siblings. She'd perfected a look most governesses would have given half their wages for. Barrett and Miss Justina Barrett shifted back and forth on their feet.

"We were just making arrangements to meet at our clubs later," the pup boldly intoned with far more braveness than Edmund would have credited.

Phoebe's frown deepened and he knew; knew because he knew the darkest parts of a person's thoughts, even when they themselves believed themselves incapable of such darkness. Though she'd done a masterful job of convincing both him and more, herself, that she didn't heed the gossips, he'd wager the use of both his legs that she now wondered about the clubs he visited, her mind lingering upon the disreputable hells.

Edmund held out an arm. "Shall we, my lady?"

She hesitated and for a moment he suspected she'd renege. Then she placed her fingertips along his sleeve and some of the tension drained from him. The butler hurried to pull the door open and with Phoebe on his arm, Edmund did something he'd not done in eleven years—launched a proper courtship of a respectable, marriageable young lady.

SINCE SHE AND EDMUND HAD made love, her body still thrummed with remembrance of his touch and her lips ached for his kiss. Now, Edmund intended to visit those scandalous clubs her brother had spoken of. Phoebe bit her lower lip. She wanted the moment in Lord Essex's gardens to hold a specialness to him, as well. Instead, he'd go off to his clubs where a sea of nameless, faceless women awaited him, all of them, no doubt, vying for a place in his bed.

"You are quiet, Phoebe."

She jumped as his breath tickled her hair. "I am." He continued to probe her with his hot, penetrating stare and she managed a smile. "Er…" Unnerved by the singular intensity of his gaze, she looked out at the busy streets and frowned, of a sudden, becoming mindful to this new, unwelcome, and unpleasant truth.

They were being stared at. *What did you expect, ninny?*

Yet, after days of their stolen meetings in the private aisles of shops and museums, and their heartachingly beautiful tryst in Lord Essex's gardens, she'd not been forced to confront the truth of Society's sick fascination—until now. And now she hated it. Hated it, for it cheapened the intimate, special connection she and Edmund shared and put them on display much like those poor creatures at the Leverian and Egyptian Hall. Guilt tugged at her. So, that was how those poor creatures spent their days.

Edmund touched his hand to the small of her back and she started, grateful for his stoic silence as he handed her up into the carriage and then followed behind her.

To give her restive fingers something to do, she fiddled with her bonnet strings.

"I detest that bonnet."

Phoebe stole a startled look up at him. The chiseled planes of his face gave no indication as to his thoughts; no hint of warmth in his eyes. She shivered, reminded of the stranger she'd met on

Lady Delenworth's terrace. She let her hand flutter back to her side. "Oh."

"Any garment that can be used to conceal your beauty should be burned."

Butterflies danced about her belly. "Oh," she repeated and then her cheeks warmed. "Thank you."

"I didn't intend it as a compliment," he said in that same cool, emotionless tone she'd learned really was nothing more than a mechanism to conceal the true parts of himself from anyone—her included.

Oh, how I love him.

She wished to be the person he could be the true Edmund Deering with. If only he'd allow her. *And what if he does not?* Then, she'd be nothing more than a young lady, devoid of her maidenhead, and...she swallowed hard, as terror reared its head once more. Why, even now there existed the possibility she carried his babe. Phoebe scrambled forward on the edge of the bench just as Edmund guided the carriage into a turn.

A black curse split his lips as he easily handled the reins and caught her against him to keep her from tumbling over the side. "What is it?"

Oh, God help her. The cool, impassive figure she'd come to expect was the one she needed now. Not the hesitant concern she detected in those hushed undertones, his gravelly voice roughened with emotion. For this gentler version he kept shielded from the rest of the world was the one she'd come to love, yet there could never be more when he was forever committed to presenting the image of an ugly, fierce vulture.

"Phoebe?" he demanded once more.

"I'm all right." Except, she lied. She would never be all right again. Not when she'd given her heart and innocence to a man who had little use of it. "Why are we here?" she blurted as he expertly guided their carriage past other fashionable lords and ladies and through the crowded path of Hyde Park.

Edmund arched an icy, dark brown eyebrow. "Because Society would not permit me to take you where I truly wish to take you," he said with the blunt honesty she'd come to expect of him.

It was all she could do to keep from asking—"Where would you take me?"

The whipcord muscles of his arm went taut in his coat sleeves, pressing hard against hers and a sound, half-groan, half-chuckle, emerged. He leveled a quick sideways stare on her. The molten heat in his eyes stole the breath from her lungs. "I would take you to the Pleasure Gardens when only you and I were there. I would see you laid upon the edge of the peering pool with that bonnet," he jerked his chin at the offending article, "gone, tossed into those waters, forever ruined, while your silken curls are fanned about you and the sun kisses your skin." Edmund deliberately shifted his knee close so the heat of him burned her through the fabric of her ivory skirts. "That is where I'd *take* you."

Phoebe managed nothing more than a breathless, broken, "Oh." He desired her, except even with his passion-roughened words and the hunger in his eyes, she wanted more from him and of him. Never once had she felt the overwhelming urge to shield herself from his gaze, the way she did the bold, impolite stares trained upon her by the men who saw her as a nothing more than the lecherous Viscount Waters' eldest daughter and therefore an easy mark. Yes, there was the hint of more; in their meetings at the Leverian and Egyptian Hall and the curiosity shops, but he'd never truly spoken of what that more was. And still knowing that, she'd given him her virginity, anyway.

The carriage rattled through Hyde Park. Occasionally, the peal of excited giggles and exuberant laughs split the spring air. Phoebe shook her head. "No," she said, startling the both of them with her one word utterance.

Edmund shot her a questioning frown.

"No, that is not what I'd meant, Edmund." To give her fingers something to do once more, she loosened the strings of her bonnet and tugged it free. She rested the ruffled scrap upon her lap. Except, the slight narrowing of his eyes and his previously shocking, quite improper words spoke to the folly of removing that protective bonnet. His gaze lingered a moment upon the top of her head. … *I would see you laid upon the edge of the peering pool with that bonnet gone while your silken curls are fanned about you and your skin is kissed by the sun…* Her cheeks burned. The heat had little to do with the warm spring sun and everything to do with his intent stare. Phoebe waved the bonnet about. "Why are we here? Why are you here? You are n-not…" She allowed those stuttered words to remain unspoken, unable to finish those damning words.

"I am not what?" he asked in that coolly detached tone.

"By your own words you are one to bring women to the pleasure gardens." Her cheeks blazed all the brighter. "Not ride through parks and not with young women in the market for a husband."

"You."

She cocked her head.

"I would not bring women to the pleasure gardens," he dipped his voice to a dangerously soft whisper. "I'd bring you there, Phoebe. Only you."

Oh, my goodness. She was no longer a virgin. She'd lain with Edmund underneath the stars in Lord Essex's gardens and still yet, shock scorched her face with heat. Phoebe raised her hand to fan her cheeks and then caught his stare. Amusement tipped his lips up in an arrogant, crooked half-grin. Did he know her every thought? Well, she'd tired of the unspoken matter between them—a matter that would mean her ruin were it discovered. She drew in a steadying breath. "Will we not speak of it?" Her quiet whisper brought his dark eyebrows together.

"Of what?" He wrapped those two words in satiny hardness.

Frustration stabbed at her. How could he be so coolly indifferent? "What happened at Lord E-Essex's." He narrowed his gaze on her. "It should not have happened, and yet it did and it cannot be undone." She spoke on a dizzying rush, her words blurring and blending. "I do not expect you to wed me." Phoebe paused and when no protestation was coming, agony and that rapidly growing panic fanned through her once more. "And yet, I must wonder what brings you here this day when you've not come 'round—"

"I want you."

Phoebe blinked several times in rapid succession. Her mind sought to make sense of those three words over the loud beat of her heart. Yes. This was not a new admission and yet her heart should flip about in this silly rhythm whenever he uttered them. Wordlessly, he guided the carriage onto a less crowded part of the path and drew the team off so they stopped with their backs presented to polite Society.

He said nothing for a long while. Instead, he remained immobile running his blank-eyed stare out over the lake. "My mother was a whore."

Those words rang a shocked gasp from her.

A hard, wry grin played on his cool lips. "Oh, she was a lady by Society's standards, but she was no more a lady than my whoremonger father was a gentleman."

For all the words he'd hurled at her in their meetings these past days, words she'd known he'd intended to shock…these were faintly different.

"Those are the people whose blood I share," he spat the words quietly into the gentle breeze. And at last it made sense. Nay, *he* made sense. Perhaps to no one in polite Society but to Phoebe, herself. Emotion swelled deep inside, filled every corner of her being, until words eluded her and movement escaped her. Edmund, the Marquess of Rutland, hadn't feigned the image of dark, unyielding lord. Rather, he'd stepped into a role he'd thought he had no choice but to claim. He saw the darkness of his life and sought to live that, failing to realize that who he was had never been inextricably intertwined with what his parents had been or, more importantly, what his parents had not been. Phoebe toyed with the ivory strings of her bonnet and treaded carefully. "My father is not a good man, Edmund."

A muscle jumped at the corner of his left eye.

"I don't expect you move in the same circles as my father," she said, filling the quiet. "But he is a shameful, loathsome, dishonorable figure. He gambles." Then she thought of her brother's intentions of meeting Edmund at their club and the gossip. "As do most gentlemen," she amended. "But my father gambles in excess and drinks in excess…" She drew in a steadying breath and pressed ahead. "And h-he carries on with women." Phoebe bit down so hard on her lower lip she drew blood. The sickly, sweet, metallic taste filled her senses and she embraced the distraction. For there were things a child should never know about one's father or mother.

They were the very shameful things Edmund himself knew. Mindful that lords and ladies moved behind them, intently studying their private exchange, she discreetly shifted her hand upon the bench and covered his gloved fingers with her own. He tensed, but did not draw back.

Encouraged by his silence, she went on. "I've known the type of man he was since I was just a girl." A bird spread its wings wide and soared gracefully upon the lake, skimming the surface. He dipped his head beneath the surface. That day as fresh now as it had been then. "I'd overheard the servants whispering about him." Her ears still burned with shame and humiliation and shock at the words no child should have ever heard.

"What did you do?" The gruff question emerged, haltingly, as though forcefully pulled from him.

Phoebe lifted her shoulders in a little shrug. "I returned abovestairs to the nursery and played soldiers with Andrew and Justina." But who had Edmund to turn to? "Did you—?"

"I did not have siblings. That was the one thing my parents did right. They knew to never bring another child into the world."

An image slipped into her thoughts, of a solitary boy with no one but himself seated on the floor with toy soldiers and silence his only company. She tightened her hold upon his hand. How lonely he must have been. "Who did you have, though?"

He peeled his lip back in a sneer. "I didn't need anyone." Still wounded and hurt as he'd always been. Perhaps as he always would be… The idea of that ran ragged through her.

"Oh, Edmund, everyone needs someone." She braced for the denial…that did not come and all the more telling than any protestation. For this man who'd crafted an image as black-hearted, relentless and unfeeling scoundrel wanted to be loved and more, he deserved to be loved. Yet, what had happened to him that he'd not trust himself to that emotion?

Finally, Edmund spoke. "How did you become," he flicked his wrist over her person, "this?"

Phoebe didn't pretend to misunderstand. The connection they shared as the children of reprehensible sires and, in his case, mothers, bonded them in ways that defied the physical and even every emotional connection to come before this. Slowly, she worked the glove free of his hand, tugging his long, powerful fingers from each place within the fabric. All the while, he eyed her through thick, impenetrable slits. She released his hand and his arm jolted, as though in a reflexive movement to draw her back to him. Discreetly, Phoebe tugged free her own glove, set it aside on the bench, and then quickly turned his hand palm side up. She laid her hand in a like position upon her skirts. "I was often fascinated by hands."

The rakish stranger, who'd once delighted in shocking her,

would have likely tossed any number of improper words to that statement. This new man, the one she'd looked close enough to see, merely studied their hands side by side with the same intensity as one who'd first stared upon a da Vinci masterpiece. "The maids had coarse hands and my mother had smooth hands and do you know what I have, Edmund?"

"What?" he asked in a gravelly whisper.

But he asked.

Phoebe pressed her palms together, steepling her fingers. "I have my father's hands."

"You don't—"

"Oh, but I do," she interrupted his harsh protestation. "I am, after all, his daughter. These hands were made by him. One day I was in the nursery and I should have been attending my lessons. Instead, I kept glancing at my nursemaid's hands. They were stained with ink and wrinkled and I was so very bored that I then began to really study my *own* hands and I noticed the lines." She turned one palm up for his inspection and trailed the tip of her finger down those intersecting lines that had once fascinated her as a child. "Do you know what I realized?"

He gave his head a brusque shake.

Phoebe claimed his hand and ran the tip of her index finger down the marks that were only his upon his palm. "They are different. *We* are different. We may have been gifted these hands by people we admire, abhor, or love, but ultimately they are our own hands and it is what we do with them that truly defines us."

Silence met her words and with it a reminder of where they were and the manner in which she held him and the humiliating admissions she'd made. His stiff, unbendable quiet made the moment all the more excruciating. She released him with alacrity, a flush climbing her neck. "Er…well, silly, I know. That is, it must sound silly to you, my fascination with hands as a child." She was prattling. "I—"

He shot a hand about her wrist, gently enfolding the smaller flesh in his more powerful grip. He drew her hand to his mouth and her pulse pounded hard there in anticipation of that caress. Then he pressed his lips to the skin and the gentle movement—sweet yet seductive—brought her eyes fluttering closed.

With Society observing this whole interlude, the gossips would bandy her name about and whisper about his kiss upon her hand at Hyde Park and yet, she could no sooner chop off that hand than she could pull free of him.

"Marry me."

CHAPTER 13

WHERE HAD THAT IMPULSIVE REQUEST come from?

There were a million reasons Phoebe Barrett should never belong to him, nay, could never belong to him. He'd fleeced her hazard-loving father of her family's possessions and properties, even as she didn't know it—including her dowry. He'd used her to advance his goals of revenge against Margaret, using the duchess' beloved niece, Miss Honoria Fairfax—who also happened to be one of Phoebe's closest friends. And yet, he'd not given a bloody thought to Margaret or Miss Fairfax or anything and anyone that was not Phoebe Barrett since he'd collided with her backside on Lord Delenworth's balustrade. He fisted his hands. Only, a relationship built upon that rather muddied foundation was but begging for a summer storm to erase anything that had been real between them.

Yes, there were a million reasons to move on from Miss Phoebe Barrett. And only one sufficient reason to make her his—he wanted her. Having known the pleasure of her body in Lord Essex's gardens had not filled this aching need for her. It had only fueled his hunger to wake her every morning with a hard, passionate loving. This wanting defied the physical and scared the bloody hell out of him. It consumed him with an intensity that got men carted off to Bedlam. Those two words he'd vowed to never speak, in fact, belonged to him.

It did not fail to escape his notice that his question met with nothing more than the rattle of passing carriage wheels and the noisy squawking of gray geese. The slight moue of surprise on her lips and her widened eyes indicated that she'd very well heard. As the silence stretched on, a flush heated his neck and climbed higher, up to his cheeks. After Margaret, he'd never weakened himself before another man, woman, or child. Yet on this day, he should so publicly humble himself before this slip of a lady and before the eyes of the passing *ton*. Why did that endangering truth not rouse unholy terror in his gut?

He fixed his gaze on her long, naked fingers, thinking of her earlier words, the tale she'd told of her fascination with hands, making him believe he was different when he could never divorce his past from his present. The lady's prolonged silence said she knew it, as well. With a growl, Edmund shifted the reins and made to guide the carriage from the copse, when she shot out a staying hand, resting her silken, soft palm over his. "You want me to marry you?"

If he were a true gentleman, he'd give her the verses of sonnets, managed by those still naïve, foolishly hopeful young swains—much the way he'd done with Margaret. Yet, where had been the honesty in any of that relationship? *Then, where is the honesty in any of this?* The snake whispered into his ear. Edmund scoffed at the taunting devil. He could give her what no other man likely would. "I have thought of the benefits in your marrying me."

Did her lips twitch with amusement? "Oh?" Had she been any other woman, he'd have offered her the finest French fabrics and expensive baubles and those trinkets would have sated the lady's greedy wants. In the days he'd come to know Phoebe, she'd proven herself an Incomparable in ways the gossips and polite Society would never understand. Incapable of the words a romantic such as she hoped for, he gave her his truth. "I will see you have any Captain Cook artifacts you may desire."

"Captain Cook?"

He didn't know what to make of her oddly tentative tone. Edmund pressed his vantage. "I'll permit you to visit whatever blasted curiosity shop or museum you desire." He slashed the air with the reins in his hand. The horses shifted, letting out nervous whinnies. "Whatever book, curiosity, or creature you desire shall be yours."

"Is that what you believe I wish?" Phoebe trained her gaze on his face. "For artifacts belonging to a man who has traveled the world?" The disappointment underscoring that question indicated his error. "I don't want those interesting, if empty, mementos, Edmund. Surely you know that?"

Then he narrowed his eyes as it at last came to him. What did she desire above all else? Uncaring of any witness who might see and the implications of his actions, he touched her chin and nudged her gaze up to his. "As your husband, I will allow you to travel." It would be enough knowing when she was gone and, more importantly, when she returned, she belonged to him.

"And will you travel with me?" There was a hesitancy to her inquiry. His answer mattered to her and scoundrel that he was, the lie should roll easily from his lips.

And yet, he stared blankly down at her delicate hand. Travel with her? The experience he had with marriage came from the sorry state shared by his parents, which had been mimicked by the philandering Society members through the years. Married women and men did not travel together. They did not even tend to move in the same circles. "And would you want me to travel with you?" he asked, in a carefully flat tone. He'd not give her an indication he wanted that answer, nay, needed that answer to be yes.

She snorted. "Well, we would be married."

By Phoebe's own experience as the daughter of a depraved lord, a man who was faithless and fickle, she should have long ago learned what that state meant to the majority of the peerage. He eyed her, this woman who with her hopeful naiveté was more peculiar than any of those creatures they'd observed at either Egyptian Hall or the Leverian. Yet, strangely, the lady had altogether different expectations of marriage.

That would change. The moment she tasted the freedom of being a wedded woman and was courted by clever rakes with glib tongues, she'd be the same.

Rage fell like a thick curtain over his vision, blinding and real. He blinked, and when he looked at her again, she bore the same innocent, unabashed openness upon her face that she always wore. "I would be there if you wanted me there," he said gruffly. "Just as I will give you whatever you desire." Phoebe stroked her fingers over the top of his hand in an almost distracted little rhythm. "You would marry me and yet you still don't know me enough to know

I don't care about any of the material gifts you might offer me? Those are not reasons to marry a person, Edmund." That accusatory edge to those words cut into the next worldly gift he would have put to her.

He raked his hand through his hair. Any other lady would think of nothing but the fact that she'd been divested of her maidenhead and, as such, had no option except that of marriage. And yet, Phoebe pressed him, relentless as a military general. She wanted more. *Demanded* more.

A desperate panic began to lick at his senses as he confronted the horrifying possibility that she intended to say no. With a silent curse, he leveled her with a stare, laying himself bare before her, even as it would likely destroy him—if not now, then later. "I need you, Phoebe Barrett. I don't know your favorite foods or even your middle name, nor do I believe that much matters as to who you are." He was making a greater muck of this. Her slight smile said as much. "Regardless, I don't want anyone and I do not need anyone, but I want you, and I'd have you marry me."

Phoebe angled her head, as though wisely searching the veracity of those words, and then a slow smile spread on her lips. "That is a reason," she whispered. The organ that had knocked around his chest all these years but hadn't felt much more than the dull beat, stirred for the first time in years, proving he was, in fact, alive.

"I will marry you."

Yet, not for any of the promises he'd already made her? What he could offer her? The stability he'd won in several games of faro and hazard opposite her father, she knew nothing of. For if she did, she'd not even now be staring at him with this glimmer in her too-trusting eyes. And for the first time, fear spiraled through him, those sentiments loathsome and potent. *I wish I'd never met you, Phoebe Barrett.* For then he'd have never known this vulnerability. The fleeting thought died a quick death. For he was more selfish than coward, and craved her still, even as she weakened him.

"You want to know why?" She settled back in her seat, calm when he was at sea.

He stiffened. When had he become so transparent that an innocent young lady could manage to read him? Edmund said nothing, instead silently pleaded with her to reply when he'd given her no reason to suspect it mattered.

"I want to marry you because, despite the life you knew as a child, part of you still clung to hope and dreamed of travel and that is the man I'd have for my husband." Her smile widened. "You shall speak to my father?"

Then, for the second time in the course of his entire life, that new emotion pricked at his conscience, a conscience he'd not even known he possessed—guilt. And all because of Miss Phoebe Barrett. "I shall speak to your father," he pledged. The other man would say nothing to her. Edmund all but owned him and therefore would own that silence, too. A surge of satisfaction filled him as with that ruthless control, he was restored once more to the emotionless bastard he'd been before the innocent Phoebe Barrett.

LATER THAT AFTERNOON AS PHOEBE sailed through the front entrance of her home, she tugged her bonnet off and handed it to the butler. She smiled and started for the stairs, feeling as though she'd worn a perpetual smile since Edmund had in his gravelly, harsh whisper professed to wanting her, nay needing her, and then he'd asked to wed her.

"My lady, you have visitors." She jumped and turned to face the old, frowning servant. He never frowned. Why was he frowning? He cleared his throat. "I've taken the liberty of showing them to the parlor and having refreshments called for."

"Visitors," she said dumbly and then gave her head a shake.

"Yes, Miss Fairfax and Lady Gillian."

Her smile dipped for the first time that afternoon and she then moved with no little reluctance through the townhouse to meet her friends. The easy relationship and friendship they'd celebrated these years had become a stiff, awkward one since Edmund had stumbled upon her on the terrace at Lady Delenworth's. Their times together now consisted of their suspicious looks and veiled warnings about his worth and value. They would never share in her regard for Edmund, nor would they celebrate the offer he'd put to her. As much as she told herself their rejection of him did not matter, she lied. It mattered very much whether they liked him and she detested that they saw him in the same black light as the rest of polite Society.

Phoebe reached the parlor and paused at the edge of the door.

"Perhaps he truly cares for her." Oh, saints love Gillian for her devotion and hopeful heart.

Honoria snorted. "He does not care for anybody. Nor will he marry her. Men such as him do not marry ladies."

Gillian's response was lost to the wall.

Phoebe frowned. She'd long known the cynicism Honoria had wrapped herself in, yet she hated to see her friend broken and bitter. And just as much, she hated that Honoria spoke words of Edmund that he himself had come to believe.

"The Marquess of Rutland is—"

Not wanting to hear any more of what Honoria felt Edmund was or wasn't, she stepped into the room, effectively ending the remainder of Honoria's sentence.

Both of her friends stared at her and then jumped to their feet. "Phoebe!" they both greeted, with far too much cheer.

"Where were you?" Honoria asked with feigned nonchalance as they all took their seats.

Phoebe leaned over and picked up the teapot, pouring herself a tepid cup of tea. "Where was I?" she asked slowly. They would find out. It was inevitable. The whole of polite Society strolling the grounds of clogged Hyde Park had likely passed word of the marquess' courtship on to the nearest peer who in turn had passed it on to servants. Yes, it was only a matter of time before they discovered his very public courtship—and his offer of marriage. She bit the inside of her cheek. Why could her friends not see the man that Phoebe did?

"Yes, as in where have you been these past few days?" Phoebe would have to be deaf to fail and hear the hurt underscoring Honoria's question. Since they'd found each other two years ago, they'd been fast friends who were always together. Until Edmund.

"The museum. I went to the museum." She was a coward. There was nothing else for it.

"Deuced dull," Gillian muttered, reaching for a raspberry tart. She added it to her plate and then proceeded to eat the confectionary treat.

Honoria's shoulders drooped. "The museum." An almost giddy laugh escaped her. "Museums are perfectly safe and a proper outing." Would she be so magnanimous in terms of those outings if she were to discover the marquess had been there?

"Whyever would a lady care to be stuck indoors at a dark, dusty building when she could instead be at Hyde Park amidst the flowers and the greens and the sunny skies." Phoebe's hand shook and liquid splashed over the sides, spilling onto the table.

"Are you all right, Phoebe? You seem very distracted." Before she could respond, Gillian looked to Honoria. "Doesn't she appear distracted?"

"She appears distracted."

They stared at her with matching expressions, teeming with suspicion. With a sigh, she set her cup down and then smoothed her palms over the skirts. They were her friends and deserving of the truth. "I—"

"It is him, isn't it?" Honoria groaned. "You're thinking of him, even now."

"I'm not." Pause. She hadn't really been. Rather, she'd been ruminating as to the best way of informing her skeptical, cynical friends of the gentleman's worth. "Er…that is, thinking about whom?"

An inelegant snort escaped Honoria's lips. "You go all wistful and starry-eyed which can only mean the marquess is occupying your thoughts."

Phoebe stole a glance at the open door and then hastened her gaze back to her friends. A desperate need to let these two people who'd been her friends when no one else had been drove back all annoyance and regret she'd carried for their narrow-minded judgment of Edmund. "He—" Phoebe tightened her fingers about her cup. "He advised me to avoid him." She began there.

Honoria blinked.

Not allowing either woman to speak, she rushed ahead. "He warned me he is dangerous." Beyond that, however, she could not share the pieces she'd glimpsed and now privately carried—intimate parts of who Edmund truly was, that she'd share with no one—not even her dearest friends. To do so would be a betrayal of this man who'd let her into his solitary world.

"Perhaps he is not altogether a liar then, *oomph*." Honoria glared at Gillian who'd nudged her in the side.

Before they could bicker with one another over Edmund's worth or even that none-too-gentle nudge, Phoebe set her cup down. "Why would he do that? Why would he warn me if there was not more to him?"

"He wouldn't," Gillian supplied helpfully.

She nodded. "No, he wouldn't." Phoebe held up a staying hand when Honoria made to speak. "I'd have you both be the first to know."

Honoria stitched her eyebrows into a single line. "To know what?"

Before her courage deserted her, Phoebe said, "The marquess asked to marry me." Her pronouncement may as well have drained the last trace of life from the room. Stark, stoic silence met her words. Honoria's shocked, disapproving stare was powerless against the excitement running through her.

The jaded young lady shook her head back and forth repeatedly and touched her fingertips to her ears as though she tried to sort through the quality of her hearing.

She started when Gillian leapt to her feet and sailed over in a flurry of skirts. "Oh, Phoebe," she exclaimed, sinking down into the seat beside her. "I am so very happy for you," she said claiming her hands and giving them a squeeze. Then her smile dipped and she looked frowningly over at Honoria. "Surely you are still not questioning the marquess' motives?"

Phoebe held her breath in anticipation of that reply. Shock, concern, suspicion all marred the delicate planes of Honoria's face. "I…" She wet her lips. "I've paid attention to the gossips and the warnings my aunt has given me to avoid him. I want you to be happy," Honoria whispered. She held her palms up as if in supplication. "I do, but it is with that reason, that fear of your happiness, I worry as to his motives. Does he love you?" Honoria held her gaze. "And more importantly, do you love him?"

Phoebe shifted under their scrutiny. "I…" There had been no talk of love. *I want you….* "I do not know if he loves me," she said at last. It would seem she had more traces of her father in her than she'd ever wished for she would wager both her happiness and heart upon the hope that he'd love her in return. "I love him," she said softly, freed by that truth. "And I believe he will come to love me."

Her friends looked at her for a long moment and then some of the tension left Honoria's stiffly held shoulders. "I do not doubt it.

How can anyone not help but love you, Phoebe? Forgive me for being skeptical. I wish you and the marquess only happiness and love."

Except, as they carried on their visit, Phoebe did not know why her friends' words had only roused the faint misgivings stirring at the back of her mind.

CHAPTER 14

THE FOLLOWING MORNING, AS PROMISED to Phoebe, Edmund drew his black stallion to a halt before the Viscount Waters' townhouse. In the light of day, with space between him and Phoebe, he acknowledged the practicality of this visit, and more, the logicalness of the offer he'd put to her father. With her gentle lavender scent no longer clouding his senses and that full, delectable mouth made for his, he'd been able to divorce those earlier, tumultuous sentiments she'd unleashed within him from the emotionless reasons to make her his marchioness.

Edmund dismounted from Lucifer and with reins in his hand, eyed the front of Waters' townhouse. The curtains rustled from a floor-length window and Phoebe peeked around the fabric. Their gazes caught and held.

There was no emotion involved in this decision. Nothing but an insatiable lust, a desire to make her his. Then she winked at him and with a slight wave of her fingertips, dropped the curtain back into place and the heart he didn't know still beat thumped hard in response. *You bloody liar.* There was nothing practical or logical in making Phoebe his wife and yet he wanted her anyway—would have her anyway. A primitive male need filled him. For in doing this, in marrying her, she would belong to him in ways she'd never belong to another. Edmund's stare landed upon the viscount's waiting servant.

The liveried groom blanched and darted his gaze about, seeming to contemplate escape, and then ultimately sidled closer to claim the reins.

Edmund started past the young man and climbed the viscount's steps. The old butler who was fast becoming a familiar face opened the door in anticipation. A slight smile lined his aged cheeks which he quickly buried. "My lord," he greeted and stepping aside, he sketched a bow.

Edmund shrugged out of his cloak then handed it off to a waiting footman. "I'm here for the viscount." He withdrew a card and held it out to the butler, who took it and eyed it a moment, before nodding and motioning him forward.

"If you'll follow me."

The other man didn't wait to see if he followed and moved at a surprisingly brisk pace down the corridor. Edmund tugged at his lapels and trailed after the man. He gritted his teeth at the quick movements that strained the muscles of his leg.

Alas, their journey was not to be a quick one. "Rutland, my friend."

He winced at the jovial greeting issued by the lady's younger brother who stepped into their path. Tamping down a sigh of annoyance, Edmund executed a stiff bow. "Barrett."

Except, that crisp, laconic utterance proved little deterrence. "Were you coming to call?"

By the hopeful glint in the young man's eyes it registered. He blanched. By God, the pup thought he was here to see him. He opened his mouth to deliver the blunt, coolly aloof response he would have at any other point in his life—before her. Edmund caught himself and forced a grin, the expression painful. "I've matters of business to attend with the viscount."

"The viscount?" Barrett scratched his brow. Then he widened his eyes with a dawning understanding. "The viscount! My father. Of course. Yes." He all but jumped sideways in his haste to clear once more the path to the viscount's office. "I'll allow you to attend your business."

Anxiety turned in his gut and he was grateful when the butler resumed the path once more. These people and their emotions, their unfettered smiles and… He shuddered, and their goodness that he did not know what to do with. All these sentiments were as foreign to him as ancient tongues. He quickened his pace and with each step that sense of disquiet grew. Until young Barrett had stepped into his path mere moments ago, he'd failed to consider that in wedding Phoebe, it brought additional connections and obligations. She brought a brother and a sister, an absent mother he'd not given thought to before now, and those friends. Guilt knotted in his belly. One of those young ladies whom he'd intended to wed and who he'd ultimately see ruined for her connection to Margaret, the Duchess of Monteith.

The butler stopped beside the viscount's office door and Edmund came to a stop behind him, staring at the wood panel as the servant rapped once.

He'd spent eleven years considering how he'd be avenged for Margaret's defection and the humiliation she'd brought him. Yet, since Phoebe had snagged herself upon Lord Delenworth's spear, revenge had been the furthest thing from his thoughts. Instead, he'd been consumed by this need for Phoebe. When she belonged to him in both name and body, then he could reclaim control of his ordered world. Only then could he know that no other bastard would lay his hands upon the satiny softness of her skin…or own her heart.

The butler shot an apologetic glance over his shoulder and then knocked once more. "Enter." The servant shoved the door open. "I said enter," the viscount thundered, his words however died at spying the figure framed behind his overly loyal servant in the doorway.

Waters' cheeks turned ashen as he remained frozen in the seat behind his desk with his fingers wrapped about a decanter of brandy.

Edmund sent a single eyebrow arching up and the decanter slipped from the man's chubby fingers as he scrambled to his feet. The butler wisely backed out of the room, pulling the door closed behind him.

"R-rutland," Phoebe's father stammered, scurrying out from behind his desk like a rodent racing about in search of a new hiding place. "I-is, d-do you require my daughter's whereabouts because I don't—"

"I do not," he intoned on a silken whisper that drained the remaining color from the usually florid cheeks. In a deliberate show of disrespect, he flicked his gaze up and down the other man's fat torso and peeled his lip back in a sneer. "I've come for other reasons, Waters." Shrewd enough to not give the viscount any indication he was in possession of the only person or item Edmund had any desire of, he flicked an imaginary piece of lint from his immaculate black sleeve and strolled over to the window. He clasped his hands at his back and peered down into the streets, presenting his back to Waters. "I'm here for your daughter."

The crystal pane of the window reflected Waters' furrowed brow. "My daughter?" The notorious reprobate scratched his bald pate. "I-I already told you I didn't know where she was. I can find out."

He tossed a glance over his shoulder. "And I've already told you I'm not looking for the lady's whereabouts."

Confusion made the other man reckless. "But you said..." Then his bulging, blue eyes went round with a slow understanding. "Ah, my daughter." His jowls shook with the force of his laughter; the sound crude and raucous, as he emitted great snorting gasps like a pig wallowing in its own filth. "You want the younger one, do you? I told you, my Justina is a lovely girl. She'll make you a good wife."

His patience snapped. Edmund spun around. "I've already told you. I want to wed your eldest, Phoebe."

Waters cocked his head. "Wed, you say?"

PHOEBE PACED A PATH BEFORE the empty hearth, while periodically stealing a glance at the loudly ticking ormolu clock. The untouched volume of her Captain Cook's work lay forgotten on the mahogany side table.

"They'll finish their discussion soon, my dear."

She paused mid-stride and glanced with some surprise at her mother. The viscountess sat with her head bent over her embroidery frame, attending her needlepoint.

"I suspect the marquess has come to make an offer for you?" At last, her mother paused and picked her head up, a twinkle lit her eyes. "Come, surely you do not believe I'm one of those self-absorbed mothers who fails to note my eldest daughter's frequently blushing cheeks and the rumors being whispered about her and a certain gentleman who—"

"She has the look of longing for," Justina said from her spot at the windowseat, absorbed in her reading.

Heat burned Phoebe's cheeks. "I do not have..." Her mother and sister both gave her a pointed look and she sighed, letting the thought go unfinished. There was no need debating the matter with them. In this, they were, in fact—correct. She glanced to the clock once more and the thin thread she had on her control snapped. "I'm going to fetch my book while I wait." Both women looked up once more. She forced a serene smile to her lips. "It is my latest Captain Cook. I thought it should help occupy my thoughts."

Justina furrowed her brow and moved her gaze from Phoebe to the unfortunately forgotten until now leather volume. "Isn't that—?"

Phoebe swung a pleading stare in her direction and her sister widened her eyes in sudden understanding.

Their mother continued working to pull her needle through the fabric on the embroidery frame. "It doesn't do to appear too eager. Not to a man as powerful as the marquess," she said, directing her words to the muslin in her hands.

"Er, yes, indeed," Phoebe agreed. "Perhaps I shall just read abovestairs until the marquess concludes his meeting."

Before her mother could say anything further on it, Phoebe hurried from the room and started down the corridor. She passed the occasional servant hurrying to attend their day's responsibilities. It wouldn't do to appear too eager. Her ever incorrect mama, in this, was indeed surprisingly correct and yet, since their exchange in Hyde Park, Phoebe had been consumed by a need to see him, be with him. This hard, unflappable man misperceived by all, broken of heart and yet daring to trust in her. With each step she took, her heartbeat grew increasingly erratic in rhythm. Phoebe turned right at the hall and tiptoed several steps past two doors, and then paused outside her father's office.

With her shoulder pressed against the wall, she strained to hear a hint of his voice. "I want to wed your eldest, Phoebe...." A grin that likely would have earned the disappointed groans of Honoria and ever optimistic Gillian played on her lips.

I don't want anyone and I do not need anyone, but I want you, and I'd have you marry me... From the moment he'd uttered those words, she'd belonged to him.

"…thought you wanted the Fairfax girl?" Her father's muffled question cut into her musings and she blinked several times in rapid succession. Surely, she'd misheard—

"Matters have changed."

Even with the wood panel between them, the lethality of his whisper cut through the door and pierced her slow-moving thoughts. Matters have changed? What was he saying? Phoebe forcibly tamped down the reservations. Of course a man who'd long protected his heart as Edmund had done would not share the depth of his feelings with one such as her father, a man he'd never before known.

"Which one do you want, you say?" Her father spoke the way a breeder would when selling horseflesh to the highest bidder.

"Your eldest."

A chill ran along her spine. Not "Phoebe". Or "the woman I gave my heart to". But rather, "your eldest".

"…you said you wanted your revenge using the Fairfax girl," her father wheedled and the dark tendrils of ice plucked at the edge of her heart. "I've done my part where that one is concerned. Wed her. I need my Phoebe to settle my debt with Allswood." The Fairfax girl? Her father's debt with Allswood? Phoebe's mind went numb as she sought to put order to those confounding words. "Or take Justina."

"You would deny me her hand?" For one beat of her heart, hope lived on where Edmund, the man she loved, battled her father for her hand. His next words slayed that fledgling wish. "I own you, Waters. I possess your eldest daughter's dowry. No one would see your girls wed with the state you've left them in. Your family will not be welcomed in even the most unfashionable halls when I am through with you. Your children's worth will be even less to you if you thwart me."

A chill went through her at that ruthless pledge of a stranger, not the man she'd lain with under the stars and given her virtue to. She folded her arms close and held tight but nothing could or would ever dull the agony twisting in her belly.

Her father cursed. "After you wed my girl, my debt to you is paid." With each word her father uttered, the cold fanned out and froze her thoughts, her words, her emotions, until she was an empty shell of a person trying to make order in a suddenly disordered world.

"You will not presume to tell me when your debt is paid," Edmund's crisp, clear command slipped into the corridor.

She shook her head slowly back and forth to rid the thick haze of confusion blanketing her mind. And then the floodgates of understanding opened and sent spiraling through her the ugly, black truth—lies. Everything. Anything between them had been based on some sickened, twisted game of revenge. To what end? The air lodged in her chest. She concentrated on the harsh, raspy sounds of her own breathing as it filled her ears to keep from focusing on those words. Her friend had warned her, seen more to the jaded lord's interest in Phoebe. She dug her fingers against her temples and rubbed hard. *Think. Think.* This did not make sense. If his was a matter of revenge, why would he enlist her? Her father was wrong. He'd been wrong about so many things through life…he'd likely misunderstood…whatever it is that had brought Edmund into his life.

Her father had been indebted to him? Edmund, the man who'd professed a love of Captain Cook and shared his dreams and hopes and worse, a man whom she'd shared her dreams and hopes with, the man she'd given her virginity to, had been the kind of man to keep company with her depraved father. Oh, God, had he seduced her all in a twisted bid to forever tie her to him? Phoebe pressed her eyes closed as nausea churned through her belly. She folded her arms across her waist and hugged tight. Who was this man she'd never known? A dissembler. A stranger. An actor upon a Drury Lane stage and she'd been an unwitting player along with him. Bile burned her throat as she fought to keep from casting the accounts of her stomach up. What had she done?

"Are we clear?" Edmund asked with a wintriness she'd never known of him. A tone that would likely strike terror in children and grown men alike. Alas, her father possessed far more courage than she'd have ever expected, or mayhap it was stupidity, for he persisted. "And you're sure you'd rather have my eldest? I can pass her off to Allswood, and you can have my youngest. Surely a man with your singular tastes would prefer the more beautiful of my daughters."

Oh, God. Bile burned her throat and threatened to choke her. A loud humming filled Phoebe's ears. Her sister. Her sweet, innocent, and all things good sister wed to this blackguard? She'd sooner kill the Marquess of Rutland with her own hands than see him destroy Justina; not as he'd destroyed her.

"I—"

Phoebe didn't want to hear Edmund's likely acceptance of her father's depraved counteroffer. She threw open the door. Both men swung their gazes toward her in unison.

Edmund stiffened and his thick, dark lashes swept low, obscuring his obsidian eyes. *Say something, anything! Deny all my father's charges.* The silence stretched on, interminable and just like a candle's dying flame, all hope was extinguished. Her heart spasmed, tightening the muscles of her chest.

Edmund's shuttered expression gave no indication as to whether he felt shame, regret, or sadness. Then, a man such as he was incapable of feeling.

"What are you doing in here, gel?" her father sputtered. "M-my daughter knows better than this." His cheeks flushed, as he seemed to realize those words even now flew in the face of that claim as evidences of her presence here.

Phoebe and Edmund ignored him. Their gazes locked on one another. She clenched and unclenched her hands into tight fists at her side. How could he be so coolly unaffected?

Her breath came in ragged spurts. She'd only thought to interrupt whatever intentions he'd utter that pertained to her sister. Except, now, as she stood a trembling, quaking mess before this man she'd foolishly loved and given her heart to, she had no grand words. She didn't have the vile epithets for one who'd speak so casually of destroying her and those she loved. Instead, she just stared at him, praying the hatred gleamed stronger within their depths than that aching agony wrought by his betrayal.

"Leave."

It took a moment to register that clipped command belonged to Edmund. Her father, unprotestingly hurried from the room as quickly as his large frame permitted. He paused beside her at the threshold of the door. "Do not do anything to ruin this, gel," he bit out.

Phoebe tipped her chin up a notch, never taking her gaze from Edmund. Her father could go to Hell and he could take the monstrous Marquess of Rutland right along with him in his travels.

Her faithless sire opened his mouth to say something further, but Edmund leveled him with a harsh stare, and her father left. The door closed. The click of it shutting thundered like a shot at night, leaving her and Edmund—alone.

The room echoed with the harsh rapidity of her own painfully drawn breaths and the hum of silence. Through it, Edmund said nothing. He did not move. He remained as frozen as his blasted heart of ice. Then, with a calm she wanted to slap his smug face for, he flicked an imagined piece of lint from his immaculate black coat sleeve. "It is unfortunate you heard that."

Phoebe narrowed her eyes. "That is what you'll say?" The shocked question ripped from her throat before she could call it back.

He paused, and for the slightest span of a moment regret flashed in his eyes, but then as quickly as a flame being snuffed out, all hint of emotion was gone, so she was left to wonder if she'd merely imagined it. "What would you have me say?" Bitterness swelled in her chest. Of course she had imagined any and all emotion from the marquess—just as she'd imagined anything and everything to pass between them these past days together.

Edmund took a step toward her and she retreated so quickly, her back thumped noisily against the door. Pain radiated along her spine and shot down her thighs, but she welcomed the discomfort for it detracted from the agony of her heart, still cracking from the truth of his ruthlessness. He continued coming and she held a hand up. "Stop!" She detested that pleading entreaty in her tone. With agony lancing through her, Phoebe turned her palms up, willing for him to deny all. "Tell me it is untrue. Tell me you would not do something so vile as destroy my family over having your desires thwarted." For none of this made any sense.

He flexed his jaw. "I cannot tell you that," he said in that flat, emotionless manner of his.

Tension spiraled through her, thick and consuming and out of control. "Why can you not tell me?" She barely recognized the high-pitched tone as her own.

His broad shoulders lifted up and down in a shrug. "Because it is true."

Of their own volition, her eyes slid closed. *It is true.* "Why?" That strangled response emerged broken and choked. Why would this aloof, emotionless stranger go to such lengths to possess her?

"I want you," he said with an icy matter-of-factness that chilled her.

She resisted the urge to rub warmth into her arms. She'd not allow him the pleasure of knowing how he'd ravaged her world with his throwaway words to her father a short while ago. Phoebe angled her chin up. "And how does Honoria fit into your twisted life, Edmund?"

A muscle jumped in his jaw. He was a man no doubt unaccustomed to anyone putting questions or demands to him and for an instant, she thought he'd ignore her question, and for an even longer moment, coward that she was, she wanted him to. She slid her eyes closed willing all of this to be nothing more than a nightmare.

"Your Miss Fairfax had the misfortune of sharing the blood of a…previous acquaintance. I intended to ruin Miss Fairfax and then wed her." Edmund's chilling words forced her eyes open. Cold stole through her as he moved an unreadable black stare over her. How coolly methodical he was in his telling. He may as well have spoken of the weather or last evening's festivities. Who *was* this ruthless stranger?

"Whose blood does she share?" That question emerged garbled.

He hesitated.

"Who?" she demanded on a high-pitched cry.

"Margaret, the Duchess of Monteith." His expression grew shuttered. "The young woman I'd once dueled for." Oh, God, it had never been about Phoebe. Edmund's kisses and whispers and promises…they'd all been nothing more than lies borne of revenge against the woman who truly held his heart. She folded her arms and rubbed her hands over them in a bid to restore warmth to the chilled limbs.

Edmund slashed the air with his hand. "Matters changed, Phoebe."

Her heart wrenched. All along Phoebe had loved him and she'd been nothing more than a secondary pawn in his scheme to hurt another. "You love her that much." Her words emerged hollow. Why should it matter that this ruthless blackguard who'd threatened her family, a man she'd given her virtue to, loved another? And yet, God help her, it mattered still.

His lips peeled back in a mocking grin. "Do not be ridiculous." The hard glint in his eyes hinted at a man incapable of loving anyone. Not even himself.

"Then why?" She shoved away from the door. "Why would you seek revenge against Honoria?" *Using me.* "She's done nothing to you."

"It wasn't about Miss Fairfax," he said with such calm she wanted to slap her hands over her ears and blot out his voice. He took another step toward her. "I always have what I want. Including," *me?* "matters of revenge." Of course, not her. He'd never truly wanted her. Not in the sweet, seductive way she'd convinced herself. That dream of a life for them, together, with their broken pasts behind them and their limitless futures before them, had belonged to her alone. He'd merely fed her the words she'd longed to hear in that carriage. A film of tears blurred her vision and she blinked back the sad, sorry, pathetic droplets. He was not worth a single shred of her emotion.

"This changes nothing between us," he said, pulling her from the precipice of her own misery.

Shock ran through her, and Phoebe cocked her head. "Are you mad?" The barely-there whisper echoed from the walls of her father's office.

"There have been worse charges leveled at me than the one of madman."

His bored, tired tone snapped the thin thread of Phoebe's self-control. She shot out a hand. The slap of flesh meeting flesh thundered around them. Heart hammering wildly, she pulled her stinging palm back and clutched at the folds of her skirts.

Edmund flexed his jaw and touched his gloved fingertips to the crimson mark left by her blow. All the while his black stare remained fixed on her. This man. This *stranger*. This betrayer with his false words and broken, empty promises and fear shot through her. Phoebe took a stumbling step away from him. "D-don't." That tremulous order came out ineffectual and she hurried to put distance between them. As he continued his advance, she moved out of his reach.

"Do you think I would harm you?" he asked in clipped tones.

Phoebe backed into the leather button sofa and her knees knocked the edge. Path of escape effectively blocked, she came to a forced stop. Not wanting him to see the hell he'd wrought upon her world, she tipped her head back. "I don't think you would harm me." Some of the tension seeped from his tautly held frame. "I know you would. You already have."

CHAPTER 15

HOW SINGULARLY ODD. TO GO through life, knowing there was nothing but cold in your veins and black emptiness to your heart, and yet to feel…this, whatever this unpleasant, harsh tightening in his chest was. Edmund looked at Phoebe, the color drained from her cheeks as she stood, pressed against the sofa. With trembling fingers, she clutched at her throat. He studied that faint quaking and then lifted his gaze to hers. She dropped her hands to the back of the sofa. Then her lip peeled back in a sneer.

Inevitably, everyone was broken. Ruined by life. For some, it was those early moments of childhood when one's father forced you, a boy of seven years, to observe the extent of your mother's depravity and faithlessness. For others, it came later with the betrayal and deception from one that was once trusted. By the icy derision in Phoebe's eyes and the cynical twist of her bow-shaped lips, she'd been broken. Yes, everyone was eventually ruined. But there was an empty, ugly ache in knowing he'd been the one to break her. The sight of her silent suffering squeezed the vise all the tighter about his chest. Apparently, he was human, after all. What an unfortunate moment to realize it.

Once again, she proved herself far stronger and more courageous than he'd ever been. She broke the silence. "I will not accept your offer of marriage. I'd rather sever my left hand than bind it to one such as you," she spat.

"It was not an offer."

She blinked several times in rapid succession.

Edmund stalked over to her. Her slender frame shook slightly and he abhorred the faint tremble that hinted at her fear of him. "I am marrying you." For even with the icy loathing teeming from her blue-eyed gaze, he wanted her, as his, and only his.

"You are m—" He gave her a pointed look and the tired accusation died on her lips.

He palmed her cheek and at his touch, she went stiff. "I always get what I want."

For a too-brief moment he believed she'd turn into his caress and angle her lips up toward his, begging for his kiss as she'd done. Then, she slapped his hand away and the foolish thought shriveled, leaving him cold. "I am not an object. I am not a material possession to be added to your collection. I am a person, my lord. You may want my body, but I will sooner bed the devil than take you as my husband and lie with you again." She made to storm around him.

Edmund stole a hand around her wrist, staying her movement. A gasp escaped her lips and Phoebe alternated her gaze between his firm hold and his face. Horror, fear, and revulsion teamed together, warring for a place with ultimately her proving triumphant. Phoebe yanked her hand hard but he held firm. This gripping need for her no less than when she'd looked upon him with hope in her eyes.

Hope that I killed. "I'll have you as my wife, Phoebe."

"Or what, my lord?" *Edmund. I am Edmund to you.* A physical hungering to hear his name upon her lips once more filled him. "You will ruin Honoria? Let Society know I'm no longer a virgin? Marry my s…" Her skin turned an ashen hue. "Marry my…" Then she widened her eyes and tugged free of him the same moment he relinquished his hold and she toppled into the seat. Phoebe flung her arms out and caught herself upon the cushions. She glowered up at him. "You would wed my sister."

That is what she believed. How could she still not know that this consuming need to possess her blotted out all rational thought and blinded him to all others? And yet, she'd showed her weakness and, with that, he'd secure her as his wife.

Only…the words would not come. He could not force the words past his lips. Not this lie. Not this time.

Except, Phoebe took his silence for unspoken confirmation. "You bastard," she hissed, shoving to her feet.

Her tangible hatred ran through him, staggering him with the extent of his own weakness in caring as he did. Edmund donned the indifferent mask he'd worn the better part of his life. "A bastard, now?" he drawled. "That is, at the very least, a deal better than a monster."

She shot another hand out and this time he easily caught her wrist. He dragged her delicate flesh close to his mouth and touched his lips to the soft skin. "You might detest me, as you should, but you desire me." Once, she'd been affected by him. The intake of her soft breath that had once stolen his sleep and entered his dreams, the tremble on her lips as she'd come undone in his arms. All gone. Regret churned in his gut.

"Do you think I should still desire you?" Incredibility underscored her question. "Do you think I'm so very weak that I would want the man who used me to exact revenge upon another? Who'd wed my sister if I reject his suit?" She scoffed. "I am not weak as the other women you've taken to your bed."

She was nothing like the women he'd taken to his bed. Everyone before her had been grasping and bitter and just as jaded as he himself was. They'd not possessed her peculiarly cheerful outlook on life, despite the ugly she'd known. There was nothing cheerful about her now. Now, she bore a shocking cynicism better suited to the person he'd always been. And yet he wanted her as she'd been, wanted her as they had been. That truth ran ragged through him, terrifying for the power of regret churning through him.

"What? Nothing to say?" she jeered.

He let her wrist go once more and she stepped around him. People had never mocked him. They'd known there were consequences in their treatment of the Marquess of Rutland. Yet, this slip of a woman was as bold and brave as Joan of Arc and his appreciation of who she intrinsically was swelled, powerful inside him. There would be time enough to worry about his reaction to her later. Now, as she stalked over to the entrance of the room, all he knew was he wanted her, regardless, just as he'd said—in any way and every way. She'd represented the last hint of possible salvation where his black, vile soul was concerned. If in his actions he'd destroyed her, would anything remain of him?

Edmund closed the distance between them in four long strides. He wrapped a hand about her waist and she stiffened at his touch as he guided her around.

"Wh—what—?" Her words ended on a startled gasp as he dipped his mouth close to hers.

"You are now bitter and aware of the truth of the world, but you are not a liar." *Not like me.* His breath came harsh and fast, a blend of desire and darkened regrets. It blended with her own. Mint and chocolate. "You still want me. And you will come to my bed, this time as my wife, my marchioness." He killed the protest on her lips by claiming her mouth for a hard, powerful kiss.

For a moment she went taut and he expected her to pull back, but then she leaned into him and that slight softening fueled his desire. It was a thrill of exhilaration in knowing even with what had come to pass between them, she wanted him still, and he could use that part of her to reclaim what he needed of her. Edmund slipped his tongue into her mouth and plundered the hot depths. Their tongues met mimicking the most intimate act of bodies joining. It conjured all manner of erotic images that involved Phoebe with her back against the wall and her skirts up while he made love to her in all the ways he still ached to.

He folded one hand about her neck and angled her head, positioning her in such a way that he better availed himself to her mouth. A ragged moan escaped her and he swallowed the sound with his own groan of hunger. Phoebe melted into his frame and with his other hand he trailed a path down the small of her back, ever lower. He caressed her buttocks, cupping the delicate swell of her derriere. She cried out and he pulled his mouth from hers, instead shifting his ministrations to the long, graceful column of her throat. Her head fell back and he exulted in her surrender. She might abhor him, but she still wanted him. And as long as he had this piece of her, it would be enough. It would be a piece of her, one he was unworthy of, undeserving to claim as his own, but then he'd always been a selfish, self-serving bastard.

Edmund ran both hands down her slender frame, reveling in the gentle curve of her hip. He needed more of her. All of her. He grasped her skirts and tugged them up, exposing the lean, lithe limbs and took in the faintly muscled calves. All manner of delicious acts that involved her legs wrapped about him slipped into his sinful thoughts. A pained desire, more agony than pleasure shot through him. Then she put her palms to his chest. And he was lost.

She shoved hard, the movement so jarring, he tumbled backward and staggered, quickly righting himself. Phoebe took several faltering steps away, her skin flushed a delicious crimson red, her lips swollen from their kiss. Edmund took in every single, subtle, jerky movement. The haste she made to put distance between them, so very similar to Society's response when he entered polite, and more often impolite, events. For years, he'd not only grown accustomed to those sentiments, he'd reveled in that fear wrapped in contempt wrapped in hatred. His gaze went to her long fingers, shaking, now clasped to her throat. Horror wreathed the delicate planes of her face.

A hollowness settled in his chest. Where was the triumph now?

WHEN PHOEBE HAD BEEN A small girl, she'd searched the house for her sister Justina in a game of Hide and Seek. Hearing faint whispers, she'd hovered outside the Ivory Parlor with her hand poised on the handle—just as the sound of voices had reached through the door. She'd stood frozen while two young servants whispered about her father's vile depravity. Heart hammering and stomach twisted with knots of sickness at the ugly truths heard, she'd run as fast and as far as her then little legs could carry her.

She'd raced down the corridors with her own breath, the servants' words, and her heart's erratic, loud rhythm pounding in her ears. She'd sought out an armoire in one of the guest chambers and shut herself away. The thick, blackness had enveloped her in the quiet and inky darkness. The silence had been deafening, until her harshly drawn breaths had robbed her of logical thought. That day, she'd climbed out of the armoire with no one the wiser of a young girl's world having been torn asunder. She'd closed the door, exited the guest chambers, and then found her siblings. Resolved to never let another person's ugliness—including her own sire's—steal her happiness or in any way fundamentally chase away the hope inside.

This moment, with Edmund before her now, was remarkably alike in that regard. The same shock, confusion, horror. And worse...the betrayal of loving one, only to find that you never truly knew the person. That everything about them, everything to come before was nothing more than flimsy lies. And yet, staring at the harsh, angular planes of his face carved in an impenetrable mask, she'd violated that great vow she'd made long ago. Not after this. Not after Edmund. Unable to bear the sight of him, she slid her eyes closed. And for this, she could not be happy again. Not truly. For she'd trusted; Edmund, herself, and given herself over to love, only to have that innocence proven foolhardy—just as Honoria had warned. Yet, that her body should still crave his kiss and hunger for his touch, sickened her with the shame of her own weakness.

"I hate you," she whispered, the words empty and meaningless. For she didn't really. If she truly hated him, her heart would not be cracking into a million shards this very instant. Instead, he'd become a blackguard, whose words and stories had been a lie. And she hated herself far more for her own humiliating weakness for this man—a dream of a person she'd dared love.

There was the faintest stiffening, the slightest indication her profession might in some way matter. Then he inclined his head. "Hate is something I am accustomed to, Madam."

In other words, he'd grown so used to those sentiments of disdain, that hers meant so very little. A chill stole through her and she folded her arms and rubbed in attempt to suffuse warmth back into the frozen limbs. "Then I daresay you'd not forever bind yourself to a woman who detests the mere sight of you," she said in a bid to hurt him.

Alas, it would take one far stronger than her to wound in any way the great and powerful Marquess of Rutland. A hard grin turned his lips. "I would have you as mine, Phoebe. It matters not that you hate me. We will have desire which is far more than all those other empty unions."

She shook her head and tried to make sense of those words. That is what he spoke of? Not love or genuine regard...but of desire? "Why?" Why with such professions of hate should he still want her?

He lifted his shoulders in a casual shrug. "Everyone hates me." In another person, those words would have been intended to ring sympathy, to inspire regret. In Edmund, however, they were delivered with a chilling matter-of-fact calm. "I might as well tie myself to one I hunger for, even if she does detest me." His square, proud jaw tensed. "And make no mistake. I want you." *And I intend to have you.* Those words danced around the air. Unspoken but no less real.

A denial sprung to her lips. Then, Justina's face flitted to her mind's eye and the false protestations withered and died. If it was only Phoebe's ruin to consider, she'd easily spit in his face and send him gladly to the devil. But he spoke of her sister; the sister whom she loved and cherished and protected. She'd not see Justina broken by life the way Edmund had been broken and the way he'd shattered her. "You will not wed my sister," she said with a resolute calm, proud of that steady deliverance.

His expression grew veiled, but he gave no response to that pledge.

Phoebe tried one more feeble grasp at freedom. "We would not suit. Not truly. The women you are…" Her cheeks blazed with heat as she recalled her friend's claims about ties and knots and bonds. Those vile, dark acts were the kind this man enjoyed. The tender meeting in the Lord Essex's gardens had been nothing more than a ruse to shatter her defenses and trap her. What would he be like as a lover now, when there were no more pretenses required of him? Unease twisted in her belly. "The women you are a-accustomed t-to," she stumbled over herself. "Are different." The *ladies* one such as Edmund would want in his life were experienced and worldly. Even in light of his betrayal, jealousy twisted like a green-edged blade in her belly. *Fool.*

The ghost of a smile played on his lips and she wanted to slap his smug face once again for being so indifferent to the talk of him with other women. "Yes, Phoebe, you are unlike any woman I've been with before now."

As she did not know what to make of that ambiguous, emotionless statement, she said nothing and waited for him to say something.

"We will be wed by special license."

To say something that was not that.

He stalked over to the door, the matter settled and panic throbbed in her breast. Phoebe sprinted over and placed herself between him and the wood panel. Her back rattled against the door. "B-but..." Her mind raced in an attempt to put her world to right and spare them both this miserable union.

"But what?" Edmund tugged out his watch fob and consulted the timepiece; the casual act, lending power to the tedium of that two-word question. "The way I see it, Madam, this is mutually beneficial to the both of us."

"How so?" A near hysterical bubble seeped from her lips. How could there be anything remotely good between them? "How can there be anything good in a marriage between us?"

With an effortless grace, he tucked his timepiece into his pocket. "I did not say good. I said mutually beneficial."

She furrowed her brow. "With the exception of saving my sister from your vile grasp, what benefit could there be to me in tying myself to one such as you?"

Edmund inclined his head. "Would you prefer the Earl of Allswood?"

An involuntary snort escaped her. "I'd prefer neither of you." His frown deepened as though he disliked being lumped in with the Lord Allswoods of the world, but that was precisely where he belonged. "I daresay there are a good many more options for me than you and Lord Allswood."

His dark eyebrows snapped into a single, hard line. He dipped his head close and she made to draw away but found retreat impossible with the hard mahogany door at her back. So, she angled her chin up and glared at him.

"Do you believe the options are so very limitless for a dowerless woman, no longer in possession of her virginity?" His words expelled the air from the room. Even with everything she'd heard and discovered, the depth of his viciousness still slammed into her with a ferocity that caused her legs to tremble. And just like that, she was the small girl, alone, in the darkened armoire "What manner of monster are you?" she asked, her tongue thick.

Silence met her question.

Did she imagine that flash of pained regret in his eyes? "You would keep my dowry, even with everything we'd shared?" Agony leant her words a ragged quality. She searched his hard face and by the unrelenting set to his mouth, needed no confirmation beyond that. A chill stole through her. Then, but for their bodies, had they really shared *anything?* Where did the betrayals end? Her father's disregard and sins through the years, she'd long ago accepted. Or thought she had. Only now, knowing not even her dowry had been valued by the wastrel reprobate who'd given her life, showed her that she was not so very indifferent to that betrayal, either.

Edmund brushed his knuckles over her jaw. "It matters not."

"It matters not?" she spat, hating that his touch somehow filled her with a reassuring warmth, hating that she still craved his touch, that special bond they'd once shared. "You'd wed a woman without a dowry, who does not want to wed you?" She could not make sense of who this man truly was or what drove him. He was a riddle wrapped in a conundrum.

"You have a dowry," he said pulling her to the moment.

"I *had* a dowry." Bitterness tinged her words. Phoebe pressed her palms to her cheeks, blotting out the intensity of his dark brown eyes. "I have nothing." *Not even my virtue*. Nausea roiled in her gut until she feared she'd cast the contents of her stomach up at his feet.

He continued to stroke her jaw and then expanded his caress to her cheek. "I possess your dowry and now I'll have you."

From the thick haze of confusion and tumult, Phoebe lowered her arms to her sides. Edmund's words came as from down a long hall. She stared at his mouth as he talked. His lips moved, but she only managed to pluck out a handful of coherent phrases from the string of words he now strung together.

"…and now I'll have you…"

Those last three words snapped her from the haze of confusion and Phoebe cried out. She ducked out from under his arm and raced away from him, placing a King Louis XIV chair between them. "What of my sister?" she demanded in a strangled tone.

His eyebrows dipped, while a muscle jumped at the corner of his eyes, as she suspected a man accustomed to not having demands made to him by anyone, didn't know what to do with her insistency.

"What of my sister?" Her cry rang about the room.

"I possess only your dowry."

She ran her gaze over his face; once beloved, now the harsh, cruel one everyone had warned her of. "I don't believe you." With the lies between them, how could she believe anything he said?

Edmund leaned a shoulder against the door and folded his arms at his chest, elegant in repose. "I have no reason to lie to you in this regard."

In this regard. Unlike all the times before this when he'd had reasons to lie to her. She smoothed her palms over her skirts. In this instance, she did not matter. Justina and her innocence and her future happiness and dowry—that is what mattered. Phoebe's fate had been settled long ago; by her father—by Edmund. "If I wed you," she began, "will you see my sister is protected? Will you see my father..." the monstrous fiend who'd sacrificed her. She took a deep breath and finished the remaining thought. "Will you see that my father does not sell my sister off to pay his debt?"

He inclined his head. "It is done."

It is done. Those three words marked this exchange as a transaction, a contract entered into. Phoebe pressed her fingers over her eyes and drew in several breaths. She could and would forever despise Edmund for his treachery, but she'd courted this disaster by continually allowing herself to meet with him and giving herself over to the notorious marquess. After their scandalous meetings had there ever really been any other recourse except marriage? Phoebe lowered her hands to her side. Edmund continued to study her in that piercing manner. A chill ran along her spine. He may as well have been a stranger she passed on Bond Street to the man she'd lain with in Lord Essex's gardens.

She eyed him warily. "Why should I trust you?" She spoke that question more to herself. "You do not," love, "care for me, therefore my sister's happiness matters less than mine, to you."

"You should not trust me," he replied, still lounged against that door. "As my wife, I'd advise you not to trust anyone." Another icy shiver racked her frame with the evidence of his cold unfeelingness. What a miserable way to go through one's existence. "But regardless of whether you believe it or not, I protect what is mine. You are mine and no one will dare hurt you or yours for your connection to me. That protection extends to those you care for."

There was something oddly reassuring in the steely edge of that promise. She'd gone through the duration of her life with a father who didn't give a jot for her. She'd been preyed upon by men with lascivious intentions for no other reason than the shameful truth of her connection to the Viscount Waters. No, looking at the icy glint in Edmund's eyes and the firm set to his mouth, he would not tolerate anyone infringing upon that which he claimed as his. For the bumble broth she'd made of her own life, knowing that Justina would be cared for would give her the courage to do this thing with Edmund. It would be the peace she found in life. Her sister would be happy and that would be enough.

At the prolonged silence, Edmund arched a single brow. "Come, Phoebe. At the very least, I would expect you to ask for something for yourself. What do you require?"

She wet her lips. "My dowry." Phoebe tipped her chin up. "I want my dowry." For eventually there would be children who she called hers and she'd not have those children dependent upon anyone the way she and her siblings were now, dependent upon their father and Edmund.

He shoved away from the door and took a step toward her. Phoebe tightened her grip upon the back of the chair. The wood bit painfully into her palms. He came to a stop six feet away and then she lightened her grip. "What will you do with your funds?"

Edmund did not say no or outright reject her request. Instead, there was a faintly mocking curiosity threading that question as though he mocked himself for putting questions to her. "That is for me to decide."

Appreciation flared in his flinty gaze. "You won't want for jewels or baubles or fabrics. Anything you desire will be yours." Anything except her freedom and happiness.

Phoebe ran her gaze over his face—this hard, implacable stranger. "Oh, Edmund," she whispered. She gave her head a sad, slow shake. "You want me, but you don't truly know me." He stilled. The dangerous narrowing of his eyes hinted at a man unaccustomed to being called out. "If you think I desire any jewels or baubles or fabrics, as you say, then you know nothing of me at all."

"Don't I?" That smooth, quiet whisper washed over her, almost tauntingly. "Do you know what I believe you'd use the funds for?"

Given his scheming machinations these days, she didn't want to feed any toying questions he'd pose and yet she wanted to know. She inclined her head, giving him a silent encouragement to continue.

"Your freedom." She started and by the triumphant glimmer in his eyes, he believed his supposition the correct one. How little they both knew of each other. "You would travel to your distant lands, like Captain Cook. Or mayhap closer. To Wales, perhaps?" He spread his arms before him. "And I shall not stop you."

Phoebe squared her gaze on his. "As your wife, you would permit me to travel?" When most gentlemen would squelch their wife's freedom, he would send her out into the world without marital strings attached? Why then, with his betrayal did his disregard pull at her heart?

"I would," he said without hesitation. "I will," he amended.

There had been so many lies between them she could not sort through them all in a weeks' time. But by the firm resolve in his eyes, she did not doubt the sincerity of his pledge. He would let her go. "You would let me go," she pressed. "Even as you insist on wedding me regardless of my feelings on the matter?"

"I would." He set his jaw at a resolute angle.

She furrowed her brow. He'd have her at any cost, but then also set her free? What sense did that make?

Edmund closed the remaining space between them, so the flimsy chair posed the only barrier. Then, he continued coming, a tiger stalking its prey and she stiffened, her body at war—conflicted with the desire for his kiss while her mind rebelled at his very nearness that threatened her reason. He stopped behind her so her back met his chest, placed his large, powerful hands upon her shoulders, and dipped his mouth close to her ear. "Do not mistake my generosity. Your freedom will not be to visit the beds of others. I will not share you." His hot breath fanned the sensitive skin at the nape of her neck and shivers of awareness shot through her.

Her eyes fluttered closed and she gave thanks that he could not see that frailty. "Y-you would demand my faithfulness?"

"Yes." He shot his tongue out and licked at the shell of her ear.

"W-would you offer the same?" She hated the stammer and question together that showed her desire for him, still.

Edmund wrapped his arm about her and stroked his hand down the front of her gown, smoothing the flat surface of her belly, as though reacquainting himself with her body. "Would you want me to offer you the same?"

He'd deliberately evaded responding to her question. He would take others to his bed. *Did you expect anything else from the notorious scoundrel, ruthless in all matters?* Why should the idea of him taking another woman to his bed eat at her like acid being tossed upon an already opened wound? Edmund's telling equivocation had the same impact of a bucket of cold water being tossed upon her ardor. She spun away from him. "Your business will be yours."

His expression grew shuttered. "We are understood then. Your freedom will be yours and mine will continue to belong to me."

At his indifference, a ball of emotion lodged in her throat and she swallowed several times to drive back the swell of pain and regret. "You offer me the freedom to travel and see the world. Don't you see? I wanted that dream with my husband at my side," she whispered. "I wanted a husband who would have torn apart with his bare hands any ship I'd ever dare climb aboard that he was not on." Edmund stilled, his face a set mask, he gave no indication that her words meant anything to him or mattered in any way. Pain cleaved her heart. She'd been a hopeless romantic, just as Honoria had charged. The hopeless part of that charge all the more aching and poignant. Phoebe took a slow, shuddery breath. "Then there is nothing else to say."

Edmund bowed. That polite, gentlemanly gesture so at odds with this feral, unrepentant blackguard, so that an image flashed to mind of him as he'd been at one time, a small boy with the lessons of polite Society ingrained into him. At what precise moment had those kind rules of decorum been coupled with this baleful, savage figure who moved by the rules of his own making?

Phoebe studied his silent departure until he opened the door, stepped into the hall, and then closed the wood panel behind him, leaving her alone. Somehow, the deal she'd made with Edmund seemed like a deal entered into with the devil. It was a deal that would see her eternally unhappy. The strength drained from her legs and she sank onto the edge of the nearest seat. She covered her face with her hands and for the first time in more years than she remembered, proceeded to weep.

CHAPTER 16

EDMUND FIXED ON THE SYNCHRONIC rhythm of his footfalls in the empty corridors of Lord Waters' home. Doing so kept him from thinking on the agony in Phoebe's eyes brought about by the edge of betrayal he'd thrust into her. She asked why he wanted her. And as he took his leave of her home, he realized—he did not know. This desire to claim her and know that no other could or would ever touch her was a consuming need that drove back all the logic and reason he prided himself upon. Yes, he wanted her. He'd prefer her as she'd been before he destroyed her innocent naiveté, but he'd have her in any way he could have her.

He turned right at the end of the corridor and collided with a small, slender figure. He immediately steadied the young woman, more girl than child.

"Lord Rutland," Justina's sunny smile ravaged at a conscience he never knew he possessed. It was winsome and innocent and hopeful. It was Phoebe's smile before this afternoon. "How lovely it is to see you."

Foolish girl. As foolish as her sister. He inclined his head. "Likewise, Miss Barrett."

An excited gleam lit the young lady's blue eyes. "Were you here to see my sister?" Her innocuous question twisted at his insides; another unwanted, unpleasant reminder that he was in fact—human. Before he could respond, she cast a furtive glance about and then returned her attention to him. She dropped her voice to a conspiratorial whisper. "My sister was ever so eager to see you." The blade of guilt twisted all the deeper—a sentiment he'd never experienced before Phoebe and, frankly, one he'd have happily gone through his life without.

"Is that so?" he asked stiffly, abhorring the image of a bright-eyed Phoebe eagerly awaiting his arrival, only to have him crush the foolish misconceptions and hopes she'd carried of him and for them.

Miss Justina Barrett gave an emphatic nod. "Oh, yes. Why, she couldn't even read her Captain Cook and then she excused herself." She lowered her voice all the more. "I think she went off to listen at the keyhole." At which point she'd heard the truth of his lies. A stone settled in his belly. "And my sister never listens at keyholes." Mischief sparkled in the girl's eyes. "I do. But not Phoebe." She prattled on and her words entered his ears and slid out, unheard. What if Phoebe had remained in the parlor with her sister, waiting and reading? Where would they be in this moment? He gave his head a shake, his lips tightening involuntarily. No, this had been inevitable. Eventually, Phoebe would have uncovered the truth of him. Better now without even more lies between them and more fanciful hopes and dreams on her part.

Suddenly, the presence of this innocent girl and her bright eyes—Phoebe's eyes—and this blasted house and the extent of his deceit, were too much. The young lady opened her mouth as though she wished to say more, but he cut into those words with a short bow. "If you will excuse me, I—"

"Rutland, my dear friend."

…am destined to be trapped here with Phoebe's siblings as a penance for my sins. He turned to greet the smiling Andrew Barrett. Of course. Tamping down impatience, he inclined his head. "Barrett, I was just—"

"I was just heading to my clubs," the man said tugging at his lapels. "Congratulations are in order, I understand." He'd wager a sum Phoebe would likely disagree with those felicitations.

He grunted as Andrew Barrett slapped him on the back. Men didn't slap him on the back and certainly not foppish dandies just out of university. Even if it was the man he'd now call brother-in-law. Alas, just like the Barrett girls, the male Barrett didn't know to be properly wary or fearful of Edmund, Marquess of Rutland.

"When is to be the happy occasion?"

Nor did they put insolent questions to him that required he share the details of his life.

Justina Barrett clapped her hands. "Oh, how splendid! A grand wedding. It shall be—"

"Justina, go abovestairs now."

They turned their heads in unison to the harsh command uttered from the entrance of the corridor. Phoebe stood with her shoulders proudly squared and glared at him with a host of loathing and fury within her blue depths.

Agony lanced at his heart and twisted the blackened organ, mocking him with the truth of some small life that resided there. He unwittingly raised his hand to his chest to rub the dull ache there. So, this was pain.

Justina's smile dipped, as she looked back and forth between Edmund and her sister. "I—I was merely congratulating the marquess on your upcoming nuptials." She wrinkled her nose. "Surely, you'd not have me be rude."

Andrew Barrett cut in before his sister could speak. "Yes, surely you'd not have her be rude. The chap," another slap on Edmund's back, "is to be our brother, after all."

A brother? Good God. Edmund dissolved into a fit of choking. Who were these people who'd welcome the devil into their fold? How, with their own father's black soul, could they not see his like soul? Phoebe narrowed her gaze on Edmund. She knew. The look in her eyes said as much. And he detested that truth with every fiber of his rotten being. "The marquess has matters of business to attend. We are to be married within the sennight."

Within the next day. By the hatred teeming from her eyes, it was wise not to point out as much.

"A sennight?" the younger Barrett's exclaimed in unison.

"Oh, well this, indeed, calls for a celebration," Phoebe's brother said and flung an arm around his shoulders.

"Andrew—" Phoebe called out.

"Isn't that right, Rutland? It only seems right as future brothers we have a celebratory drink at the clubs."

It was Phoebe's turn to dissolve into a paroxysm of coughing. The shock stamped in the lines of her face far preferable to the hatred from moments earlier and he welcomed that crack in her veneer. He held her stare. "A trip to our clubs, then." Her gasp was lost to her brother's eager response. Knowing her need to protect her sister and brother from the truth of her own circumstances, Edmund took a bold, calculated step closer, and another, until he stopped before her.

"What—?"

He captured her hands, silencing her with that subtle movement. "A pleasure, as always, Phoebe," he whispered.

If a single look could kill, he'd have been a dead heap at her furious feet. He raised her fingers to his lips and dropped a kiss atop her knuckles. A faint tremor shook her frame and he delighted in that slight quake that hinted at her awareness of him still. He dropped his lashes and studied her, wanting her, reveling in the knowledge that soon she would belong to him. What had come to pass between them could never be forgiven, but there would still be passion, and her body's desire for him, and that would be enough. His gut clenched. It had to be.

Edmund released her hand. She blinked several times and then snapped her hands to her side and buried those long fingers in the folds of her skirts. With a knowing smile that only sparked a glint of outrage in her eyes, he bowed his head and with an unwanted shadow at his side, took his leave of Phoebe.

As he exited the viscount's home, Andrew Barrett prattled on and on at his side until his ears ached. The young man accepted the reins for his mount and looked to Edmund as he swung his leg over his horse, Lucifer. "I daresay a visit to Forbidden Pleasures is in order."

He said nothing but merely nudged his horse into forward motion and rode alongside Phoebe's brother. Who was still prattling. A lot. On and on until he allowed his mind to move away from the incessant noise about the cut of his collar and tie of his cravat and instead fix upon his circumstances with Phoebe. Her profession of hate was not inconsistent with anyone else's opinion of him and that antipathy had never before mattered when the sentiments had been expressed by others. In fact, he'd quite reveled in the disdain for it kept people away. It protected him from hurt and feeling, because as a boy he'd once felt and he'd decided early on he didn't like what went with that. Her disdain, however, mattered. He guided his horse onward. Andrew Barrett fell quiet, having either run out of discourse on his garments or at last taken hint of Edmund's total lack of interest.

The crowded streets grew more and more sparse as they continued along the cobbled roads to the less fashionable end of London. They reached the front of Forbidden Pleasures and dismounted, tossing their reins to waiting servants.

Barrett rushed forward with an eagerness Edmund had never felt about any aspect of life. He started for the same five damned steps he'd climbed too many times over the years. Had he always been bored by these senseless amusements? A servant opened the door of the famed hell and he moved forward. Suddenly, a tiredness with the depravity of it all consumed him. He cast a glance back at his mount, filled with a desire to return to his own, empty home which, for the first time, was preferable to the familiarity of his clubs, when from the corner of his eye his gaze collided with two statues adorning the small brick columns framing the opposite side of the entrance. He stared unblinking at two adornments he'd passed many, many times before. Not once had he given them much notice—until now. Of their own will, his legs carried him over and he paused beside one of the ghastly pair. The hideous creature sat atop a skull and a collection of bones. His heart started.

"...On the outside, you are correct, they really appear quite fearsome. But they're not really. When you know them, when you learn all those pieces about them that you'd not ordinarily know..."

The world tilted and swayed beneath him and he gripped the edge of the column.

"Rutland?" Phoebe's brother's concerned question came as though down a distant corridor.

Instead, Edmund stood while the strong, secure walls he'd constructed about himself proved how ineffectual they'd truly been these years, cascading into a heap of useless stones about his uneven feet. Phoebe's disdain mattered because *she* mattered. He wanted to be more...because of her; more worthy, more honest, more...everything. Not the material anything, over the years that had never filled the emptiness within.

"I say, Rutland, are you all right? You have a ghastly pall about you."

He blinked back the haze of madness that clouded his vision and glanced about. Wide-eyed patrons hurriedly stepped around him. Amidst all those cowering dandies rushing by stood Andrew. Concern etched the planes of the young man's face.

He'd be concerned about him. The man who'd broken his whimsical sister's heart and illusions. It was not every day that Edmund found himself humbled by his own unworthiness. "Fine," he managed on smooth, modulated tones that could only come from years of perfecting that apathy. Relinquishing his grip upon the stone pillar, he started up the steps and entered his clubs, somehow not the same man he'd been before.

PHOEBE PACED BEFORE THE HEARTH wishing she'd donned something other than blasted slippers so there might be some kind of furious, frustrated rhythm to match the turbulent emotions swirling through her. "To the blasted clubs," she muttered to herself. "With my brother."

The audacity of him. She growled. Then, an unrepentant blackguard like Edmund, the Marquess of Rutland, was guiltier of far worse crimes than making friendly with her impressionable brother, after he'd shattered her heart and hopes. For them. Of them. She clung to the outrage of him going off with her brother, to one of those notorious hells, for it kept her from dissolving into a crumpled heap of despair over his betrayal. She fed the rage, gave it life, allowed it to become her breath. Otherwise, drawing any other air with ragged pain would be impossible and she'd cease to be.

"Why should he not be with Andrew?"

Her sister's befuddled question rang a startled shriek from her and she spun around. "Justina." *I forgot you were here.* "I—" She scrambled in search of a response other than the truth. How could she impart the truth of Edmund's deception without also destroying her sister's illusions of life? "I don't want Andrew at those hells," she easily amended. No, Edmund had stolen her innocent hope. He'd not take her sister's, too. She firmed her jaw. Just as she'd not allow him to sully her brother with his rakish ways.

From her seat upon the ivory sofa, with her knees pulled up to her chest, Justina appeared girl-like in her artless pose. "I daresay it's not the marquess' fault Andrew seeks out those clubs. He is quite scandalous in his pursuits."

Phoebe frowned. Her sister's pronouncement provided a momentary, welcomed distraction from the sting of Edmund's behavior. "Not Andrew." Her brother was good and honorable and—

Her sister snorted and swung her legs over the edge of the sofa. "Come." The fabric of her white muslin dress settled noisily at her feet. "Never tell me you'd be as trusting as Mama to fail and see the truth about Andrew." The truth about Andrew? "He really has become quite the scapegrace."

"Justina!" The exclamation burst from her. Andrew was but eighteen and just out of university. He was not one of those gentlemen to create gossip and break hearts and care about nothing more than his own pleasures. And yet...she chewed her lower lip. There was the garish attire and his mention of seeing Edmund at their clubs and... She widened her eyes. How could she have been so very blind? Over the years, her brother had become someone she didn't recognize. She turned away from her sister's sunny smile and stared down into the empty hearth. Then, as evidenced by Edmund in his scheming had made a total mockery of her feelings and love, thus showing Phoebe had a remarkable lack of insight where anyone was concerned.

She started as her sister patted her on the back. "It is all right. It does not mean he is a bad person. It just means he is a...person who enjoys things he should not enjoy," Justina finished with another one of her patent grins.

Regret pulled at her. In listening to Justina, it was much like glimpsing back at the hopelessly hopeful woman she herself had been. With that humbling thought came the aching reminder of Edmund's treachery. She ran a tired hand over her face. She'd made him out to be more than he was. The actuality of Edmund, the Marquess of Rutland, was that he was just a man broken and ruined beyond repair by life. A life she didn't truly know anything of. *But how I wanted to...* The hole where her heart had been could never be healed. She expected to always feel this knife-like agony cutting through her, mocking her for the innocence that had clouded her vision to the warnings leveled at her by Honoria.

Justina lightly squeezed Phoebe's shoulders, forcing her attention back around. "You...you do not seem unabashedly joyous at your marriage to the marquess," she put forth tentatively. "I do not understand. Why do you seem so sad if you are to wed a gentleman you very much love?"

She was so sad because she was to wed a gentleman she very much loved but knew not at all. He was someone as real as a mere wisp of a dream. Mustering a smile for her sister's benefit, Phoebe said, "I am happy." She was happy Justina would be spared from wedding one such as Edmund. Happy she would have the funds for her and her future children's freedom—if he did not merely lie to her once again with that promise. Her heart tugged with the thought of a tiny, trusting babe, born to her and Edmund's cold, empty marriage. The muscles of Phoebe's face hurt from the false smile on her lips. "I am abundantly happy," she said turning around and taking Justina's hands in hers. She shook them back and forth the way she had when playing rhyming songs in the nursery with her younger sister. "I am merely sad about leaving you." Which was not altogether untrue. Her sister, mother, and brother completed the part of her heart that had not been broken this day.

"Don't be sad about that, Phoebe. Think of it as a grand adventure!"

A pang struck her chest. How very much alike she and Justina were in that regard—both dreaming of life beyond the one that existed for them. Only now with Edmund's betrayal, the absolute naiveté of that dream mocked her. There was nothing grand about this journey she'd embark on as Marchioness of Rutland. But then, the great Odysseus' journey had proven that not all grand adventures were good ones.

A knock sounded at the door. They looked to the door as the butler appeared. "Miss Honoria Fairfax and Lady Gillian," he announced the young women and then backed out of the room.

Phoebe stared at her two friends—one ever cautious, the other always of sunny disposition—and a lump swelled in her throat. On this agonizing day, with her world ripped asunder, she needed the honesty of her emotions, of confessing all without fear of recrimination or smiling when her heart was broken.

"Hullo, Justina. Phoe—," Gillian's words trailed off as she glanced at Phoebe. She looked quickly to Honoria. The intensity of that young woman's friend's stare hinted at a jaded knowing. How much wiser and intuitive Honoria had proven to be. Not like the fanciful fool Phoebe had been.

"Hello," Justina said and dropped a curtsy. She waved to Phoebe's friends.

"Dear, will you allow me to share the splendid news with Honoria and Gillian?" she asked softly, that great lie of a request spoken for her ears.

"Of course," she said cheerily. She skipped past the young ladies and then closed the door behind her.

With her sister gone, Phoebe's shoulders sagged at the relief in not having to fake a smile or construct lies to spare her sister's sentiments. Tears welled once more.

"Oh, dear," Gillian whispered and raced over. "What is it?"

Fury flashed in Honoria's eyes. "It is the marquess," she hissed. Could there be another reason? "What did he do?"

Phoebe opened her mouth to let forth the words she needed to share, but they would not come. She pressed steepled fingers to her lips and wandered over to the window, then offered the shortest piece of the truth. "You were, indeed, correct about the marquess," she whispered.

A black curse escaped Honoria's lips; words no lady should know, and words no gentleman should even hear, and for a moment amusement warred with her inner agony. She braced for the "I-told-you-so" Honoria was entitled to…that did not come.

Her friends drifted over, but hesitated, hovering just beyond her shoulder and for that she was grateful. If they touched her or said even the wrong word she'd dissolve into another round of hopeless, useless tears.

"What happened?" Gillian prodded.

Phoebe pulled back the edge of the curtain and stared down distractedly into the busy streets below. "It was all a lie," she whispered. "All of it." The chance meetings, the moments shared, the love of Captain Cook. Had any of it been real? She quickly recounted the conversation she'd heard between her father and Edmund, every black, vile piece, only withholding that once beautiful, now shameful, act in Lord Essex's gardens. When she finished, silence met her recounting.

Honoria was the first to break the quiet. "You do not have to wed him."

She drew in a shuddery breath. "My father will allow him to

wed Justina if I do not."

"That bloody bastard." This from the usually mild-mannered Gillian. There was not a friend in the world for Edmund, the Marquess of Rutland, and with good reason.

Phoebe wiped a tired hand over her face. "It is my own fault. I was properly warned." She looked to Honoria, who slid her gaze away.

With an aggravated sound, Gillian slapped her fingers into her opposite palm, making a loud thwack. "What was your fault? That you loved him? That you believed in him when the world said not to?" She gave her head a hard, swift shake. "No, that is not your fault. That is the marquess' and it is a crime he will have to live with."

"A man such as he doesn't feel regret for those sins he adds to his collection like a lady with too many fans," Honoria said gently. "He wanted what he wanted and he's acted." Her jaw hardened. "And now Phoebe is to pay the price."

Except…Phoebe looked out to the street once more. A black lacquer carriage rumbled past, even with the distance noisy in its forward journey. Except, there had been a momentary flash of emotion in his eyes. If she didn't know the blackness of his soul, she'd believed it was pain, regret, and shame. She scoffed, immediately shoving back such foolish musings. "You are right, Honoria," she said, suffusing steel into her words. "He doesn't feel any regrets. But it is done." Their fates would be forever sealed.

Odd, how just yesterday the thought of an eternal union with him had flooded her with a heady happiness and now felt like a death knell made by an executioner. She squared her jaw. "I will be his wife, but he will never control me." Not again. Not more control than she'd already given him. He'd deceived her and that was a sin she could never, would never, forgive.

Gillian gave a pleased nod. "That is the spirit you should possess. Not this weepy, broken figure we came in to see."

Honoria nodded in agreement. "That is correct." She moved over and claimed the windowseat. "He demanded you wed him, but he also promised you your freedom should you wish it. And do you know what you will do now, Phoebe?"

She shook her head slowly and looked down at her friend.

"You will deny him any more pieces of you. Live your life. Travel, attend whatever events you wish to attend. All of them. None of them." Her friend meant to convey the greatness at Phoebe's fingertips—a freedom often denied to young ladies. But oh, how very lonely she made it all sound. "Let him have his mistresses." Oh, God. Her heart wrenched. Why did her heart wrench in this agonizing way if she did not care?

"I'll not take a lover." Not even for revenge.

Honoria grimaced. "Egads, no. We don't require anything of a gentleman. You don't want a lover."

"No," she murmured in agreement.

As the trio sat in silence, she considered Honoria's accurately spoken words. No, she didn't want a lover.

She'd only wanted love.

CHAPTER 17

THE FOLLOWING MORNING, THE CARRIAGE rocked to a halt before the Marquess of Rutland's townhouse—soon to be her new home. Phoebe's stomach turned over as she peered out the window at the white façade. Two statues, vicious lions reared on their legs, framed the entrance of the townhouse. Those same, snarling beasts adorned the knocker. A panicky laugh bubbled up her throat. Even his blasted townhouse was menacing.

"I still do not see why the marquess would not allow the marriage to take place at our home," her mother's vocalized musings drew her attention. "Highly unusual the marriage taking place so quickly and at the bridegroom's residence, no less." She wrung her hands together. "The gossips will talk."

Alas, courtesy of the viscountess' philandering husband, the gossips spoke about the Barrett family with a regular frequency. "They are already talking, Mama," Phoebe said tiredly. And they'd been since the Marquess of Rutland and his whirlwind attentions to a proper lady had earned curious stares and questions. Her gut clenched. Oh, why hadn't she paid attention to those warning hints?

"Nevertheless," her mother frowned. "The gossips will speak even more." Phoebe looked out the window once again, a hollow shell of the person she'd been. "What does it matter what they say?" Just as her mistakes could not be undone, those whispers would never be silenced as long as the ruthless Marquess of Rutland roamed amidst polite Society.

"Stop asking questions, woman," her father snapped. He dabbed his sweating brow.

She recalled the traces of the conversation she'd overheard between her father and the marquess. The tremble in her father's words, the pleading in his tone…an inherent fear of the marquess likely accounted for the perspiration now.

Her mother frowned and folded her hands primly on her lap. "I was merely asking why—"

"The marquess wants what he wants and it's not your place to question it."

From the corner of her eye, Phoebe detected the widening of her sister's shocked eyes. Fury burned in her heart for the humiliation and shame her mother had endured these years. She balled her hands into fists, so tight her nails left crescents upon her palms through the thin fabric of her gloves. Her patience snapped. "No, it is yours."

Three pairs of eyes swung to Phoebe. Her father opened and closed his mouth several times like a trout floundering on the shore.

She glared at him, willing him to see all the loathing, all the resentment, disappointment, and outrage she'd carried over the years for the useless sire he'd been. "It is your place to question," she taunted. "And your place to know all the things that matter about your family."

"Phoebe," her mother said, shock in her tone. "Do not speak to your father so."

Which only added to her fury. How dare her mother be this weak-willed, spineless figure she was. Where was her pride? Phoebe jabbed a finger out at her father's hateful face. "You have an obligation to care for us. All of us." *And you failed.* The words tumbled out of her, freeing after years of being kept buried just under the surface. "It is your place to know whether someone's intentions are honorable and to care whether those intentions are dishonorable because you care for, nay, love your children." But where had been the love in any of his dealings with Edmund?

"Put your finger down, gel," her father boomed.

A servant rapped on the carriage door. "Just a moment," Phoebe called out and her father's flushed cheeks turned all the more red at her highhanded dismissal of the driver. "I am not through with you, Father." Her marriage to Edmund represented an eternal prison, binding them and yet, there was something cathartic in knowing she would be free of her father. "You have an obligation to protect all of us. And you failed." Her mother's shocked gasp rang through the carriage. "But I will not see you fail Justina." Her dowry was to be protected. Not as he'd squandered hers on a man who had no heart and only black intentions.

Father and daughter stared at one another in silent mutiny. At one time, his withering glare would have riddled her with fear. Not any longer. For as much as Edmund's betrayal had destroyed her, it had, in other ways, strengthened her.

Justina looked between her silently fuming father and Phoebe. She furrowed her brow in confusion. "I don't understand. Don't you want to wed the marquess?"

That innocently spoken question snapped her from her furious reverie. Phoebe nodded, praying the subtle gesture was convincing enough to her ingenuous sister. "I do." *Or I did at one time.* That was close enough to add some truth to the lie.

Another rap sounded at the door, more tentative than the previous. With a dark curse, the viscount leaned over and tossed the door open. He didn't wait for the assistance of the servant but leapt from the carriage with a surprising agility for such a cumbersome man. Her mother lingered. She continued to wring her hands together, her face twisted with unease. She looked as though she wished to say something, but then avoiding Phoebe's eyes she accepted the servant's assistance and allowed him to hand her down from the carriage.

She made to follow her mother down when her sister quietly called out. "I will miss you, you know." Phoebe paused. A sad smile formed on her sister's lips. "Our house is really quite dreary when you are not in it and I dearly wish you didn't have to go, but certainly understand you must and envy you more than a little," she finished, speaking more to herself with those last handful of words.

Phoebe's heart wrenched. "I will always be here."

"No, no you won't," Justina said with that calm practicality that hinted at the woman she was becoming. "You will be here." She motioned to the menacing townhouse. "But that is fine. It is time for you to live your life free of us." She held Phoebe's gaze. "We are not yours to protect and care for." She leaned across the carriage and placed a kiss on Phoebe's cheek. "But I will love you forever for always trying." Tears flooded Phoebe's eyes. God, she was turning into a veritable watering pot. "Bah, no tears. Now, go." With a flick of her hand, she motioned to the open doorway. "It is your wedding day. Mustn't keep the marquess waiting. I suspect a man such as he is unaccustomed to being made to wait."

A man such as he...

How often were those same words uttered about Edmund? A man such as he... Society, the *ton*, her friends, her family, even Phoebe carried so many conceptions of who he was. None of them favorable. But who was he really?

She slowly disembarked from the carriage and lifted her gaze up the tall shadow of his home. The faintest flutter at the top right window caught her notice. Bold, unrepentant and unashamed Edmund stood at the floor-length crystal pane with his hands clasped at his back, his possessive gaze trained on her. A shiver ran along her spine at the coldness that was so a part of him, evident even with the space between them. She made her way toward the handful of stairs framed between those snarling lions. She'd wager her very soul that no one would ever truly know who Edmund, the Marquess of Rutland, was.

"Well, come along," her father wheedled from the opened doorway.

Squaring her shoulders, she continued her same, sedate pace, refusing to allow her father, or any man, to have one aspect of control of her decisions.

The irony of that was not lost on her as she climbed the steps and was permitted entry by the ancient butler. In a matter of moments, she would, by English law, belong to a man in every aspect that her mother belonged to her father. Her insides twisted into pained knots as she shrugged out of her cloak and scanned the expansive foyer. Phoebe studied the black marble floor flecked with white, the gilt handrail, and then she raised her gaze to the sweeping ceiling with a crystal chandelier at the center. How did anyone dare light the candles upon such a place? She swallowed hard at the dark opulence of Edmund's world.

Her skin pricked with the feel of someone's eyes upon her and she lowered her stare.

The wizened butler, with his shock of white hair and wrinkles that marked his face with the age of time, looked at her with a surprising gentleness. She fisted her skirts. Then, this man of advanced years in the marquess' household likely knew she entered the devil's lair. "If you will follow me," he spoke in even tones, conveying no hint of his thoughts or feelings. Much like his employer.

Wordlessly, her family followed along behind the butler, down corridor after corridor, turning right and then left, until she was spun around. Would she ever find her place in such a dark mausoleum? For all the ugliness that came in being the daughter of the Viscount Waters, her home had been a happy one. She peeked at the row of portraits she passed of ancestors with chiseled cheeks and aquiline noses that marked them as ancestors to the current marquess. All equally cold and unfeeling on the canvas, captured by an artist from long ago. How could there ever be happiness here with this man who would have her at all costs but for no reasons that were beautiful or, at the very least, good or honorable. His had been a matter of revenge and possession and now…ownership.

With each footfall, the panic pounded harder and harder in her breast until her feet twitched with an involuntary need to flee. The butler drew to a stop before an open door. And they arrived. Phoebe passed her gaze around the massive library. She located her brother who'd arrived earlier by horseback. Andrew grinned widely like a madman who'd just found his way out of Bedlam. Her throat tightened at the trusting innocence of even her brother who believed in the worthiness of Edmund. Unable to meet Andrew's smiling visage, she looked to the gentleman beside him who stood with a book in his hands. The vicar. The man who would say the words to forever link her to Edmund, the man whom she'd given her heart to and had only been fed lies and deception for that gift. Her panic redoubled and she looked quickly away from the bespectacled man of God. Her gaze collided with Edmund's. The butler opened his mouth to announce her family, but then dissolved into a fit of coughing. His wizened face turned red from the force of his efforts.

From where he stood, at the window with his arms still folded, Edmund gazed at Phoebe with a hard, inscrutable stare. He shifted to the servant struggling to breathe. "That will be all," he said with a harshness that brought a frown to her lips.

The servant inclined his head and then turned and left.

Her mother, ever the consummate smiler and maker of peace entered deeper into the room. She sank into a curtsy. "My lord, what a beautiful day it is for a wedding."

He cast a dubious glance out the window at the gray skies but said nothing on her mother's polite pronouncement, for which Phoebe was grateful. Her mother dealt with enough unkindness. She'd not tolerate it from this man.

"Rutland," her father said smoothing his palms over the front of his jacket. "A pleasure to see you this day."

Her bridegroom flicked a bored gaze over her father. With the sneer on his lips and the loathing in his eyes, her soon to be husband looked upon the viscount as though he were sludge dragged in on his boot. For all that had passed between them, at least they could come together in this regard. Edmund didn't return the greeting. Instead, shifting his attention to Phoebe, he spoke to the vicar. "It is time to begin."

As her family sought out chairs arranged at the front of the room, Phoebe's pulse pounded in her ears, deafening. She eyed her family seated in a neat row like geese in Hyde Park on a spring day and then cast a last, desperate glance at the door. What if she left? Surely, the marquess could not very well proceed to marry her sister, this day or any other day, not after he'd been jilted by the eldest sister.

Her gaze locked on his harsh, unrelenting stare one more time… and she knew—this was not a man who'd give a jot for Society's opinion. If he wished to wed, her, Justina, or the queen herself, the woman's fate would be sealed. With a slow, steadying breath, she walked the remaining distance over to Edmund and the vicar—ready to be married to the man who'd shattered her heart.

EDMUND STARED AT A POINT beyond the vicar's head as the man rambled on and on with the words of God and fidelity and love and trust. Words that his parents, all of Society, had proven were worth nothing more than the pages of that black book they were written upon.

"Edmund William Amery Deering, wilt thou have this Woman

to thy wedded Wife, to live together after God's ordinance in the holy estate of Matrimony? Wilt thou love her," his stomach twisted. He loved no one. "comfort her," what did an emotionally deadened man know of comforting anyone? "honour, and keep her in sickness and in health;" She would never fall sick. He'd not allow it. "and forsaking all others, keep thee only unto her, so long as ye both shall live?"

He paused to study this woman who would be his wife—his marchioness. Proud, silent, unmoving, she'd not cast another glance at him since she'd taken her place beside him in front the vicar. Fidelity, in a world where there was no honor, was a laughable clause put forth by the Church of England in an age-old vow. And yet, looking at the crown of her thick, auburn tresses and the smoky blue of her gaze…he'd not thought of bedding another and could not. Perhaps someday when he didn't burn with this fierce need only for Phoebe. For now, she was all he wanted. Terror twisted in him.

"My lord?" the vicar prodded, giving him a pointed look.

"I will."

The man nodded and then carried on with the same silly vows. There was the faintest pause before she pledged herself to him with that simple "I will".

"Who giveth this woman to be married to this man?"

The viscount inclined his head. "I, her father."

At the immediacy of that disloyal cur's words, a blanket of rage fell over Edmund's vision. How easily this man would turn Phoebe over to him—an unworthy, undeserving bastard. How easily it could have been another. A growl climbed up his throat and the vicar swallowed audibly. The book slid from his fingers and he and Edmund and Phoebe knelt to retrieve it simultaneously. From their positions upon their floor, their gazes locked. She searched his face and he knew she was looking for words of him, from him. And he wanted to be the man to give her those words she deserved and more.

But he was not that man. Edmund swiped the book and climbed to his feet. He held a hand out to Phoebe and then turned the small, black volume to the other man's care.

The ceremony continued without further interruption and with a final statement from the vicar he'd managed to rustle up, Edmund was at last married. He looked at Phoebe, frozen, her expression wan. His lips twisted in a bitter smile. Married to a woman who would rather see him to the devil than call him husband, but then she was his. And that would have to be enough to satisfy this hungering to possess her in all ways.

He grunted as Phoebe's brother slapped him on the back. "Splendid day, splendid day. Days ago I called you friend." He stuck his hand out. "Now I'll call you brother."

Edmund choked on his swallow. He didn't have brothers. Or friends. Or family. Hell, he didn't even have a single person he could bring to scratch to stand beside him on his wedding day.

"And you shall call me sister." The youngest skipped over with her hand outstretched. Oh, God this one would find herself ruined within days of her entry into Society in a handful of years if she was not carefully guarded.

Phoebe stepped between Justina and Edmund and glared at him. Her sister slowed to a halt and looked with confusion back and forth between Edmund and Phoebe. "Phoebe?"

"It isn't polite to take a gentleman's hand," his wife bit out between clenched teeth.

He took in the tight, white lines formed at the corners of her mouth and then a slow dawning understanding registered. Yesterday, when she'd overheard his discourse with her father, she'd believed he would wed Justina to settle a debt between them. But there was more to it. By God, she believed he desired her sister—a mere child. At one time that weakness would have proven useful; a seed of truth to manipulate and weaken her. Now, he detested the idea that she believed he could ever want another who wasn't her.

An awkward pall of silence descended over the room and an eager desire to be rid of the entire Barrett brood with their misguided, misplaced beliefs in him. "If you will excuse me," he said coldly eying each of the Barretts staring at him with such an eclectic array of emotions he was nearly dizzy—adoring younger brother, fearful viscount, uneasy mother, confused younger sister, and irate Phoebe. Suddenly, these five people, six with the vicar, was five too many. "If you'll excuse us," he said stiffly.

"Excuse us?" her mother parroted back. "The wedding breakfast," she blurted.

"There will be no wedding breakfast." There was no need to fuel this family's erroneous conclusion as to the man he was. No, the sooner they were gone from his townhouse and life, the sooner he could go back to reclaiming his solitary world—with now just Phoebe in it.

Mother and youngest daughter looked back and forth between each other as though in a desperate bid to make sense of his words. Andrew Barrett's faltering smile conveyed his disappointment. The viscount's fleshy jowls communicated relief. Only Phoebe's newly cynical eyes hinted at a woman not at all surprised that the man she'd just wed hadn't the decency to coordinate a celebratory feast with her family.

By their recriminating silence, he'd achieved the very goal he'd set out in through the avoidance of that meal. He never hated himself more than he did in that moment.

"Come along then," the viscount ordered his family. When no one immediately moved, he gave his wife a sharp look that propelled her into movement. The woman dropped a curtsy and a murmur of polite felicitations and then started toward her husband.

"But I don't understand." Of course the unabashed Justina Barrett would voice the very words thought by all—including Edmund himself.

A soft smile so pure and still unsullied turned Phoebe's lips as she looked on at her sister. That gentle tilt of her lips, as potent and powerful as it had been from their meeting on the Delenworth's terrace, froze him. And with it went all logical thought. His wife crossed over to her sister and took her hands. "There is nothing to understand," she said, while he stood there in silent torment over her masterful hold upon him. "The wedding breakfast is a mere formality and ours was a hastily thrown together affair. There was no time for those small details."

"Just like your gown," Justina Barrett complained.

Phoebe nodded. "Just like my gown."

Just like her gown. And the breakfast. And the whole bloody day. One more mark upon his soul. What was a missing wedding breakfast and denying a woman her wedding trousseau and the lavish affair dreamed of by most? Guilt knifed at him. Why did this fault seem the most egregious of all the other sins against him?

"Oh, very well," the younger Barrett sister said with a sigh. She gave Edmund a disappointed look and then made her way over to her parents. All but his wife and Andrew Barrett took their leave.

The younger man rocked on his heels, more hesitant than he'd proven in all their exchanges. Then, he walked over. He stuck his hand out again. "My congratulations." He cleared his throat. "My sister is a good person. An honorable one." In short, everything that Edmund was not.

He eyed it a moment and then took the offering.

"Take care of my sister," the young man finished.

"Indeed," he drawled, infusing as much bored nonchalance into those words, all the while panic churned through him. It was far easier having wed a woman whose body he craved and whose presence he wanted when he'd not stopped to think on what she meant to him. He let go of Andrew Barrett's hand swiftly and then clenched and unclenched his fingers into a fist. The other man turned to his sister and then, much like the boy he was, wrapped his arms about her and held tight. She returned that innocent embrace and patted him on the back.

She looked around her brother's shoulder. "I will be all right," she spoke quietly, those words reached over to Edmund, spoken just as much for his benefit as Andrew Barrett's. The lady had learned the skill of lying at his hands. He should be proud of that one gift he'd given her. So why did agony rip through his chest?

As though embarrassed by his show of emotion, the young man quickly released her. With flushed cheeks, he beat a hasty retreat.

And just like that, Edmund and Phoebe were alone, married—until death did part them.

The room filled with the harsh drawn breaths of his bride; the first indication she'd given of her unease. She ticked her chin up a notch and glared at him. "Now what?"

Edmund quietly pressed the door closed, leaned against the wood panel, and folded his arms at his chest. He smiled slowly. She might despise him, but he would give her more pleasure than she'd ever known possible. "And now, the wedding night, Phoebe."

CHAPTER 18

PHOEBE WIDENED HER EYES AND stared unblinkingly at the terrifying dark, tawny stranger she'd bound herself to. "The wedding night," she repeated blankly. On the heel of that came rushing forth charges made by Honoria, who'd been so very skeptical of his intentions from the moment of their first meeting. Honoria's concerns had proven right in this. What if she'd also be proven correct about the whole tying ladies up business? In Lord Essex's gardens, he'd sought to seduce Phoebe's mind and body. Now, there were no longer pretenses for him to keep up. "With you?" *Of course with him, you goose.*

"With me," he spoke on a smooth, dangerous whisper. His feral grin widened and he shoved away from the door, stalking over to her. "Certainly not another." He stopped before her, so she was forced to either crane her head back to meet his gaze or retreat.

Overwhelmed by the sheer masculinity of his broad, powerful frame, Phoebe made to edge around him. He propped his hip on the arm of the sofa and effectively killed her retreat. She wet her lips. Not in any part of his offer, nay threat, that forced her into this marriage did she ever believe theirs would be a union in name only. Most especially not after their passionate joining under the stars. "But it is not n-night." She'd naively expected the wedding night, would come…well, at night.

He brushed his knuckles along her cheek and involuntarily, her lashes fluttered. Warmth shot through her at his touch and she detested her body's weakness to him, despite his betrayal and the lies between them. "No, it is not." He lowered his mouth to hers.

A startled squeak escaped her and she ducked down and scooted past him. "I…" She searched her mind for some plausible reason to delay the consummation of their vows. This intimate act would bind them in ways far deeper than mere words alone and even more than their tryst in Lord Essex's—this represented the consummation of their marital vows. It would be a tangible linking of two beings that bound them forever in ways that moved beyond any sexual joining.

Edmund moved toward her with the lethal, predatory grace of a sleek panther. She knocked against a side table and the delicate mahogany piece tipped and swayed. Phoebe shot her hands out to steady the table and then rooted her feet to the floor. She'd not be cowed by him or unnerved by this nonsensical hold he had upon her. She would however delay…this. He was not the man in Lord Essex's gardens. And she was no longer the innocent miss who'd come to him trusting with stars in her eyes, desperate for his kisses and more.

"Surely not now. There is…" She searched the room. "Breakfast," she blurted. The ceremonial meal he'd not even deigned to have her family attend. Not that she necessarily wanted her family here on this sham of a union.

He paused. "Breakfast."

Even so, a twinge of regret pulled somewhere inside that their marriage should begin in this cold, lonely way. Why should it matter how little he cared about their wedding? After all she'd not truly given a single thought about this *special* day. And yet, he'd been so very insistent upon having her for his wife. She cleared her throat. "Breakfast. A slight repast to begin one's day." Then their marriage had begun the day more than anything. Still, there was something a good deal less terrifying in eggs and cold breakfast meats than in lying with this man whose expert touch had robbed her of her senses and awakened yearnings she'd never known a person could feel. Phoebe folded her hands together in front of her. He continued to eye her through thick, curled lashes no man had a right to, and then with a veiled look, spun and started for the door.

He was leaving? Where was the sense of victory at his rapid

departure? Why should she want to spend a moment with the heartless fiend who'd forced her into marriage…and who would have just as easily taken Justina to wife? Edmund strode over to the bell pull and tugged once.

He was *not* leaving, then.

No, he turned around and started back in her direction.

Her belly fluttered with nervousness. "What are you doing?"

A knock sounded at the door and she gave silent thanks for the momentary interruption. "Enter," he called out.

The door opened and a servant stepped inside. The young maid dropped a curtsy and cast a curious gaze momentarily in her mistress' direction before then turning her attention to her employer. "My lord?"

"A tray of breakfast," he put in coolly. A meaningless gesture from a man who did for none. This simple request was nothing more than a chore. A useless bother. "For my wife." For his wife.

The woman gave a quick nod and then backed out of the room.

He respected her so little he'd not even introduce her to his staff. Then he turned back to her and her body burned at the powerfully hot stare he trained upon her. And the matter of his staff and her breakfast and their wedding really was quite secondary to the wedding night business. For this stranger was a man who liked his ladies bound. Not the man who'd laid her down gently amidst the roses and made gentle love to her. She gulped.

Edmund took another step toward her and she held her palms up. "Stop."

Surprisingly, he did.

In an attempt to right her racing heart, Phoebe drew in a breath between her lips, filling her lungs and released it slowly. He winged an expectant black eyebrow upward. "I will not let you tie me up."

Edmund stilled.

"I-I am c-certain those are merely rumors," she stammered in a bid to fill the quiet. Phoebe cast a glance about, searching the room for those whispered about ropes, and then swiftly returned her attention to his implacable face. "I do not see. Ropes, that is." She bit her cheek at that silliness. Of course he'd keep those wicked cords in his chambers. "But I've…heard the rumors and I will not let you tie me up."

The ghost of a smile tugged at his lips, softening him in ways that were mere illusory in nature. There was nothing gentle about him. "They are not rumors." Except his silken whisper. *That* was smooth and washed over her like a hot sun on a midsummer's day. And then she registered his words.

Involuntarily, her eyes flew wide, but she was saved from responding as he pulled the door open and allowed the servant entry with a silver tray. Breakfast. She swallowed hard. As though she could entertain thoughts of food with that shocking admission. The maid averted her gaze and then quickly rushed out, pulling the door closed behind her.

Edmund turned the lock and they two were alone—again.

Suddenly, this effort he made of going through the world terrifying all—men, women, children—and her, grated on her already frayed nerves. She settled her hands on her hips and glared at him. "I will not be afraid of your lies."

"It is not a lie—"

"Or your angry whispers and hard stares and surly disposition. I—" *It is not a lie.* As in Honoria had, in fact, been correct and Edmund, the Marquess of Rutland, did, in fact, tie up women. "Oh." In light of all the treachery he'd practiced upon her, should she truly be surprised by that admission? And yet, disappointment stabbed at her. Her arms trembled and she swiftly lowered them back to her side, lest he see the effect his words had on her and take some unnatural delight in disapproval.

So lost in her thoughts, she failed to notice his approach. She stiffened as he ran the pad of his thumb over her lower lip. "Those women wanted it." The flesh quivered at his caress. He brushed his lips over hers once. "And you will, too."

That is what he'd say? He'd speak of the scandalous ladies who'd occupied a place in his bed, on their wedding night, no less? She glanced at the long-case clock tick-tocking away. Rather, their *wedding night* morning. Bitterness swelled deep inside. It churned in her belly and turned her insides in knots until pain melded with regret and anger. How had her mother managed to smile all these years? Phoebe wrenched away. His hand fell back to his side. "Then you should have wed one of those women, Edmund, for I am not one of those who will delight in your dark deeds and shameful acts. The man I'd want is good and does not want me bound in any way, but free and strong and happy." She gave her head a shake. "And that man is not," nor will ever be, "you." With stiff legs, she stalked past him, turned the lock, and slipped from the room. She'd been wrong. It appeared there were more parts of her heart to break. For with his casual talk of others on her wedding day, he had managed to break the rest of that foolishly hopeful organ.

EDMUND STARED AT THE DOOR his wife had disappeared through. He'd hurt her. Again. He scrubbed his hands over his face and cursed roundly.

This, the seduction of his wife, was to have been the easy part. He was bloody rot with all the warm endearments and gentleness she both desired and craved, but the matter of her body—that he knew. He knew how to make a woman scream with pleasure, knew just how much pressure to apply to each crevice until she pleaded for more. The memory of Phoebe's breathless cries and whispery moans were testament to his mastery of her body. And yet... *I am not one of those who will delight in your dark deeds and shameful acts...* Such would never be enough for Phoebe. Edmund dropped his hands to his side. Then, with this shiftless, shapeless, amorphous world she'd thrust him into, there was nothing easy anymore in his life. He no longer knew up from down or left from right.

She'd cared that he'd spoken of other women on their wedding night. Even if it was to have been a matter of assurance. Each one of those scandalous ladies had begged to be tied and bound and then ultimately pleasured...and not a single one of them had minded he'd been with any others. In fact, they'd seemed to delight in taking the feared Marquess of Rutland to their beds.

Phoebe, however, had clearly minded. That damned hurt had glowed in her eyes so that he would have gladly removed his own right arm if it would have spared her from the pain bleeding through the fathomless blue irises. Before her, he would have said the worst thing was *caring* whether or not he'd hurt her. That no longer held true. Now, the worst thing was not knowing how to stop her from hurting.

Footsteps shuffled in the hall and he looked up expectantly. Disappointment settled like a stone in his belly. He'd welcomed the prospect of Phoebe returning, spitting mad and her finger wagging…than not at all. "Wallace," he greeted his stubbornly loyal butler with wooden tones.

"My lord," the older man said and inclined his head. "I have taken the liberty of having one of the maids show Her Ladyship to her chambers."

He stared blankly at Wallace. The man tilted his head forward and gave him a direct look. His butler expected something of him where Phoebe was concerned. Short of reversing time, there was little he could do regarding his mention of previous lovers. On his and Phoebe's wedding day. Wallace wagged his bushy brows. Edmund shook his head.

A rheumy smile twinkled the older servant's eyes. "Perhaps Her Ladyship would care for her morning meal."

He gave a tired sigh. "I will have a servant bring it up."

Wallace coughed into his hand. "My lord, I think it is best if you bring Her Ladyship her meal."

He cocked his head. "Me?" Aside from his miserable company, the last thing or person his wife cared for was the morning meal.

The servant nodded. "You."

Edmund looked to the tray and then to the door and then back to the old butler. The man was loyal and faithful and really the closest person he had to a friend in this world, but he was going mad in his advancing years if he suspected Phoebe wanted to share the same room with him. Then, Wallace hadn't overheard the exchange involving bondage and mention of previous lovers. He cringed. Yes, in retrospect that really wasn't a matter fit for a lady's ears—on her wedding day. From her husband, no less.

Determined as he was faithful, Wallace reached for the tray. Edmund sighed and intercepted the man's slow movements. "I have it," he muttered. With the burden in his hands, he started for the door.

"And perhaps, if I might be so bold," Wallace called after him, staying his movements. "A wedding gift, my lord, perhaps?"

A wedding gift. Of course, women adored baubles and trinkets and would expect glittering gemstones as some kind of token. *Then you should have wed one of those women, Edmund, for I am not one of those…* Wallace quietly took his leave.

Tray in hand, Phoebe's words churned around his mind, Edmund scanned his gaze over the library. Practically a room unused during his parents' living years, it was free of memories of his youth and for that he came here often for silence and the privacy of his thoughts. He shifted the burden in his hands and eyed the room. Edmund set down the tray; a tray of rapidly cooling food and eyed the floor-length walls of leather bound volumes. He started over to one shelf and perused the titles. A collection of blue leather tomes etched in gold lettering brought him to an immediate stop. Edmund pulled the book from the shelf and flipped it open to read the author's note at the front. His heart started in a peculiar way. Over a blasted book. "You are driving me, mad, Phoebe Barrett," he muttered. Nay, not Barrett. Deering. He snapped the book closed, and then with his meager offering set, it down upon the tray and resumed his march to her chambers.

With each footfall that brought him closer, the blasted uncertainty and indecision grew. He gritted his teeth. How much simpler his life had been when he didn't feel or worry about anyone but his own pleasures. But now he cared and that could not be undone. Edmund drew to a stop beside his wife's chamber doors, recalling back to another time he'd come to a halt outside the guest chambers. His father at his side, his strong, commanding hand on his smallish shoulder. He'd looked up at his sire, who'd stared at the wood panel, and hadn't understood the vitriol, the loathing which burned from his eyes. Until he opened the door. And then Edmund had known. From then on, he had known all—about his parents and love and innocence and, more importantly, the ugliness of life. Violently thrusting aside those musings he'd kept buried for the better part of his life, he pressed the handle. Surprise shot through him when the handle easily turned.

He stepped inside and immediately located her. His body was attuned to her body's nearness, as it had been from their exchange that moment beside her Captain Cook's exhibit. She stood with her shoulder angled to him, pressed alongside the window with the curtain peeled back. For a moment he suspected she'd not heard his entry, but then she spoke in a tired tone that indicated she'd heard, and worse, didn't care. "What do you want?"

He shifted on his feet, feeling like a boy who'd been caught nipping some gent's purse of coin. *You. I want you. Only you.*

At his silence, her narrow shoulders stiffened, but she still did not turn to face him. "I suspect you've come to consummate our marriage."

One time, that would have been the most important, nay the only important, aspect of their relationship. He would rut himself to ecstasy between her sweet thighs. She would take him keening and crying with desire. They would have been sated. Now that was no longer enough. He wanted more of her than that quick coupling in Lord Essex's garden. In ways he still did not fully understand, nor could piece together with his sullied spirit. No, despite her otherwise apt opinion, it was not what brought him here.

Edmund tried to form words, but for some reason he could not coordinate the blasted movement between his brain, his mouth, and his heart. His fingers tightened reflexively about the edge of the tray. "I am sorry." The words burst from him, explosive and harsh.

At his gruff apology, Phoebe stiffened, but otherwise gave no indication that she cared. And why should she? The man he was, who'd never humbled himself after Margaret Dunn had made a fool of him on a field of honor, wanted to turn and run at being flayed open before Phoebe now.

He tried again, gentling his tone. "I am sorry." The man he was now would not let him leave. Those words still emerged gravelly and hardened, but then that is who he'd been for the better part of his life. He could not change who he was in all the ways he wished he could, not even for Phoebe.

She wheeled slowly around to face him, but still she remained silent torturing him with the quiet. He slid his gaze to a point beyond her shoulder. "There have been women before you." Lonely, miserable ladies as cynical and jaded as himself. Women trying to fill their own empty, meaningless lives. Edmund returned his gaze to her heart-shaped face. How had he once thought her plain? How had he not seen the fire of her spirit or the luxuriant auburn tresses that marked her as a very real Athena? "But I have not been with a woman since the moment I met you." Initially, he'd been so preoccupied with his scheme involving Margaret Dunn's niece and his quest for revenge. Now, he barely remembered there had been a woman named Margaret in his past. "And right now, all I know is I want you." *Only you.* At his admission,

Phoebe remained frozen, unblinking; those eyes that had once been a window into her soul and thoughts, this time blank. Her gaze alighted on the tray in his hands and then flew back to his face. Surprise lit her blue irises.

He hastily set down the burden, feeling exposed by her silent scrutiny. To give his hands something to do with purpose, he picked up the book and held it aloft. "I brought you a book. For our wedding." He winced, as the words left his mouth at how ineffectual a gift this was. An old book taken from his already existing library.

She fluttered a hand about her breast and just touched the tips of her fingers to her chest.

"It is merely a book that was already a part of my collection," he felt compelled to point out. There were enough lies that he, at the very least, owed her the truth of this book's origins. Edmund studied the gold lettering a moment and then held it out to her. "I thought you might like it."

They remained like that. He with his hand outstretched with the damned book in his hands, and she with her hand clasped to her chest. When she made no move to accept the offering, he forced his hand back to his side. He tossed the book down upon the tray where it landed with a thump. The silver clattered noisily, rattling the porcelain plate and silverware arranged by Cook. He dug deep and worked at hastily reconstructing the broken walls she'd shattered with her presence in his life. "If you'll excuse me," he said stiffly and made to go.

"Don't!" she called out. He stopped and shot a backward glance at her.

Phoebe's chest rose and fell with her slow, deliberate breaths. His gaze wandered lower and he proved himself the selfish bastard he'd always been, for he took in the exposed cream of her décolletage. A hungering to possess her slapped at him once more. When he forced his gaze away from the generous mounds of her flesh, he found her bold stare trained on him.

"Don't leave." She wet her lips and then said, "Stay."

CHAPTER 19

STAY. WHAT MADNESS WAS THIS in asking him to stay? He, the unrelenting, unforgiving Marquess of Rutland had come with an apology and a gift? She eyed him suspiciously. "Is this another of your games, Edmund?"

He gave his head a brusque shake. "No game," he said, the words a terse statement of fact.

Phoebe took several tentative steps toward this stranger she was now wed to; a man she'd loved in error and folly. She came to a stop beside him and the tray he'd brought and glanced down at his offering. Her heart turned over. Which was really quite odd, when her heart had been so thoroughly broken and shattered, destroyed beyond repair. And yet, in this instance, staring down at John Britton's *Beauties of England and Wales*, her heart felt very much alive. With hesitant fingers, she scooped up the book and ran them over the gilt lettering.

"It is about England and Wales." His gruff statement filled the silence.

She lifted her eyes from the small volume. "I see that," she murmured.

"You'd spoken of traveling to Wales and—" He dragged a hand through his dark, unfashionably long locks. There was a faint tremble there hinting at his unease; this stoic, unflappable man became, just then, very human. "It is not new," he rambled on. "As you can see. It should have been new," he said under his breath. "At the very least it—"

"It doesn't have to be new and shiny and perfect to be a worthy gift, Edmund," she said, pulling his offering close to her chest. He still did not understand. "It is not the outer piece that matters, but rather what is underneath. That is what matters."

A flush stained his cheeks as he clearly interpreted the words she meant for him to hear. Then he tugged at his lapels. "Yes, well—I will leave you to attend your meal and your reading, my lady." *My lady*? She cocked her head while he backed away from her as though she were a viper poised to strike Then, on the heel of that was his earlier talk of women and their ties and ropes, and an ugly niggling played at the edges of her mind. "Are you going to one of your ladies?" She should be glad if he did and yet unwelcome jealousy twisted at her insides. Phoebe folded her arms close and tried to dull the pain of his inevitable betrayal. To no avail.

Her words brought him to a slow halt. Edmund lowered his eyebrows and with slow, languid steps closed the distance he'd placed between them. "Would you like that?" There was a clipped harshness to his question that hinted at the truth—her words mattered to him in some way.

Phoebe wanted to strike out at him. A flippant response formed, but then stuck in her throat. For all the lies and deception between them, it would break her in ways her mother had never been broken the day Edmund took a lover. Not for the shame that would come with that, but for what that said of the end of a dream she'd once had for them. She gave her head a jerky shake. "No. I would not like that."

With his open palm, he caressed her cheek. "You still do not know," he whispered.

She leaned into his touch, hating herself for her weakness, and hating him more for this hold he had upon her. "Kn-know what?"

Edmund leaned down, so their lips were a hairsbreadth apart. The faintest trace of coffee and mint clung to him and she inhaled deeply of that sweet and potent scent and allowed it to fill her senses. He brushed his lips faintly over hers and she wanted to cry out at the fleetingness of that exchange as he drew back. He folded his large hand over the nape of her neck and angled her head. "I only want you," he said, his tone harsh, as though angry with himself and her for that admission.

Her heart flipped unto itself and then he claimed her mouth under his in a hard, punishing kiss. Passion exploded between them as he slanted his lips over hers again and again. She moaned and with that slight parting of her lips, he thrust his tongue deep into her mouth. Her legs weakened, but he easily caught her to the hard wall of his chest, anchoring her against him, preventing her from dissolving into a puddle of nothing but hot sensation at his feet. He stroked her tongue with his and she met that determined movement, returning his kiss. There would be time enough for regrets later for surrendering to this—to him. For now, there were only this moment and them.

Edmund swept her up and with long, quick strides carried her to the bed. As he laid her down, he broke contact with her lips, and she cried out, aching for his kiss. His thick, smoky black lashes swept low, but not before she saw the hot flare of desire in his chocolate brown eyes—desire for her. For everything that had come to pass between them, she exulted in this small sliver of power she had over him. He shrugged out of his jacket and tossed it to the floor where it landed with a noisy thump. Next came his snow white cravat. Phoebe propped herself up on her elbows. She should look away. Any polite, proper, and decent young lady would avert her gaze from the sight of man disrobing before her.

Then, her wild abandon in Lord Essex's gardens was proof that there was nothing polite, proper, or decent about her. Phoebe could no sooner tear her gaze away from Edmund as he pulled the white lawn shirt over his head, than she could slice off her smallest left finger. She was a wanton. There was nothing else for it. Edmund tossed his shirt atop the rapidly growing pile of clothes and climbed on the bed, prowling forward much like that sleek, black panther, forever frozen at the oddities shop, back when the world had been right for her and Edmund. Except this man, who now guided her up and set to work unfastening each tiny button along the length of her back. would never be so weak as to be trapped. Not like that poor panther. Edmund, with his strength and power, could reign over even the strongest of those jungle creatures. He slid button after button free of its delicate eyehole. Then the cool air slapped her back through the thin, flimsy fabric of her chemise.

"So beautiful," he whispered, placing his lips to each inch of skin he exposed.

Tingling shivers of awareness shot down her spine and she arched her neck. "N-no," she managed to rasp out. "Th-there doesn't have to be lies in this. Let this be the one h-honest thing between us." She at the very least wanted this of him. He dragged her hand to his lips and pressed a firm kiss to her wrist, and then placed it on his chest. The rapid pounding beat of his heart thumped beneath her fingers; a testament to his need for her. "My heart does not lie." Not in this. Just in the ways that mattered. As though sensing the bitter path her thoughts had pulled her down, he claimed her lips once more. There was nothing gentle or apologetic about this kiss. It was a man branding a woman as his, and she pressed herself against him, taking his mouth with an equal intensity, marking him as hers. If just for this moment.

A breathless moan escaped her as he expertly slid the gown downward, moving it past her legs, and leaving her in nothing but her undergarments. That moan became a sharp cry when, through the fabric of her chemise, he cupped her right breast. As he weighed that round flesh in his palm, her head fell back and she gave herself up to the sensation. He captured the swollen peak between his thumb and forefinger and teased the sensitive flesh. Pleasure ran through her and she shot her quaking fingers to his head and gripped his long, dark hair and held him to her. Edmund continued to tease at the tip until a scorching heat spiraled through her and pooled at the juncture of her thighs, filling her with such hunger she'd go mad if he didn't alleviate the empty ache within.

Phoebe groaned in protest when he pulled away. The tense set of his mouth and the agony reflected in his eyes might as well have been a mirror into this desperate hunger she herself now knew. "From the moment I met you, I longed to have you naked, with your hair draped about our entwined limbs," he whispered, and disentangled one hair comb from her intricately arranged hair.

"S-surely not the first moment." After all, their first meeting had been born on the wings of a lie.

"Yes, the first." He tossed it to the nightstand and then paused to run his gaze over her face. "I just didn't realize it." He reached for the other gold comb and freed her hair.

Yet this was not the first time they'd join their bodies as one. "B-but you already had me."

"Not like this, Phoebe," he said, his gravelly voice, harsh with desire? Regret? Surely he was incapable of that sentiment.

SHE'D DESERVED HER FIRST MOMENT to be made more than that quick coupling in Lord Essex's gardens. Edmund swept his lashes low. Yes, that time could not be undone… but he would take his time loving her and learning every contour of her delicate frame.

Phoebe's auburn tresses tumbled in a shimmering cascade about her naked shoulders and the sight of her, an olive-skinned, lithe beauty to rival those spiteful Greek goddesses, stirred his emotions. Never before and never again would he hunger for a woman more than he did her. His ears filled with the raggedness of his own breath and hers as they joined their hands as one.

With an almost physical pain at his body's surging awareness of her, he ran a hand down the satiny smoothness of her forearm, lower and lower. With sure movements, he enfolded her hand in his and slid his fingers into hers so they were joined in unison—interlocked in ways he'd never before been. His vision was transfixed by the sight of the union of their hands, her fingers graceful, long, and delicate and his hard, dark, and scarred—an unlikely pairing—and somehow all the more perfect for it.

The muscles of his throat moved in a reflexive swallow. Until Phoebe, he'd never bothered to hold a woman's hand in bed. There had been no need. Nothing but a mindless, soulless desire had driven his past. Until now. Until her hand. Her fingers.

"What is it?" Phoebe's hoarse question brought him to the moment.

He gave his head a shake and raised her fingertips to his lips. "You are perfect," he said again. With swift, sure movements he removed her chemise and the remainder of her undergarments. For every woman who'd come before her melted away into a faceless, nebulous shape so all he saw, all he wanted to see, was Phoebe.

Her cheeks pinkened under his stare. "You no doubt say that to ev—"

Edmund crushed her lips under his once more, swallowing those words, willing her to feel the truth, when her mind could not believe it. In one fluid movement, he laid her down and came over her. He reached between them and teased the damp auburn curls that shielded her womanhood.

Her hips arched off the bed. "Edmund," she gasped and bucked into his touch.

She might despise him for his crimes against her, but her body hungered for his. That would be enough. It had to be. "Do you want this, Phoebe?" he reveled in her panting, raspy moans of desire. He teased her pleasure nub until she cried out. "Tell me," he demanded harshly, pressing the heel of his hand into her. "I do," she moaned, her hips arching back, seeking, searching.

Edmund drew his hand back to her sharp cry of protestation, but moved slowly down her body. He dragged his mouth over hers, trailing kisses down her neck, lower.

Phoebe shot her hands out and clasped her fingers in his hair. With a wanton urging that sent blood racing to his shaft, she dragged his head to her right breast. He hovered with his mouth poised over her soft skin, gleaming with moisture. "Do you want my mouth on you here, Phoebe?" he whispered and brushed a faint kiss over her nipple.

Her thick lashes fluttered open. "I do," she rasped.

Masculine triumph ran through him and he darted his tongue out teasingly and, to her cry of protest, he continued lower. He lowered his face between her thighs.

She came up on her elbows. "Wh-what are you doing—?" Her words ended on a shattered scream and she fell back on the bed, as he pressed his mouth to her core.

Edmund slipped his tongue inside and caressed her, laving her hot, throbbing center until she thrashed her head wildly upon the pillow. The taste of her sweet and more potent than any spirit he'd consumed drove him to the edge of madness. He pushed his tongue deep inside, working her until she pumped her hips toward his mouth in swift, jerky movements that indicated she was nearing that point of her body's surrender. Edmund drew back. "Please," she begged and ran her fingers down his back in a bid to pull him close, but in a frantic need to free himself, he shoved off his breeches and kicked them over the bed.

Her lips parted on a soft moue and with that softening, he drew her up, flush to his frame. A harsh groan escaped him, broken and shattered at the burn of her satiny soft skin against his. With an ache to feel her hand upon him, he drew her small palm to his chest.

She toyed with the mat of hair on his chest and then the same bold woman who'd danced away from Society's reach at Lord Essex's rubbed the flat circle of his nipple.

He hissed and she picked her head up. "Did I hurt you?" Several lines creased her brow.

In response, Edmund took her hand and brought it lower, guided it down to the burgeoning member that stood out in reach for her. He paused and studied her; aching to know her touch on his naked flesh, without the barrier of cloth between them this time. But he'd not take his own pleasure at the expense of her uncertainty.

The air left him on a swift exhale as Phoebe stroked the head of his shaft. She looked up quickly, as though to ascertain whether she'd caused him more than this pleasure-pain, and then swiftly returned her attention to exploring the size and feel of him. She ran the tip of her index finger up and down the length of him; that feathery, light caress an exotic torture he'd have given his entire landholdings, his title, and every material possession to forever know. And since he'd already consigned himself to Hell for many sins before this, with his hand, he guided hers about his hardened member and showed her the slow, up and down rhythm.

His head fell back on a pained groan as she began working him with a seductive hold both innocent and brazen that he nearly spent in her hands like some inexperienced youth.

He wrenched away and she furrowed her brow. "I'm sorry—"

Edmund kissed her hard, momentarily silencing her and then pulled back. He ran his gaze along her face, memorizing the delicate planes as well as the faint birthmark on the lobe of her right ear. In an imperfect world, she was the only piece of perfection. "You never have to be sorry for anything that happens here in this bed, between us. Ever," he said on a gruff command and then closed his mouth over the turgid bud of her breast once more.

Phoebe cried out and tangled her fingers in his hair, holding him in place, and urging him on with her pleading moans. Gently, he drew the swollen tip between his lips and then swirled his tongue over it until the room filled with her cries. Passion licked away anything but the feel, scent, and sounds of his wife in her unrestrained pleasure.

Guiding her down onto her back once more, he came over her, and parted her thighs with his knee. Edmund worked his eyes over her flushed cheeks and then locked his gaze squarely with hers. "I have ached for this moment since Lord Essex's. I will never have enough of you."

Those were the closest words of endearment he could or would ever give her. In response, Phoebe splayed her legs open. A wall of emotion slammed into him, humbling him with her unwarranted offering in light of his betrayal. Her arms came up and she wrapped them about him, holding tight.

Then with a groan he slid himself into her welcoming, wet heat.

Phoebe cried out and wrapped her arms about him.

This meeting was not the gentler, more tentative meeting when he'd last joined his body with hers in Lord Essex's gardens. Now, they moved with a primitive savagery. He thrust himself hard and deep inside her. Over and over again. And she lifted her hips in perfect rhythm to his body's movements.

Low, hungry moans slipped past her lips. "Edmund."

Sweat beaded his brow and dripped into his eye. He fought the surge of desire threatening to take him under and urged her onward to her pleasure. "Come for me," he demanded. "Come."

Phoebe's body went still and then her eyes flew wide. "Edmund?" His body stiffened as he crested the precipice of release and then he was hurtling forward, careening in a blinding flash of light and color, and Phoebe was coming with him. He stiffened, his shaft spurting his hot seed deep inside her womb, filling her.

Dragging in great, gasping breaths, Edmund collapsed atop his wife. He lay there, eyes closed, relishing in Phoebe's own shuddering breaths. *I will never have enough of you…*

Phoebe's gentle caress up and down his back brought his eyes slowly open. "Edmund," she whispered.

"Yes, love?"

She stilled at the endearment that had slipped out unheeded, unchecked. A slow smile formed on her lips, terrifying him with the emotion there. "You are crushing me."

With a curse, he immediately rolled off her. He pulled her into the fold of his arm and drew the blankets over them. There would be time for the resentment and anger that had brought her to this union later. For now, there was peace. With Phoebe's auburn tresses a silken curtain wrapped about them, Edmund closed his eyes.

CHAPTER 20

THE FAINTEST RUMBLE AT HER back penetrated Phoebe's slumbering. Her body hot like the kiss of a sun on a summer's day, she wanted to close her eyes and lose herself in that soothing warmth once more. Then a loud snore filled the room. Her lids fluttered open and she stared at the pale yellow wallpaper—the unfamiliar pale yellow wallpaper. She tried to make sense of her surroundings: the heat, the snoring, and then she remembered.

God in heaven. She was married. To the notorious Marquess of Rutland, who'd only begun a false courtship to bring him closer to Honoria and who'd threatened to destroy her family if she did not wed him. That truth still ran through her heart with the same raggedness as the moment she'd overheard him speaking to her father yesterday morn. Had it only been yesterday?

She scooted out from under the fold of his powerfully strong, well-muscled arm and turned on her side to look at him. Something pulled inside at the peaceful, unguarded evenness of the chiseled planes of his face. A loose, black curl tumbled over his brow, softening him. She propped her head in her palm and continued to examine this man she'd married.

A slight smile twitched at the corners of his lips and there was nothing hard or cynical and practiced in this most honest of reaction of his sleep. What did a man like Edmund dream about that brought him to smile? Another shuddery snore escaped those lips and in his sleep, he rolled onto his back. The sheet slid down his frame further revealing the broad wall of his naked chest matted with tight, black curls.

She slid her gaze over to the tray he'd brought in earlier; the food forgotten upon it, and that small leather book there, a conundrum wrapped in leather with gold lettering. What need had there been for him to select a book for her and deliver a tray of breakfast to her? A man so viciously methodical and whispered about by Society for his ruthlessness would not worry over his wife's hurt feelings. That man Society loathed and feared wouldn't give a jot if his wife had been hurt by talk of the women who'd come before. Nay, that man would delight in the weakness shown. Phoebe returned her attention to Edmund. But he'd not delighted in her hurt or sought to use it as a weapon with which to further manipulate her. He'd come with an apology. She inched closer and trailed the tips of her fingers over his bare chest.

My heart does not lie...

"Who are you, Edmund?" she whispered. The man who'd have his revenge at all costs? Or the man who knew her interests and in an attempt to right her hurts, would humble himself with an apology.

As though disturbed by her questioning even in his sleep, he shifted. That slight movement further dislodged the sheet and it slid lower. She reached for the soft fabric to pull it back into place and a horrified gasp escaped her. A vicious, white, puckered scar traversed from the corner of his right hip down to the middle of his thigh. She shoved herself up from her reclining position and came to her knees. The angry mark upon his otherwise perfect skin displayed a vicious injury. *I dueled for a lady's heart...* This was the mark he bore, as a testament to that former love. Agony swept over her at the prospect of this tall, powerful, commanding figure forever silenced. With the pain he'd caused her, she cared for Edmund still. Phoebe reached tentative fingers to that mark when a powerful hand shot out and circled her wrist.

Her heart thundered hard and her gaze flew to Edmund. He eyed her through thick, hooded, black lashes that revealed little of his thoughts. She swallowed hard and mustered a smile. "G-good morning."

"Afternoon. It is afternoon."

"Is it?" Her voice emerged on a high squeak.

"And the same day."

She looked to the window. She'd been Miss Phoebe Barrett, then found herself wedded to Edmund and now titled the Marchioness of Rutland, and had made love to him...and this had all been the same day? How many changes a person could undergo in so very little time. Phoebe pulled her hand back and he quickly released her. Her skin pricked with the heated intensity of his stare.

"Surely you'll ask the question?" His harsh baritone belied the just previously resting gentleman with a smile in his sleep.

A man who snored like a bear in winter and grinned like a naughty boy while he slumbered did not evoke the same fear a man such as the Marquess of Rutland's legendary ruthlessness did. Phoebe skimmed her fingers over his scar once more. "Is this from your duel?" For another woman. A woman he'd loved. He stiffened at her touch, but made no attempt to pull away. Otherwise, he remained stoically silent and she suspected he did not intend to answer. Disappointment swelled at the boundaries he'd keep between them, even married as they were. She stared at that angry scar. It should not matter, his silence. There were no illusions of love on his part; not the way she'd foolishly, optimistically hoped during his pretend courtship. She pulled the sheet close and swung her legs over the edge of the bed then made to rise.

"It is."

Phoebe froze. She glanced over her shoulder to gauge his reaction to that admission. As usual, his inscrutable expression gave no indication to his thoughts. "Who did you duel for the lady's love?" She could not keep the bitterness from her words and hated it for the weakness it revealed for this man, still with his treachery.

Edmund sat up and the sheet dipped lower. "The Earl of Stanhope."

The name meant nothing to her. Recently wed to Lady Anne Adamson, there was a scandal surrounding their own marriage, but she'd never bothered with the details of scandals and such. Now, in this, she wished she'd attended more closely.

He settled his hands upon her shoulders and she stiffened. "In the end she chose neither of us." His hot breath fanned the skin of her neck, stirring the loose curls that hung haphazardly over her shoulder. "It was for naught. It did not earn me the lady's love."

It did not earn me the lady's love. If the duchess had, in fact, chosen Edmund, what a very different man he'd be than this twisted creature bent on revenge. That somehow made her agony all the more painful. Her belly twisted in a hard knot. Edmund stroked his hands up and down her forearms in a seductively soft, soothing rhythm.

"I was young," he confessed, touching his lips to her neck.

Was she so very transparent in her thoughts? How unsophisticated she must be to this worldly, jaded man.

She hated that she craved his kiss as she did, hated that she was so attuned to his every caress when she meant so very little to him. "How old were you?"

"Twenty-one."

The same age as she was now. Old enough to know one's heart. Her throat worked. She pulled back, but he applied a gentle pressure to her arms, as though willing her to stay because he needed her there, which was madness. "How very much you must love her."

"I don't love anyone," he replied with an icy automaticity that lashed at her weak heart. Of course he couldn't love anyone—her included. Even knowing the ruthless scoundrel he was, why should that cause this vicious agony in her breast? She looked sadly back at him. "Everyone loves someone. Even if it is only themselves."

A slight scowl marred his face, a slight indication he'd detected her unintended barb. "I did not love her," he said setting his jaw at a mutinous angle.

Phoebe pulled away again and this time he made no move to stop her. She stood and tugged at the coverlet, holding it close to her naked frame, shielding herself from his eyes. "You protest any time I mention your loving your Margaret—"

"She is not my Margaret."

"And yet you'd involve me and Honoria and my father and," she slashed the air with one hand. "God knows whoever else so you might exact some revenge on the woman." She tipped her chin up. "Do you still intend to have your revenge on her for a past hurt?" Phoebe held her breath, bracing for his response. He remained silent and with his lack of words, provided all the answer she required. "I would ask that you set aside this vengeful life you've set for yourself, Edmund." Otherwise, it would destroy the remaining part of him that was still good. The part of him that could say sorry and carry silver trays with meals for a wife he'd inadvertently hurt, and a gift of a book that spoke of a man who'd listened to her interests and hopes.

An impatient sound escaped him; part growl, part moan. "You do not understand."

"Then make me."

A muscle jumped at the corner of his mouth. A man who evoked fear in the hearts of most in Society was likely unaccustomed to having orders put to him. She released the breath as disappointment filled her. "Simply saying you did not love her does not make it true." Phoebe readjusted her hold on the coverlet, tightening her grip. That slight muscle continued to tic away at the right corner of his lip. "And you still don't realize that loving someone doesn't make you weak." She dropped her gaze to the rumpled sheets. Or perhaps it did. After all, was she truly any stronger for loving? "Is she why you ceased believing in love?"

Edmund came up to his knees in one fluid motion. Unrepentant in his nakedness, he brushed his knuckles along her jawline. At that slight caress, she started. "I ceased believing in love long before Margaret." His use of the woman's Christian name somehow made this aching hole in her chest all the wider. Edmund paused that gentle caress and his mouth tightened. "I learned early on at my parents' marriage. There is no love. There are simply people who would have their pleasures and take them. Love is an empty, useless emotion."

"My parents' marriage is not a happy one," she reminded him.

"My mother took my father's brother as her lover," he said bluntly.

She gasped. For her father's shamefulness, this level of treachery Edmund spoke of was foreign.

The unholy smile on her husband's lips mocked her for her innocence and she recognized it as a protective grin he adopted to shield himself from inquiries into his life. "What, nothing to say?" He captured a loose curl between his thumb and forefinger and rubbed the tress almost distractedly. "Will you have me tell you how my father ordered me from the nursery and forced me to the room where my mother and uncle rutted like beasts?"

Nausea churned in her belly. *Oh, God.* He'd once claimed she knew nothing about him. And Lord forgive her, these were the pieces of Edmund Deering she'd not known. Pieces that explained the puzzle of the man he'd become. "Would you hear more?" A hard glint sparked to life in his eyes. "Or shall I not sully your innocent ears any further?"

The taunting barb, no doubt, was intended to silence her and end his telling, and yet…the pleading in his eyes, begged for her to hear these parts he'd shared with no one. "I would hear it all, Edmund."

His eyebrows shot up, but then he quickly smoothed his features.

"Very well, then you'll have me tell you how my father forced me to stand and watch them?" Bile climbed up her throat until she feared she'd cast the contents of her stomach at his feet. "Or how they were so enthralled with one another they failed to see me or my father at the doorway? How when my mother and uncle found their release, they finally saw me, and laughed."

He would have been just a boy. At his deadened tones, she pressed her eyes closed. There was an ugliness in her own soul, for she wanted to drag the now dead marquess and marchioness from their graves and choke them for shattering a boy's innocence. His fingers tightened upon her shoulders in an almost reflexive manner. "From that point, I became a pawn used by my parents to inflict hurt upon one another. I decided at that moment I would never be used by anyone. I would never be hurt by anyone in any way." He flexed his jaw. "I am no pawn and I will have vengeance on those who think they might inflict hurt. For if I do not, then my weakness will be used against me."

Phoebe dropped her gaze to his scar; the angry, vicious reminder of what had happened when he'd trusted that there could be more than ugliness in the world. What a warped, sad way to go through life.

"Don't do that," he commanded harshly.

She picked her head up.

Edmund released his hold on her and she mourned the loss of his touch. "Do not pity me."

"I do not pity you." She didn't. Her heart ached for him and she wanted to take away a child's pain so mayhap he might grow into a man who'd not been scarred by his parents' depravity.

"And with everything you've heard, you still believe in love."

She bristled at the cynical twist to that statement. "Just because you can't love me, does not mean there aren't others who d—" Her words ended on a startled squeak as he swiftly turned her around and brought her down beneath the wall of his chest. Her back burrowed into the downy soft mattress.

Powerful emotion burned from Edmund's eyes, scorching her with the strength there. "There will not be another," he commanded, his tone gravelly.

She blinked. "Another what?"

He lowered his brow to hers so the brown of his irises bore into hers. "A lover."

Her heart started. He was jealous. "You are jealous." Shock leant her words a breathy quality.

Edmund ceased blinking, but he did not deny the charge.

How could this man, who'd used her for nothing more than a pawn in his twisted, illogical plot against the Duchess of Monteith, care at all about anything? His reaction could be one of a man who'd have, as he said, revenge on those who sought to hurt him. However, something in his eyes spoke of a different tale. Her heart hitched. For even as she hated the ruthless man who wanted her at all costs, who would have destroyed her family if it so suited him, that blasted, weak organ would belong forever to him. She stroked her fingers down his jaw. "I will not take a lover," she said softly. "Not because you command it," his jaw flexed once more, "but because I will not become my father or your mother…" *Or you…*

Edmund raked a gaze over her face as though seeking the veracity of her words and then he covered her mouth with his in a hard, possessive kiss. This was not the gentle searching of earlier that morning. This was unrestrained and explosive. He thrust his tongue deep and she moaned at that primitive kiss which set her body ablaze with a hunger for more of him.

Her husband groaned and he found her wet center with his fingers. Then in a move made to, no doubt, torture, he pressed the heel of his hand against her until Phoebe tossed her head back and a sharp cry slipped from her lips. Edmund continued to work her, toying with her nub, even as he lowered his lips to the swollen tip of one breast. He captured the bud and drew the pebbled flesh deep, suckling until all rational thought fled and she became nothing more than a bundle of nerves and sensations. A whimper stuck in her throat and she parted her legs for him; hungry for the promises he'd made with his body earlier that morning. Edmund settled himself between her thighs and then with a gentleness she'd not known him capable of, moved slowly inside her. She braced for a hint of the earlier pain she'd known, but all discomfort faded at the slow, steady drag of him filling her, entering her, and then he plunged deep.

Phoebe cried out and raked her nails down his back; holding him closer, wanting to bind her soul with his so there was no darkness within him and only light. With his mouth clenched in a tense line and sweat dripping from his brow, Edmund continued his steady thrusts. Retreating. Plunging forward. Retreating. Plunging forward. And Phoebe held on tight to him as she climbed that pinnacle and then a garbled cry burst from her throat as he increased his rhythm and then she plunged over the edge of all reason, falling, falling into the bliss of his sure movements. Then with a primitive, triumphant shout, he arched back and flooded her with his seed.

And this time, as he collapsed atop her and then swiftly rolled off, pulling her into the fold of his arms, she knew that for the hurt he'd caused, her heart was in even greater peril where her husband was concerned. For it did not escape her that he'd not responded to her request for him to set aside the life of revenge he'd lived all these years.

CHAPTER 21

THE FOLLOWING AFTERNOON EDMUND SAT in his office. A ledger lay opened and forgotten upon his desk, buried under a familiar leather book.

I would ask that you set aside this vengeful life you've set for yourself.

He swiped the book from his desk and fanned the pages that contained years' worth of men who'd wronged him, men who owed him debts and who, through those debts, could hold no power over him. Phoebe asked him to forget who he'd been for the past thirty-two years. In the whole of his life, he'd not been happy. Not truly happy, but he'd felt nothing and feeling nothing was far safer than feeling something. He'd made that mistake but once—with Margaret Dunn. On her, he'd pinned the fleeting hope, the whimsical belief, he could perhaps be different than his parents. With her faithlessness, and in her quest for power and the title duchess, she'd killed that foolish, fleeting weakness.

Until Phoebe. He gripped the leather book hard in his hands. In her, she'd made him feel things he'd not allowed himself to feel in more years than he could remember. Nay, emotions he'd not wanted to feel. With her effervescent spirit, she was spring to his dark winter. She represented life and hope and happiness he'd long ago given up on. He drew his desk drawer open and tossed the book inside. Slamming it shut with a decisive click, Edmund swiped a hand over his face. And yet, for years he'd protected himself by making himself stronger as others grew weaker.

Could he just set aside the years he'd spent trying to survive on the request of a woman? A dry laugh escaped him and he dropped his hand to the book. Could there be any greater weakness than that? Except—was it truly weakness if making his wife happy also brought him more happiness than he knew what to do with?

Abandoning his work and tumultuous thoughts, he shoved back his chair and stood. He needed a visit to his clubs. He needed to clear his thoughts and restore order. With determined purpose, Edmund strode to the door, yanked it open, and took his leave. Yes, in his clubs he plotted and schemed. It was there he was comfortable. With those thoughts fueling him, he made his way through his quiet townhouse.

"Oh, my." The faint, whispery words carried through the still corridor and he slowed his steps, beckoned back toward the sound of his wife's voice. He froze outside the closed door and listened at the panel.

Like a blasted child at a keyhole. He blinked as with that he was transported years earlier to a different door. The muscles of his stomach knotted as his past converged with his present. Phoebe's words called him back from the memories.

"That is splendid. So very splendid." What in blazes? Edmund threw the door open so hard it bounced off the wall and nearly closed in his face once more. He stuck his arm out to keep it from shutting.

His wife shrieked and dropped the book in her hands. She swung her legs over the side of the chair and settled her feet on the floor. The taffeta of her gown wrinkled noisily as a wide-eyed Phoebe leapt to her feet. "Edmund," she greeted. "What are you…?" her words trailed off as he stepped into the room and looked about.

He blinked slowly. There was no one here. He returned his attention to her.

"Are you looking for someone?" she asked furrowing her brow.

"No." *Yes.* A dull flush burned his neck. Had he expected Phoebe the day after their wedding to be rutting with some stranger or servant in his library? His answer, based on his own experience should be an emphatic yes and yet it was not. "What are you doing?" he asked, hearing the accusatory edge of his question.

Phoebe stooped down and retrieved her book. "Reading." She paused. "What are you doing?"

Which was, of course, the far better question. "I was—" Going to my clubs. The words stuck in his throat and he remained rooted to the floor.

"Did you know the Green Bridge of Wales is not really a bridge?"

He cocked his head.

"It is an arch. A naturally formed arch. It is approximately eighty feet," she said animatedly and opened her book. She skimmed through the pages. "Though I don't know how anyone can measure that with any real certainty." There was something so very enchanting in the excitement in her tone and eager movements. "Do you know?"

"Do I know what?" His tone emerged sharper than he intended. That handful of words were roughened by embarrassment.

"How they measure such a thing?"

Edmund gave his head a shake. He cast a glance over his shoulder at the opened door and then looked back to her. He should really leave.

"Have you been to the Pembrokeshire Coast?" she called out, unwittingly staying him with her question.

"I have not.

Phoebe flipped her book open to a certain page. "Aha! Here it is." She turned it around to face him. "Do you believe there is grass atop the arch?" She caught her lower lip between her teeth and nibbled at it contemplatively. At any other point and any other time, all he would think about was his own sexual gratification and what pleasures that delectable mouth could be used for.

Not now. Now, standing before her with that damned book, he was infected by her contagious enthusiasm—for life. Pressure weighted his chest and he made to flee once again.

"I think I shall go here."

And he froze once more. Agony lanced through him. So, she would leave. *You offered her freedom. You said you only wanted her as your wife and have since had her body twice. That should be enough.* With a growl he stalked over. Yet it was not. He made to take the book from her hands to see what rival he now fought.

Phoebe looked around his arm at the book he now held in his hands. "I suspect it must feel like the ladder to heaven, broken just shy of the gateway."

Was there a heaven? For people like her there would be and

suddenly her cheerfulness grated. "Why aren't you enraged?" The question ripped harshly from his chest.

She picked her head up; confusion riddled her brow. Phoebe alternated her attention between Edmund and the book in his hands. "I daresay I will eventually go there. There is nothing to be—"

"With me?" he snapped. She'd sworn her hatred not even two days earlier.

"Do you want me to be enraged with you?" she asked hesitantly.

Edmund thrust her book back into her fingers and dragged a hand over his face. "You made your feelings quite clear two days earlier, Madam." *When I forced you into marriage.* He'd foolishly thought having her would be enough. How wrong he'd been. He wanted all of her. "Do you still not feel that hatred?"

He didn't realize his breath was bated, until a somber look settled over her face. Pulling the book close to her chest, she took a step away from him, and then retreated, giving him her back. "I want to hate you." Some of the tension lessened in his chest. For her words hinted she still cared for him in some way. She shot a sad look over her shoulder and just then he'd give her everything he had to erase that glint that had no place in her eyes. "Should I go through life frowning and snarling because you've hurt me? Because you've forced me into a marriage?" *That I did not want.* Her words were like a dull blade in his gut. "I don't want to become you, Edmund," she said at last. "I don't want to be destroyed by my misery. I will not have your love, nor will I want it as long as you are on a quest of revenge against anyone and everyone who you perceive as having wronged you. But neither will I be destroyed." *By me.*

"But you do not still fancy yourself in love with me?" He cringed as soon as the question left his mouth. God, he'd been transformed into a weak, mewling, pathetic excuse for a person.

Phoebe took a step toward him. "You don't fancy yourself in love with someone." She gave her head a little shake. "You either are or you aren't. And I fell in love with you alongside a Captain Cook exhibit at the Royal Museum. Now, it is just a matter of knowing if any part of that man is truly real."

He opened and closed his mouth several times and then like the coward he was, turned on his heel and fled.

IF EVER THERE HAD BEEN an indication as to her husband's true feelings, his swift retreat this moment was it.

"Did you expect he loves you?" she muttered. "Just because he wanted you?" Now he'd had her in the only ways he'd wanted her. What need had he of her any longer?

"What was that, my lady?"

Phoebe spun about and flushed at the butler who stood framed in the doorway. "Er, nothing…." The poor ancient servant was everywhere she turned.

"My lady, forgive me. I did not have the honor of a proper introduction." He bowed. "I am Wallace."

She bit the inside of her cheek. No, her husband hadn't bothered to perform those necessary introductions with the members of his staff. But then, a man so consumed on revenge and bent on hatred wouldn't bother himself with such social niceties.

The butler, Wallace, stood in stoic silence.

She cleared her throat and broke the awkward quiet. "Have you been in the marquess' employ long?"

He inclined his head. "I began working for the previous Marquess of Rutland ten years before Lord Edmund was born."

Her mind raced. Why, that must make the gentleman at the very least—

"I am seventy years old, my lady," he supplied, his aged voice laced with amusement. "I've been in the employ of the Marquess of Rutland's family for forty-two of those years."

Her fingers tightened reflexively on the edge of her book. For his dedicated service, the man had not been properly compensated with a deserved retirement. How could her husband not have generously rewarded the man for his years of service to his father? "I am sorry," she said at last.

Wallace's aged brow wrinkled. "My lady?"

"I expect for your dedicated service that, at the very least, you'd be deserving of a generously settled pension." Disappointment filled her at Edmund's lack of regard for the old servant. "I," she held her palms up. "I will speak to His Lordship if you wish." As soon as those words left her mouth she grimaced at the futility of them. She'd never hold any sway over Edmund; not in the ways that mattered, nor the ones that did not.

"Speak to His Lordship?"The ghost of a smile played on his lips.

"On the matter of your retirement. I…" At his growing smile, her words trailed off.

"I do not wish to retire, my lady."

She cocked her head. "You do not?" Surely, all people not only deserved, but wanted, some rest at the end of their years.

Wallace gave his head a vigorous shake. "I do not." He leaned close and then dropped his voice to a hushed whisper. "Oh, His Lordship has fought me on any number of scores about the very matter."

"He has?" Shock filled her tone.

"He has," he concurred. "But I ultimately always prevail with His Lordship." Phoebe eyed him with incredulity. No one prevailed where Edmund was concerned. With his ruthlessness and steely resolve, he was indomitable in all matters.

She continued to study Wallace a long moment. Yes, no one emerged triumphant over Edmund—except, it would seem this ancient servant. Intrigue stirred in her breast and she felt like she had been handed a thousand jagged pieces of a puzzle and tried to put it to rights. "Why do you wish to remain at your post?" She could not call the question back, nor did she wish to. The old man's smile slipped. Sadness wreathed his wrinkled cheeks. "I vowed I'd not abandon my post until His Lordship was happy."

Those words struck at her heart; an unexpected, painful jab. But twelve words, and yet they conveyed so very much. They recalled the parts of his past he'd shared yesterday. "Surely," she wet her lips. It was the height of impropriety to speak on personal matters with a servant; to speak of one's husband, madness. "Surely, he's been happy at some point these years." Yet, this man also had known Edmund from the moment he'd been born. She tried to imagine Edmund as he'd been once—innocent, trusting, and dependent upon others for his care and love. Who had first failed him to make him this empty shell of a person?

"Oh, he was once very happy." Wallace said nothing more on it, dangling that morsel so she was forced to either remember what was expected of a proper lady or feed the questions on her lips. He sketched a bow and a moment of panic besieged her, a fear that he would leave and so would end her only opportunity to ask the one person with answers about the stranger she'd married, but then he said, "Will you allow me the honor of showing you about the townhouse, my lady?"

"I would appreciate that, Wallace," she said suddenly glad her husband had not seen to that polite detail. She hurried after the butler as he turned on his heel. They continued down the hall. The older man walked with slow, shuffling footsteps with the soles of his shoes dragging quietly on the floor. Together, Phoebe and Wallace moved through the corridors with Wallace pointing out a Blue Parlor, a Pink Parlor, and a Green Parlor.

It would seem in this new, grand, spacious labyrinth she called home, there was no shortage of parlors. She troubled her lower lip and searched for a polite way, or at the very least, less obvious way, to inquire about her husband and coming up empty, she settled for blunt directness. "What was he like as a child?"

Wallace slowed a moment. She stole a sideways peek at him. The fond gleam in his eyes was better suited to a proud parent. Then, he resumed his pace. "He was quite mischievous, my lady. Always ready with a smile but a handful to his nursemaids and tutors."

Phoebe drew forth an image of Edmund as a small boy—a boy with a thick crop of chestnut, slightly curled hair and a wide grin. Her heart pulled painfully at the image.

The butler motioned to another room. "His Lordship's office."

She paused beside the closed door and stared at the wood panel.

"He is not in his office at this moment."

No, she knew as much. He'd fled her the way one might have fled the burning city of Rome. They continued on, when a portrait in an elaborate gold frame caught her notice. She paused, and Wallace momentarily forgotten, wandered over to the canvas upon which a boy, mayhap no more than ten or eleven glared back at her. He stood beside a leather button sofa with his hand curled on the arm. The virulence in his brown-eyed stare beckoned her forward. She inched closer and then came to a stop. A chill went through her. She'd never before thought a mere child could invoke fear and upon a painting, no less. Yet, there was something menacing about the boy. A dark strand of hair tumbled over his brow and the hardness of his lips marked this too-old-for-his-years child as her husband. "When did he become so…so…?" Cold, unfeeling, ruthless.

"Serious?" Wallace supplied from just over her shoulder.

She nodded, transfixed by her husband forever memorialized as an angry child. Serious would suffice. When silence met her inquiry, she shot a glance back.

Lines of sadness wreathed Wallace's face. "He was seven."

Phoebe swiftly returned her attention to the canvas. She raised tentative fingertips to the grim child. *Seven*. Her heart sputtered. Oh, God. "Seven," she repeated. That was the piece he'd not shared yesterday. He'd been just a babe. Her throat worked spasmodically. "Did he…ever know happiness after?" At least with his Margaret. For as much as she hated the other woman for having what Phoebe herself wanted, she would be grateful if, even for just a short time, he'd smiled again.

"That is a question best reserved for the marquess, my lady."

As she stood there, the ten-year-old Edmund continued to bore his angry, hardened stare into her soul. She swallowed hard and once more managed words. "Wallace, thank you so very much for showing me about." Phoebe forced her focus to the older servant and managed a smile. "May we continue our tour at a later time?"

"Of course, my lady," he said. With a bow, he turned and shuffled down the hall.

Phoebe stared at Wallace's slow-moving frame as he retreated. This ancient servant was just one more piece in the puzzle that was her husband; a piece that did not fit within the jagged frame of his life. Who was this man she married? Monster or just a complex man who hid the good parts of himself from the world? She gave her head a rueful shake. Or perhaps that was nothing more than the fanciful ponderings of a woman so desperately wanting to see more. She turned to make her way abovestairs and then froze. Unbidden, her gaze traveled back to Edmund's office door. With hesitant steps, Phoebe wandered to the door and froze. She worried her lower lip and then cast another glance down the opposite end of the corridor. It wasn't really wrong entering his empty office. This was now her home and surely she was permitted the luxury of moving freely within any and every room. Before her courage deserted her, she pressed the handle and stepped inside.

Silence rang in the grand space and she quietly closed the door behind her with a soft click. She scanned the empty room. The mahogany Chippendale furniture and broad, immaculate desk in their deep, cherry hue perfectly suited Edmund's dark personality. Phoebe took a cautious step forward and then another. Crimson velvet curtains hung closed, as though her husband barred the passersby below even a glimpse into his world. She skimmed her fingers along the leather button sofa and the cool of the fabric chilled in an otherwise warm space. She came to a stop at the foot of his desk and rested her palm along the surface.

The room for all its costly pieces of furniture was otherwise devoid of life and cheer. Dark, cold, sterile. Phoebe moved around the desk and claimed her husband's tall, leather, winged back chair. She shifted in the seat testing the folds of his chair and then laid her palms on the smooth surface. In a distracted manner, she rubbed them back and forth along the cool wood.

"So this is where you see to your business, Edmund Deering," she said into the quiet of the room.

The familiar silence of the room echoed as her only response. Phoebe ran her gaze about the office again. For a man who evoked terror in the hearts of most gentlemen, there was something rather ordinary about this space that he made his. She made to rise and then stilled. With the tip of her finger she played with the gold latch on the long desk drawer. It really wasn't her place to snoop through her husband's affairs.

Phoebe looked to the closed door and then back to the drawer. But then, neither had he given her much choice in the matter of their marriage. Surely one as ruthless and relentless as her husband would not object to such behavior in his own wife? Guilt niggling at the back corner of her mind, she thrust aside those misgivings and pulled out the drawer.

She stared disappointedly down into the meager contents. Though she didn't know what she'd truly expected to find, there had been the sliver of hope that there would be some piece of his business that gave a glimpse into who he was and what he did. Not unlike the book and the breakfast and now the childhood painting. But for a small, black leather ledger and a handful of pens and a sheaf of parchments, there was nothing personal or at all distinctively Edmund's.

Absently she pulled out the book and fanned the pages, admiring his neat, meticulous scrawl. There was a boldness and power to even the ink markings he left upon his pages. She flipped through the small ledger and then blinked slowly as the words inked upon those pages registered. The leather seat groaned in protest as Phoebe sat forward in the chair. With trembling fingers, she brought the book close to her face and buried her nose in its loathsome pages as she rapidly scanned the words in her husband's hand.

Lord Exeter. Weakness Faro and French mistresses. Debt one thousand pounds.

Nausea turned in her belly.

Lord Donaldson. Weakness diddling his servants. Whist. Debt country cottage in Devonshire.

She quickly worked her gaze over the names of men and women indebted to Edmund in some way.

Miss Honoria Fairfax?

Bile climbed up her throat.

Miss Phoebe Barrett—weakness? Her friends and family.

Oh, God.

For everything she knew about her husband's fierce pursuit of power, and his ease in taking what he wanted, and when he wanted it…seeing that ruthlessness enumerated on these pages by him, the way he might record a mundane shopping list, spoke to a depth of his hard-heartedness. Gooseflesh dotted her arms and the book slid from her fingers. It tumbled unceremoniously to the desk with a loud thump. She sat frozen, staring at the book open on its spine with her name glaring mockingly up at her. These words, they were not the words belonging to a man who carried breakfast trays and books of Wales. Rather, these black marks upon the page belonged to that sneering, snarling child who'd jeered her for daring to look at his painted likeness.

"Have you found anything of interest in my office?" a harsh voice drawled.

For a moment, she stared numbly at the page not understanding why the damning leather book should be speaking, in her husband's tone no less. The office door closed with a soft click, bringing her head up.

Edmund stood at the entrance of the room, a hard, undecipherable look stamped on the harsh features of his face. Her husband stalked over like a sleek, lethal panther, moving around the desk and stopping beside her.

He reached for her and she flinched. His ever-narrowing eyes took in that subtle movement and then with a growl, he swiped the book from the desk, snapped it closed, and set it back on the desk. He laid his hands on the arms of her chair, blocking escape. A vein pulsed at his right temple and her heart thumped, reminded once more that Edmund, the Marquess of Rutland, was nothing more than a stranger. "Did you think I would hurt you, Phoebe?" he jeered.

Even with her heart aching and a void of emptiness in her chest, Phoebe managed to tip her head up. "You still have not realized that you don't need to use your hands to inflict hurt upon," me, "a person. You manage that just as effectively with your words."

They remained locked in a silent battle of wills; he seething and simmering like an angered dragon prepared to snarl flames, she proud and defiant, refusing to be cowed by him.

Shockingly, Edmund conceded defeat. He shoved himself to standing and took several steps back, allowing her to rise. Unable to bear the heated emotion in his eyes, Phoebe looked away, peering down at the book. She ran her fingers over the surface of that vile book. "Do you know, Edmund, I am a fool." He stiffened, but otherwise made no attempt to refute or confirm her claim. Acrimony had a bitter taste like acid on her tongue. As she fanned the pages, her skin pricked with awareness of his studious attention to her movements. "I heard everything outside of my father's office. Your intentions for me, your plans for Margaret, your…" Pain choked off those words and she cleared her throat. "Your ruthlessness in wedding even my sister should I not relent." Phoebe raised her eyes to his. His mouth tightened. White lines formed at the corners of his lips. "What does it say about me and the extent of my weakness and folly that I continue to believe in you?" *In us.* Phoebe released the book once more and dusted her hands together. "All my life I was determined to not be my mother. I would wed an honorable gentleman who'd respect me. He would be kind and he would be faithful." The dreams of that fictional gentleman flashed to her mind's eye. "I would dream of who he would be but he never had a face." She drew in a broken breath and looked into her husband's eyes. "For a while that man's face belonged to you. No more, Edmund. You are not that man."

OVER THE YEARS, MANY VILE epithets and black obscenities had been leveled at him that they'd ceased to matter. They hit him and rolled off his impenetrable back without leaving so much as a hint of a mark. Standing there with Phoebe's discovery between them, her words ravaged him more than Stanhope's blade or any of those other ugly charges to be heaped upon his worthless shoulders before.

For standing here, staring at Phoebe with the delicate planes of her cherished face etched in grief and acceptance, whatever she might have felt for him that wasn't loathing had clearly died with the discovery of that book.

He dug deep, searching the dismissive response that would send her fleeing, but he did not want her to go, for when she left, after this, Phoebe would be gone in ways that he could never, ever again find her. Edmund stared blankly down at the book; a book he'd not etched a single mark in after the moment he'd put Phoebe's name down.

With a sound of disgust, Phoebe made to step around him. He shot a hand out, staying her movement. She glanced down at his hold upon her person with such potent disgust, he released her suddenly. "I have not written another name in that book since yours." *Since you.*

She eyed him as though he'd escaped from Bedlam. "Am I supposed to find honor in that? Reassurance?" She scoffed. "So you have not written another name in it since mine. There will be others after me. Mayhap not today or tomorrow, but you will find others. People's weaknesses you use to build up an artificial strength." Her words slashed through him, powerful with their accuracy. "But you are not strong," she said, cutting his legs out from under him. She jerked her chin toward the door. "You are that angry, scared child in the painting—"

"I do not know any other way!" he shouted, his voice thundered from the ceiling and echoed around them.

Phoebe placed her palms on the edge of the desk and leaned toward him, shrinking the space. "Then try. What happened to you as a child was horrid," she said, her tone gentler, bearing more hints of the warmth usually lining her every word. "It truly was. Your parents, like my father, were rotten, horrid, dishonorable people. But that happened to you, just as it happened to me, and you need to move on from it."

Move on from it. There was something seductive in those four words. Move on… He'd spent the course of his life with manacles holding him to the past. As she'd said, a child hurt and wounded nursing those hurts in a bid to never be hurt again. He wanted to be more. And yes, he wanted to be more for her because that is what she, at the very least, deserved, but for him.

Silence stretched on eternally between them and then Phoebe pushed away from the desk. With resigned steps, she walked away from him.

"I want to change," he called out, staying her as she reached the door. "I want to be more." *For you.*

Phoebe wheeled slowly back, her face curiously expressionless. "Unfortunately, Edmund I'm not entirely sure you can."

Long after Phoebe had gone, Edmund stood fixed to the spot. He stared at the wood panel, clenching and unclenching his fists into painful balls at his side. Then, moving behind his desk, he sat down. With slow, methodical movements he flipped open the familiar book and then pulled open his desk drawer. Dipping his pen into the crystal inkwell he etched one more name onto the pages and stared blankly down at the name marked there.

CHAPTER 22

LATER THAT DAY, PHOEBE STARED up at the façade of a familiar stucco townhouse. Her skin pricked with the gazes trained on her by rabidly curious passersby. She rapped once on the front door. In light of this latest betrayal by Edmund, surely she should feel some great torrent of emotions. Except, she didn't think she could shed another tear for her husband, the Marquess of Rutland. She raised her hand to knock again, when the door was suddenly opened.

Surprise wreathed the old butler, Manfred's face, reminding her of another loyal, devoted butler. "Miss Barrett," he greeted with a smile and then remembered himself as she stepped through the doorway. "My Ladyship," he amended.

Phoebe shrugged out of her cloak and handed it off to the waiting servant. "I daresay a dear family friend who knew me when I was putting rose water in my father's cologne is permitted calling me by my Christian name, still."

"Did you now?" A twinkle lit his old eyes. "I do not recall you as anything but perfectly behaved."

She managed her first laugh that morning and then looked about.

"Her Ladyship is in the Pink Parlor," he said correctly interpreting the reason for her visit. He motioned with his hand. "If you'll allow me to—"

"That won't be necessary," she said with a murmur of thanks. "I've been gone but two days," which felt like twenty years. "I still remember my way about," she assured him.

Manfred grinned and inclined his head. "As you wish, my lady… Miss Phoebe," he said when she gave him a pointed look.

With a last small smile for the servant who represented a tie to her past, she made her way through the quiet townhouse, onward to the Pink Parlor. She came to a stop at the open doorway. Her mother sat at the edge of a mahogany shell chair. Head bent over an embroidery frame, she attended the stitchery in her hand, pulling the needle through the stark white fabric.

"I did not expect a visit so soon after you'd been married," her mother welcomed, not picking her head up from her work.

"Mother," she greeted. Phoebe stepped into the room, hesitated, and then pulled the door closed behind her. That soft click brought the viscountess' attention up and her wide smile withered and died on her lips.

"What is it?" She tossed aside her frame, work forgotten, and climbed to her feet.

There was such a gentle, maternal concern in that inquiry that if Phoebe hadn't already cried every last possible tear for Edmund and their future, she would have dissolved into an empty puddle of weepy nothingness at her mother's feet. Phoebe gave her a shake and motioned to the chair she'd just vacated. Wordlessly, she claimed the seat opposite her mother. She drummed her fingertips on the arm of her chair, examining this woman who'd smiled through so much darkness. "How did you do it?"

Her mother angled her head.

Phoebe ceased the distracted tapping. "Marriage to Father. How did you do it all these years and smile? Why aren't you…?" She closed her mouth.

The viscountess picked up her embroidery frame. "Why aren't I…?" she prodded, setting her stitch work on her lap.

"Unhappy? Bitter? Angry?" Everything Phoebe herself was this moment.

Her mother furrowed her brow. "What do I have to be unhappy about?"

"Come, Mama," Phoebe chided. "Surely you know what I speak of?" She glanced at the silver needle dangling from the frame. "You can't possibly be happy wedded to Father."

A dawning understanding lit the other woman's eyes. "Ahh," she said, settling back in her chair. She sighed and glanced over at the closed door as though ascertaining there was no one at the entrance, before then returning her attention to Phoebe. "No," she said softly. "My marriage has not been a happy one, but my life has been a great one."

Phoebe wrinkled her brow. "That seems a contradiction," she scoffed. How could one not preclude the other?

Light danced in her mother's blue eyes. "Does it? Is my marriage to your father a happy one?" She shook her head once. "No, it isn't," she said with more candor than Phoebe ever recalled. "It is not the marriage I imagined for myself." Those words an echo of Phoebe's earlier thoughts ran through her, tightening the pain. Yet there was no spiteful resentment deserving one such as her mother. Her mother began tugging her needle through the frame once more. "My life is a happy one, Phoebe, and I'd have it no other way." She glanced up and must have seen the disbelief on her daughter's face, for she smiled. "You think I lie?"

Phoebe shifted. "No…I…" At the knowing look, she settled back in her seat with a sigh. "Yes," she mumbled, feeling like a recalcitrant child. "Surely there must be a lie."

"Oh, there is no lie," her mother said instantly. "Perhaps regret, yes. But not a lie. My life is a happy one."

Filled with a restive energy, Phoebe jumped to her feet and began to pace. "How did you do it? How do you go through life with a smile and laughter?" When Phoebe herself thought she could never smile again. She spun back, pleading with her eyes for an answer.

Her mother set aside her frame again and then came to her feet. She came over and took Phoebe gently by her shoulders. "How can you not know why I smile and laugh? I have you and Justina and Andrew. My heart is full because of you three and someday, when you are a mother, you will understand that," she said giving her shoulders another slight squeeze.

Phoebe's throat worked spasmodically. "That cannot be the same as having a husband's love."

"No, no it is not." Her mother brushed a kiss on her forehead. "I would be lying if I didn't say there was a void, but you and your brother and sister, you fill that."

She drew in a shuddery breath and a strand of hair fell over her brow. The viscountess brushed it back and tucked it behind her ear. "This is about your Lord Rutland."

And because Phoebe would wager her very life that Father didn't speak to his wife on any matter, even the topic of her own children, she told her the truth. "He won my dowry in a game of cards against Father."

Her mother stilled her soothing caress. "And?"

"And he would have wedded Justina if I did not marry him." That part stung more being breathed aloud so that she resisted the urge to rub her hand over her aching chest.

Mama snorted. "You believe Lord Rutland would have wed Justina, to what end?"

Phoebe opened and closed her mouth several times and then frowned. Odd, until this moment, she'd not truly considered how Justina fit into his madcap scheme. Or…for that matter, why he even wanted Phoebe. After all, marriage to her had effectively quashed his plans for Honoria.

"Do you know what I believe?"

She shook her head, wishing someone had answers to put her world to rights.

"Your husband cares for you. When he looks at you, there is no other person in the room." She stroked her hair. "No, that man would have never wed Justina." Her lips turned in a wry smile. "I am not excusing his behaviors, but I am saying there is more there than your modest dowry."

Hope stirred at her mother's words and, for an instant, she willed them to be accurate and true. Then she recalled that blasted book and her name scratched casually upon the pages as though she were any other person he'd use in his scheme of life. "Edmund doesn't care for anyone," she said tiredly. She drew in a breath and before her mother could debate the point with her, she hurriedly said, "I should return home."

"Yes, you should."

Phoebe kissed her mother on the cheek. "I love you."

"And I love you."

She started for the door when her mother called out stopping her. "Phoebe?" Phoebe glanced over her shoulder. "Lord Rutland is not your father," she said simply.

Phoebe managed a smile and with that, left. As she made the

short carriage ride back to Edmund's townhouse and entered her new home, her mother's words danced around her mind. Wallace opened the door granting her entry and she paused in the foyer.

The servant cleared his throat. "His Lordship has gone to his clubs."

His clubs. Of course.

His clubs. Those vile, despicable dens of sin. It should come as no surprise that a man with a book containing peoples' weaknesses would take to his clubs not even two days after he'd married. She curled her hands into tight, painful fists. After he'd lain in her arms and shown her more pleasure than she'd ever known her body capable of, he'd today sought out his clubs, which was really not dissimilar than any gentleman might do—if he were to visit White's or Brooke's, but this was different. Hurt throbbed in her chest and she swiftly turned to go. "Thank you." Phoebe made to climb the stairs to seek out the sanctuary of her new chambers.

"My lady, you have visitors."

Foot poised on the step, Phoebe spun about, nearly toppling herself in her haste. "I have taken the liberty of showing Miss Fairfax and Lady Gillian to the drawing room." Her friends! Joy filled her at the prospect of seeing the two women who'd been friends to her when no one else had and then her happiness quickly receded with all the secrets she'd kept from them. She'd not even given them the courtesy of speaking to them of her wedding. Granted hers hadn't been a joyous affair, but still they would have expected and surely deserved an invitation to act as guests and friends.

Wallace again spoke, calling her attention back. "If you wish me to inform them that you aren't receiving—"

"No!" the denial sprung from her lips. She winced at the desperate edge to that one word utterance. Phoebe took a calming breath. "That is, thank you. I will join them."

He bowed his head, but did not leave. Phoebe stared questioningly at him.

"Lady Rutland," he said this time. "If I may be so bold? You looked at the painting and wondered as to His Lordship's happiness. He has not been happy in more than twenty years, but I do believe he is happy, *now*." Wallace gave her a pointed stare, his meaning clear: Edmund could be happy because of Phoebe. Which was madness. It would take far more than her to ever fill the vast void inside her husband. She managed a small smile and before she made a cake of herself and cried useless tears in front of the servant, hurried off to the parlor. If she were a good friend she'd be properly focused on the regret she had for abandoning them the moment she'd met Edmund. But she was not a good friend. For with each footfall that brought her away from that child's portrait and to the drawing room, Wallace's words haunted her; echoing around her mind, calling forth thoughts of Edmund as a child of seven, once smiling—and then three years later, in a picture so bitter and cold in his portrait.

Phoebe came to a stop outside the drawing room and froze at the threshold.

Gillian and Honoria stood shoulder to shoulder with their arms folded at their chests and matching expressions of disappointment stamped in their face. If there had been anger, it would have been easier than—*this*.

She stepped into the room and quietly closed the door behind her. To break the recriminating silence, she said, "Would you care for—"

"If you offer us refreshments, I'm going to clout you," Honoria interrupted. She stitched her eyebrows together.

Phoebe fell silent. The trio of friends once inseparable stared at one another, each daring the other to speak.

With a sigh, she clasped her hands together. "I understand you are upset." And rightly so.

"I understand if you'd not share the details of your marriage with the *ton*, they are horrid," Gillian gave a sniff. "But we are your *friends*."

"I shared with you what I knew during your visit." They gave her dark frowns. Guilt needled at her conscience and she crossed over. "I didn't know we would wed so quickly," she said as she came to a stop before them.

The concern faded from Honoria's stare, replaced now by dark suspicion. "Did he force you to immediately wed?"

"Yes. No." She pressed her fingers to her temples. How could the answer be both? She'd not debated him on the point of when the event would take place. "It mattered not whether it was the next day or next week, my marriage to him was inevitable." She'd courted ruin in meeting him all those days. She sank onto the edge of a red-velvet sofa and directed her stare at her lap. "I know what you think of me. I know you believe me an awful friend for shutting you out of my life these ten days," and she was. "And I am." Pain filled her throat and made words difficult. "But I fell in love with him," or rather she'd fallen in love with the lies he'd fed her. "And he was all I thought of." Phoebe forced her gaze to Honoria. "You were right." Her voice emerged a broken whisper. "I was hopeful and foolish, and he was everything you claimed he was." Only that wasn't altogether true. Confusion stabbed at her mind and played havoc on her heart. There was also a man capable of apology and who'd brought her a tray of food and a book. Nay, not just any book. The book of Wales.

The sofa dipped slightly with the addition of Honoria's weight as she settled into the spot beside Phoebe. "Do you believe I would judge you so harshly?" Honoria chided, a stern reproach threading her words. "I love you," she said simply. "You are my friend. And I love that you are hopeful in the face of your father's horridness." She claimed Phoebe's hands and gave them a squeeze. "You retained that important piece of your soul when others," Honoria, "are less successful at such a feat."

Gillian claimed Phoebe's opposite side. "It is true. I would have dearly loved to attend your wedding and be there for you. But I would never resent you for finding and knowing love." Her lips pulled in a grimace, as she seemed to recall the inevitable deception Edmund had practiced upon an unsuspecting Phoebe.

Honoria scrutinized her in that assessing manner of hers. "Has he…" Her cheeks pinkened and with that hesitancy of her question and the color on her face, her meaning became clear. "Hurt you?"

"No!" The words burst forth.

They eyed her skeptically.

She drew in a breath. "Not…in *that* way." He'd been a patient, careful, gentle lover. Bitterness turned in her heart. Then, his expert touch had merely proven just how very many came before her. Even now he could be with one of those women. How she wished his had merely been a physical pain inflicted, instead of this twisting, aching regret.

Honoria applied pressure to her fingers. "What is it?"

She gave her head a small shake, not wanting to breathe the truth aloud to these two women. Some things had no place between anyone, but one's own tortured musings.

Gillian looked about. "Where is His Lordship?"

And with that simple inquiry, she was proven a liar. There were more tears. The gates opened up. Phoebe buried her face in her hands and wept noisy little tears, detesting the shuddery sobs that shook her frame.

"Oh, Phoebe," Honoria said with such a gentle kindness, Phoebe quaked all the more.

She cried with such force she soaked the fabric of her friend's muslin gown. "I-it sh-should not matter that he's gone—" Especially after that blasted book.

"Where has he gone?" Gillian put in and it made the tears come all the harder and faster.

"T-to his s-scandalous clubs. B-but it does. And I d-don't know why."

Gillian settled her fingers on Phoebe's back and rubbed small, soothing circles. "Why, you love him, sweet. That is why," she said gently.

Phoebe wrenched away. She staggered to her feet and gave her head a horrified shake. "I-I don't." She couldn't. Not with the lies between them. "He betrayed me, forced me into a marriage I did not want. No, I do not love him." She brushed her hands over her cheeks, recognizing the lie of her own words.

As did Gillian. "You cannot simply erase the ten days where you did fall in love with him."

Phoebe spun around and strode over to the window. "Nothing was real," she said, more to herself. She yanked the edge of the curtain back and stared out at the passing conveyances. The crystal windowpane reflected back her grief-ravaged face and she winced at her own weakness. She'd become her mother. Phoebe pressed her eyes tight. God help her.

The rustle of skirts indicated one of her friends had moved. "Some of it had to be real," Gillian said.

In the window she detected the hard stare Honoria gave their still hopeful, dreamily optimistic friend. "It matters not," Honoria said and crossed over. She settled her hand on Phoebe's shoulders. "You will do precisely as I said. You will live your life, he will live his, and along the way you will steal happiness for yourself where you can. Lady Wentworth has her annual ball this evening. It shall be good fun and even more so for you, as a wedded woman. Promise you'll come. Present yourself as the proud, bold Marchioness of Rutland."

"I don't want to go to a ball," she said, her voice tired.

Honoria snorted. "No one does—"

"Some do," Gillian put in.

"But it shall be far better to go together. We shall face Society with you a married woman, no different than any other wedded lady of the *ton*." Phoebe released the curtain and it fluttered back into place. She'd long abhorred the crush of balls and the inanity of soirees. Except when presented with the option of remaining alone in Edmund's home with her broken heart and morose thoughts, the ball sounded a good deal more preferable. She sighed. Who knew?

CHAPTER 23

EDMUND SAT AT THE BACK table of Forbidden Pleasures. Through the years, this was the place he'd felt most at home. When he'd needed to strategize on a man's destruction, this is where he'd come to organize his thoughts. In this instance, however, he scratched and clung to his very survival. Since yesterday morn, after he'd made love to his wife and awakened beside her lithe, naked form, Phoebe had turned his mind inside out with a hungering for her that went beyond the physical. He'd never slept beside a woman. There had been no need. No, his relationships with women had served one purpose—his and his partner's sexual satiation. Edmund damned his wife for making him want more. He looked over the club, determined to put logical thoughts back to right.

Except now, the din of raucous laughter and the clatter of coins hitting the faro tables of this once stable hell blared loud in his head. He raised his snifter of brandy to his lips and welcomed the familiar burn of the fine, French liquor as it blazed a trail down his throat. Frustration turned within him as he skimmed his gaze over the lords with a scantily clad beauty upon their laps; some of them with two or three. At one point, he'd felt a sense of belonging in the decadent hall of sin. His gaze collided with the fat, sweating frame of the Viscount Waters and Edmund clenched his snifter so hard, his knuckles turned white. He took in the man, his father-in-law, more importantly, Phoebe's father. With the lush, blonde beauty on his lap, nuzzling his neck, the man was no different than really any other married man of the *ton*. Edmund continued to study him. And yet, this was Phoebe's father, a man who'd visited shame upon her. He warred with the sudden urge to storm across the crowded club and take the man apart with his bare hands.

He studied the contents of his glass a moment, rolling the snifter back and forth between his hands. For the course of his life, he'd allowed his parents' depravity to define him. Destroy him. He'd taken the sight his father forced him to witness and used that as an excuse to live an equally immoral existence.

And yet, Phoebe's life had not been unlike his. Both born to shameful sires who opened their eyes to vileness in a person's soul, they'd each let that shape their lives but in entirely different ways. He had embraced a cold, unfeeling world in which he'd never know hurt and only feel that which brought him satisfaction. Phoebe, however, had moved through the world with a positive hope in others and her future. He'd prided himself these years on his strength, but he'd not been strong. He'd been merciless and ruthless, but that was not strength. The inherent ability to smile through life's ugliness and not allow it to turn one bitter and cold—that was strength. He was merely the monster he'd proven himself to be these years. His insides twisted in agonized knots. And in his need to possess her, he'd destroyed her. With a curse Edmund downed the remaining contents on a long, slow swallow. His lips pulled in an involuntary grimace and he set the empty glass down with a hard thunk.

What manner of pathetic fool had he allowed himself to become, sitting here with a club of eager beauties and coin to be won, waxing on with his maudlin thoughts about his childhood and his wife? He swiped the bottle from the table and splashed several fingerfuls into his empty glass. This hold Phoebe had upon him was too great. He could not give her more of him than this—it would weaken him and destroy him in ways he'd not been destroyed. She already hated him. He swirled the contents of his glass in a small circle. History had proven what happened to those who hated. Soon, that bitterness would drive his wife to seek out another and he would not be the angry, hurt man staring at her tup another, the way his father had been.

A young beauty sidled up to him. "My lord," she purred. "Are you desiring company?" Clad in a black lace confection, she was sin wrapped with the crimson bows that held her slip of a dress loosely tied. The lush woman fingered her low décolletage in invitation. At any other point, in any other time before Phoebe he'd have unhesitantly taken the woman. He would have slaked his desire, brought her release that left them both sated. Edmund gave his head a curt shake and with a moue of disappointment, she sauntered off. Now there was Phoebe and nothing made sense any longer.

"Rutland, my good man."

At the cheerful greeting, Edmund stiffened. *Bloody brilliant.* "Barrett," he said warily. "I was just—"

The young man was as undaunted as his older sister. "Glad to keep you company." He tugged out the chair opposite Edmund and slid into it. "Enjoying marriage?" His wry grin indicated he'd already arrived at an opinion on Edmund's thoughts of his wedded state.

He frowned and remained silent.

Undeterred, Andrew Barrett stuck his hands into the edge of his waistcoat and tipped back on the legs of his chair, balancing haphazardly. "A bit surprised I am, if I can admit as much."

Edmund battled back wary annoyance. "Surprised at what?" Of course, he should expect his brother-in-law would take offense with him abandoning the newly married Phoebe. Still, visiting his clubs was not uncharacteristic of a wedded gentleman. Mayhap not a just wedded gentleman, but it was quite the norm.

Barrett shrugged and then leaned abruptly forward as his precarious positioning nearly landed him on his backside for his attempt at nonchalance. "A man such as you would hardly be content with Pheebs." A cocky grin pulled his mouth up at one corner. "A bit mouthy and motherly, I was surprised that you were so determined to have her."

A growl worked its way up Edmund's chest and he narrowed his eyes into thin slits.

Barrett wasn't wholly stupid, for he bristled. "Not that I'm not glad to have you as a brother." No, perhaps he was wholly stupid after all. "And Phoebe will make you a good wife. She is loyal and devoted."

Edmund reached for his bottle and poured himself another

brandy. The man spoke of her as though she were a damned spaniel. Yes, she was loyal and devoted as the other man claimed, but she was so much more than that. She was spirited and passionate and intelligent. "She is not a blasted dog," he snapped, then set the bottle down hard and picked up his glass. He took another much needed drink.

Barrett blinked rapidly. He scratched his brow. "Er...I didn't call her a dog. I called her devoted." Glancing about, the young pup located a fiery-haired lightskirt and motioned to her. The woman sauntered over with the flimsy, crimson satin fabric molding to her every curve with each slow, inviting step she took.

The young woman stopped beside their table and settled a glass on the smooth mahogany surface. Then, planting her palms on Barrett's lap she leaned close and flicked her tongue over the shell of his ear. "Do you require anything else?"

The young man's throat bobbed up and down.

Edmund swiped his free hand over his face. Oh, Christ. The last thing he cared to do was sit here with this man who had his wife's eyes while he took a whore in public for all to see. He made to shove back his chair.

"I was surprised I didn't see you with her tonight."

Edmund froze and probed Phoebe's brother with a hard look.

The young man paused in the midst of nuzzling the prostitute's neck. She giggled and swatted at him in protest. "At Lord and Lady Wentworth's," he clarified. "Came from there a short while ago."

The knot twisted all the more in his gut. She'd gone out to a polite Society event. *Did you expect she should stay at home, alone, while you sought out your clubs?* Yes, yes he had. Because the selfish bastard that he was, he'd not considered what she'd be doing. But now he knew. She was at the bloody Wentworth's ball. If they were to live their own lives such a detail didn't really matter. She'd attend with—

"Was there with her friends," Barrett supplied, as he ran a hand down the whore's thigh.

Edmund came to his feet earning a confused look from his brother-in-law. "Where are you off to, Rutland?"

He gave a slight bow. "Barrett," he muttered. Regardless of their connection through marriage, and by Phoebe, he still wouldn't answer to this man or anyone. He spun on his heel and he who'd sworn to avoid polite Social events unless they suited some larger purpose took his leave from Forbidden Pleasures and made his way to the damned Wentworth ball.

"I DO SAY THEY ARE leering more," Gillian said on an annoyed moan.

"Yes, yes they are," Honoria glared at Lord Pratt who eyed the trio of her, Gillian, and Phoebe.

Phoebe sighed as the young earl ran a lascivious stare over her person, before ultimately settling his hot gaze upon her bosom. She caught her lower lip between her teeth. "I daresay it is my fault," she muttered. For apparently with this whole marital business came open advances and interested stares from bold gentleman no longer restricted by the polite bounds of unwed, virginal lady and gentleman. Lord Allswood caught her eye across the ballroom and gave her a slow, lingering grin. She scowled and jerked her attention away. She'd wager the title of Marchioness of Rutland did not help with the whole respectability end of everything.

Gillian groaned and together Phoebe and Honoria followed her stare to the other woman's fast-approaching father and another prospective suitor at his side. "Go," Phoebe whispered out of the side of her mouth.

On cue, Honoria positioned herself between Gillian and the determined pair marching through the crowd, and with a last grateful look, she all but sprinted away, weaving and darting past curious lords and ladies, and then she disappeared.

Suddenly, the marquess stopped. He scratched his head and then turned off in search of his daughter.

"Surely, there is more to life than this," Honoria muttered at her side.

At her friend's hopeless words, regret filled her. One time she would have had proper words of hope and an optimistic thought for the cynical one of their trio. Not this time. Phoebe stared above the heads of the dance partners now performing the steps of a quadrille. It was deuced hard to be optimistic or truly happy when you found yourself wed to a man who'd merely used you in some convoluted scheme and then was content to let you carry on your life, while he carried on his.

"He is not worth it, you know." Honoria's quietly spoken words brought her back from her despondency.

She didn't pretend to misunderstand. However, neither could she force out words of concurrence. The loyal butler, Wallace, had seen more in him and, at one time, so had she. Surely, some of that had been real?

"Phoebe." She looked to Honoria once more. "Not all people can be fixed."

"I know that," she said quickly. Because she did. Some people were broken beyond repair and could not be healed, no matter how much you willed it, no matter how much you wished it. It didn't, however, stop you from hoping.

She was never more grateful than when Honoria changed the subject to a far safer matter. "You know they aren't *really* staring at you any more than you think they are."

A small laugh burst from Phoebe's lips.

Honoria leaned close and dropped her voice to a low whisper. "Only you and…and…the marquess know the true circumstances of your marriage. Why, for all intents and purposes," she motioned to Lady Wentworth's guests. "You may as well be any newly married woman here."

"Without the wedding trip," she said dryly.

"Without the wedding trip," her friend said with a nod, either failing to hear or deliberately ignore the sarcasm lacing Phoebe's words. "They still see you as a love match." Which is what she'd believed they would be not even three days ago after rides through Hyde Park and afternoon visits and stolen interludes at curiosity shops. Phoebe closed her eyes a moment and willed back the pain.

Her friend discreetly slid her hand in hers. "Oh, Phoebe. Not here. You are to live your own life."

"I didn't want to live my own life," she said on a ragged whisper, damning Society for hovering on the fringe of her broken heart. *I wanted a life with him. I wanted to be loved and happy and everything my own mother was not, nor ever would be.*

The column of Honoria's throat moved and she looked beyond Phoebe's shoulder. Recognition flared in the other woman's eyes and Phoebe followed her stare.

Her heart plummeted to her toes as she assessed the tall, regal lady approaching them. Phoebe had seen her before, on numerous occasions. At every one of those meetings, the woman had been polite and smiling, and cloaked herself in more than a little bit of sadness. Now, as Honoria's Aunt Margaret, the Duchess of Monteith, approached, jealousy knifed through her being and slashed a trail of hurt in its wake. This was the woman Edmund had loved so very much that he'd have involved not only Honoria but Phoebe in his sick, twisted game of revenge.

The duchess came to a stop before them.

Honoria dropped a curtsy and greeted the too-young-to-be-a-widow duchess. "Aunt Margaret."

Phoebe dropped a belated curtsy and stood a silent observer to the warm exchange between aunt and niece. Love shone through their similarly shaped eyes. She drew in a slow breath as understanding settled around her brain. This was why Edmund would have used Honoria, because the only person who'd possessed his love so very clearly loved Honoria. She curled her fingers into tight balls, hating herself for her own pettiness. But God help her, she loathed this woman for having possessed the only real sliver of Edmund that had existed in the twenty-five years since he'd last truly smiled.

As though feeling her intense focus, the duchess shifted her attention to Phoebe. She gave a small, sad smile. "I understand congratulations are in order."

Incapable of words, Phoebe managed a shaky nod.

For a moment the other woman looked at her with an aching understanding and pity, a look she'd worn when she'd stared upon her own mother. Phoebe's breath escaped her on a swift exhale. God help her. In just a handful of days, she'd transformed herself into—her mother. She lurched backwards and knocked into the Doric column at her back.

Honoria looked questioningly at her, concern radiating from her eyes.

She mustered a smile for her friend's benefit. "I-I need but a moment," she managed to squeeze out and then before Honoria could press her further, she spun on her heel and disappeared down the same path Gillian had taken a long moment ago. With each hasty, uneven step, lords and ladies looked at her with rabid curiosity in their cruel gazes. Phoebe collided with a young woman.

The lady shot her hands out and steadied her, momentarily halting her retreat. Phoebe stared blankly at the woman with glorious blonde curls piled atop her head, who now looked at her with unexpectedly kind eyes…and pity…there was pity there, too. For everyone knew that Phoebe had gone and wed a gentleman who spent his days and nights at his clubs. A man who'd had to have her at any cost and, yet, at the same time, didn't want her. She bowed her head and sought the proper apology but emotion balled in her throat and she swallowed convulsively.

Spinning on her heel, she continued her retreat; the young woman forgotten. A loud hum filled her ears and the crowd's cheerful laughs and gossip exploded into an ugly menagerie of sound within her mind, until her heart kicked up a frantic, panicked tempo. She reached the edge of the ballroom and then with each freeing step away from polite Society, the sound receded and her heart resumed its normal cadence. Still, Phoebe continued walking the length of the hall, onward through her host and hostess' empty corridors. The lit sconces cast flickers of eerie glow that danced off the gold damask wallpaper. A loud creaking, as though a depressed floorboard echoed in the silence and she froze. Footsteps sounded down the hall, and with her heart thundering, Phoebe shoved the nearest door open and stumbled inside. Hurriedly, she pressed the door closed with a soft click and then leaned against the hard wood panel.

She blinked several times in a bid to adjust to the darkened room and then took in the sanctuary she'd stolen. Distractedly, Phoebe tugged off her white gloves and tossed them down onto a nearby table.

White stared back at her. White walls, white upholstered sofas, white marble. A white parlor. Phoebe shoved away from the door and started tentatively about the room. She wandered absently over to a nearby side table and picked up a pale blue porcelain sheep. With a wry shake of her head, she turned it over in her hands studying the unexpected splash of color. In a world of white, the sheep had been painted blue. Surely, there was more to the oddly colored glass figurine. She skimmed the tip of her nail over the creature's ears. Had the glass sheep began as white with one mistake by the artist resulting in an entirely different shade to the piece? Or had that always been what it was intended for it?

An inevitable fate of…color. How very similar Edmund was—standing out, different than all other members of the *ton*, but not necessarily for reasons that were good or honorable. When had he been a white sheep?

With the silence of Lord Wentworth's parlor as her only company, she set the figurine back upon the side table and confronted the true nature of her upset—it wasn't the humiliation at being left the day after they'd wed, it wasn't the whispers and stares of polite Society, it was her. She hated that for his betrayal she still wanted him to be more, needed him to be more. Phoebe folded her arms close and hugged herself. She wanted him to be the uncomplicated person Wallace had spoken of who'd once smiled; not that cynical, angry, and cold child who'd been ruined by life.

Her gaze went unbidden back to the blue sheep. Except, he could never be that person again. He'd been painted, and that could not be removed. Edmund would remain forever—blue. He would seek out his clubs and carry on with his women. He would exact revenge on those he felt deserving of some warped sense of justice for crimes mayhap real, mayhap not. And what would become of her?

A loud, creak rent the quiet and slashed into her ponderings. She swung her gaze to the door. Her heart jumped at the stranger who stepped inside. The gentleman, she vaguely recalled as the Viscount Brewer was not unpleasant looking; quite handsome, in fact, with thick, dark unfashionably long blond curls better suited to that archangel Gabriel. It was the glint in his eyes that marked his soul black.

"Lady Rutland," he drawled with what most women would likely find a charming grin on his hard lips. "A pleasure to see you."

CHAPTER 24

ANNOYANCE STIRRED IN PHOEBE'S BREAST at the gentleman's bold perusal and she resisted the urge to fold her arms protectively across her chest to hide her breasts from his leering stare. "My lord, forgive me," she said, squaring her shoulders. She took a step around the table and made for the exit of Lord Wentworth's parlor. "I'd intended to steal a moment for myself. I shall leave you to..." Her words trailed off as he slowly closed the door behind him.

"What if I don't want you to leave, my lady?" He dropped his voice to a teasing whisper. At his boldness, annoyance slipped away, replaced with a burning anger.

She tipped her chin up. "If you will excuse me," she said again this time firming her tone with the same steel she'd detected in Edmund's words so many times, now knowing why he'd affected that icy cool. It gave one strength. Even if it was merely an artificial one. There was something protective in that detachedness.

Phoebe made to step around the viscount, when he shot out a hand blocking her retreat. "Come, my lady, you arrive alone, Rutland's wife, just newly married." He captured a loose curl between his thumb and forefinger and her mouth went dry with fear at the boldness of that touch.

"Do not touch me," she gritted out. She swatted at his fingers, but he merely laughed.

"Am I to believe you are not here in search of a lover who will fill the void left by your absent husband?" His hot breath fanned her cheek. Icy fear snaked down her spine as she registered for the first time the precariousness of her situation.

Phoebe made a grab for the door handle when he grabbed her wrist, capturing it in a hard, punishing hold. She winced at the tightness of that grip. "Release me this instant." And as Society quaked with the fear of her husband's name, she boldly tossed the reminder of Edmund. "My husband, the Marquess of Rutland, will not tolerate you putting your hands upon me."

The viscount tossed his head back and the room thundered with his laughter; that cold, mirthless sound chilled her. "Oh, something tells me your husband will not much care."

Phoebe pursed her lips. "You are wrong," she snapped. For Edmund's ruthlessness and lack of regard where she was concerned, she still did not doubt he'd destroy any man who infringed upon that which he viewed as his—including her. "He will care." She yanked at her hand again, but the viscount held firm. "If you believe he'd allow any man to touch his wife, then you do not know Lord Rutland."

"Then you, my lady, do not know your husband." He released her with such alacrity she stumbled back. Phoebe tripped over herself in a bid to put distance between them. With a sneer on his lips, he advanced. "A man who takes his pleasure with married women—mine—" Oh, God. Agony lanced her heart. "—others, why he surely will not care when you take your pleasures where you would." Her heart twisted at this glaring truth of the man Edmund had been…mayhap, in fact, still was. One who'd make love to a married woman. She drew in a ragged breath and hastily put a chair between them. "So, that is what this is about," she charged. "Your attempt to inflict the same shame and hurt on my husband for having dallied with your wife?"

For a moment rage flared in his eyes and she thought he might strike her. Then, a feral grin turned his lips. "I assure you, you will quite enjoy it." And then he continued walking.

At the prospect of letting this dissolute nobleman touch her the way only Edmund had, a shudder of revulsion racked her frame. "I am sorry." That softly spoken apology brought him to a swift stop. "I am sorry that my husband…" Her cheeks blazed with heat. "C-carried on with your wife." For everything she didn't know about Edmund, there were important pieces she did know.

He would not force himself on an unwilling woman the way the viscount attempted. "But I do not want your attentions." He narrowed his eyes, as her meaning became clear—his wife had.

With a curse, he shoved the small barrier between them away with the tip of his heel and grabbed her at the waist. "A woman who'd willingly wed herself to Rutland would like it rough," he said crudely as he captured her wrists within one of his larger hands. He ran his free hand down her body.

At each careless caress, her body turned first cold and then hot with sick shame. She bucked against him. "Let me go, sir" she hissed twisting and turning, she managed to yank a hand free. Phoebe raked her fingernails down his cheek and a sharp cry escaped him as he released her suddenly and she went sprawling backward upon the floor. A finger streak of crimson blood marred his cheek.

He touched the wound and then stared at the stain on his fingers. "You bitch," he spat.

Phoebe gave her head a clearing shake and shoved to her feet. She darted past him and then raced for the door. A cry rang from her lips as he pulled her by her hair and yanked her against his chest. Tears sprung behind her eyes at the cloying fear and desperation that coursed through her. "Let me go," she cried out, as he ran a trail of hot, wet kisses down the curve of her neck. In response, he nipped at the flesh. "P-please, stop." Her desperate entreaty emerged as a broken sob.

Panic sucked her in a vortex and threatened to drag her in. Phoebe bucked and twisted against him in a bid to free herself, but he tightened his manacle-like grip on her.

"How sweet to have Rutland's wife pleading," he whispered cupping her right breast in his hard, punishing grip. And fury lit to life, blotted out her hopelessness.

"You bastard," she hissed at the violation and jabbed her elbow back hard against him, but he laughed, that cold, merciless sound indicating he delighted in her struggles. She landed a hard jab to his midsection and the air left him on a whoosh. The viscount lost his grip on her. She ducked out from under his arms and sprinted for the door. Her heart pounded loud in her ears, the rapid, staccato beat deafening.

Phoebe stretched her fingers to the handle of the door.

Lord Brewer wrapped an arm about her waist and hauled her back so her feet left the floor and she kicked at the floor with the tips of her slippers. "You bitch," he said with such emotionless calm that terror stabbed at her insides. The viscount threw her down upon the sofa with such force the seat knocked the mahogany side table. The rapid movement unsettled the blue, porcelain sheep. Lord Brewer grinned cruelly down at her and then came over her, shifting his larger frame atop her smaller one. He covered her mouth with his and she gagged as he thrust his tongue into her throat. The weight of him, coupled with his cruel kiss, crushed off her airflow and she scrabbled at his back in a futile attempt to remove him from her person.

He cupped her left breast this time and a groan escaped him. "You will enjoy it, I promise," he said on a guttural whisper.

She bucked and twisted against him and his erection dug painfully into her belly. A convulsive shudder racked her frame. By God, what manner of man was he that he should be so aroused by her struggles? Her blank gaze slid momentarily from the monster above her as he worked a hand between them and undid the front flap of his breeches. Phoebe bit the inside of her lip so hard the sickly, sweet, metallic tinge of blood filled her senses. He shifted himself between her thighs and in one last frantic bid at freedom she punched him in the temple, landing an ineffectual blow.

God help me. A sheen of tears blurred her vision and, in this moment, she hated Lord Brewer as much as she hated herself for her inability to stop his assault. With blood pounding loudly in her ears, she stared hopelessly up at the white-wash ceiling and she braced for the viscount's swift, painful entry when he collapsed. Phoebe froze in shock and then she registered the slack-jawed man atop her frame. She swung her gaze to the stranger above her with her fingers outstretched, the blue sheep clasped tightly in her hand. The kindly-eyed blonde woman she'd seen earlier in Lady Wentworth's ballroom stood above her, her mouth set in a furious line. With a slight cry, Phoebe struggled with Viscount Brewer's powerful weight.

The woman sprang to action. She set the sheep down hard on the table. "Here, allow me to help you," the woman offered and then with a grunt, tugged the viscount by the back of his jacket and rolled him unceremoniously to the floor where he landed with a loud thump.

Phoebe scrambled to an upright position. With shamed mortification burning her skin, she averted her gaze and attempted to right her gown and hair and a sob escaped her which she buried into her trembling fingers. She struggled to her feet and made a bid to step over the prone form. Then a dawning horror crept in. Her gaze flew to the other lady.

"He is not dead," the woman said dryly. "Though it would hardly be a loss if he was," she muttered. She held her hand out. "My name is Jane. I am the Marchioness of Waverly."

Phoebe's eyebrows shot up. Though she'd yet to meet the marchioness, she'd heard whispers of the scandal that had found this illegitimate daughter of the Duke of Ravenscourt wedded to the marquess. There was a slight challenge in the woman's eyes, as though she expected Phoebe to find her in some way wanting. Alas, the young lady did not realize that she had long ago learned to look to each person's worth. Phoebe eyed the other marchioness' gloved fingertips a moment and then placed her hand in the woman's, allowing her to help her over. "Th-thank you," she murmured. Phoebe alternated her gaze between the unconscious man at their feet and her slippers. "I-I it was not…I…" She dropped her gaze to her mussed gown and captured her lower lip between her teeth.

"It was not your fault," the woman put in. There was a steely strength to those words that rang with conviction and somehow calmed her. And this woman who'd weathered her own scandal rose even higher in her estimation. "No, it was not your fault." The Marchioness of Waverly kicked the man with the tip of her slipper at his lower back. In his slumberous state, he groaned. "There are some men, however, who think a woman is there for their pleasures and it matters not what that woman wishes."

That matter-of-factness spoke of a woman who knew. Phoebe's throat worked at the sudden kindred connection she felt to this stranger. "Thank you," she said quietly. With quaking fingers she struggled to put her hair to rights. "Please, let me." Placing her gentle but firm hands on her shoulders, she turned her about and set to work rearranging the tangled tresses. "I'm sorry," she murmured, as Phoebe flinched.

At their feet, the viscount emitted a long groan and she jumped.

The marchioness took her by the hand and guided her over to the door. "Come with me. I will call for your carriage. Is your...?" *Husband.* Pain knotted Phoebe's belly. Pink bloomed on the other woman's cheeks. No doubt she recalled that Phoebe was the famed Marchioness of Rutland. Of course her husband was not present. "Do you have someone to escort you home?" the woman amended.

Phoebe gave her head a jerky shake, her gaze fixed on the gleaming, gold pendant at the woman's neck. She stared absently at that heart. Her unwed friends had come with their chaperones and respective parents. Jane pulled the door open and peered out into the hall. With Phoebe in tow, she all but dragged her from the room, down the hall, and onward away from the White Parlor. Each step that carried her from Lord Wentworth's and the remembrance of the viscount's assault left her more and more freed.

They turned the corridor just as a tall, commanding figure stepped into their path. A startled shriek escaped them as the frowning, dark-haired gentleman looked back and forth between them with a question in his eyes. His gaze lingered a moment upon Phoebe's torn gown and a dark glint flared in his eyes.

The marchioness slapped a hand to her heart. "Gabriel." She looked to Phoebe and gave her a reassuring smile. "It is just my husband." The woman returned her attention to her husband. "Gabriel, this is my friend," her throat worked, "Phoebe, the Marchioness of Rutland." His eyebrows shot up in surprise, but he gave no other outward indication as to his shock at the legendary marquess' new wife.

"My lady," he greeted.

Phoebe managed to sketch a hasty curtsy. A panicky laugh bubbled up in her chest at the ridiculousness of the pleasantries here in the hall, following the viscount's attack. Then, they were members of polite Society and were to wear a cool smile and calm expression even if the world was tipped upside down.

The marchioness cleared her throat. "Gabriel, will you see that Lady Rutland's carriage is readied? I will remain here."

He narrowed his gaze and looked down the hall, as though searching out the one responsible for her current state. She pressed her eyes closed at the humiliation of having this indignity witnessed by not one, but two, strangers. With a short bow, the gentleman turned on his heel and left.

A short while later, Phoebe boarded her carriage. As the conveyance rumbled away from Lady Wentworth's ball she recalled the viscount's words, the vile accusations about Edmund lashing at her mind like venomous barbs. She pulled back the velvet curtain and stared blankly out. Edmund had promised that marriage to her would, at the very least, provide her protection. With an arrogance that could only come from being the feared, famed, Marquess of Rutland, he'd expected his reputation should offer her a semblance of polite courtesy from the *ton*.

It appeared he'd added one more lie to the mountains of others to come before.

WITH A GROWL OF IMPATIENCE, Edmund took the steps of his townhouse two at a time. After an infernal night at his club, and then a blasted appearance at Lady Wentworth's tedious ball and then upon discovering his wife had the good sense to leave the infernal affair, a swift departure, he wanted to see his damned wife. Wallace, faithful as the day was long, pulled the door open in anticipation of his arrival. And he didn't like that he needed to see Phoebe. Giving a quick search of the foyer, he shrugged out of his cloak and handed it over to a waiting footman. But more than that, he didn't like that he hadn't seen her.

He looked up the staircase.

"Her Ladyship arrived earlier this evening, my lord. She's taken to her chambers."

Edmund made to go, but something in the man's rheumy eyes gave him pause. "Say whatever it is you would, Wallace," he snapped. He knew he was being a foul-tempered bastard in taking his frustrations out on the loyal servant, but he'd have the man out with his disappointment and not this vague game he'd played through the years of hoping he would suddenly become the man he wanted him to be.

Wallace looked off to the waiting footman and with a polite bow, the man left. "Her Ladyship did not seem herself," Wallace said when he returned his attention to Edmund.

"What do you mean she did not seem herself?" he asked with

a frown. Furthermore, Wallace had known Phoebe but two days. How much could he truly know where the lady was concerned?

The butler cleared his throat. "She was crying."

Guilt turned in his gut and cleaved at his conscience. It twisted inside him, forming a pebble in his belly that sat hard inside. This deuced caring business was blasted awful. By the tilt of the other man's head, Edmund knew there was something Wallace wished him to say. "Crying," he forced himself to respond.

"Yes, my lord. Crying. Tears."

"I know what crying is, Wallace," he said with a touch of impatience.

"Of course, my lord."

He cast another glance up the stairs. It was because of him. *Of course it is because of me.* From the moment he entered her life, he doomed her to despair. The pebble became a stone. "And how did you…know Her Ladyship was crying?"

"Red eyes, my lord. Very red."

With a black curse, Edmund took the stairs two at a time, then strode down the hall, coming to a stop outside Phoebe's chambers. He laid his forehead against the door. That afternoon he'd run from all her earlier talk of love and hope and happiness. Like the bloody coward he'd been all these years, only to hover at her doorway like a child with his ear to the keyhole, only to find he could not escape it. All the walls he'd erected these past years had been nothing more than sugar towers, toppled with the first hint of true warmth and goodness in his life. She'd asked him to set aside years of who he'd been. Could a person simply change?

He pressed his eyes closed. He wanted that answer to be yes. A shuddery sob split the wood panel and gutted him worse than the tip of Stanhope's rapier those eleven years ago. He'd have taken that blasted blade to his heart this instant if it would mean Phoebe did not know pain. He didn't know if he could be what she deserved or who she deserved—but he wanted to, at the very least, try. Edmund turned the handle and stepped inside.

It took a moment for his eyes to adjust to the darkened chambers. The faintest glow of a lone candle atop Phoebe's nightstand cast an eerie shadow upon the wall. He closed the door with a faint click and her sobs immediately ceased. She lay on her side with her back to him and made no move to look at him. "What do you want, Edmund?" she asked, her tone ragged with resignation.

Edmund shifted back and forth on his feet. *I want you*. Except, years of protecting himself kept those words back. "I came to… Wallace said…" His lips pulled in a grimace. "I visited Lady Wentworth's ball," he settled for.

Her slender back went taut, but she otherwise gave no outward reaction that she'd heard him.

He cleared his throat. "I came to see you, to attend with you."

"Not with me," she said, directing her words to the wall.

Edmund stiffened.

"You did not attend *with* me."

Edmund held his palms up, but with her back presented, she could not see them turned out in supplication.

"Is there anything else you wish to say?" Those blank, emotionless words did not belong to Phoebe. But this is what he'd made her. Agony speared at his stomach.

He let his hands fall to his side and cleared his throat. "That is all," he said tersely.

"Then go," she said on a harsh whisper.

Tugging at his lapels, Edmund turned on his heel and did the first honorable thing of his life—saved Phoebe from his useless offering of love.

CHAPTER 25

THE FOLLOWING MORNING AFTER ATTENDING to business with his man of affairs, Edmund returned to his townhouse. He strode up the steps with a heaviness to his footsteps. As diligent as always, Wallace pulled the door open in faithful anticipation of his employer's arrival. With a murmur of thanks, he shrugged out of his cloak and handed it over to the old servant. He looked expectantly at the man more friend and father than his own sire had ever been.

"She is in the drawing room receiving visitors," Wallace supplied. "A Miss Honoria Fairfax and Lady Gillian."

Edmund glanced down the corridor leading to his office. Following his meeting, there were really matters he must attend to. He needed to speak to his servants and see to his ledgers. He lifted his head and then started for his office. He intended to continue to said affairs. To move right past the closed receiving room door where his wife met with her friends. He really intended to. "That bastard."

If that muffled curse didn't reach through the door panel and freeze him in his tracks. As it was, he'd learned long ago the perils of listening at doors, but the fury lacing that word no polite lady ever uttered kept him rooted there. Not that he needed to remain outside, eavesdropping on his wife and her friends to know which gentleman earned the "that bastard" curse. Phoebe's friends were loyal and likely well knew the extent of Edmund's evil.

He turned to go and allow Phoebe her privacy.

"There *could* be benefits of marriage to him," one of the young lady's comments brought him to a stop outside the parlor. He wasn't eavesdropping. He didn't partake in such silly, nonsensical endeavors as…

"Marriage shouldn't be about benefits, but rather love and caring."

Edmund pressed his ear closer to the door. His wife's oddly detached words brought a frown to his lips. Granted, she was, indeed, correct but grating nonetheless.

"Surely there is some good in him," his unwitting champion said defensively. He gave his head a rueful shake. Foolish girl.

Phoebe laughed and this was the joyous, unadulterated sound he once remembered of her, before he'd gone and trapped her and shattered that exuberance with his ruthless plan for revenge. Pain tugged at his heart.

"What is it?" the other young lady asked, concern lacing her tone.

"Good in him? In a man who should use me in a game of revenge he'd exact against Honoria's aunt, his former lover? I think not."

His frown deepened. He'd not taken Margaret as his lover. Which he supposed was neither here nor there, and yet, Phoebe believed that untruth and he wanted her to know that despite the many lovers he'd taken, her friend's aunt had never been one of them. *As though that would bring his innocent young wife any consolation*, a voice jeered.

He really should go. There was no point in visiting a room of three ladies who'd likely rather have his blood than his company. Edmund turned to go, again.

"I for one imagine even one such as him would care a great deal." The loyal defender of his worthless self, intoned. "You should tell him," she added as an afterthought. The lady was incorrect in this regard. He didn't care a great deal about anything. Except her. He cared about Phoebe. His wife's murmured response was lost to the walls dividing them.

As the garrulous one carried on, Edmund took a step toward his office. "A gentleman doesn't like to have his wife going about being kissed by other men."

He froze. A crimson rage descended over his vision, momentarily blinding him and he wheeled slowly back around. *That.* He cared very much about that.

"I for one agree with Gillian," the more jaded, of the ladies chimed in. "A heartless cad such as the marquess will hardly tolerate another gentleman forcing his attentions on his wife."

The muscles in his body went taut. The crimson fury turned black until he breathed, tasted, and smelled the death of the man who'd touched Phoebe. A muscle jumped at the corner of his eye. The moment he discovered just who touched his wife, he'd hunt the bastard down and choke the breath from his worthless body for daring to put his hands upon the person that belonged to Edmund. A growl rumbled up from his chest.

"What was that?"

Silence reigned.

Christ. Edmund turned and peered down the hall plotting his escape just as the door opened. A young lady peeked her head around the edge of the frame. Her eyes went wide. A dull flush heated his neck.

"Oh, hullo," the young lady said with a smile as though she hadn't just discovered one of the darkest, most black-hearted lords in the realm listening at the keyhole. She turned back and called over her shoulder. "It is merely your husband, not some gossiping servant," she said with such innocent cheer he winced.

Edmund moved woodenly through the doorway, keeping his face an expressionless mask. At his presence, the previously talkative ladies fell silent. He remembered to sketch a bow but remained with his attention fixed on his pale wife. Edmund recalled his visit to her chambers last evening. She had lain with her back presented to him. Now in the light of day, he took in those details that had escaped him the previous evening. The cut at the corner of her mouth. The bruise on her neck. Then with a dawning, creeping horror all the darkest, ugliest possibilities slipped in of Phoebe on her back with some bounder above her, rutting between her thighs while she fought and cloyed for freedom. *I was at my clubs. I was at my clubs while she was alone.* He drew in a slow, calming breath, one heartbeat from madness. When that had no effect, he drew in another.

From the corner of his eye, he saw Miss Fairfax and Lady Gillian exchange looks and then wordlessly the two young ladies hurriedly took their leave.

That sprung Phoebe back to movement. She jumped to her feet. "You do not have to go," she called after them, her voice a high squeak. Edmund stepped aside allowing her two silent friends to slip from the room like white ruffled geese in matching steps until he and Phoebe were alone. He reached behind him and drew the door silently closed.

"Who?" he asked quietly.

She slid her gaze away from his and made a show of studying the tips of her slippers. "I don't—"

"Who?"

Phoebe picked her head up. "Does it matter?" She lifted her shoulders in a little shrug. "It could have been any number of irate husbands who sought revenge on the man who took their wife as his lover."

His stomach churned with nausea. Bile climbed up his throat, until he thought he might be ill. "Is that what happened?" he hardly recognized that strangled, garbled tone as belonging to him.

Her hesitancy served as his confirmation. Edmund closed the distance between them in several long strides and hovered before her. In a world where he was decisive and moved with purpose, now he was at sea. So *this* was what it was like to be preyed upon.

He stretched a hand out and brushed his fingertips over the mark on her neck. His heart pounded loudly in his ears, nearly deafening. When he trusted himself to speak he asked the question he didn't really want an answer to. "Did he—?" Ah, God help him for a coward. One single utterance would shred what was left of his worthless soul.

Phoebe fisted the fabric of her skirts. "No." She gave a brusque shake of her head. "He did not." Edmund slid his eyes closed and sent a prayer skywards to a God who apparently did exist. He opened them again just as his wife touched her fingertips to a heart pendant at her neck, an inexpensive bauble that gleamed bright. "The Marchioness of Waverly came upon us…him…and she clouted him over the head. The marquess saw to my carriage. And then I returned home."

How coolly emotionless she spoke and yet the faintest tremble to her lithe frame indicated the mark left by the monster who'd touched her. And Edmund had not been there. He stared at the crown of her dark tresses. He'd promised that she'd be afforded the protection of his name. Instead, he'd left her dependent on the timely arrival of strangers. Edmund had never hated himself more than he did in this moment. The Marquess of Waverly, brother to Lord Alex Edgerton, a man whom he'd sought to publicly humiliate for perceived injustices after Margaret's betrayal, no less. For this, Edmund would eternally owe that family his fealty. What a humbling, shaming moment. "Who?" She paused and for a long moment he suspected she'd withhold that name, and it would forever haunt him knowing that a gentleman who moved about polite Society had dared kiss her mouth and marked her skin.

"Lord Brewer."

"....I've had so many other men's wives in my bed, surely you don't expect me to remember yours...?"

Oh, God. Not trusting himself to speak, Edmund turned on his heel and left. A volatile fury with a lifelike force fueled his movements. He strode through the corridors and with each angry step he took, he lashed at himself with the memory of his wife, injured, assaulted, nearly raped for his crimes. Rage roiled in his belly and he fed the familiar, safe emotion. He reached the foyer and bellowed for his horse.

A short while later, his mount was readied and he swung astride the magnificent black beast with one purpose in mind. Edmund guided Lucifer through the crowded streets, the fashionable end, onward to the hallowed halls of White's. He dismounted before the famous, white façade structure and tossed the reins to a nearby street urchin. The boy accepted the reins and waited with the promise of coin as Edmund strode inside the legendary club. The club he'd taken membership at for the company it afforded him, but had studiously avoided through the years, unless it suited his purpose of revenge. As such, Edmund knew all those men who owed him a debt and where they spent their afternoons. He stepped inside the respectable club feeling like the sinner stepping through the church doors for Sunday sermon. Ignoring the buzz of whisper generated by his presence, he strode through the crowd, scanning the crowded tables, in search of one.

And then he located him at the far right corner of the room, with a bottle of brandy and tumbler before him. Thoughts of

Phoebe and her tear-stained cheeks and her marked neck filled his mind, and Edmund increased his stride. Just then, Lord Brewer glanced up and his gaze landed on Edmund. All the color leeched from the bastard's face. The faint trail of fingernail tracks upon his cheek stood as a stark contrast.

Madness lapped at Edmund.

Phoebe's fingers. Fighting when she shouldn't have had to.

He came to a stop at Brewer's table.

With courage he didn't know the other man possessed, or perhaps it was mere idiocy, Brewer gave a cocksure grin. "Rutland." He raised his glass in salute. "How is the marchion—?"

Edmund hauled the man from the seat by the lapels of his jacket and dragged him so they were eye to eye. "If you ever touch my wife again, by God I will kill you dead. I will take you apart with my bare hands and relish the sounds of your screams while I do it."

The muscles of the viscount's throat moved up and down. "Y-you who've made a c-cuckold of most gentlemen in this room would issue that threat?" In the absence of a pledge to steer clear of Phoebe, Edmund buried his fist in the other man's nose. Brewer cried out as blood spurted from the broken appendage and he stumbled into the table and then landed hard on his back.

The viscount pressed a hand to his face. Blood seeped through his fingers and he continued undeterred. "If it is not me, it will be another," Brewer spat and a chill ran through him at the final reckoning of his sins. He would not pay the price, but rather Phoebe. By God, she'd not pay for his crimes. "And you will be no different than any other m—" He cried out as Edmund came over him and punched him in the face again. Edmund rained down his fists, pummeling the other man so that crimson stained his face and through it, he saw this man's frame atop her. Her cries. Her pleas. *Because of my sins.* He reached for the barely moaning, limp viscount's neck, when hands scrabbled at his back. Powerful hands hefted him from Brewer's frame and dragged Edmund back. He kicked out at Brewer with the toe of his boot and fought against the stranger's powerful hold.

"By God, Rutland, I detest you but I'd still not see you spend your days in Newgate for offing one like Brewer."

Edmund wrenched free of the man's hold and turned to face the Earl of Stanhope. Panting from his exertions, the earl's hair fell over his brow and he glared at Edmund.

Edmund glowered back and Stanhope must have sensed his intention to go and finish Brewer for he wrapped a powerful hand around his forearm and forcibly dragged him through the club. Edmund fought against his hold. "By God, let me go, Stanhope," he hissed.

The earl, this man who'd competed with him for another woman's affections eleven years ago ignored his commands and continued propelling him through the club.

They reached the front of the club and a majordomo pulled the door open in eager anticipation of Edmund's departure. He braced for the other man to toss him, but the earl followed behind him out into the street. They stood at the front steps of the club with passersby casting the rumpled pair curious looks. "I well know this isn't your usual choice of establishment, nor will you find yourself welcomed with this showing," the earl muttered, as he yanked a kerchief from his jacket and dusted off his brow.

Edmund eyed the doors, contemplating entering the club once more and destroying Brewer. He took a step toward the club.

"Do not," Stanhope said in clipped tones, anticipating his efforts.

He flexed his jaw. "He touched my wife," he said on a hushed whisper.

The earl arched an eyebrow and stuffed the white fabric back into his jacket.

A dull flush heated Edmund's cheeks as Brewer's charge melded with Stanhope's accusatory look. In a bid for revenge against the man who'd dueled him for Margaret's hand, he'd orchestrated his own wife's ruin and then sealed that ruin with his own kiss. He swiped his hand over his face. Who had he been?

Stanhope slapped a hand on his back. "Come with me." It was not a question.

And the man Edmund had been fifteen days ago would have sneered at Stanhope and had a mocking rejoinder for that request. The man who'd been shaped by Phoebe's good and his own desire to be more followed the earl to his carriage. One of Stanhope's grooms pulled the door open and then motioned him inside. He hesitated, as too many years worth of wariness reared its head. Perhaps it always would.

Edmund climbed inside.

But then mayhap he was strong enough to battle that guardedness. He claimed a seat on the bench and through hooded lashes studied Stanhope who whispered something to the groom. The young man nodded and closed the door behind him. The earl claimed the opposite bench, rapped once, and the carriage rocked into motion.

He sprung forward on the edge of his seat. "My—"

"My man will see to your horse," he assured him.

"What the hell do you want?" he snapped fisting the edge of his seat.

"To talk."

He blinked several times. "What could you have to say to me?" By rights, Stanhope should attempt to bloody Edmund the way Edmund bloodied Brewer just moments ago.

"Other than go to hell?" Stanhope drawled. "You'd be surprised." The ghost of a smile died on his lips. "I have hated you for years, Rutland."

With that statement the earl could keep company with most of polite Society.

"I do not any longer."

Edmund went still.

"I pity you."

There it was. That unwanted, loathsome emotion. It was on the tip of his tongue to say he didn't need anyone's pity, but yet, the truth was, he'd been a pitiable creature these years. A soulless beast.

"I let go of my past," Stanhope continued quietly. "While you," he nodded his chin at him. "You remained firmly stuck there and I would have been stuck there right alongside you if it wasn't for my wife. Whom I love. And any man who reacts the way you did this afternoon at White's is also very much in love with his wife."

The air slipped from his lips on a hiss as Stanhope, this longstanding enemy found his weakness. He braced to have that discovery turned against him as a weapon to inflict a lethal blow. Stanhope winged a blond eyebrow upwards. "You are wondering how I'll use that information against you." A crooked grin formed on his lips. The carriage rocked to a slow halt and he rapped once on the roof of the carriage. "I'll use it against you by helping you. Go to your wife and put your past behind you."

Before Phoebe had entered his life, Edmund would have scoffed at Stanhope or any man who dared believe he could change. Or, for that matter, that he'd *want* to change. The muscles of his throat bobbed up and down. His wife had forced him to look at the parts of himself he'd long buried; his secret hunger to be viewed as more man than beast...and more than that, a man capable of being loved and loving in return.

Edmund looked out the window at the façade of his townhouse. He looked at Stanhope squarely. "Why?"

"Oh, do not mistake me," the earl said rolling his shoulders. "I still think you're a miserable bastard but life does that to all of us, then. And if we are fortunate, then we can accept saving in the unlikeliest place."

He furrowed his brow.

"With the love of a lady." Stanhope's driver pulled the door open. "Now get the hell out, Rutland." He eased those words with a half-grin.

As he stepped down, Edmund tried to force out the appropriate words. He turned back and stuck his hand inside the carriage. "Thank you."

This man who'd battled him for another years ago, looked at the offering a moment, and then put his hand in his. There was something freeing in the broken chain that tied him to a dark, ugly past he no longer wanted a part of. "Go," Stanhope said again.

With that, Edmund turned from his past and stepped toward his future.

CHAPTER 26

FROM HER PERCH ON THE windowseat overlooking the streets below, for the tenth time, Phoebe read the familiar words in The Times.

In a not uncharacteristic show of ruthlessness, the Marquess of R, violently assaulted the Viscount B. No one can glean the details surrounding the incident, however…

She tossed aside the paper where it landed in a soft thump at her feet. Phoebe knew precisely the details surrounding that particular incident. Following her admission yesterday afternoon, he'd stormed off and she'd not seen a glimpse of him since.

His defense could be explained by purely self-serving reasons as her friend had suggested. Edmund's concern for being viewed as weak and made a cuckold of before other gentleman could surely explain away the vicious fire in his eyes or the primitive growl as he'd stormed from the room. Yet, Phoebe had seen more there. A more that indicated this had not been entirely about him, but rather her.

A knock sounded at the door and she glanced up.

"His Lordship has requested your presence in his office," the servant politely informed her.

Phoebe swung her legs over the edge of the bench and settled her feet on the floor. He would summon her. Her heart slipped. Edmund could not be bothered to find her himself and speak to her on whatever matter he wished to speak to her. With a murmur of thanks, she woodenly shoved herself to her feet and made her way from the room, through the halls, and to Edmund's office. As she walked through the corridors, servants rushed past her, arms filled with valises and trunks. Her trunks. Edmund's request forgotten, with a frown on her lips, Phoebe followed the flurry of activity to the end of the hall. The front doors opened, sunlight streamed into the marble foyer as servants carried her belongings outside.

It appeared as though her husband had tired of her. What did bored gentlemen do with new, unwanted wives?

"My lady, do you require any help?" a servant asked at her shoulder.

Phoebe gave her head a clearing shake. "Er, no. Thank you," she added absently and then turned on her heel, making her way to Edmund's office.

The office where he plotted the ruin of men. She thought of her own name in that book. Honoria's. And young ladies. No one was spared from, as the gossip columns called it, his ruthlessness. Who knew the gossips could be correct about anything. Phoebe stopped outside his closed door. She should be glad he wanted her gone. And yet, regret stabbed at her sharp and painful as a dull dagger sticking at her heart. *You are a fool, Phoebe Eloise.* She raised her hand to knock and then thought better of it. Edmund could send her away but regardless, this was now her home. She pressed the handle. And she'd not rap on the door like a recalcitrant child summoned by her father. Phoebe opened the door and stepped inside.

Her heart started. Edmund stood with his hip propped along the edge of his desk, arms folded at his chest, elegant in his repose. Why did he have to be so blasted handsome? Phoebe pushed the door closed behind her and then leaned against the wood frame, borrowing support from the wood panel. "You wished to see me?" she asked quietly. Having seen her belongings being packed up, she rather knew what this meeting pertained to. Hurt twisted her belly in knots.

Edmund remained casually leaning, so impossibly cool and calm when her every fiber thrummed with awareness and regret.

"I did," he said simply.

Her gaze fell to the loathed, damning black leather book at his side.

He followed her stare and, picking up the book, shoved himself to standing. With the leather tome in his hands, he strolled over to her, fanning those pages as he walked. "I lied to you again." Phoebe stiffened.

"I pledged that I'd never again write a name in this book, but that was a lie."

Her heart slipped.

His thick, black lashes swept downward. "Here." He held out that detestable book.

Phoebe clutched a hand at her throat. She didn't want to see that name. Didn't want to know that he could not, nay *would not*, change.

"Take it," he urged, his tone a blend of steel and warmth. Wetting her lips, she accepted it with numb fingers and scanned past name after name.

Miss Margaret Dunn

The Earl of Stanhope

Lord Alex Edgerton

She continued turning page after page.

The Viscount Waters

Miss Honoria Fairfax.

Phoebe. She paused on her name, her own weaknesses staring back at her. He'd known her so very well that he'd known precisely what mattered to her and forever marked it upon his page. With a drawn sigh, she turned the page—

And froze.

Phoebe shot her gaze to his and found his face a blank, expressionless mask. She quickly looked to the page and read and reread the two sentences. One name. Nine words marked in his hand.

Edmund Deering, the Marquess of Rutland. ~~Weakness my wife~~.

Emotion swelled in her throat and she quietly handed the book back over to him. He refused to take it and she let it fall to her side. So that is why he'd send her away. A man like Edmund who thrived on power and resented all hint of weakness, would not want to be riddled with the constant reminder of a person who inspired anything less than ruthlessness in him. "I don't want to be your weakness," she said softly. She wanted to be his partner through life, making one another stronger with love.

He brushed his knuckles along her jaw, forcing her attention back to him. "Turn the page."

"What game do you play, Edmund?" she asked, shaking the book. "Why can you not say what it is that you want me to read in these pages?"

"There is no game," he said, his tone gruff. He took the book from her hands and tossed it aside where it landed with a noisy thwack upon the hardwood floor. "Would you know what those words say on the next page? They say Edmund Deering, Marquess of Rutland. My strength is my wife."

Her heart stilled a beat as with infinite gentleness he took her face between his palms. "You are my strength. You do not make me weaker. You make me stronger just by your spirit and courage and convictions."

She shook her head, trying to make sense of his words. "I don't understand." Her voice emerged as a breathless whisper.

"How can you not know? I love you," he said softly.

No. He couldn't. "But you do not—?"

He silenced her words with the pad of his thumb; rubbing the flesh of her lower lip. "But I do. I spent all my life fearing any emotion that could weaken me and do you know what I discovered, because of you, Phoebe?"

She managed to shake her head.

"I didn't like the man I was—a man who took his pleasures where he would." With women who'd been equally miserable and lonely. By the flash of regret in his eyes, she knew he'd followed that unspoken thought. "I do not want to be that man again. I will not be that man." He brought her hand to his chest and placed it where his heart beat. "What I feel for you, this love, it fills me with lightness, it lifts me from darkness, buoying me in ways I've never been." He lowered his brow to hers. "How can this emotion be worse than the darkness that has weighted me down all these years? It is freeing and healing and makes me stronger, not weaker."

Phoebe pressed her eyes closed and a tear squeezed past her lashes. Edmund brushed it away with the pad of his thumb. "I love you," he said again. "And I do not expect after my treachery that you should return those sentiments—"

"Why are you sending me away?" she blurted. Why, if he loved her would he let her go?

"I want you to have what you've always wanted. I've arranged for you to have your Captain Cook Adventures, your travels to Wales." He drew in an audible breath. "I would go with you," he said on a rush, as though fearing her response, "because if you were to board a ship without me, I would take it apart with my bare hands before I let you leave."

At those words she'd once given him, a sob escaped her. He drew her into his arms. "You deserve a gentleman, a lord with pretty words and an honorable soul, and I know there is little use with the heart of a scoundrel, but I'd give it to you, anyway."

"Oh, Edmund." Phoebe captured his face between her hands and looked into his eyes. His eyes slid closed a moment, as though with her words, she'd given him an absolution of sorts. She waited until he looked at her once more. "I love *you*." She managed a watery smile. "I don't need the heart of a gentleman with pretty words. I just need the heart of a good man who loves me."

A slow smile turned his lips up at the corners and this was pure, honest, devoid of all cold artifice and pretense. "Then that is what you will have," he whispered. He claimed her mouth under his in a gentle kiss.

And *that* is all she'd ever wanted.

EPILOGUE

Spring 1817
One month later

"AT LAST YOU RETURNED."

Curled up at Edmund's side, Phoebe looked up at the door to where her brother and sister stood. A patent smile lined Justina's face. Andrew, however, wore a dark scowl. "It is lovely to see you, as well," she drawled, making to rise, but Edmund wrapped a possessive arm about her and held her at his side. Since he'd discovered she was expecting in Wales, he'd ordered their belongings packed and rushed them back to the confines of their townhouse. He'd not left her side since. Despite her assurances and the assurances of his family physician, he'd not gathered that this expecting business was really quite natural.

Either failing to hear or care about Phoebe's droll tone, Andrew sailed into the room. He plopped down on the chair nearest Edmund. "You've been gone an infernally long time." His lips settled into a petulant frown.

"It was but a month."

"It was a month and one week," Justina muttered, and gave her brother an accusatory glance. "And I should know. *That* one spoke of it. Every day." She looked to Phoebe. "Every. Day."

At his sister's pronouncement, embarrassment turned his cheeks red and Andrew tugged at his lapels. "Well, is there something wrong with a chap missing his friend?"

A smile twitched at Phoebe's lips. "Your sister?"

Her brother furrowed his brow in consternation. "Did I say my sister? I was referring to Rutland, there."

"Ah, of course," Phoebe said with mock solemnity. She stole a glance up at her husband. A pained expression marked the chiseled planes of his face. Another smile tugged at her lips. For the gentleness and love he'd shown her this past one month and one week as her siblings had aptly pointed out, there would always be, she suspected, a bearish gruffness to him around others and the affection shown him. She slipped her hand into his and gave a slight squeeze.

Edmund glanced down at their interlocked digits and raised it to his lips. A look passed between them and warmth filled her heart. It spiraled through her with a blazing heat.

Andrew leaned forward in his chair and waved his hand about. "Are you two listening to me?"

"No, they are not." Justina slid into a mahogany shell chair beside her brother. Her blue eyes twinkled with mirth. "They are giving one another the look of longing."

"The look of longing?" her brother wrinkled his nose. "What in blazes is that?"

Edmund wrapped an arm about Phoebe. "Someday you will discover precisely what that is, Barrett."

Andrew gave a dismissive wave. "Regardless, I've not come to talk about Phoebe's odd looking business." It did not escape Phoebe's notice that he'd very deliberately left Edmund out of that odd looking business. "I've missed you at the clubs. Not the same there without you."

Annoyed by his visiting those shameful sins, Phoebe frowned at Andrew. She opened her mouth to deliver a stinging lecture on those very clubs, when Edmund folded his ankle at his knee.

"I no longer visit For…those clubs," he amended, glancing over at his young sister-in-law and then wife.

The man he'd been would have not given a jot about talking about those scandalous clubs before anyone and everyone. The man he truly was, however, cared…about Phoebe, her family, their life.

Andrew blinked in rapid succession. "You no longer visit Forbidden Pleasures."

Edmund gave a somber shake of his head. "I do not."

"Never tell me you attend," He gave a shudder. "Brooke's or Whites?"

Edmund's silence stood as his answer.

A pained groan escaped the younger man and he threw himself back in his chair. "You've ruined him, Phoebe. Utterly and completely ruined the Marquess of Rutland."

Edmund raised Phoebe's fingertips to his lips once again and placed a lingering kiss on the inner portion of her wrist where her heart pounded wildly. "Ah, but that is where you are wrong, Barrett. Your sister saved me."

And ignoring the painful groan of her brother, Phoebe leaned up and kissed her husband.

THE END

OTHER BOOKS BY CHRISTI CALDWELL

TO ENCHANT A WICKED DUKE

Book 13 in the "Heart of a Duke" Series by Christi Caldwell

A Devil in Disguise

Years ago, when Nick Tallings, the recent Duke of Huntly, watched his family destroyed at the hands of a merciless nobleman, he vowed revenge. But his efforts had been futile, as his enemy, Lord Rutland is without weakness.

Until now...

With his rival finally happily married, Nick is able to set his ruthless scheme into motion. His plot hinges upon Lord Rutland's innocent, empty-headed sister-in-law, Justina Barrett. Nick will ruin her, marry her, and then leave her brokenhearted.

A Lady Dreaming of Love

From the moment Justina Barrett makes her Come Out, she is labeled a Diamond. Even with her ruthless father determined to sell her off to the highest bidder, Justina never gives up on her hope for a good, honorable gentleman who values her wit more than her looks.

A Not-So-Chance Meeting

Nick's ploy to ensnare Justina falls neatly into place in the streets of London. With each carefully orchestrated encounter, he slips further and further inside the lady's heart, never anticipating that Justina, with her quick wit and strength, will break down his own defenses. As Nick's plans begins to unravel, he's left to determine which is more important—Justina's love or his vow for vengeance. But can Justina ever forgive the duke who deceived her?

One Winter with a Baron

Book 12 in the "Heart of a Duke" Series by Christi Caldwell

A clever spinster:

Content with her spinster lifestyle, Miss Sybil Cunning wants to prove that a future as an unmarried woman is the only life for her. As a bluestocking who values hard, empirical data, Sybil needs help with her research. Nolan Pratt, Baron Webb, one of society's most scandalous rakes, is the perfect gentleman to help her. After all, he inspires fear in proper mothers and desire within their daughters.

A notorious rake:

Society may be aware of Nolan Pratt, Baron's Webb's wicked ways, but what he has carefully hidden is his miserable handling of his family's finances. When Sybil presents him the opportunity to earn much-needed funds, he can't refuse.

A winter to remember:

However, what begins as a business arrangement becomes something more and with every meeting, Sybil slips inside his heart. Can this clever woman look beneath the veneer of a coldhearted rake to see the man Nolan truly is?

To Redeem a Rake

Book 11 in the "Heart of a Duke" Series by Christi Caldwell

He's spent years scandalizing society.
Now, this rake must change his ways.

Society's most infamous scoundrel, Daniel Winterbourne, the Earl of Montfort, has been promised a small fortune if he can relinquish his wayward, carousing lifestyle. And behaving means he must also help find a respectable companion for his youngest sister—someone who will guide her and whom she can emulate. However, Daniel knows no such woman. But when he encounters a childhood friend, Daniel believes she may just be the answer to all of his problems.

Having been secretly humiliated by an unscrupulous blackguard years earlier, Miss Daphne Smith dreams of finding work at Ladies of Hope, an institution that provides an education for disabled women. With her sordid past and a disfigured leg, few opportunities arise for a woman such as she. Knowing Daniel's history, she wishes to avoid him, but working for his sister is exactly the stepping stone she needs.

Their attraction intensifies as Daniel and Daphne grow closer, preparing his sister for the London Season. But Daniel must resist his desire for a woman tarnished by scandal while Daphne is reminded of the boy she once knew. Can society's most notorious rake redeem his reputation and become the man Daphne deserves?

To Woo a Widow

Book 10 in the "Heart of a Duke" Series by Christi Caldwell

They see a brokenhearted widow.

She's far from shattered.

Lady Philippa Winston is never marrying again. After her late husband's cruelty that she kept so well hidden, she has no desire to search for love.

Years ago, Miles Brookfield, the Marquess of Guilford, made a frivolous vow he never thought would come to fruition—he promised to marry his mother's goddaughter if he was unwed by the age of thirty. Now, to his dismay, he's faced with honoring that pledge. But when he encounters the beautiful and intriguing Lady Philippa, Miles knows his true path in life. It's up to him to break down every belief Philippa carries about gentlemen, proving that not only is love real, but that he is the man deserving of her sheltered heart.

Will Philippa let down her guard and allow Miles to woo a widow in desperate need of his love?

The Lure of a Rake

Book 9 in the "Heart of a Duke" Series by Christi Caldwell

A Lady Dreaming of Love

Lady Genevieve Farendale has a scandalous past. Jilted at the altar years earlier and exiled by her family, she's now returned to London to prove she can be a proper lady. Even though she's not given up on the hope of marrying for love, she's wary of trusting again. Then she meets Cedric Falcot, the Marquess of St. Albans whose seductive ways set her heart aflutter. But with her sordid history, Genevieve knows a rake can also easily destroy her.

An Unlikely Pairing

What begins as a chance encounter between Cedric and Genevieve becomes something more. As they continue to meet, passions stir. But with Genevieve's hope for true love, she fears Cedric will be unable to give up his wayward lifestyle. After all, Cedric has spent years protecting his heart, and keeping everyone out. Slowly, she chips away at all the walls he's built, but when he falters, Genevieve can't offer him redemption. Now, it's up to Cedric to prove to Genevieve that the love of a man is far more powerful than the lure of a rake.

To Trust a Rogue

Book 8 in the "Heart of a Duke" Series by Christi Caldwell

A rogue

Marcus, the Viscount Wessex has carefully crafted the image of rogue and charmer for Polite Society. Under that façade, however, dwells a man whose dreams were shattered almost eight years earlier by a young lady who captured his heart, pledged her love, and then left him, with nothing more than a curt note.

A widow

Eight years earlier, faced with no other choice, Mrs. Eleanor Collins, fled London and the only man she ever loved, Marcus, Viscount Wessex. She has now returned to serve as a companion for her elderly aunt with a daughter in tow. Even though they're next door neighbors, there is little reason for her to move in the same circles as Marcus, just in case, she vows to avoid him, for he reminds her of all she lost when she left.

Reunited

As their paths continue to cross, Marcus finds his desire for Eleanor just as strong, but he learned long ago she's not to be trusted. He will offer her a place in his bed, but not anything more. Only, Eleanor has no interest in this new, roguish man. The more time they spend together, the protective wall they've constructed to keep the other out, begin to break. With all the betrayals and secrets between them, Marcus has to open his heart again. And Eleanor must decide if it's ever safe to trust a rogue.

To Wed His Christmas Lady

Book 7 in the "Heart of a Duke" Series by Christi Caldwell

She's longing to be loved:

Lady Cara Falcot has only served one purpose to her loathsome father—to increase his power through a marriage to the future Duke of Billingsley. As such, she's built protective walls about her heart, and presents an icy facade to the world around her. Journeying home from her finishing school for the Christmas holidays, Cara's carriage is stranded during a winter storm. She's forced to tarry at a ramshackle inn, where she immediately antagonizes another patron—William.

He's avoiding his duty in favor of one last adventure:

William Hargrove, the Marquess of Grafton has wanted only one thing in life—to avoid the future match his parents would have him make to a cold, duke's daughter. He's returning home from a blissful eight years of traveling the world to see to his responsibilities. But when a winter storm interrupts his trip and lands him at a falling-down inn, he's forced to share company with a commanding Lady Cara who initially reminds him exactly of the woman he so desperately wants to avoid.

A Christmas snowstorm ushers in the spirit of the season:

At the holiday time, these two people who despise each other due to first perceptions are offered renewed beginnings and fresh starts. As this gruff stranger breaks down the walls she's built about herself, Cara has to determine whether she can truly open her heart to trusting that any man is capable of good and that she herself is capable of love. And William has to set aside all previous thoughts he's carried of the polished ladies like Cara, to be the man to show her that love.

The Heart of a Scoundrel

Book 6 in the "Heart of a Duke" Series by Christi Caldwell

Ruthless, wicked, and dark, the Marquess of Rutland rouses terror in the breast of ladies and nobleman alike. All Edmund wants in life is power. After he was publically humiliated by his one love Lady Margaret, he vowed vengeance, using Margaret's niece, as his pawn. Except, he's thwarted by another, more enticing target—Miss Phoebe Barrett.

Miss Phoebe Barrett knows precisely the shame she's been born to. Because her father is a shocking letch she's learned to form her own opinions on a person's worth. After a chance meeting with the Marquess of Rutland, she is captivated by the mysterious man. He, too, is a victim of society's scorn, but the more encounters she has with Edmund, the more she knows there is powerful depth and emotion to the jaded marquess.

The lady wreaks havoc on Edmund's plans for revenge and he finds he wants Phoebe, at all costs. As she's drawn into the darkness of his world, Phoebe risks being destroyed by Edmund's ruthlessness. And Phoebe who desires love at all costs, has to determine if she can ever truly trust the heart of a scoundrel.

To Love a Lord

Book 5 in the "Heart of a Duke" Series by Christi Caldwell

All she wants is security:

The last place finishing school instructor Mrs. Jane Munroe belongs, is in polite Society. Vowing to never wed, she's been scuttled around from post to post. Now she finds herself in the Marquess of Waverly's household. She's never met a nobleman she liked, and when she meets the pompous, arrogant marquess, she remembers why. But soon, she discovers Gabriel is unlike any gentleman she's ever known.

All he wants is a companion for his sister:

What Gabriel finds himself with instead, is a fiery spirited, bespectacled woman who entices him at every corner and challenges his age-old vow to never trust his heart to a woman. But... there is something suspicious about his sister's companion. And he is determined to find out just what it is.

All they need is each other:

As Gabriel and Jane confront the truth of their feelings, the lies and secrets between them begin to unravel. And Jane is left to decide whether or not it is ever truly safe to love a lord.

Loved By a Duke

Book 4 in the "Heart of a Duke" Series by Christi Caldwell

For ten years, Lady Daisy Meadows has been in love with Auric, the Duke of Crawford. Ever since his gallant rescue years earlier, Daisy knew she was destined to be his Duchess. Unfortunately, Auric sees her as his best friend's sister and nothing more. But perhaps, if she can manage to find the fabled heart of a duke pendant, she will win over the heart of her duke.

Auric, the Duke of Crawford enjoys Daisy's company. The last thing he is interested in however, is pursuing a romance with a woman he's known since she was in leading strings. This season, Daisy is turning up in the oddest places and he cannot help but notice that she is no longer a girl. But Auric wouldn't do something as foolhardy as to fall in love with Daisy. He couldn't. Not with the guilt he carries over his past sins... Not when he has no right to her heart...But perhaps, just perhaps, she can forgive the past and trust that he'd forever cherish her heart—but will she let him?

The Love of a Rogue

Book 3 in the "Heart of a Duke" Series by Christi Caldwell

Lady Imogen Moore hasn't had an easy time of it since she made her Come Out. With her betrothed, a powerful duke breaking it off to wed her sister, she's become the *tons* favorite piece of gossip. Never again wanting to experience the pain of a broken heart, she's resolved to make a match with a polite, respectable gentleman. The last thing she wants is another reckless rogue.

Lord Alex Edgerton has a problem. His brother, tired of Alex's carousing has charged him with chaperoning their remaining, unwed sister about *ton* events. Shopping? No, thank you. Attending the theatre? He'd rather be at Forbidden Pleasures with a scantily clad beauty upon his lap. The task of *chaperone* becomes even more of a bother when his sister drags along her dearest friend, Lady Imogen to social functions. The last thing he wants in his life is a young, innocent English miss.

Except, as Alex and Imogen are thrown together, passions flare and Alex comes to find he not only wants Imogen in his bed, but also in his heart. Yet now he must convince Imogen to risk all, on the heart of a rogue.

More Than a Duke

Book 2 in the "Heart of a Duke" Series by Christi Caldwell

Polite Society doesn't take Lady Anne Adamson seriously. However, Anne isn't just another pretty young miss. When she discovers her father betrayed her mother's love and her family descended into poverty, Anne comes up with a plan to marry a respectable, powerful, and honorable gentleman—a man nothing like her philandering father.

Armed with the heart of a duke pendant, fabled to land the wearer a duke's heart, she decides to enlist the aid of the notorious Harry, 6th Earl of Stanhope. A scoundrel with a scandalous past, he is the last gentleman she'd ever wed...however, his reputation marks him the perfect man to school her in the art of seduction so she might ensnare the illustrious Duke of Crawford.

Harry, the Earl of Stanhope is a jaded, cynical rogue who lives for his own pleasures. Having been thrown over by the only woman he ever loved so she could wed a duke, he's not at all surprised when Lady Anne approaches him with her scheme to capture another duke's affection. He's come to appreciate that all women are in fact greedy, title-grasping, self-indulgent creatures. And with Anne's history of grating on his every last nerve, she is the last woman he'd ever agree to school in the art of seduction. Only his friendship with the lady's sister compels him to help.

What begins as a pretend courtship, born of lessons on seduction, becomes something more leaving Anne to decide if she can give her heart to a reckless rogue, and Harry must decide if he's willing to again trust in a lady's love.

For Love of the Duke

First Full-Length Book in the "Heart of a Duke" Series
by Christi Caldwell

After the tragic death of his wife, Jasper, the 8th Duke of Bainbridge buried himself away in the dark cold walls of his home, Castle Blackwood. When he's coaxed out of his self-imposed exile to attend the amusements of the Frost Fair, his life is irrevocably changed by his fateful meeting with Lady Katherine Adamson.

With her tight brown ringlets and silly white-ruffled gowns, Lady Katherine Adamson has found her dance card empty for two Seasons. After her father's passing, Katherine learned the unreliability of men, and is determined to depend on no one, except herself. Until she meets Jasper…

In a desperate bid to avoid a match arranged by her family, Katherine makes the Duke of Bainbridge a shocking proposition—one that he accepts.

Only, as Katherine begins to love Jasper, she finds the arrangement agreed upon is not enough. And Jasper is left to decide if protecting his heart is more important than fighting for Katherine's love.

In Need of a Duke

A Prequel Novella to "The Heart of a Duke" Series
by Christi Caldwell

In Need of a Duke: (Author's Note: This is a prequel novella to "The Heart of a Duke" series by Christi Caldwell. It was originally available in "The Heart of a Duke" Collection and is now being published as an individual novella.

~★~

It features a new prologue and epilogue.

Years earlier, a gypsy woman passed to Lady Aldora Adamson and her friends a heart pendant that promised them each the heart of a duke.

Now, a young lady, with her family facing ruin and scandal, Lady Aldora doesn't have time for mythical stories about cheap baubles. She needs to save her sisters and brother by marrying a titled gentleman with wealth and power to his name. She sets her bespectacled sights upon the Marquess of St. James.

Turned out by his father after a tragic scandal, Lord Michael Knightly has grown into a powerful, but self-made man. With the whispers and stares that still follow him, he would rather be anywhere but London…

Until he meets Lady Aldora, a young woman who mistakes him for his brother, the Marquess of St. James. The connection between Aldora and Michael is immediate and as they come to know one another, Aldora's feelings for Michael war with her sisterly responsibilities. With her family's dire situation, a man of Michael's scandalous past will never do.

Ultimately, Aldora must choose between her responsibilities as a sister and her love for Michael.

Once a Wallflower, At Last His Love

Book 6 in the Scandalous Seasons Series

Responsible, practical Miss Hermione Rogers, has been crafting stories as the notorious Mr. Michael Michaelmas and selling them for a meager wage to support her siblings. The only real way to ensure her family's ruinous debts are paid, however, is to marry. Tall, thin, and plain, she has no expectation of success. In London for her first Season she seizes the chance to write the tale of a brooding duke. In her research, she finds Sebastian Fitzhugh, the 5th Duke of Mallen, who unfortunately is perfectly affable, charming, and so nicely… configured… he takes her breath away. He lacks all the character traits she needs for her story, but alas, any duke will have to do.

Sebastian Fitzhugh, the 5th Duke of Mallen has been deceived so many times during the high-stakes game of courtship, he's lost faith in Society women. Yet, after a chance encounter with Hermione, he finds himself intrigued. Not a woman he'd normally consider beautiful, the young lady's practical bent, her forthright nature and her tendency to turn up in the oddest places has his interests… roused. He'd like to trust her, he'd like to do a whole lot more with her too, but should he?

A Marquess For Christmas

Book 5 in the Scandalous Seasons Series

Lady Patrina Tidemore gave up on the ridiculous notion of true love after having her heart shattered and her trust destroyed by a black-hearted cad. Used as a pawn in a game of revenge against her brother, Patrina returns to London from a failed elopement with a tattered reputation and little hope for a respectable match. The only peace she finds is in her solitude on the cold winter days at Hyde Park. And even that is yanked from her by two little hellions who just happen to have a devastatingly handsome, but coldly aloof father, the Marquess of Beaufort. Something about the lord stirs the dreams she'd once carried for an honorable gentleman's love.

Weston Aldridge, the 4th Marquess of Beaufort was deceived and betrayed by his late wife. In her faithlessness, he's come to view women as self-serving, indulgent creatures. Except, after a series of chance encounters with Patrina, he comes to appreciate how uniquely different she is than all women he's ever known.

At the Christmastide season, a time of hope and new beginnings, Patrina and Weston, unexpectedly learn true love in one another. However, as Patrina's scandalous past threatens their future and the happiness of his children, they are both left to determine if love is enough.

Always a Rogue, Forever Her Love

Book 4 in the Scandalous Seasons Series

Miss Juliet Marshville is spitting mad. With one guardian missing, and the other singularly uninterested in her fate, she is at the mercy of her wastrel brother who loses her beloved childhood home to a man known as Sin. Determined to reclaim control of Rosecliff Cottage and her own fate, Juliet arranges a meeting with the notorious rogue and demands the return of her property.

Jonathan Tidemore, 5th Earl of Sinclair, known to the *ton* as Sin, is exceptionally lucky in life and at the gaming tables. He has just one problem. Well…four, really. His incorrigible sisters have driven off yet another governess. This time, however, his mother demands he find an appropriate replacement.

When Miss Juliet Marshville boldly demands the return of her precious cottage, he takes advantage of his sudden good fortune and puts an offer to her; turn his sisters into proper English ladies, and he'll return Rosecliff Cottage to Juliet's possession.

Jonathan comes to appreciate Juliet's spirit, courage, and clever wit, and decides to claim the fiery beauty as his mistress. Juliet, however, will be mistress for no man. Nor could she ever love a man who callously stole her home in a game of cards. As Jonathan begins to see Juliet as more than a spirited beauty to warm his bed, he realizes she could be a lady he could love the rest of his life, if only he can convince the proud Juliet that he's worthy of her hand and heart.

Always Proper, Suddenly Scandalous

Book 3 in the Scandalous Seasons Series

Geoffrey Winters, Viscount Redbrooke was not always the hard, unrelenting lord driven by propriety. After a tragic mistake, he resolved to honor his responsibility to the Redbrooke line and live a life, free of scandal. Knowing his duty is to wed a proper, respectable English miss, he selects Lady Beatrice Dennington, daughter of the Duke of Somerset, the perfect woman for him. Until he meets Miss Abigail Stone…

To distance herself from a personal scandal, Abigail Stone flees America to visit her uncle, the Duke of Somerset. Determined to never trust a man again, she is helplessly intrigued by the hard, too-proper Geoffrey. With his strict appreciation for decorum and order, he is nothing like the man' she's always dreamed of.

Abigail is everything Geoffrey does not need. She upends his carefully ordered world at every encounter. As they begin to care for one another, Abigail carefully guards the secret that resulted in her journey to England.

Only, if Geoffrey learns the truth about Abigail, he must decide which he holds most dear: his place in Society or Abigail's place in his heart.

Never Courted, Suddenly Wed

Book 2 in the Scandalous Seasons Series

Christopher Ansley, Earl of Waxham, has constructed a perfect image for the *ton*–the ladies love him and his company is desired by all. Only two people know the truth about Waxham's secret. Unfortunately, one of them is Miss Sophie Winters.

Sophie Winters has known Christopher since she was in leading strings. As children, they delighted in tormenting each other. Now at two and twenty, she still has a tendency to find herself in scrapes, and her marital prospects are slim.

When his father threatens to expose his shame to the *ton*, unless he weds Sophie for her dowry, Christopher concocts a plan to remain a bachelor. What he didn't plan on was falling in love with the lively, impetuous Sophie. As secrets are exposed, will Christopher's love be enough when she discovers his role in his father's scheme?

Forever Betrothed, Never the Bride

Book 1 in the Scandalous Seasons Series

Hopeless romantic Lady Emmaline Fitzhugh is tired of sitting with the wallflowers, waiting for her betrothed to come to his senses and marry her. When Emmaline reads one too many reports of his scandalous liaisons in the gossip rags, she takes matters into her own hands.

War-torn veteran Lord Drake devotes himself to forgetting his days on the Peninsula through an endless round of meaningless associations. He no longer wants to feel anything, but Lady Emmaline is making it hard to maintain a state of numbness. With her zest for life, she awakens his passion and desire for love.

The one woman Drake has spent the better part of his life avoiding is now the only woman he needs, but he is no longer a man worthy of his Emmaline. It is up to her to show him the healing power of love.

A Season of Hope

A Danby Novella

Five years ago when her love, Marcus Wheatley, failed to return from fighting Napoleon's forces, Lady Olivia Foster buried her heart. Unable to betray Marcus's memory, Olivia has gone out of her way to run off prospective suitors. At three and twenty she considers herself firmly on the shelf. Her father, however, disagrees and accepts an offer for Olivia's hand in marriage. Yet it's Christmas, when anything can happen…

Olivia receives a well-timed summons from her grandfather, the Duke of Danby, and eagerly embraces the reprieve from her betrothal.

Only, when Olivia arrives at Danby Castle she realizes the Christmas season represents hope, second chances, and even miracles.

"Winning a Lady's Heart"
A Danby Novella

Author's Note: This is a novella that was originally available in A Summons From The Castle (The Regency Christmas Summons Collection). It is being published as an individual novella.

~★~

For Lady Alexandra, being the source of a cold, calculated wager is bad enough...but when it is waged by Nathaniel Michael Winters, 5th Earl of Pembroke, the man she's in love with, it results in a broken heart, the scandal of the season, and a summons from her grandfather – the Duke of Danby.

To escape Society's gossip, she hurries to her meeting with the duke, determined to put memories of the earl far behind. Except the duke has other plans for Alexandra...plans which include the 5th Earl of Pembroke!

Tempted by a Lady's Smile
Book 4 in the "Lords of Honor" Series

Richard Jonas has loved but one woman—a woman who belongs to his brother. Refusing to suffer any longer, he evades his family in order to barricade his heart from unrequited love. While attending a friend's summer party, Richard's approach to love is changed after sharing a passionate and life-altering kiss with a vibrant and mysterious woman. Believing he was incapable of loving again, Richard finds himself tempted by a young lady determined to marry his best friend.

Gemma Reed has not been treated kindly by the *ton*. Often disregarded for her appearance and interests unlike those of a proper lady, Gemma heads to house party to win the heart of Lord Westfield, the man she's loved for years. But her plan is set off course by the tempting and intriguing, Richard Jonas.

A chance meeting creates a new path for Richard and Gemma to forage—but can two people, scorned and shunned by those they've loved from afar, let down their guards to find true happiness?

"Rescued By a Lady's Love"

Book 3 in the "Lords of Honor" Series

Destitute and determined to finally be free of any man's shackles, Lily Benedict sets out to salvage her honor. With no choice but to commit a crime that will save her from her past, she enters the home of the recluse, Derek Winters, the new Duke of Blackthorne. But entering the "Beast of Blackthorne's" lair proves more threatening than she ever imagined.

With half a face and a mangled leg, Derek—once rugged and charming—only exists within the confines of his home. Shunned by society, Derek is leery of the hauntingly beautiful Lily Benedict. As time passes, she slips past his defenses, reminding him how to live again. But when Lily's sordid past comes back, threatening her life, it's up to Derek to find the strength to become the hero he once was. Can they overcome the darkness of their sins to find a life of love and redemption?

Captivated by a Lady's Charm

Book 2 in the "Lords of Honor" Series

In need of a wife…

Christian Villiers, the Marquess of St. Cyr, despises the role he's been cast into as fortune hunter but requires the funds to keep his marquisate solvent. Yet, the sins of his past cloud his future, preventing him from seeing beyond his fateful actions at the Battle of Toulouse. For he knows inevitably it will catch up with him, and everyone will remember his actions on the battlefield that cost so many so much—particularly his best friend.

In want of a husband…

Lady Prudence Tidemore's life is plagued by familial scandals, which makes her own marital prospects rather grim. Surely there is one gentleman of the ton who can look past her family and see just her and all she has to offer?

When Prudence runs into Christian on a London street, the charming, roguish gentleman immediately captures her attention. But then a chance meeting becomes a waltz, and now…

A Perfect Match…

All she must do is convince Christian to forget the cold requirements he has for his future marchioness. But the demons in his past prevent him from turning himself over to love. One thing is certain—Prudence wants the marquess and is determined to have him in her life, now and forever. It's just a matter of convincing Christian he wants the same.

Seduced By a Lady's Heart

Book 1 in the "Lords of Honor" Series

You met Lieutenant Lucien Jones in "Forever Betrothed, Never the Bride" when he was a broken soldier returned from fighting Boney's forces. This is his story of triumph and happily-ever-after!

~★~

Lieutenant Lucien Jones, son of a viscount, returned from war, to find his wife and child dead. Blaming his father for the commission that sent him off to fight Boney's forces, he was content to languish at London Hospital… until offered employment on the Marquess of Drake's staff. Through his position, Lucien found purpose in life and is content to keep his past buried.

Lady Eloise Yardley has loved Lucien since they were children. Having long ago given up on the dream of him, she married another. Years later, she is a young, lonely widow who does not fit in with the ton. When Lucien's family enlists her aid to reunite father and son, she leaps at the opportunity to not only aid her former friend, but to also escape London.

Lucien doesn't know what scheme Eloise has concocted, but

knowing her as he does, when she pays a visit to his employer, he knows she's up to something. The last thing he wants is the temptation that this new, older, mature Eloise presents; a tantalizing reminder of happier times and peace.

Yet Eloise is determined to win Lucien's love once and for all… if only Lucien can set aside the pain of his past and risk all on a lady's heart.

ONLY FOR THEIR LOVE

Book 3 in the "The Theodosia Sword" Series

Miss Carol Cresswall bore witness to her parents' loveless union and is determined to avoid that same miserable fate. Her mother has altogether different plans—plans that include a match between Carol and Lord Gregory Renshaw. Despite his wealth and power, Carol has no interest in marrying a pompous man who goes out of his way to ignore her. Now, with their families coming together for the Christmastide season it's her mother's last-ditch effort to get them together. And Carol plans to avoid Gregory at all costs.

Lord Gregory Renshaw has no intentions of falling prey to his mother's schemes to marry him off to a proper debutante she's picked out. Over the years, he has carefully sidestepped all endeavors to be matched with any of the grasping ladies.

But a sudden Christmastide Scandal has the potential show Carol and Gregory that they've spent years running from the one thing they've always needed.

Only For Her Honor

Book 2 in the "The Theodosia Sword" Series

A wounded soldier:

When Captain Lucas Rayne returned from fighting Boney's forces, he was a shell of a man. A recluse who doesn't leave his family's estate, he's content to shut himself away. Until he meets Eve…

A woman alone in the world:

Eve Ormond spent most of her life following the drum alongside her late father. When his shameful actions bring death and pain to English soldiers, Eve is forced back to England, an outcast. With no family or marital prospects she needs employment and finds it in Captain Lucas Rayne's home. A man whose life was ruined by her father, Eve has no place inside his household. With few options available, however, Eve takes the post. What she never anticipates is how with their every meeting, this honorable, hurting soldier slips inside her heart.

The Secrets Between Them:

The more time Lucas spends with Eve, he remembers what it is to be alive and he lets the walls protecting his heart down. When the secrets between them come to light will their love be enough? Or are they two destined for heartbreak?

Only For His Lady

Book 1 in the "The Theodosia Sword" Series

A curse. A sword. And the thief who stole her heart.

The Rayne family is trapped in a rut of bad luck. And now, it's up to Lady Theodosia Rayne to steal back the Theodosia sword, a gladius that was pilfered by the rival, loathed Renshaw family. Hopefully, recovering the stolen sword will break the cycle and reverse her family's fate.

Damian Renshaw, the Duke of Devlin, is feared by all—all, that is, except Lady Theodosia, the brazen spitfire who enters his home and wrestles an ancient relic from his wall. Intrigued by the vivacious woman, Devlin has no intentions of relinquishing the sword to her.

As Theodosia and Damian battle for ownership, passion ignites. Now, they are torn between their age-old feud and the fire that burns between them. Can two forbidden lovers find a way to make amends before their families' war tears them apart?

My Lady of Deception

Book 1 in the "Brethren of the Lords" Series

This dark, sweeping Regency novel was previously only offered as part of the limited edition box sets: "From the Ballroom and Beyond", "Romancing the Rogue", and "Dark Deceptions". Now, available for the first time on its own, exclusively through Amazon is "My Lady of Deception".

~*~

Everybody has a secret. Some are more dangerous than others.

For Georgina Wilcox, only child of the notorious traitor known as "The Fox", there are too many secrets to count. However, after her interference results in great tragedy, she resolves to never help another… until she meets Adam Markham.

Lord Adam Markham is captured by The Fox. Imprisoned, Adam loses everything he holds dear. As his days in captivity grow, he finds himself fascinated by the young maid, Georgina, who cares for him.

When the carefully crafted lies she's built between them begin to crumble, Georgina realizes she will do anything to prove her love and loyalty to Adam—even it means at the expense of her own life.

NON-FICTION WORKS BY CHRISTI CALDWELL

Uninterrupted Joy: Memoir: My Journey through Infertility, Pregnancy, and Special Needs

The following journey was never intended for publication. It was written from a mother, to her unborn child. The words detailed her struggle through infertility and the joy of finally being pregnant. A stunning revelation at her son's birth opened a world of both fear and discovery. This is the story of one mother's love and hope and…her quest for uninterrupted joy.

BIOGRAPHY

Christi Caldwell is the bestselling author of historical romance novels set in the Regency era. Christi blames Judith McNaught's "Whitney, My Love," for luring her into the world of historical romance. While sitting in her graduate school apartment at the University of Connecticut, Christi decided to set aside her notes and try her hand at writing romance. She believes the most perfect heroes and heroines have imperfections and rather enjoys tormenting them before crafting a well-deserved happily ever after!

When Christi isn't writing the stories of flawed heroes and heroines, she can be found in her Southern Connecticut home chasing around her eight-year-old son, and caring for twin princesses-in-training!

Visit *www.christicaldwellauthor.com* to learn more about what Christi is working on, or join her on Facebook at Christi Caldwell Author, and Twitter *@ChristiCaldwell*